MW00882171

JAGGED HARTS

KATELYN TAYLOR

Jagged Harts

Written by Katelyn Taylor

Cover art by To All The Books I Love

Interior Formatting by LJDesigns

Published by Katelyn Taylor

Warning: This book contains several potential triggers including, physical and sexual abuse, coarse language and violence. Please proceed with caution. This story is raw, gritty and at certain points deliciously dirty. If you are still reading this then I guess that means you are in, enjoy!

CHAPTER ONE

Aubrey

Cold hands wrap tightly around my throat. My eyes spring open as I desperately look for my attacker, but all I see is darkness. The fingers dig deeper as my breaths become shorter. Help. I need help. I open my mouth to scream but no sound comes out.

Panic floods me as I grasp the hands holding my throat. The feel of his skin under my fingers sends my stomach retching. One of his hands lets up and my heart soars in relief. He is going to let me go.

But oh, how wrong I am.

The now free hand trails down my body, leaving a vile wake in its path. Like a million of bugs crawling across my skin, the feeling skitters across me as my heart leaps into my throat. No. No. Help. I need help. But no one is coming. No one ever comes. The only person who can save me is me and I can't. Not against him. I am too small, too weak, too broken.

Blinking my eyes rapidly, my head swivels to take in my

surroundings. It takes a moment before I let out a ragged sigh of relief when I see that I just dozed off in my car. Glancing at the clock on my dash it looks like I was only asleep for a few minutes. That is all it usually takes for the talons of my nightmares to sink into me, never granting me more than a minute or two of dreamless sleep before they creep in.

I coasted my car into this parking lot about 10 minutes ago. After an over two thousand mile drive it was like a weight had been lifted from my shoulders. I was running on fumes for the last 15 miles and couldn't believe that I had actually made it. I should have known that Betty wouldn't let me down, though. Me and this old girl have been through a lot together. Rubbing my hand appreciatively on the dash, I blow out a deep breath before stepping out of the car.

Flicking my eyes around, my gaze settles on the looming building in front of me. My eyes trail over the sprawling campus with scattered buildings that look more like skyscrapers than school halls. Damn. Whitman University, I made it. Fucking finally. It took over two days of driving and an obscene amount of coffee, but I am finally here.

I reach into the backseat and sling the lone duffel bag over my shoulder. Perk of having practically nothing to your name, you are able to travel light. Though, even I can admit that it is pretty damn pathetic that I can fit my entire life into a single yellow bag that most people would use for a weekend trip. Soon that will all change. I mean, that is why I am here in the first place. Change, a fresh start, a new life.

I know that I am ridiculously lucky to have been selected for the full ride scholarship that I was given. There is no way college would have been on the books for me otherwise, but I knew I had to figure it out somehow if I wanted to make something of myself. These days being hardworking just isn't enough. No matter where you turn, every job wants you to have a fancy piece of paper that costs six figures to get.

I busted my ass for years to be eligible for a scholarship like this and it is finally starting to pay off. I am going to get an expensive ass degree, get a good job and fucking thrive. I have a future waiting for me that doesn't include rotting away in Sunny Crest Trailer Park back in LA. It's a fate unfortunately most suffer, but not me. My new life begins tonight, in Glenfield, Alabama.

With classes starting tomorrow I know that I have to haul ass to get settled in. Stepping quickly through the main entrance I see a crotchety old lady at the receptionist desk. I am not sure if her snooty bitch attitude is because of my showing up at 8:30PM or my slapped together appearance. What does she fucking want from me? She would look like a hot damn mess if she just drove across the country too.

After I show her my ID and paperwork, she wrinkles her nose up at me as she hands me a map of the campus and what must be my dorm room key. Her eyes continue to trace over me with a disapproving gaze. Baring my teeth at her in what I hope is one of my more intimating smiles, I give her a mock salute before turning on my heel in search of my dorm. Fucking bitch.

Some girls might be worried about walking around a college campus in the dark. You never know who could be lurking about, but I welcome the monsters of the night. I challenge them to come for me. Just fucking see what will happen if they do.

Most people look at me and see a petite girl at a whopping 5'4 with platinum blonde hair and bright blue eyes that are closer to turquoise most days. To the majority, I look small, weak. Their first mistake is underestimating me. More people than I can count have made that mistake and paid the damn price for it.

I only get lost once before I make it to my dorm room, which I count as a win because this place is fucking crazy big. When I open the door, I practically fall to my knees as I give a silent thank you to the big man upstairs while I take in the single room in front of me. Sure, it is probably smaller than most of the others dorm rooms that have two students in it, but this place is still twice the size of the room that I called home for the last 18 years of my life. Cleaner too.

Dumping my duffel onto the plain white desk in the corner of the room, I plop down onto the twin mattress on the other side. The place is basic and everything apart from the sporadically stained carpet is crisp white. It almost has a sterile feel to it which is honestly kinda perfect. It doesn't reek of cigarettes or cheap whiskey, and I know for a fact that no one is coming through that door without my say so. That is more than I have ever had so this place is practically paradise.

My stomach audibly groans, causing me to remember that the last thing that I had to eat was a pack of 98 cent powdered doughnuts somewhere in Dallas. I pull out my wallet and see that I have a single 20-dollar bill left. That's it. That is all I have left to my name. I was saving it for an emergency which is why I almost ran out of gas just getting to campus.

First priority after classes tomorrow will be to get a job somewhere. I could shovel horse shit for all I care, as long as it puts money in my pocket, I am good. Keeping in mind that money will be coming to me soon one way or another, I decide to shove my shit into my pockets and head out the door in search of some food. If I had gotten here earlier like I planned to, I could have just hit up the cafeteria since I am on the meal plan, but it is well past eating hours by now, so I am shit out of luck.

I snort. What's new?

The map that the old hag gave me shows a few restaurants that are within walking distance of the dorms. I'm sure one of them will be decent enough. It doesn't take me long to make it across the street and down the road a bit where I see a white and black neon sign over a rustic looking bar that says, 'The White Oak Pub'.

The smell of greasy burgers and fries waft through the air and my stomach grumbles in approval. I should probably find a cheap fast-food place so that I can save as much of my money as possible, but with a painful growl of protest from my stomach I decide against it and walk up to the pub.

When I step in, I notice instantly the pleasant low lighting and soft rock playing through the speakers around the room. There are too many delicious smells to even name as they all flood my senses at once, causing my mouth to literally water. It isn't a huge place which I dig. It has an almost intimate vibe to it, like you could come and hang out here anytime. These hole in the wall places are always the best.

As I step up to the front counter, a messy head of light brown hair pops out around the corner accompanied with a friendly grin.

"Well, hello darlin'. What can I do for you?" The guy asks with a flirty twinkle in his baby blue eyes.

He can't be more than a couple years older than me, but he is well over 6 inches taller than me as he towers behind the counter. I try to hold back my amused snort at his words. I don't know how long it will take to get used to these crazy ass accents down here. I feel like I am in a damn western movie with the way people talk.

Glancing up at the illuminated menu behind him, I settle on the first thing I set my eyes on.

"Can I get a rodeo burger with some fries, to-go?"

"Sure thing," he grins as he rings in my order. "Anything else?"

I shake my head as I pull out my wallet as $10.79 flashes on the register screen. I have to physically push aside my perpetual frugalness as I begrudgingly hand over the money. The guy takes it and quickly gives me my change and a receipt before he leaves with a wink and dashes to the back.

Pocketing my money, I step to the side and lean against the wall as I take in the room around me. There definitely aren't places like this out in LA. I think it makes me like this place that much more. There won't be anything out here in bumfuck Alabama that will remind me of where I grew up, which is a blessing in its own.

Not even five minutes pass before the flirty guy is holding my bag and walking around the counter to hand it to me.

"Thanks."

"No problem. What's your name?"

I cock an eyebrow at him before I snatch the bag out of his hand. "What's it to you?"

He holds his hands up in surrender. "Just wanted to know the name of the girl that I have been dreaming of my whole life."

Now I can't hold back my derisive snort. "That line usually work for you, buddy?"

The guy grins and shrugs. "You tell me. You are the first one that I have used it on."

I look him up and down slowly. He is cute in a boyish charm kind of way, I guess. He looks like the wholesome all American golden boy. I'd bet my left tit that he played football in high school, maybe even in college too if he goes. His family is probably right out of a Norman Rockwell painting and everything. His blue eyes are nice, but he is too soft, too pure. Definitely not my type.

"I'd say you need new material, golden boy."

Before he can respond, I spin on my heels and walk out the door. It is surprising to me how it is significantly warmer outside than in the bar even at this time of night. I am used to warm weather back in California, but this shit is humid and almost unbearable. I can practically feel my body break out into a sweat after only a few steps outside.

Just as I am coming up to the crosswalk to campus, a large hand grips my bicep like a vice. Without hesitation, I spin around quickly and cock my arm back to lay whoever just grabbed me the fuck out. Unfortunately, before I have the chance to, I notice the rough looking middle-aged guy gripping me being tossed away like a rag doll as he lands on his back with a sickening thud.

In an instant, a dark hooded figure is on top of my would-be attacker, beating the absolute shit out of him. I hear the whimpers and pained cries of the man on the ground as the hooded figure practically pulverizes him. I can't help but watch with sick fascination at the excellent form the hooded figure has. My knuckles itch to get a few hits in myself but it doesn't look like there will be much left by the time this guy gets done. Pity.

When the piece of shits whimpers quiet and his arms stop flailing, I finally speak up.

"I think you got him."

The hooded figure stops mid punch and goes rigid before he stands up slowly and turns around to look at me. I suck in a sharp breath as my stomach drops when two sharp green eyes that are so vivid they look damn near radioactive collide with mine. Now that he is standing at his full height, I would guess that he is at least 6'4 and based on his wide frame he has to be well over 240. He would be in the heavy weight class at my gym back home for sure. The guy is a fucking tank.

Moonlight softly casts down on him making me notice the dirty blonde hair that is gelled up underneath his hood. His chest is heaving, and blood is splattered across his knuckles and sweatshirt. For a moment we don't say anything, neither one of us seemingly being able to look away or willing to snap out of whatever this weird trance is. There is something about his eyes that speaks to me, a pain that seems to match the same kind that I am hiding, like two broken pieces from the same window.

Something shifts inside of me as I continue to stare at him, assessing him. He is clearly gorgeous, anyone can see that, but instead of traditional good looks like the golden boy inside, there is an undercurrent of something dangerous in him, something dark.

His darkness seems to draw me in like a moth to a flame which is a huge fucking red flag. Nope. Fuck that shit.

"Are you alright?" His gravelly voice rumbles.

I suppress the shiver that begs to run through my body at the sound. Fuck. If there was ever a voice that could make a woman come from sound alone, it would come from this guy's mouth. I'm torn between telling him off for coming to rescue me like some helpless damsel or asking him to speak again. Mentally slapping myself, I go with the former, screwing in my signature sneer as my eyes connect with his.

"Of course, I am. I could have taken care of the asshole myself, though. I didn't need your help. Maybe you should mind your own business next time."

He scoffs and crosses his thick arms across his chest. How is it possible for a hoodie to wrap around forearms like a second skin like that?

"Most people would just say thank you," he scowls.

Now it is my turn to scoff.

"I'm not most people."

Turning on my heel before the douche can spout anymore bullshit, I look down the street before I jog across it and head back to my dorm. I tell myself that I am hustling to get back so that I can eat and get to bed, but I think it has more to do with the fact that I am trying to get as far away from the hooded man as possible.

He elicits something inside of me that I have never felt before, it took me all of two seconds to realize that whatever it was would only lead to trouble. I pride myself on having great instincts, it is what has kept me alive this far. Right now, my instincts are only screaming one thing about that guy. Run.

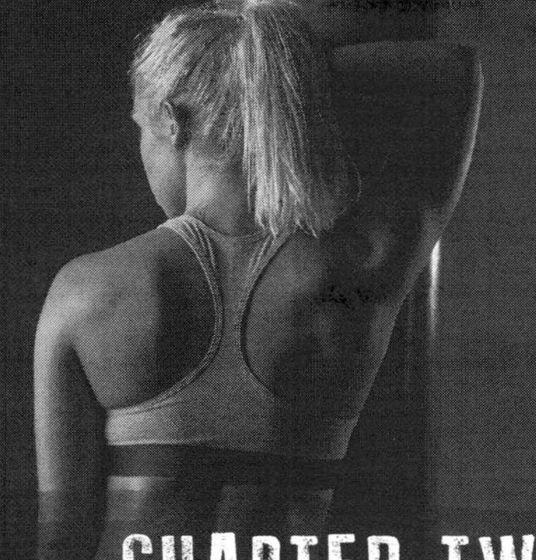

CHAPTER TWO

Aubrey

A heavy body weighs down against my chest, effectively immobilizing me. I try to squirm out from under it, but it is no use. I am being crushed. My cries are muffled and fall on deaf ears. No one can hear me. No one will come. I am on my own.

Pushing on the body with all of my might, I am able to free myself by an inch or two before the heaviness falls back against me. A dark chuckle suddenly fills my ears, sending fear ridden goosebumps racing across my skin.

Oh. God. It's him. Not again. Please, God. Not again.

I jolt forward, gasping for air as my eyes wildly flick around the room. My heart is pounding violently against my ribcage as I take in the crisp white walls, the stained carpet and the white desk in the corner.

I'm not there. I'm safe. I'm safe.

Blowing out a shaky breath, I slowly peel the sweat-soaked

sheets from my body before I grab my bathroom stuff and make my way to the showers. I turn the water to the coldest setting and relish the chill it leaves me with. If I can feel then this isn't a dream. If I can feel then no one can hurt me.

Once I am showered, I throw my hair into a quick braid before I slip into a pair of faded blue jeans and my favorite Zeppelin t-shirt. I finish the *high fashion* outfit off with a white pair of sneakers that are really closer to brown at this point.

I swipe on some drugstore mascara that I picked up in Arizona before calling it good. I am about the furthest thing from a girly girl. I much prefer bloodying up my knuckles over going on shopping trips. Hell, the only reason I even wear mascara is to keep my annoyingly long eyelashes out of my eyes.

Before I step out the door, I spray on some vanilla body spray that I have had for almost two years. Even I am impressed that I have been able to make this stuff last as long as it has. Soon I won't have to ration and stretch every cent that comes my way. Starting today shit changes and thank fuck for that.

I stumble around campus for a little while as I search for my first class of the day, quickly realizing that my first mistake was not scoping out where my classes were ahead of time, because this map that was so graciously provided to me does absolutely jack shit. With my head buried in the useless piece of paper, I don't see the brick wall like figure right in front of me as I barrel straight into it.

"Whoa there, darlin'. If you wanted to touch me all you had to do was say so."

The lame remark comes from the flirty brown-haired guy from the pub last night. His eyes twinkle with amusement as he gives me a smile that is filled with mirth. Being so close to him, I'm overwhelmed with the smell of laundry detergent and fresh pine. He is still douchey but at least he smells good, I guess.

Rolling my eyes, I move to sidestep him when he mimics the

move so that he is still very firmly in my way.

"I didn't know that you were a student. My lucky day. Where you headed, darlin'?"

"None of your fucking business."

"Aw, come on. Don't be like that, darlin'."

"Aubrey," I grit through clenched teeth as I try to step around him again.

"Aubrey?" He furrows his brows in confusion as he blocks my path once more.

"My name. It's Aubrey, not darlin'," I snap. "And I'm late to class. Move."

I step to the left briefly before pulling a quick right and shoulder checking him on my way past as I continue walking through the quad.

"What building you going to? I'll walk you," he says, not missing a beat as he hustles to keep up with me.

My jaw ticks in irritation as I stop mid stride and exhale heavily before turning towards him. I could just knock him out, but I don't think that my scholarship would stay intact after something like that, so I settle for verbal resolution. That's what all those annoying as fuck counselors used to try to preach at school, so why the fuck not?

"Look, despite your fucking pathetic pick-up lines, I am sure that you are a nice enough guy. If I was any other girl, I bet I would be swooning at the thought of a good-looking guy going out of his way to show me around, but I'm not. So, if you would leave me the hell alone, that would be fucking awesome."

He looks down at me, stunned into silence for a moment. Then a brilliant smile spreads across his face showcasing a perfect set of pearly whites. Is this guy insane? In what world did anything I just say warrant a fucking smile?

"You think I'm good looking?" Amusement laces his voice as he takes a step closer to me.

I snort. "That's what you got out of all of that?"

I shake my head and turn around to keep walking. A few seconds later, I notice that he falls right into step with me yet again. Are all southern boys this persistent or is this guy just particularly skilled?

"I'm Cole Simmons," he says after a few steps.

I nod as I keep my pace, making sure not to respond. I could honestly give a shit. I really don't want to encourage this guy. Maybe if I ignore him, he will get bored and just go away.

When I finally find my first class, I open the door and pause. Cole is still following me. I turn towards him and give him a look that would make a lesser man shit a brick.

"Can you fuck off now? I am trying to get to class."

That twinkle from last night returns to his eyes as he speaks. "Me too. Econ with Braxton. Lead the way darlin'."

He makes a sweeping gesture for me as he reaches over my head to hold the door open. The way his accent draws out my unwanted nickname has me rolling my eyes. Whatever. I scan the room for an empty seat and start heading up to the back row, plopping down into the first available seat. Of course, golden boy chooses the seat right next to mine.

"So, where ya from darlin'?"

I close my eyes for a moment before I blow out a deep breath and turn to look at him. He has officially worn me down. Maybe if I just answer his stupid fucking questions, he will leave me the hell alone.

"California. Any other questions, golden boy?"

"Plenty," he beams back at me. "But I'll save the rest for tonight when we hang out."

A laugh escapes me before I can choke it back down. "Yeah. That won't be happening. Despite my *total* lack of interest, I will be job hunting all day after classes."

His smile stays firmly intact, not at all deterred from my

rejection. "Oh yeah? Where you applying to?"

"Anywhere that will take me," I mumble more to myself than anything.

I have scraped and saved for years, waiting for the moment that I could take off and never look back. My move from LA to Alabama officially drained me all in one swoop. Now in order to survive, I am at the mercy of anyone who will give me a job.

"Well, you sure are lucky to have met me, darlin'. We are looking for a server at The White Oak. I have a shift starting today at 4. Come with me and I'll introduce you to the manager. I'm sure he'll hire you."

I pause for a second before turning to face him, eyeing him skeptically as I do.

"Really?"

"Yes, really," he smirks. "You seem like a cool girl. Maybe a bit prickly on the outside but I am betting that makes you all the sweeter on the inside." He tosses me a wink while he stares at me expectantly.

I would normally throttle assholes for just speaking to me the way that he is but for some reason all of his lines come across sadly pathetic as opposed to sleazy. It's clear that the suave cool guy thing is more of an act than his real personality. Probably why I haven't shoved his balls down his throat yet. My subconscious has already deemed him as harmless.

I bite the inside of my cheek as I contemplate his offer. What could it hurt, right? I have waitressed before and it wasn't the worst. Plus, you get tips. Maybe I could make enough to eat name brand ramen, now *that* was the American dream. Maybe I need to reign in the bitchiness for a bit, at least until I can see if this guy is going to be able to hook me up with a job or not.

After a minute of weighing my options, I stick my hand out to Cole.

“Friends?” I smile. Well, my best version of a smile, which from the look on his face I imagine is closer to a grimace.

He looks down at my outstretched hand and shakes it, caressing the back of my hand with his thumb.

“Friends…for now.”

He finishes with a wink as I roll my eyes and pull my hand away before turning to the front of the class as the professor walks in.

“Can you start tonight?”

“Fuck, yeah! Shit, fuck. Yes, I mean. Of course, thank you,” I ramble.

I can’t believe it was that easy. Golden boy must have more clout than I gave him credit for. Who gets offered a job after a glossed over two-minute conversation?

“Great. Have Cole give you the tour and we will fill out all of the paperwork after your shift tonight.”

The owner, Marcus, looks to be in his late 40’s. He has light blonde hair with hazel eyes and a smattering of blonde stubble across his sharp jawline. He also looks to be well over 6’2 at least with arms the size of cannons. The guy is a total silver fox. I’d bet he has half the female population of Glenfield coming in this place for just a chance to catch his eye, though he doesn’t really seem like the type. He doesn’t exactly give off warm and cuddly vibes but then again neither do I so maybe that is why he gave me the job on the spot like that. Kindred spirits and all that shit.

“Hey there, darlin’. Told you we would be together tonight,” Cole says with a teasing smirk on his lips as he comes to stand next to me while Marcus heads to the back.

I roll my eyes and bump my shoulder into his. “Seriously though, thank you. I appreciate it.”

“I’m sure you will find a way to make it up to me.”

He waggles his eyebrows, and I can't hold back an amused smile. This guy is admittedly starting to grow on me, like a fungus or a flesh-eating disease.

8 hours later and it is officially the end of my first shift. It was a little rough in the beginning. I mixed up a few orders at first and dropped a plate on the ground just before I got to the table, but I was able to get into the swing of things by the end. I turn the open sign off and head to the back to grab my stuff.

"Hey, darlin'. Nice work today. Let me walk you home," Cole says coming up to me as he bumps his hip into mine.

I eye him warily, searching for any hints of malice but just as I originally concluded, he is harmless, so I relent.

"Alright, sounds good."

As we walk down the road towards the dorms, we start talking. Well, Cole does most of the talking, I mainly just listen. Cole is a senior at Whitman, born and raised in a small town a couple of hours away and from the sounds of it, I nailed it on the head with the whole Norman Rockwell thing and the football in high school part. We discover that we are both hardcore fans of Harry Potter and ice cream, cookie dough flavor to be specific.

"Kramer's has the best ice cream in town. We will have to go sometime," Cole suggests.

Cole seems like a nice guy, once he puts the flirting bullshit aside, which usually isn't for long. Despite his flirtations I can tell that he is a genuine person. He didn't have to hook me up with a job, but he did even when I was a bitch to him. For a moment, I wonder if what he is offering is really payment. Where I come from you don't get something for nothing. Does he want to take me out in exchange for getting me the job?

"Look, I'm sorry I was such a bitch today. I am not very good with people. But I don't think-"

"Oh, don't worry, darlin'. I'm not asking you out. You've

already rejected me too many times for my fragile male ego to take in 24 hours." He throws me a wink before continuing. "*When* you want to go out, you are gonna have to ask me. We are just friends, until you make your move."

I chuckle and nudge him as we make our way up to my building. "Don't hold your breath, golden boy."

"So, what brings you to Glenfield?" He asks, turning to face me when we get to the doors.

I give him a deadpan look as I tilt my head to the side. "School."

He rolls his eyes and smiles. "Yeah, smartass. I figured. But there are thousands of colleges all around the country. What made you come all the way from California to Alabama?"

My brows furrow as I hesitate. Why does he have so many fucking questions? Part of me wonders if this is just how normal people are. I wouldn't know a thing about that, so I settle on a vague enough answer that still holds some truth.

"This was the first place that offered me a full ride, so I accepted. Pretty simple."

"That's awesome! Congrats on the scholarship. You must have had to work your ass off."

He's got no fucking idea.

"Well, do you like it so far? Alabama? Glenfield? Whitman?"

I shrug. "It's as good of any place for a new beginning."

I freeze as soon as the words leave my mouth. Fuck. Did I seriously just say that out loud? This damn guy and all of his incessant questions are seriously fucking with me. I need to get to my room and away from this nosy fucker.

He doesn't comment on my answer, instead just smiling and nodding before he leans down and hauls me into a tight hug. I freeze in place as my breath stalls and my head starts to spin. Oh no, shit. Not again. Slamming my eyes closed, I do my best to talk myself down.

It's okay. I'm safe. I'm safe.

My body starts to slowly relax, and my breathing begins again as I blow out a soft breath. Fuck. I haven't had a mini freakout like that in a while. Cole must be able to sense my discomfort because he gently untangles himself from me and takes a healthy step back, finally allowing me to take in a cleansing breath.

"Night, darlin'," he smiles softly before turning on his heel and heading back the way we came.

Blowing out a long breath, I quickly head inside and don't stop until I am in my room, door locked and face down on my bed. Panic attacks suck. The worst part about them is how weak you feel during and after them, not just physically but emotionally. I promised myself a long time ago that I would never be that weak little girl ever again. That girl died a long time ago and from her ashes I rose. Never again will I be her, never again.

Aubrey

My first week of my new life practically flies by. I am getting better at my waitress gig with every shift, and I have even been able to stay ahead in all of my classes, though since it is the first week, I guess that isn't all that impressive. It is Friday night, and my shift is almost over, thankfully. My feet are throbbing, I'm hungry and so ready to go home. With 5 minutes left to close, I start my end of the night tasks so that I can get out of here as soon as possible.

Suddenly, the door bursts open as five rowdy college kids make their way inside and head towards a booth in the back.

"Seriously?" I grumble under my breath.

Guess my bed will have to wait.

I gather up the last bit of customer service that I can before I walk over to the group with a smile screwed in place. I am sure it looks just as fake as it feels. Good, maybe they will take the hint

"Hey guys. What can I get you?"

The two girls in the group look up at me and wrinkle their noses like they smell something bad. I can relate because their god-awful perfume makes them smell like baby prostitutes. Maybe that was the goal? The girl's skimpy outfits cling to them like a desperate second skin. Leather miniskirts and tops that more closely resemble headbands than actual shirts with sky high heels that can't possibly be comfortable.

The bubbly blonde snuggling up to a tall guy with sandy brown hair speaks in a nasally voice.

"Can I get a sex on the beach?" She asks as she starts to giggle uncontrollably while giving 'fuck me' eyes to sandy boy.

The dark-haired guy sitting next to sandy boy scoffs and rolls his eyes, I automatically determine that I like him best. The redheaded girl speaks next.

"Can I get a Cosmo? And make sure that it's made like really good?"

I internally roll my eyes. *Well, I was gonna make sure it was really bad, but if you insist.*

Looking past the girls, I lock eyes with a familiar pair of green eyes. The hooded guy that beat the shit out of the dude in the parking lot on Sunday is staring up at me with what looks like surprise, but he quickly masks it as he slings a casual arm around the redhead's shoulders. Now that I can see him better in the light, I see that his dirty blonde hair is almost buzzed completely on the sides while styled longer on top. His jaw line is strong and sharp that only highlights his assessing gaze as he practically burns holes straight through me.

I also notice that the shadow of a bruise is starting to form on the left side of his face. Looks like Mr. Hothead makes it a habit of getting into trouble. He is wearing a t-shirt that hugs his arms like it's wrapped around a set of tree trunks, and pair of black workout shorts that seem to fit him just as well as the shirt.

A glint of silver catches my attention around his neck. It is so dainty that it almost looks like a woman's chain. Odd. Now under the fluorescent lighting my previous suspicions are confirmed. This man is sexy as sin and way too fascinating for my liking. His eyes narrow on me in a way that some may consider intimidating but I know what that dark glint in his eyes really is, curiosity.

Whatever he is looking for it seems he found it or found something because I watch as his eyes flicker for a moment before the hard shell of his perfectly placed mask cracks slightly. He must be able to feel it cracking though because he quickly rights it as he continues staring at me with his previous stoic expression.

Wanting to be done with our intense stare off, I peel my eyes away and face the rest of the group. I can't believe we just sat there and stared at each other like that in front of all of these people. Thankfully, no one outside of the dark-haired guy seemed to notice.

"We will take two pitchers of beer and eight cheeseburgers," Sandy boy states from the other side of the booth.

"Sorry, kitchen is closed. I can get you those drinks though," I offer. What do they expect coming in here 5 minutes to close?

He tosses his head back and starts to laugh like I made a joke. When he realizes that I'm not laughing, the smile slowly slides off his face.

"Wait, are you serious?"

"As a heart attack," I quip.

He shakes his head in what looks like disbelief as he leans forward and places his elbows onto the table.

"You are new here, clearly. Marcus always keeps the kitchen open for us on Fridays. It's fine."

"Yeah, well, the cook already went home so it looks like food isn't on the menu tonight. Sorry," I deadpan.

Green eyes flicks his gaze up to me and though I hate to admit it, my stomach dips for a moment with his attention sitting heavily on me. He cocks his head ever so slightly and squints as if he was studying an insect.

"Hey, y'all. Is there a problem?" Cole chimes in, coming to stand next to me with a friendly smile.

Sandy boy swings his gaze to Cole with a sneer firmly fixed across his face.

"Your new chick doesn't know her ass from a hole in the ground. She says you guys aren't going to serve us food."

I notice green eyes shoots a look at his buddy as his hand resting on top of the table tightens into a fist before he settles his gaze back on me. The dark-haired guy on the other side of the table is giving the guy a similar look and Cole is now sporting a scowl before he lets it fade into a bull shit smile once again.

Guess no one appreciated that comment.

"Sorry about that guys. This is her first Friday shift. The cook already went home but I can whip up anything you want."

"Thanks, man," Sandy boy replies before he goes back to nuzzling Blondie at his side.

When I glance around the group, I notice that green eyes is still staring at me. Since I've never been one to back down from bullshit intimidation tactics I meet his stare with a cool one of my own. Cole touches my elbow and starts guiding me back towards the bar despite my resistance. The guy's eyes laser in on where Cole's hand is currently holding me and then flick back to my eyes for a moment before he raises a questioning eyebrow my way. I don't even want to know what that look is about, so I turn and walk away.

"What the hell was that about?" I ask, irritated by our late-night visitors.

Cole looks down at me while he leads us behind the bar.

"*That* is Dax Hart and his inner circle."

I cock one eyebrow up at him. "Is that supposed to mean

something to me?"

He chuckles and shakes his head. "I forgot that you aren't from around here. Dax is a big deal in Glenfield. He is a senior at Whitman and is the one to beat in the underground MMA scene. The guy is a beast, you never recognize his opponents when he is finished with them, and he rarely leaves with more than a bruise or a scrape. Their group always comes in after his fights on Fridays. He is Marcus's nephew, so they get special treatment around here." He shrugs saying this like it is common knowledge and just something to accept.

I perk up at the mention of MMA. I was a permanent fixture at the MMA gym near my house growing up and I have been itching to find a new place. I turn to catch a glimpse of their table before looking back to Cole.

"Quite the ladies' man too," Cole tacks on. "He usually has a different girl with him every time that I see him. Guess everyone wants a piece of the talent."

I nod. That is usually a ring bunny's MO. I have seen it too many times to count with the guys from my old gym. Needless to say, I have been in my share of fights with jealous women thinking that just because I hangout with the guys they are trying to fuck means that I want to fuck them too.

"So, does that mean there is an MMA gym around here? Is that where the fights are held?"

"Yeah, the MMA gym on second hosts under the table fights in the basement on Fridays. Fight night gets pretty wild. We should go sometime, that is if you are ready to ask me out?" He teases, the corner of his eyes crinkling with delight.

I throw back my head letting out a full belly laugh. "Oh my god. Seriously, get new material. This shit is just sad."

He throws me a wink as he heads back to the kitchen to start the burgers. I start loading up my tray with their drinks when I look up to see Dax towering over me.

"Can I help you with something?" I ask dryly.

I don't like the way that he is looking at me. It isn't in a skeevy way like most men would be doing but it is intense. The way he is looking at me makes me feel bare and exposed and that is way worse than being eye fucked.

His eyes meet mine, but he says nothing, he just…stares. Doing my best not to squirm under his scrutiny, I lift my chin a little higher and make sure my resting bitch face is firmly intact. We stand there silently for a few more moments before he lifts a single eyebrow.

"What are you doing here?"

"Working. You?" I bite out.

I watch as his jaw ticks at my answer before he crosses his arms across his chest. "I didn't realize my uncle hired anyone."

"I didn't realize that it would be any of your business," I snark.

From the low growl rumbling through his chest and the menacing look on his face, I think I just poked the bear, metaphorically and maybe literally, but I couldn't help it. Who the hell comes up to a perfect stranger and starts questioning them like this? Fucking asshole.

"What's your name?" He practically barks when he looks down to the blank place of my uniform where a name tag should be. I have never been so grateful for a back order in my life.

"None of your damn business," I scoff as I finish pouring the last pitcher of beer.

He is quiet for a few seconds and despite knowing better, I glance up to see why he has all the sudden gone quiet. I see a fire lit in those sharp green eyes and watch as his hands repeatedly clench into fists and unclench. He looks like he is hanging on by a thread and as intimidating as he does look, I can't help but want to see what he would be like when he loses control. To see what happens when his darkness consumes him and what would remain in his wake. My bet is not much.

"If I would have known you were such a bitch, I wouldn't have even bothered with saving your ass the other night," he spits lowly.

Suddenly, my temper flares to life as my eyes widen. Lifting my hand up I jab a finger into his steel like chest as I come unglued.

"First of all, you didn't save me, you got in my way. I was just about to lay that fucker out when you came along. Next time, why don't you mind your own fucking business! Second of all," I seethe as I jab another finger into him. "How dare you say something so fucking vile. So, you are saying that if you would have seen any other woman that more than likely couldn't have defended herself, but you thought was a bitch, you would have sat back and watched as a man robbed her, killed her, or worse? You are disgusting."

Something in his fiery eyes dims momentarily at my words. I am not sure what part of my rant got to him but whatever it was it obviously hit him where he didn't expect. Good. Fucking piece of shit. I am about to open my mouth to keep handing this motherfucker his ass when Cole calls out to me through the kitchen window.

"Aubrey! Can you grab the cheese from the walk in for me?"

Dax continues to stare at me as I glare at him. I let out a short scoff and shake my head before turning on my heel to head to the kitchen. When I push through the doors, Cole is next to me instantly.

"Hey," he says in a hushed tone. "Are you okay? Things looked tense out there."

My eyes flick over to the kitchen line where I see Cole already has the cheese set out. He was just giving me an excuse to get away from Dax. Without thinking too much into it, I lean in and give Cole a quick hug, thankful that it doesn't send me into a near tailspin like last time.

"Thanks. I'm fine. He is just an ass. Do you need any help? I just want them to get out of here so that I can go home."

Cole's smiles understandably before he shrugs. "Nah, I'm good.

If you could just take the drinks out to them. This stuff is almost done."

I give him a mock salute causing us both to chuckle as I walk back through to the front. When I step up to the counter, the small smile that I was wearing drops when I see that Dax is now behind the bar mixing the girls drinks. I roll my eyes but don't protest. His uncle owns the place, I am sure it isn't the first time that he has jumped behind the bar.

When he is finished, he places the drinks onto another tray and takes it while I take the one with the beer and glasses on it. Staring at him with a blank face, I begin to follow behind him towards the table. If he wants to make my job easier, so be it, you won't see me throwing a fit.

We reach the booth quickly, and he sets his tray down on the table as he resumes his spot next to the redhead. As he settles back, she curls a possessive hand around his bicep and practically crawls into his lap while shooting me a scathing look. I roll my eyes to the back of my head.

Marking our territory, are we?

Dax looks down at the desperate girl before looping his arm around her tiny waist and hauling her fully into his lap as he looks back up at me. His eyes immediately come to my face, almost like he is searching for a reaction. *Please.* The guy is hot, I'll admit, but his shit personality brings him way down in my book. I barely contain my snort before I set all of their drinks down onto the table. I can feel his eyes on me, watching me carefully as I pick up the trays, but I don't spare him a second glance as I head back to my closing tasks.

Cole brings their food out to them and thankfully they eat pretty quickly. Soon they all start to stand and make their way out of the restaurant. *Fucking finally.* As I am walking around the front counter to grab their dishes, I am stopped by a hand gripping my elbow.

Dax looks down at me seriously, an impassive look that seems to be perfectly practiced on his face before he leans in just a fraction of an inch away from my ear.

"That mouth of yours is going to get you in trouble one day, Aubrey," he whispers.

The way his voice draws out my name sends goosebumps across my skin and causes my heart to race. I quickly shove away all of those disgusting feelings and focus on his thinly veiled threat. Narrowing my eyes, I rip my arm out of his hold as I roll my shoulders back and take a step forward until our chests brush. I have to crane my neck up just to look him in the eye which admittedly takes away some from my intimidating stance.

"So will yours," I promise as I flex out my knuckles that are just itching to connect with this dicks face.

His jaw ticks as his eyes flare to life once more before he steps back and storms away, slamming the door so hard as he goes that I half expect the glass to shatter.

Someone has a temper.

Shaking my head, I continue moving over to their now abandoned table. I did not travel over two thousand miles to let some asshole think that he can intimidate me just because everyone else says he is top dog. If he thinks I will take his bullshit laying down, he has another thing coming. Dax Hart may be the self-proclaimed badass in the octagon, but I am the motherfucking queen and if he gets in my way of my fresh start, I will fucking end him.

CHAPTER FOUR

Aubrey

I am walking home the next day after a long ass shift. I have been getting consistently steady hours which I am grateful for, but I am on my fucking face. I'm not sure if it is the fact that I have been spending all my time when I am not working studying that is wiping me out or maybe it is having to put on a bullshit customer service smile for entitled asswipes. Either way I need to sleep for like two weeks.

When I walk past Greek row I see several houses thumping with loud music and drunk shouts. I used to party quite a bit in high school, anything to get an escape even if it was just for the night, but the appeal quickly wore off. I hook a left and make my way to my dorm when I hear a muffled shout.

"Stop!" A girl's voice rings out through the night before the sound of scuffling feet comes from my right.

Pausing in place, I turn my head towards the noise to see a girl being pinned against the back of one of the houses by a large guy.

There is no one else around the back of the house except for them. It is practically pitch black back there, so it takes a few moments for my eyes to adjust to what I am seeing.

When they finally do, I see the guy grab the girl by the throat before he smashes his lips against hers. Her body locks up instantly as her hands frantically try to shove him off, but he doesn't stop. Instead, he takes his free hand and snakes it up her mini skirt before a ripping noise sounds as he tosses a torn scrap of lace to the floor.

As quietly as I can, I slowly make my way towards them. A choked whimper comes from the girl as the guy pulls back and his hand under his skirt begins moving.

"Stop playing hard to get, baby girl. Look at what you wore just for me? How do you not expect me to bend you over when you are looking this sexy? Just sit back and let me make you feel good," he purrs, though it is probably the least attractive sounding purr that I have ever heard.

"No! Get away from me! Don't touch me!" The girl snaps out as she begins struggling against him again.

Unfortunately, she is severely outmatched and looks to not have a freaking clue how to defend herself against the guy. Disgust rolls through me as he keeps her pinned against the house with his large body before his hands reach down and bunch her skirt up around her waist. Fuck no.

Closing the remaining few feet between us I shout out venomously to the guy.

"Hey!"

His head whips over to me, fear filling his eyes before irritation replaces it. He sneers at me before turning back to the poor girl.

"Fuck off. This isn't a free show!"

"No means no, motherfucker!"

Before he can respond, I am winding back and hitting him across the face with everything that I have. He crumbles to the ground like a fucking pussy as I continue raining punches down on him. He is rolling from side to side, cradling his broken and bleeding face as I lift my leg up and stomp down onto his rapist dick. Normally, I don't land cheap shots like that if I don't have to but what better way to stop a man from raping women then mutilation, right?

He squeals like a pig at the pain before he continues blubbering and groaning. I am honestly so fucking sick of hearing this piece of shit, so I rear back and hit him right on the magic spot that knocks people out in an instant if done right. When I know that he won't be waking up for a bit, I turn my head up to see a shaking half naked girl, staring down at me with fear filled eyes.

Slowly, I stand up and walk towards her, keeping my hands where she can see them and stopping a few feet away so that I don't invade her space.

"Are you okay?" I ask softly.

"H-how did you do that?" She asks as her eyes flick down to her unconscious attacker.

I smirk softly. "It wasn't much. That guy is a little bitch compared to guys that I have taken on. Did he hurt you? Physically?"

She rubs her throat gently before she shakes her head. I nod. That's good.

"If you want to file a report on him, I'll write a witness statement. Anonymously of course. I'm not looking to catch a misdemeanor for beating the piss out of him. Motherfuckers like him don't deserve to be out in society though. In my opinion, they should all be put down like dogs but that's just me."

She looks unsure as her eyes flick around while she starts righting her clothes, picking up what is left of her shredded underwear with as much dignity as she can have before she stuffs them into her clutch. I watch her patiently until her shaking has slightly lessened.

"Do you live on campus?" I ask.

The girl nods as I take step closer to her.

"Well, if you don't need the hospital and you don't want to do a report at least tonight, how about I walk you home?"

Breathing out what seems like a sigh of relief she nods.

"Thank you," she whispers softly.

I give her an understanding smile as I usher her past the guy that is starting to rouse. Her eyes harden as she looks down at him before she pulls her leg back and kicks him right in the dick. Fuck yeah. I think I like this girl.

Reaching into my purse, I get an idea. I uncap my permanent marker before crouching down and writing across the guy's swollen forehead 'rapist' in bold letters. Hopefully others will take it upon themselves to rough him up once they undoubtedly piece together what he tried to do, and no doubt has probably done in the past.

The girl looks down at my artwork with a satisfied glint in her eyes before we silently walk to her dorm. She is just in the building next to mine, so we get there soon. I walk her all the way up to her door before she turns to me. In the lit hall I am able to see her better. She is gorgeous with lush light brown hair and matching brown eyes. Her killer body and obviously expensive clothes make her look more like a supermodel ready for the runway than a college girl.

I can tell that she wants to say something but isn't sure what. My eyes flick down to her rapidly bruising neck and I grimace before I gesture to it.

"You may want to take a picture of that for evidence, just in case you ever do decide to fill out a report. Keep the panties too."

She nods numbly as her eyes begin to water. I slowly reach forward and squeeze her shoulder. I fucking hate physical contact with others on a normal day but I feel like she needs some type of reassurance. She practically sinks into my touch as I give her a sympathetic nod before I turn on my heel and head to my room. Fuck. Did I mention that it has been a long fucking day?

On Monday, I make my way through the cafeteria on campus, grabbing the closest edible thing that I can before I head over to an empty table and crack open my English lit book. Getting in any extra study time I can manage is crucial. I am here on a scholarship, and I am not gonna screw up my one shot for something stupid like not making enough time in my schedule to study.

After a few minutes, a random tray plops down next to me, shaking me out of my study fog. I glance up at the owner to see a familiar petite brunette with big brown eyes and a kind smile.

"Hi. After you left the other night I realized that I never got your name."

I nod. "Aubrey."

She smiles softly as she nods. "I'm Mckayla but most people call me Kayla."

"Good to meet you," I say as I take a bite of my food.

We quietly eat our food for a few moments before she speaks.

"Thank you, for everything. I can't remember thanking you the other night and I need to. I owe you a lot."

I wave her off before crossing my arms across my chest.

"Forget about it. You don't owe me shit. Any decent person would have done the same thing."

"Not just anyone could have taken down one of the starting linebackers of the school's football team like that though," she points out.

Linebacker? Makes sense. The dude was a fucking ogre. I shrug as I turn my head back to my book. A few more minutes go by before she says something again.

"Are you going to the clay banks this Saturday? The upperclassman are hosting a back-to-school thing. It should be really fun."

I give her a blank stare for a few seconds as I blink at her.

"Do I look like the type of girl that goes to the clay banks and throws back some wine coolers with a bunch of co-eds?" I deadpan.

I know I sound like a bitch, but I don't understand what she is still doing sitting next to me? I get that she wanted to say thanks which is cool and all, but it isn't like she has to stick around any longer. If she needs me to fill out a report I am sure she will hit me up. If not, we are pretty much done here.

My eyes trail over her, taking in her perfectly crisp outfit that no doubt cost several hundred dollars, perfectly glossy hair and her fancy ass purse that no doubt has a shiny black credit card inside with her daddy's name on it. She is the perfect southern belle princess no doubt. We couldn't be more different if we tried which only solidifies my want to be left the hell alone.

I'm surprised when she takes my brash attitude in stride and shrugs simply. The meek scared girl from the other night quickly falling away before my eyes as a strong confident woman takes her place.

"I'm not sure. I don't judge people based on appearances, unlike some people," she says, giving me a knowing look before continuing. "But do you look like you are in desperate need of some fun? Definitely."

Narrowing my eyes, I shoot her a murderous glare in return. Instead of blanching or running for her life like she should be doing, she meets my glare head on with an unimpressed raised eyebrow as she seemingly waits for me to respond.

I have to admit, having her point out the fact that I judged her before she could even get a chance to judge me makes my stomach twist. I've been on my fair share of judgmental comments and looks just because of where I lived or who my mother was. It's a shitty ass feeling and suddenly, I feel like a huge fucking asshole.

"Sorry," I mutter under my breath, so softly that I doubt she could hear it.

She shrugs, seemingly completely unbothered by me as she happily munches on her rabbit food before delicately dabbing at her mouth with her napkin.

"So, are you coming?"

At first it sounds like the worst thing in the world, but the way this girl is handling my less than friendly attitude has me mildly impressed and slightly curious. Despite our initial encounter she seems to ooze this laid-back confidence that I really dig. The way she claps back at me has me giving a little respect for her which is way more than I can say for every other girl that I have met since I came here. And who can't love a potential victim kicking her assailant in the dick?

Fuck it.

"Sure. Why not?"

Mckayla smiles before she scribbles down her name and number on a piece of paper as she slides it over to me.

"Here is my number. Shoot me a text and we can ride together."

Before I can respond, she is already out of her seat and sashaying across the cafeteria to a table filled with guys, making herself right at home with a wide smile and flirty eyes. The guys all practically drool on her as her attention flits to each guy equally. She has the whole table practically eating out of the palm of her hand.

Damn. I am actually kind of impressed. Usually, people that go through what she did just the other night withdraw at least for a little while. Not this girl though. She seems to not be letting what happened bothered her or change her life any more than it has to.

Good for her.

I think I might actually like that girl. I pocket her number before I turn back to my book. Look at me, making friends and shit.

CHAPTER FIVE

Aubrey

My life has been consumed with work, class and very little sleep this week. I know it will all pay off in the end but damn, I am fucking exhausted. As much as I would rather be in bed right now, somehow I instead find myself riding in a hot pink Jeep that would make Barbie jealous as Mckayla drives us to the clay banks.

Mckayla rapidly burns through topics the whole way, occasionally asking me questions that I am pretty sure are rhetorical. I look out the window and look down at the side of the car before I chuckle to myself. I really have never seen such an obnoxious looking car in all my life. McKayla must be able to guess what I am thinking because she just shrugs as she takes another turn.

"Daddy insisted that I drive a Jeep and since he wouldn't get me the little Miata that I had my heart set on, we compromised on a custom paint job."

Yeah, custom. It looks like the body shop dipped the damn thing in Pepto Bismol. I prefer my '97 Ford Aspire, personally. When I offered to drive, Mckayla wrinkled her nose at the sight of Betty like it offended her to be in the same parking lot as her. Sure, Betty wasn't fresh off the showroom floor or anything, but she is 25 years old, a classic some would say!

Okay no one would call a '97 Ford Aspire a classic, but still.

I mean, yeah, the red paint is bubbled and chipped. And I have a black passenger side door since it's all I could find from the scrap yard after some asshole t-boned me last year. The tires are all different brands and different ages since I used to get flats every other week on the shit roads back home. And hey, the engine ticks once in a while like an impending bomb but that's it. Besides the horrific cranking noise that she makes when she first starts that sounds like it's better suited for background music in a horror movie. Other than that, she is in great shape and has yet to let me down.

I bought Betty with my own money when I was 16. I was sick of taking public transportation and rideshares hit the bank account way too hard. She was the one thing that I had in this world that was actually worth something and all mine. She made it the whole trip out here just fine, and I'm sure that I will be able to get at least another five years out of her. And you can bet your ass that I am gonna milk her for all that she is worth.

I snap back to reality, catching the tail end of a story Mckayla was telling about how she won Miss Teeny Alabama when she was 6 and continued competing up until she came to college. It makes sense, the girl is stunning.

"So, what about you? What is your story?" She asks.

I turn and cock my head to the side as I look at her. Why is everyone around here so fucking nosey? Shrugging off her question, I look out the window again.

"No story. Just your average college freshman."

"Hmm, why do I find that hard to believe?" Mckayla wonders out loud.

"Think what you want," I snap a little too harshly.

Instead of getting offended at my aggressive change in attitude, she chuckles lightly.

"Alright, so backgrounds are firmly off the table for discussion. Works for me."

At least we can agree on something. We drive for a few more minutes before she speaks quietly.

"I'm going to report Kyle."

I turn to look at her. So, the rapist has a name. I think I will just keep calling him rapist in my head though, it fits better.

"I don't want you to file a witness report. I don't want you to get in trouble for saving me, but I just wanted to tell you. I wasn't sure if I was going to at first because it will probably turn into a big thing once my parents hear about it, but I don't want him to try to do it with another girl who isn't lucky enough to have you walking by."

I nod my head in agreement.

"Guys like him will never stop. They are rotten to the fucking core and deserve to be locked up or shot. But everyone has gotten so fucking touchy with capital punishment so I guess locked up will have to do."

A bubbled laugh escapes her as she nods. "Knowing daddy, as soon as he finds out, he will be cleaning his gun before paying Kyle a visit, more than likely before a trial can even begin."

"You got a good dad then."

She smiles and nods before she throws the Jeep into park on the side of the road, and she pushes her movie star sunglasses on top of her head and turns to face me.

"You ready?"

I nod and slide out of my side, reaching back to grab my towel and sunglasses. Mckayla struts over to me, looping our arms together before she starts dragging me away. I wait for the normal freak out to come from the contact since I usually cannot stand being touched, but for some reason it doesn't come.

Mckayla must have stripped off her swimsuit cover at some point because now she is only wearing a white bikini that looks like a 10-year-old attacked it with a bedazzler paired with wedged heel sandals. If she was hoping to attract every male eye within a five-mile radius, then she couldn't have picked a better outfit.

My bathing suit is much plainer in comparison. It's black with not much detail to it. My mother may have never given me much but the one good thing that she did give me a decent sized chest. I have a full C cup or a small D which makes my bathing suit look extra nice. Normally I would never wear something as revealing as a bathing suit in public, at a water hole or not, but I am really struggling to adjust to this humid heat and couldn't bear the thought of jeans, so bathing suit it is.

I don't even know what I am doing here, honestly. I can't remember the last time that I hung out with another girl. Maybe 7th grade. Sarah Brennon? Yeah, that sounds about right. Girls don't typically like me and that is alright because I have not been a fan of the ones that I have met. I have never focused too much of my life on trying to be friends with anyone really. It is too hard to maintain a friendship with anyone when I had to take care of myself first and foremost. God knows no one else was going to.

"Hey ladies!" A voice in the distance shouts.

We both spin around to see Cole bounding up to us wearing only a pair of swimming trunks and a goofy smile. His skin is sun kissed which only enhances his bright blue eyes. I had a feeling the guy was in good shape, but damn. I can't help but let my gaze fall over his broad shoulders and drop down to see his defined chest and toned abs. He looks surprisingly good and based on the look on his face I would say that he knows it too.

"Hey, darlin'. I didn't know that you were going to be here," he says, sweeping me into a tight but brief hug.

When he pulls away his eyes flick to my face, seemingly looking for any sign of distress. I am just as thankful as him that I haven't had a freakout since that first day. Look at me being all normal and shit.

"Mckayla, this is Cole. Cole, this is Mckayla," I introduce, doing my best to get Cole's inquisitive stare off of me.

"Well, hello there," Mckayla purrs as she does her own inspection of his body before settling back on his face.

"Hey," he replies, giving her a polite smile but keeping his eyes on her face the whole time before he turns his attention back to me.

Mckayla doesn't seem put out at all. She just shrugs and pulls me along so that we start walking again.

"Well, let's get going before the drinks get warm!"

Cole slips his arm over my shoulder casually like it's a normal thing we do as he falls into step with us. When my body doesn't tense and my stomach doesn't turn over from the touch, I decide to go with it. I don't get any bad vibes from him and even though he is taller and obviously stronger than me I am fairly confident that I could take him down if needed.

We walk through a wooded trail for a bit before it pops out to a clearing with a crisp blue lake and clay rocks varying in size surrounding the edges. Scattered every two feet are college kids either sunbathing, swimming or playing some type of drinking game.

"Oh! I'm gonna go say hi to my friend from high school over there, be right back!" Mckayla calls out as she hurries to sidle up next to a lean guy with dark auburn hair. Well, I am sure that is the last that I will see of her today.

"You do realize that she isn't coming back, right?" Cole says with an amused smile.

I huff out a short laugh. "Yeah, I gathered. Looks like I've been officially abandoned."

His grip around my shoulders tightens as he pulls me in to a side hug. "Oh, darlin'. Don't worry. I won't leave your side."

"Until a bouncy little thing in a tiny bikini requires your attention," I smirk.

His smile slips just slightly, and his eyes look into mine earnestly. "The only girl I'm interested in spending time with today is you." His sincerity hits me square in the chest and the look in his eyes has me directing mine anywhere but him.

I start scanning the crowd again before they stop on a familiar pair of emerald green eyes that are apparently already locked on me. A scowl is etched across his face before he breaks eye contact with me and pulls the redhead from the pub down onto his lap. She squeals and throws her head back like she is embarrassed, but the fuck me eyes she is throwing him shows that she is anything but.

I look away and roll my eyes. I came here to have a good time and damnit that is what I am going to do. I won't let that asshole's presence ruin my day. Looking up to Cole who is watching me with a soft smile, I lean up onto my tip toes as I glance at his mouth. His eyes darken with desire as he takes a half of a step towards me.

When I am only a hairs width away from his lips I whisper, "Race you," and take off running towards the water. I hear his heavy footsteps following close behind only a second later and before I can toss out my next insult, I am thrown over his shoulder and we are diving into the water.

I let out a sharp yelp when I emerge to the surface, feeling the full effect of the brisk water wrap around me. Kicking my legs up, I lay on my back so that I float on the surface, basking in this current feeling. The feeling of being free, with no worries or fears. The feeling of just, living.

Cole and I spend the day laughing, splashing in the water and me drinking him under the table. Golden boy can't hold his liquor for shit. McKayla started an impromptu dance party that I was strong armed into and pretty soon everyone followed.

Towards the end of the night several bonfires have been set up all around with different groups of people around each. I'm sandwiched in between Cole and some guy as they animatedly discuss this year's football season and what is to be expected. They sure take their sports seriously around here. Must be a southern thing. Stretching out my legs, I settle back onto my hands as I stare at the fire, watching the top of the flames lap at the night sky.

Damn, I don't think that I have ever seen stars like this before. Living in a big city my whole life the night was usually lit up from skyscrapers and businesses and what was left of the sky was covered in a haze of smog. It's pretty gorgeous.

Suddenly, I feel the air around me change and realize that Cole and football dude have vacated their spots and someone else is now sitting down next to me. I look over to see Dax eating up the space between us with a beer in his hand.

Fucking hell.

"Nice night," he remarks to no one in particular as he stares up at the sky.

I choose not to respond because I honestly have nothing to say to this prick. I should honestly deck him for the shit that he said last week and move to another spot, but my curiosity is too great to see why the hell he would directly approach me. We sit there for several minutes in silence. It is heavy with obvious tension but also a sense of peace. I have no explanation for it, and I am actually glad that he speaks so that I don't get the chance to go down that particular rabbit hole.

"You looked like you were having fun today," he says hollowly with a hint of something that I can't quite pin down. Irritation? Accusation? *Whatever.*

I drop my gaze from the sky to look at him, my eyes narrowed into slits.

"Yeah, I did. Is that a fucking problem?" I snap.

He turns his head down to look at me, lifting a single eyebrow as he does. "Are you always so fucking angry?"

"Only when I have to talk to egotistical assholes," I say with an ugly sneer.

His face remains perfectly unfazed, and I can't help but feel disappointment that I didn't rile him up like last week. It was an almost powerful feeling to push a man like him. To most people it would probably also be a death sentence, but I'm not scared of this asswipe.

My eyes flick over him and I notice that just below the collar of his t-shirt, dark black ink is peeking up. I can't see what the tattoo is since most of it is obstructed but I can't say that I am not super fucking curious what a man like Dax would get inked on his body permanently. He is a fucking asshole. But an intriguing asshole, nonetheless.

"I was a dick the other day," he rumbles lowly.

My eyebrows knit together in confusion at his words. Is he actually admitting it? Eyeing him warily, I slowly agree.

"Yeah, you were."

"You pissed me off, so," he shrugs like that is all the excuse needed for his behavior.

"Well, you pissed me off too, so," I mock with a shrug before rolling my eyes.

He narrows his eyes as he leans forward, resting his thick forearms on top of his thighs. "Do you even know who I am?"

Unfortunately, I know a lot more about Dax Hart than I care to. It's hard not to overhear gossip while working. The shit some people say in public honestly blew me away at first. I know that I was a little off about the whole self-proclaimed badass thing, from the talk that I have heard he *is* actually pretty badass. He had another fight last night and apparently destroyed the guy, broke his jaw and snapped his leg in half in the first minute of the fight.

I also learned that he was born and raised here and was for a brief moment in the UFC, like only a few fights brief. Apparently, his fight name is Angel of Death, don't know why but it sounds cool. I didn't hear why he no longer fights on the circuit, instead in a dingy gym basement after dark, but I honestly didn't care enough to bother for more.

A few girls also talked about some other skills that he possessed that were not inside the octagon, those details were ones that I was even less interested to hear. Overall, it seems that everyone had something to say about Dax Hart. You can tell that every guy wants to be him, and every girl wants to be with him. He is *that* guy. The only part of his background that I have any amount of respect for is his record, undefeated since he started fighting underground. Not that I would ever let on that anything about this man could impress me.

"I know enough," I say coolly. "From what I have heard, I don't really see what the big deal is." I only have to partially lie about that part.

His eyes stay narrowed as his head tilts to the side in what looks like contemplation. I meet his stare head on, refusing to show an ounce of weakness in front of him. I know all too well what men with power do with weaknesses. Exploit. Manipulate. Destroy.

"You are different," he murmurs, almost to himself like he is mulling over the thought and didn't mean to say it out loud.

I give him my best saccharine smile as I nod. "Yeah, I am. But you're not."

My smile instantly drops as I push myself up to stand and walk away without another word. I tip back the last of my beer before tossing it into a nearby trashcan as I stumble a bit, making my way through the groups of remaining people, looking for Mckayla. I want to get as far away from Dax Hart as physically possible.

"Hey, darlin'. Whatcha doing?"

I turn around to see Cole standing to the side of me with a group of people that I haven't seen before. I swear he knows everyone, and if he doesn't know someone, he is friends with them in like two minutes of meeting them.

"Just looking for Kayla. Have you seen her?"

He smiles and waggles his eyebrows. "Yeah. She went home with Mr. Friend From High School. She asked me to give you a ride when you were ready."

"Oh okay. Do you mind if we head out soon? I am opening tomorrow, and I still need to finish my lit paper," I lie easily.

I finished that paper two days ago, but Cole doesn't know that. He smiles down at me and takes a step closer.

"Not at all. Let's head out."

Cole says his goodbyes to everyone before he slips an arm around me as we walk away. While we weave our way through all of the party goers, I can't help but discreetly look to see if Dax is still here. Sure, enough he is still here, and those hypnotic eyes are tracking me like a predator tracks its prey. His jaw is tight and his face thunderous. Who knows what or who has pissed him off this time?

Not my fucking problem.

CHAPTER SIX

Aubrey

Since I opened this morning, my shift was shorter than usual. I was able to clock off by 3PM which was nothing short of a miracle with the insane lunch rush we got. I didn't have anything else planned to do today so I decided to look up some local gyms and see if I could train somewhere close by. It isn't like I am interested in actually entering fights or anything, though I wouldn't say no if something came up, I guess. I just want to spar and keep my skills sharp. It is more like therapy for me than a workout. When I go for too long without being in a gym, I feel like I can't breathe. It gives me the control I crave, the release I need.

I pull up to the gym on second street that Cole told me about. It is strictly an MMA gym where the other ones that I looked up only had MMA classes. Before I left work, I slipped into a workout tank top and my sports bra before I threw on a pair of black spandex. My hair is in a high ponytail, but it is so long that it still swishes against my upper back as I walk up to the front door.

When I step into the gym, the smell of leather and sweat fills my senses. To most it probably isn't the best of smells, but to me it is home. A safe haven. As I walk towards the front desk, I look around to see several different sections throughout the gym with different heavy bags, speed bags as well as a weightlifting area, some treadmills and a couple of designated sparring mats. All of it surrounds the large octagon that takes center stage in the middle of the gym. My knuckles twitch in anticipation. Okay, maybe I lied. I think I am totally down for a fight today.

A guy in his early 30's looks up to me from a pile of papers as he stands behind the front desk.

"Hey there. Looking for someone?" He asks with a polite smile.

I barely contain my eyeroll at the fact that he assumes I am just here to see one of their guys instead of wanting to join their gym.

"No. I am looking to join."

His eyes crinkle a little as he looks at me curiously. "We aren't a regular gym. This is an MMA facility."

"I know, I can read," I say dryly. Their damn sign literally says Glenfield Mixed Martial Arts.

Now his eyebrows shoot up to his hairline.

"Oh, yeah. Of course. Sorry. We don't normally get many women interested. We offer a few introductory classes if you are wanting to get a feel for things," he says as he grabs some membership papers and hands them to me. I take a pen and start filling them out immediately.

"I'm good. You got anyone available to spar today?"

"Like I said, we don't get many women in here. Actually, I think you will be our first."

I cock a brow at him while I continue filling in the forms. "So?"

"Well, you would have to spar with a guy."

This fucking guy, I swear. Didn't we leave this sexist bullshit back in the 20th century?

"That's fine. Just don't give me some rook. I want an *actual* challenge."

"I don't think you know what you are asking for," a familiar voice calls out from behind me.

My body tenses in recognition before I turn around to face him. Dax is standing a few feet away from me with his arms crossed over his chest and a dubious look on his face as his eyes rake over me like I am less than satisfactory.

"You following me or something, short stuff?" Dax asks as several of his buddies surround us. I recognize sandy boy from the diner and their other friend with the dark hair. He looks bored while all the others have smug smiles on their faces. Let me repeat, the dark-haired guy is my favorite of their group by far.

I snort and shake my head as I push my completed papers to the receptionist dude.

"Short stuff? How fucking original. And no, I'm not. This may come as a shock to your delicate ego, but the world doesn't revolve around you. I came to train and to fight. So, why don't you get the fuck out of my face."

"Ohhh, she sure has a mouth on her. I got something to keep that mouth busy, baby," sandy boy winks as he grabs his junk.

Without hesitation I take a healthy step forward, angle my body just right and throw every ounce of muscle I have into one solid right hook. I connect perfectly with his jaw and the piece of shit drops like a sack of potatoes as he goes out like a light.

Good. Maybe the prick will learn a lesson in respecting women from now on.

The room is silent for a moment as I take a step back, rolling my shoulders out as I casually glance around like I didn't just drop a dude nearly twice my size. All the guys around us are flicking their gazes from their knocked-out buddy to me. Some looks are shocked, some are pissed off and I notice that by the look on Dax and the dark-haired guy's face they seem impressed, though Dax makes quick work of masking his appreciation.

"What the fuck is going on out here?" A man who looks to be in his 50's calls out as he comes from a back office.

Before I can open my mouth to defend myself, Dax cuts me off.

"Chase was talking shit to our newest member. She delivered a fucking brutal hook right to the button. He is gonna have a hell of a headache when he wakes up."

The man, who I am assuming is the owner, looks over to me with equal parts fascination and irritation.

"Because you are new, I will let it slide. But everyone knows the rules, no fighting on the concrete," he says as he gestures towards the ground. "You fight on the mats. I don't need someone cracking their head open and making a damn mess."

"Yes, sir," I say respectfully.

He nods seemingly pacified. "What's your name?"

"Aubrey Davis."

"Cameron Smith," he says as he holds out his hand. I shake it and nod to him in greeting. "What are you looking to get out of coming here? Clearly you know how to throw a punch."

"I just want to train. Maybe spar occasionally. Make sure that I keep in shape and don't get rusty."

Cameron nods. "Alright. Well let's see what you got when you don't have the element of surprise on your side. I am sure Josh already told you that we don't have any other women that are members so you will have to be okay with sparring against men."

"More than okay."

He smirks a little before he nods. "Alright. Cane, you up for a fight?" He asks a guy that can't weigh more than 140lbs.

Granted, he is probably the only one that is even remotely close to my weight class, but the dude is stick thin with hardly any muscle to him. It will be over before we even start.

"No offence, but I would like more of a challenge," I cut in.

The Cane guy doesn't seem offended at all, he almost looks relieved. Maybe he realizes that I would have whooped his ass and is glad that I don't have to embarrass him in front of all of us buddies. Cameron opens his mouth to say something before Dax interrupts.

"Think you can take me on, short stuff?" He asks with a challenging look in his eyes.

This is probably dumb. Not only does he have well over eight inches on me as well as probably 100lbs of muscle, but he is a skilled fighter, brutal from what I hear. This wouldn't be an easy fight, not even close. Then again, I never could say no to a challenge.

I give him a short nod as I roll out my shoulders again. Dax looks at me through narrowed eyes for a second before he turns and quickly strips off his shirt, only leaving him in his workout shorts before he jumps into the octagon and starts strapping on his gloves. Ink catches my attention instantly. Dax's body is covered. I knew that he had some from what was peeking out at the clay banks, but I didn't realize that he had so much. His entire back has black wings stretched across it, making him look like some avenging angel. Like an Angel of Death. I guess I know where the nickname comes from now.

The familiar dark-haired guy tosses me a pair of gloves and I catch them quickly just before they hit me in the face.

"These should fit," he says as he walks up to me.

"Thanks," I nod.

"You know, that might not have been a smart thing to do, getting on Chase's shit list. He has been known to hold a bit of a grudge."

I peek over his shoulder to see a now conscious Chase holding an icepack to his jaw as he glares at me from across the room. I shrug unaffected as I start slipping on the gloves.

"I am not worried about it. Besides, I never claimed to be smart."

The guy smirks. "No, I guess not. I am Blake."

I give him a tight smile and a quick nod. "Aubrey."

He gives me a kind smile before glancing over his shoulder and taking a step closer to me as he bends his head down next to my ear.

"Watch Dax's feet. He always takes a step before he punches."

Keeping my face trained in a neutral expression, I give him a nod as he claps me on the back before he walks away to stand with the others. I do some light stretching to loosen up my muscles since I really wasn't expecting to spar after only 10 minutes of being in the gym. I glance around the room to see that it is quickly filling up. I swear there wasn't this many people in the gym when I first showed up. Looks like we are drawing quite the crowd.

"Got to say, I think we deserve a cut of the admission to the show, Cameron," I call out.

He looks around as every person in the building is now circled around the octagon. Chuckling he rubs his jaw and nods.

"We'll talk about it."

Dax regards me respectfully from across the cage. He isn't talking shit like most would. He isn't demeaning me because I am a woman. Sure, he called me short stuff, so I owe him a few hits for that bullshit alone, but I am surprised that that is all he has thrown at me so far.

"Tap out and I will back off immediately. I don't want to hurt you," he says seriously.

I give him an amused look and my lips kick up slightly. "I can't promise the same."

Dax's eyes spark to life with some type of emotion that I don't have time to name as he watches me carefully. I pop my mouth guard in while he does the same before I walk to the middle and get into position. I hear Cameron yell fight in the background and my adrenaline skyrockets. I wait for Dax's initial strike, but it doesn't come. He is waiting for me to make the first move.

Knowing that I can't catch him off guard like I did with Chase, I decide to test the waters a little bit. His reach far exceeds mine so I know that I will have to work around that. He may be stronger with a larger reach, but I am quick. I throw a few lack luster punches that he easily blocks, but that's alright. It's all about assessing your opponent and thanks to Blake's little insider tip, I know what I need to win.

I throw a left jab to his torso and just as he twists to block it, he opens himself up perfectly for me on his right. As quick as I can manage, I bring my leg up and deliver a hard kick to his ribs. He jumps back and grunts in pain before his eyes widen in surprise. I see recognition flash across his face, like he finally understands that I am not some silly little girl trying to play with the big boys, but an opponent. Being the condensing bitch that I am, I crook my finger in a come hither motion before giving him a cocky smirk.

He effortlessly makes his way to me and finally starts throwing some jabs and hooks. I dodge them all as my eyes frequently flick down to watch Dax's feet. If I wasn't watching as intently as I am, I don't think that I would stand much of a chance, honestly. He swings a lot faster than the guy's back home do. Cole said that he was a big deal around here, I see why. His form is excellent and if he were actually *trying* to fight me, which I know he is not right now, then his blows would be pretty damn devastating.

I notice that he hasn't gone for a face shot yet. I am not sure if that is just not done during sparring in this gym, or if that is special treatment on my account. Either way, I am not interested in being treated like a China doll.

Taking a step forward, I open myself up on my left side, knowing that it will be all too tempting for him to send a hit there. Predictably, he does and while he is busy hitting my side with a good amount of strength, I wind my right arm back to connect with his jaw, just like I did with Chase. Unlike his little shit of a friend, Dax doesn't drop, though he does flinch and stumble backwards a few steps before he rights himself. I see him working his jaw slightly as he shakes his head.

Don't worry, I didn't break it, sweetheart. Not that I couldn't have if I really wanted to.

Finally, Dax seems to be over the little cat and mouse game we have going. He holds his arms a little wider as he advances on me and I already recognize what he is trying to do, he is trying to take this to the floor. He is at least twice my size and if he gets me to the ground, it is as good as over.

I am a purple belt in Brazilian Jiu Jitsu, which translates to me to being a badass and since BJJ is mostly grappling techniques, usually I wouldn't be too concerned about being taken down. I am so much smaller than my usual opponents that I can typically wiggle myself out of people's holds easy enough. I have a gut feeling though that tells me if Dax gets me on the ground, I won't be getting up until he decides that I can.

He takes another large step until he is only a few feet from me. I toss an aimless blow as I back up to try to keep him out of arms reach, but he easily takes the hit and grabs me. I send a few direct jabs to his ribs. Each one earns me a feral grown that rumbles up from his chest. I don't want to admit that the sound was probably the hottest thing that I have ever heard, so I push that thought away and contemplate how I can knock this fucker out.

Driving his right leg in between mine, he hits his knee against mine before expertly twisting our bodies so that I am off balance and fall to the ground. Being the cocky fucker that he is, he thinks that just because I am on the ground that I am going to call it quits, but he really doesn't know me. While he is leaning over me, seemingly waiting to see if I am going to give up or not, I bat my eyes seductively and watch as his body relaxes just slightly and leans in just a little bit closer. Fucking idiot.

I quickly wrap my arms around his neck and pull him down into me. In the same moment, I twist around so that my leg has his right bicep locked down tight and my foot is pushing his face away. The move is called Omoplata, one of my favorites.

I can feel Dax begin to panic as he starts to struggle while I put more and more pressure on his arm. He tries to get out of it, but I am bearing down and putting everything I have into this move. I am channeling everything that I possibly can into this one moment. I am only maybe an inch or two away from breaking his arm, but the stubborn ass is refusing to tap out. Oh well, hope he isn't right-handed.

Just before I can finish him off, I hear Cameron shout out to us. "That's enough!" I look up around Dax's body to see Cameron standing right next to us on the other side of the cage, his face carefully neutral. "You guys are done."

Rolling my eyes, I scoff as I untwist myself from Dax and effortlessly stand up. Dax scrambles up to his feet as he shoots me an irritated glare. He isn't able to hold it for long though. I see a small amount of humble admiration shine through the cracks of his façade. I give him a knowing but respectful smirk as we move to the edge of the cage.

"Do you know what you just did?" Cameron asks me gruffly.

I look between him and Dax before my eyes skate over all of the guys in the gym. Everyone is looking at me with shocked expressions except for Chase who looks like he wishes I would just drop dead, and Blake who is giving me a thumbs up as he grins from ear to ear.

"Almost broke his arm because he was too damn stubborn to admit that he had been beaten by a girl."

Dax scoffs but his mask slips further, and he actually smiles. It is one of those barely there smiles, but it is a smile, nonetheless. It hits me then that I don't think I have yet to see him smile since we met. It's a shame because it is a sinfully sexy smile.

Fuck, shit. No. Not going there.

"You almost broke the arm of my undefeated Friday night fighter," Cameron says as his stoic expression turns to an amazed smile.

I let out a dry laugh and lightly shake my head. "Damn, I guess you guys need some new competition then if a girl can come out of nowhere and get him into a position like that."

A few chuckles sound through the room as Dax rolls his eyes. "Don't let your head get too big, short stuff. I wasn't actually trying to hurt you, unlike someone," he says as he rubs his jaw.

I knew that one hurt him pretty good. I am damn proud of it too.

"Well, that is your first mistake. You fight with everything you have, or you don't at all. Don't step on that mat if you aren't going to show up," I say as I condescendingly pat his cheek before stepping down to the ground.

Blake tosses me a water bottle and I accept it happily, draining the entire thing in seconds.

"Nice work, Aubrey," he says as he crosses his arms over his chest.

"Thanks for the tip," I wink.

"What tip?" Dax growls from behind me.

Blake and I trade a secretive smirk before I shrug my shoulders. Blake however seems to want to rub this in his face, so I kick back and watch.

"Oh, nothing, man. You know how I am always telling you about how you need to be careful what your feet give away? Just thought it was fair that I share some of that info with Aubrey here. I mean, in all of our minds she was a complete rookie that had no business being in there and she was taking on the champ. She needed an edge."

Dax scoffs and crosses his tree trunk arms. "Yeah, well clearly she isn't some rookie. I think she cracked a fucking rib," he spits, though his tone holds no venom.

His eyes flick down to mine before he sticks out his hand. My eyes flick to his, waiting for the trick, but when I see no ill intention, I shake it hesitantly. He dips his head so that it is only me and him that can hear his next words.

"Nice work, short stuff. I am impressed and that doesn't happen often. Just know that the next time that I get you on your back, you will be staying there until we are both satisfied."

I whip my hand away and shove him as hard as I can. He seems to have predicted my reaction because he barely even moves an inch as he smirks down at me.

"In your dreams, asshole."

"Ever since that first night," he quips.

The seriousness of his tone catches me off guard. I am not sure what to make of his words or how to even respond, so I just don't. I walk over to one of the empty mats and start stretching out. If I don't stretch after a match like that then I will be walking stiff legged for days. Cameron walks by and drops $200 in my lap. I furrow my brows as I glance up to him.

"Your winnings. The guys were taking bets before you two even got in the octagon. The only one that bet on you was Blake."

I glance over to see Blake shaking a few bills around and giving me a wink across the room.

Yep. Definitely my favorite.

I laugh and slip the money into my bra. "Sweet, thanks."

"No problem. Look, if you are ever looking to make some money, come by on a Friday night. I won't pair you up with someone like Hart but that should make winning that much easier, right?"

I smirk and nod. "I'll think about it. Thanks for the offer."

"No problem."

Cameron strides over to a group of guys and jumps into training.

I smile as I watch them for a little while. It may seem weird that a place like this is where I feel most at peace, but I do. Maybe it is from my original memories of a place not too different from this one, maybe it is from the power and confidence I feel when I walk through a set of gym doors. Either way, this is as close to true peace as I ever feel.

I know that if Dax wanted to take me out early in our fight he could have, everyone knows that. But everyone also knows that I held my own and caught him off guard a few times and I can go home proud of that.

After I am done stretching, I hop up to my feet and head for the door. Several people call out my name and say bye. I haven't met any of them obviously, but I guess they all think it is in their best interest to get on my good side. Whatever. I toss a general wave in the air before I reach the door.

Just as I touch the handle, I feel a tingling at the base of my neck. I turn around to look over my shoulder and see Dax standing in the middle of the octagon as he watches me intently. Our eyes connect for a couple of seconds and my heart beats rapidly out of rhythm in my chest.

Playing it off like I am completely unaffected by him, I open the door and make my way to Betty. The delicious ache that begins to seep into my muscles tells me that today was a good workout and something that I was in desperate need of. I will definitely be back, if anything, to make sure Dax fucking Hart stays humble.

CHAPTER SEVEN

Aubrey

We are slammed at work tonight. Everyone and their mother called out with the flu, so it is just Cole bartending while I work the floor and Freddy in the kitchen. Apparently, all the residents of Glenfield also decided that it was a good idea to get some food from The White Oak tonight. We are currently maxed out on capacity with not one free seat in the whole damn place.

"Hey!" A guy in his mid-twenties calls out from a booth in the corner.

I stop what I am doing and turn around, slapping on my fakest smile before I get to him and his buddy.

"Hi, everything alright?"

He scoffs. "No, everything is not alright. You fucked up our order! We wanted whiskey sours, not straight whiskey." His voice drips with disdain at the fact that he even has to talk to me right now.

Trust me, the feeling is mutual.

I could have sworn that they ordered two neat whiskeys because I remember thinking that they didn't look like the sipping whiskey type. Honestly though, I am drowning out here. So maybe I did screw it up.

"I am sorry about that," I say making my voice come across way more apologetic than I actually am. "I will get you some new drinks right now."

"Damn right you will, honey. Maybe next time use that thing in your pretty little head when you show up to work."

I don't respond to that as I walk away, heading for the bar while checking over the latest order I have to punch in. Working in a customer service job like this has forced me to tolerate way more bullshit than I normally would. But if I want a paycheck, I gotta grin and bear it. Walking up to the bar top, I place my hands on it and lean over to Cole so that I can re-order douche bag #1 & #2's drinks.

"Hey, Cole. I need two whiskey sours. The assholes at table six…" My voice trails off as I look up to see not Cole but Dax bartending. He is standing there with a raised eyebrow, no doubt amused at my surprise. He glances at me and then to the guys in the booth and then back to me.

"Need me to take care of the assholes?" Dax offers as he sends the guys a dark look, though it's wasted since they aren't even paying attention to us.

"No, I've dealt with worse. Just the drinks…please."

He looks at me for a second before he nods and starts making the drinks quicker than I would have guessed he could. I step around him to ring in the multiple food orders that I haven't had a chance to place yet. Once they are all sent through, I walk back over to the bar top to take the drinks, but Dax brushes past me and heads for the douche bag booth. I keep trying to take them from him as he walks, but he blocks all my attempts.

"What are you doing?" I huff in frustration.

He looks down at me with a serious expression and a deep tone. "Fixing an issue."

Dax steps up to the booth as the guys look up to see us approaching. Recognition flashes in their eyes when they see Dax, so they must know him or something. It seems like he really is some type of local celebrity. For an underground fighter a lot of people sure seem to know about him.

"Hey guys. I hear there was some issue with the last round of drinks?" He asks, setting down the drinks

D-bag #1 looks up at him and nods. "Yeah. Barbie over there gave us the wrong drinks. I know she is a hot piece of ass and all man, but she's totally incompetent. She shouldn't even be working here. You only keep girls like her around for one thing, ya know?"

Disgust fills me as he continues to spew shit. I would love nothing more than to throttle his ass right now. Unfortunately, Dax beats me to it. In a flash he has lifted the guy out of the booth and has him pinned to the wall by his throat. The look on the guy's face is one of sheer terror, while Dax wears a deep scowl and practically stares into the dude's soul.

"Apologize," Dax growls.

His tone is icy and hard. His arms are trembling, and it looks like he is barely containing his rage at this point.

"Hey! Fuck you ma-"

Dax cuts him off by bringing him off the wall and slamming him against it again.

"Say you're sorry, you little shit, and then get the fuck out of my bar," he roars in the guy's face.

D-bag #1's eyes dart back and forth between Dax and I before they settle on me.

"I-I'm sorry. Maybe I ordered the wrong drinks. Just a misunderstanding," he pushes out, his voice strained, probably from Dax's grip tightening by the second.

Dax drops him to the ground and watches as the guy falls into a crumpled heap. D-bag #2 quickly helps him up as they scramble out the door like they are running for their lives. Maybe they are, Dax does look pretty pissed. I saw that look in his eye. The pure undiluted rage that was begging to be set free, the darkness begging to envelope him and carry out its dark purpose. The Angel of Death.

Slowly, Dax turns around to look at me as if he is waiting for my words of praise and thanks, but he has another thing coming if that is what he is hoping for, he should know from the last time that he pulled this shit. I don't let people fight my battles for me and this guy has interrupted not one altercation but two. Who the fuck does he think he is? Pure fury is burning inside of me while my hands ball up into fists by my sides. I go to open my mouth, the anger ready to boil over before I hear a booming voice shout across the bar.

"Dax, out!"

The words are short and clipped as I turn to see Marcus glaring at Dax. Dax shrugs like his behavior is to be expected and Marcus shouldn't be surprised. As Dax makes his way out of the bar, he looks back at me one more time with an almost confused expression, like he genuinely thought I would be happy that he barged in and made me out to be a dainty little princess who got her feelings hurt. Obviously, this man doesn't have a fucking clue.

The next day, I'm making my way through the courtyard when I spot Dax talking with Blake and Chase. I storm up to him as the fury from last night begins to rise inside of me. Almost instantly I feel just as pissed as last night. When I reach him, I push him with all of my might. He stumbles a step before he catches himself which wasn't nearly as satisfying as I was hoping. His angry expression swings around to look at who dared to put their hands on him.

In the same instant, I reel my arm back, ready to deck him when he grasps my wrist mid-air before I can make the connection. *Shit.* The anger on his face fades and a stoic mask replaces it, which pisses me off even more for some reason. I let out a frustrated grunt before ripping my hand out of his grasp as I ball both of my fists at my sides, ready to take another swing if the opportunity arises.

"What the fuck was all that about last night?" I seethe.

"What part? The part where I saved you from the jackass talking shit or the part where you got pissed off for God knows what reason this time?" He snaps back, a little glimpse of that temper from last night peeking through. He doesn't scare me though, not even close.

I let out a humorless laugh as I shake my head.

"Saved me? You made me look weak! Now them and anyone else who witnessed your little tantrum thinks that if I fuck up, I can't own up to it. That I have to have someone come fight my battles for me, that isn't me. And news-fucking-flash. I don't need saving, ever."

He looks at me thoughtfully and his mask slips just barely as he speaks.

"Everyone needs saving once in a while. I think the words you are really looking for are thank you."

"Nope, I was thinking more like fuck you. Next time, just make the fucking drinks and let me handle my shit, got it?"

I don't give him time to respond before I shoulder past him, storming away. Maybe some chicks would be thankful for the bullshit hero routine, but where I am from you handle your own and if you don't you are labeled weak and then shit only gets worse from there. I don't know what the fuck possessed him to pull what he did last night but one thing is for sure, if he pulls anything like that again I will break his fucking arm.

The next few weeks pass by in a blur and fall comes out of

nowhere. Thank God for that because I thought the heat was going to kill me. Most of my days have been spent either in class or at work but the occasional free time I have is usually spent at the gym or hanging out with Cole and Mckayla. Cole took me to Kramer's one day after class and he was right, their ice cream is fucking delicious.

I have made a couple of acquaintances at the gym that I spar with when I go there which is cool. They are a pretty chill group of guys. They all seem to have major respect for me since I took on their almighty leader, except for Chase of course who just as Blake predicted seems to have a massive grudge against me.

There have been a few times that I have run in to Dax around campus, always with a different girl perched on top of his lap. We have passed by each other a few times at the gym too, but he never pays me too much attention, which is fine by me. Our eyes will meet, and he will stare at me with that mask of indifference, but I see right through that shit. He is so far from indifferent. Whether he is or not doesn't really matter to me though.

I am hanging out in my room one night working on a paper when I hear a knock come from my door. I jump up and pull it open to reveal Cole's easy smile.

"Hey, darlin'. I thought you might be low," he says, raising a bag that has two gallons of ice cream in it.

I smile and give him a mock irritated glare. "Yeah, *someone* keeps eating it all."

I open the door more to let him in. He walks in and heads for my mini freezer that I bought after last paycheck before putting the ice cream away. Once he shuts the door, he flops onto my bed, sprawling out like he always does. I swear the guy makes himself at home everywhere he goes. I start to gather my books and papers together since I know that I won't be getting anymore work done with Cole here.

"So, what have you been up to?" I ask as I move around my

room, putting things away as I go.

"Just got off the phone with my family. The twins were in some play, and they wanted to tell me all about it." He looks at me with an exasperated face. "For 45 minutes," he deadpans before breaking out into a wide toothed grin.

I roll my eyes at his dramatics and shove him to the side. He loves his sisters so much the guy is a total sucker for them. I am pretty sure *he* talked about them for 45 minutes the first time that we talked about his family.

"Oh, man. They sound like a handful."

He scoffs. "You have no idea. One year, they wanted to help Mama make Dad's birthday cake. They did a pretty good job, except they put salt instead of sugar in it."

"Oh shit," I cringe.

He starts laughing. "Oh yeah. But Dad powered through not one piece but two, at the girl's insistence, of course. Mama was so mad she wouldn't let the girls into the kitchen for a year after that."

I chuckle before something twinges in the typically empty hole known as my chest. My smile slips just for a moment but it's enough for Cole to notice.

"Darlin'?" He asks gently

I pretend to be really busy straightening my bed spread so I don't have to make eye contact.

"Mhmm?"

He reaches over and places his hand on top of mine, forcing my attention to him.

"Why don't you ever talk about your family?" His voice is soft, and maybe a bit worried.

I have done a really good job of steering clear of my past while still getting to know him and Mckayla. I thought they just hadn't noticed. Now I see that they have been waiting for me to bring it up. Poor guy will be waiting a while.

I shrug. "Nothing to tell. I am just a plain girl with a plain life. I don't have any rowdy siblings sabotaging birthday cakes," I say teasingly, desperately trying to get the spotlight off me.

A serious look flashes across his face and his jaw hardens in resolve. "You, Aubrey Davis, are anything but plain."

Sincerity is written across his face like he genuinely believes it. I reach over and wrap him up into a tight hug. I have gotten better about physical touch with others, not that I had much of a choice. It seems both Cole and Kayla are huggers, and it doesn't even make me cringe anymore. Progress. Thankfully, Cole drops the subject, and we move on to talk about some ridiculous customers that he dealt with last weekend.

My past is something that I plan to keep very firmly in the past. I like that I have been able to reinvent myself here and have the life that I finally deserve. For me it doesn't matter where I have been, just where I am going. Besides, what is the point in reliving nightmares?

CHAPTER EIGHT

Aubrey

The next day I decide to take my new paycheck to the store and stock up on essentials. I take a quick shower and toss on a pair of ripped jeans and my favorite Metallica sweatshirt before I add a few sprays of perfume and head out the door. When I go to start Betty up, she makes her typical whining noise, but it lasts a lot longer than normal.

"C'mon baby, you can do it. C'mon, c'mon."

Finally, she gives in and starts. I blow out a rough sigh of relief. *Good girl.* When I get to the store, I grab a cart and pile it full of non-perishable foods. It is really all that I can afford, besides that is all that college kids eat anyways, right?

I have been doing surprisingly well with tips at The White Oak, despite the fact that I am a shit waitress. Not sure if people tip me because they feel bad for me or they feel obligated, either way it is

It doesn't take me long to finish up in the store and check out before I head back to my car. When I step out of the store, I pass by a guy in his early 20's playing guitar while he sits on the curb. It looks like he is homeless. His hair is scruffy and greasy, his clothes are rumpled and stained and the bags under his eyes tell me that he hasn't slept well in God knows how long.

I pause and hang back a few feet away from him as I listen to him play. While he is strumming, his rough voice begins to sing. The song is hauntingly beautiful, talking about the choices you make in life and how to move on when you know it is too late.

I knew a lot of good people back home who made one bad choice and ended up on the streets. Some didn't even make a bad choice. Life had just dealt them a shitty hand and they couldn't get back on their feet. One thing we all seemed to have in common, we are survivors. Fighters. You get knocked down you get back up until you make it to where you want to be.

People walk past him without a second glance, like he is just background noise. Don't people see what kind of talent and potential is sitting right here in front of them? He is a person who is trying to make something of himself. Instead of feeling sorry for himself and wasting away at the bottom of the bottle or a needle he is here, giving what he can in exchange for a chance to turn things around.

I reach into my wallet and grab every single dollar that I have left, not bothering to count it before I drop it into his case, which was previously empty. I bought enough stuff to get me through my next paycheck anyways.

He stops playing suddenly when he sees the cash fall into his case before he whips his head up to me, astonishment splashed across his face. I give him a small smile and lean down before I put my hand on his shoulder. He flinches away for a moment, like he is used to every touch causing him pain.

I know the feeling.

"I'm Aubrey," I say softly.

His eyes search mine for a moment before he gives me a small nod. "Seth."

The guy's voice is raspy and worn, it's clear he hasn't been able to take care of himself the way he should be able to.

"Nice to meet you, Seth." I pause for a second. "I was where you are just a couple of months ago. It gets better, man. Keep fighting."

I expect him to get pissed off at me trying to relate to him. Or maybe embarrassed that I am acknowledging that he is down on his luck. It isn't an easy thing to go through, especially in front of strangers. Instead of all that though, tears fill his eyes as he bites his lip and gives me a short nod. He looks away quickly and brushes at his eyes casually.

"Thanks," he croaks.

I give him another smile before I stand back up and head to Betty. It's the little things in life that can make you realize how far you have come. I can practically still feel my stomach twisting in pain from hunger more times than I could count growing up. The musty smell of our run down trailer that used to make me nauseous from the moment I stepped through the door still fills my nose at unexpected times. I am just thankful all of that is nothing more than a memory now.

When I am about ten miles away from campus, it starts to rain. The sky begins to darken as the rain gradually increases. I glance through my windshield to see that the clouds that are rolling in look black and ominous. It must be one of those southern storms that I have heard so much about.

I don't even finish that thought before Betty starts making this horrible sputtering noise. My stomach drops to the floor as panic fills me. My eyes swing down to see that my heat gauge is in the red. Does that mean the car is too hot? I hear a loud pop as steam starts billowing out from under the hood. *Well, that's not good.*

Betty instantly slows down to a practical crawl. I am barely able to steer her to the side of the road before she finally gives out.

"No, no, no, no, no!" I slam my hand against the steering wheel before I rest my head against the back of my seat. *Fuck.*

I can't afford a tow truck, let alone a shop, especially after I just gave all my cash to Seth. *Really Karma?* I decide that I really have no other choice. I have to get Betty home on my own. Looking out the window, I see that the rain has now picked up to a steady down pour.

Heaving a rough sigh, I flip up my cotton hood and make a break for the trunk where I keep a few tools. I am not sure how to use them or what they should be used on, but I will figure that out later. The rain batters against me, soaking me in an instant. I grab the first thing that I see in my bag of tools which is a crescent wrench. Maybe something needs to be loosened? Or tightened?

I make my way to the hood with less urgency than before, seeing as I am already completely soaked to the bone. When I pop the hood, more steam billows out causing my situation to really sink in and force me to realize how utterly fucked I am. A car drives next to me slowly as if they are reveling in my misery. I flip them off and turn back to stare at my car, as if I can intimidate her into starting or at least telling me what the hell I need to do to fix her.

"Aubrey? Are you okay?" A voice calls out.

I tighten my grip on the wrench for a second before I recognize the voice. I see an old school mustang is now pulled over on the shoulder just ahead of me as Dax jogs over with his hood up.

"Dax?" I stupidly question. Of course, it's him. I would recognize him anywhere.

When he comes up beside me, he is looking back and forth between me and Betty.

"Car problems?"

I let out a humorless laugh and shake my head as I look up at the sky briefly before looking back to Dax.

"Yeah, guess so. I'm not sure what happened. I think it got too hot and let out a lot of steam or something."

He tries to muffle a laugh as he softly shakes his head. "What? You don't know a lot about cars, do you?"

"I know you put gas in it to make it go, and you have brakes to make it stop. And every year or so I put a quart of oil in it."

His eyes widen for a second before he shakes his head.

"I'm not even going to comment on any of that." He moves around me to get a better look under the hood, which is still billowing steam. "Have you called a tow yet?"

"Ah, uh no. I can't really afford it. I was hoping to just patch her up and get her back to campus at least."

He shakes his head at me, a surprisingly remorseful look on his face.

"I hate to break it to you, short stuff, but this thing isn't going anywhere anytime soon. Not unless it's hooked up to a tow truck."

My heart falls at his words. I knew that was the case but having someone else say it out loud makes it so much worse. He must see the panic and heartbreak on my face. He turns and looks out across the darkened wet road for a second before turning back to me.

"I have a buddy who owes me a favor, he drives a tow truck. I can have him take it to whatever shop you want him to drop it off at? Lou's is really good place."

"Yeah, I don't really have the finances to take care of something like that…Could he maybe just drop it off at campus? I will try to figure it out from there."

I bite back the emotions that are beginning to flood me. The gravity of my situation is starting to weigh down on me and I honestly have no fucking clue what I am going to do. Dax looks at me for a moment as if contemplating something before he speaks again.

"Well, how about I take a look at it? I am a pretty good mechanic, restored my baby myself," he says, gesturing to his car.

"No, that's okay," I answer quickly.

He rolls his eyes and raises his voice to speak over the rain which has now become even heavier. Can rain be heavier than a downpour? Because right now it definitely is.

"Don't be stubborn. You need help and I'm offering. If I can fix it, I will. You buy the parts, alright?"

I look at him skeptically. No one is nice for nothing, what is he playing at? Honestly though, am I even in a position to argue regardless? Reluctantly, I nod my head.

"Alright, let me give you a ride to campus and I will call my buddy."

"Okay, let me just grab my stuff."

"You go. I'll grab your things," he says as he shoos me towards his car.

If I wasn't shivering from being drenched, I might protest. Instead, I practically run to his car. I am immediately greeted with the smell of leather with a hint of mint, most likely from the smooth black seats and the pack of peppermint gum in the center console. I don't know much about cars, but I know that this must be a classic and has been taken care of as one. I glance over to the back seat, finding myself wondering how many girls have been back there.

Why would I even waste my time wondering that? The number is probably too high to count.

Dax jumps into the car quickly, snapping my attention forward once again. He sets my purse and bags at my feet before starting the car and cranking up the heat, turning all of the vents towards me before he turns back on to the road. A funny feeling spreads across my chest at the small seemingly natural gesture. I am pretty sure I don't like it.

After a few minutes of silence, I blurt out, "Thank you for this.

You didn't have to help me. I know we don't really like each other but I appreciate it."

He raises that single stupid fucking eyebrow at me as he splits his attention between the road and me.

"I don't dislike you. Though I am sure you can't say the same."

A laugh escapes me before I can push it down because honestly, he isn't too wrong. Ever since we sparred at the gym, I haven't outright disliked him, except for when he pulled that hero bullshit. Looking back now I feel like I may have overreacted a bit. He is probably just used to damsely girls that need saving. That just isn't me though. In this fairy tale, I save myself.

"I don't dislike you when you mind your own business," I say with a shrug as I stare out the front windshield.

Dax barks out a rough laugh that has my head whipping over to him. A full smile is spread across his face as his shoulders shake. Damn, if I thought that smile at the gym was good this one is knock you out cold good. He doesn't even look like the surly brawler that I have come to know.

"That doesn't sound overly warm. So, are you saying that I should just toss your ass out of my car and let you solve your own problems then?"

I frown at his words before crossing my arms. Well, when he puts it like that…

"I'm kidding," he says with a slight laugh. "I'm happy to help."

I narrow my eyes at him. "Why?"

He opens his mouth to speak but hesitates. His brows furrow as he looks out the window before shaking his head.

"Not really sure, honestly. This is a first for me."

Not knowing how to respond to that, I choose to stay quiet. To my surprise the silence doesn't feel awkward at all, it almost feels natural which weirds me the fuck out. He has been really helpful and surprisingly nice today. He is right. If he would have listened to all of my 'mind your own business' talk then he could have left my ass stranded on the road, but he didn't. I try to remind myself that this is the same asshole that I have had nothing but problems with ever since coming here but he is making it kind of hard right now.

Soon we are pulling up to campus just before he puts the car into park.

"Well, give me your number and I'll let you know when your car makes it to my place. Then I can let you know what we are dealing with."

I narrow my eyes slightly. "Was this all an elaborate ploy to get my number?"

He scoffs and rolls his eyes. "Short stuff, you are hot as fuck, but I am not hard up for pussy by any means. Don't flatter yourself."

I give him a short nod, feeling oddly pacified with that answer before I take his phone and punch in my number.

"Thanks again, really. I appreciate it."

He nods and though he isn't smiling, he isn't scowling either which is basically the Dax Hart equivalent of a smile.

"No problem."

I give him a quick wave before I hop out of the car and make a run for my dorm. After a scalding hot shower and a warm cup of tea, I change into a dry pair of pajamas and pop in a movie. I have gotten really ahead in almost all of my classes, so I don't have to worry about any homework, thankfully. Soon, I find my eyes drooping just before I drift off to sleep, the last thing that I remember seeing when I close my eyes is the image of a man with sharp green eyes and surly scowl on his face.

CHAPTER NINE

Aubrey

The next morning, I am woken up by a text. I look at my phone bleary eyed to see that it's from Dax.

Dax: Your car just got here. You sure you don't want to just scrap it? I think the poor thing needs to be put out of its misery.

Fucker. Betty is a great car. She just needs a little TLC and some money put into her. Unfortunately, I don't have tons of extra money at the moment, so she will have to settle with my love. How can he even suggest scrapping her?

Me: Betty has always been reliable and has taken great care of me.

Dax: Until now.

Me: Shut up. Just let me know when we are tearing into her.

Dax: We?

Me: Yeah. I want to learn what's wrong and

how to fix it. Then if something like this ever happens again, I can get myself out of the situation and I won't need help from anyone.

Dax: You really hate relying on other people, huh?

Me: I'd rather gouge my eyes out than willingly depend on someone.

Dax: Seems extreme but I get it. Alright, I am gonna tear into it now. Come by whenever. 425 Park Lane, second driveway all the way down.

Me: On my way.

I peel myself out from under my toasty warm blankets and get ready before I order a ride. About half an hour later, I am pulling up to a garage in the back of someone's property. Maybe this is Marcus's place?

Getting out of my ride, I walk towards the open garage door, hoping I am at the right place. If Dax sent me the wrong address to fuck with me or something I will murder his ass. As I make my way inside the garage, I spot Dax quickly tossing a beer bottle into the trash. He is wearing a pair of oil-stained jeans and a beat-up white t-shirt. Even like this he still looks sexy as sin, but you'll never hear me admit it out loud. I am sure the hordes of women he entertains blow up his ego plenty as is.

When he sees me in the doorway, I notice his gaze skates over me from head to toe. I look down at my outfit and shrug. I am only wearing my leather jacket hoodie and a pair of jeans with my chucks. A far cry from the usual primped and polished outfits I see the girls he is with squeeze themselves into.

To his credit, instead of looking disgusted by my lack of fashion sense he almost looks like he is admiring me. Like I am so brave to come see this dude without caring what he thinks. I can't help but scoff at the thought of that.

“Hey,” I finally say, dropping down onto a bar stool and setting two coffees and a box down on the table.

“Krispy Kreme?” He asks, raising his eyebrows with a disapproving look.

“Breakfast of champions,” I retort.

“Yeah, well, I don’t eat that shit.”

“Good. They aren’t for you. I brought a coffee for you but keep your meaty paws away from my breakfast.”

I reach over and open the box of doughnuts before I pull one out. I am mid bite when I see Dax has his mouth slightly parted in shock. What is his deal? I only got half a dozen.

“Are you seriously going to eat all of those?” His tone is one of disbelief and it instantly pisses me off.

I scowl at him after finishing one and shove him to the side.

“Hey. Don’t fat shame.”

He throws his hands up in surrender as he shakes his head.

“That’s not what I meant. I am just surprised that you can eat all of that and still look the way you do.”

My eyes are still narrowed on him as I cock my head to the side.

“And how is that?”

He shrugs and answers like it’s the most obvious thing in the world.

“Hot.”

Dax is just another womanizer, his opinion of me shouldn’t matter. So why did my heart stutter for a moment when he said that? Nope, not going down that road.

“So, you ready to dive in?” Dax asks, effectively breaking my inner monologue.

“Yeah, let’s do this.”

After a couple minutes of poking around to get an assessment, he sighs heavily and runs a hand down his face.

“Well do you want the good news or the bad news first?”

"Good."

"Well, the good news is that I am a badass mechanic." I give him a derisive snort and stare at him, waiting for the rest. "The bad news is that your car is a piece of shit."

"Hey!" I interject. He chuckles lightly and holds up a hand so I will let him continue.

"So, you need all new fluids, obviously. Your alternator is about to go out, your tires are bald as hell and your brakes are almost metal on metal. I can't believe this thing was running at all, but the thing that effectively killed Billy-"

"Betty," I snap.

"My apologies, Betty, was a blown head gasket. To fix that, I am going to have to rebuild the engine."

I cringe. "Is that expensive?"

My voice is meek, probably for one of the first times in my life. I am already mentally calculating how much disposable income I have and trying to figure out a way to scrape up the funds to patch Betty back together. Spoiler alert, it isn't looking good.

Dax shrugs as he buries his hands into his pockets and leans against Betty.

"Nah. I am pretty resourceful. I'll do it for as cheap as possible."

"Why are you doing all this? I mean, it was the decent thing to do not leaving me on the side of the road in the middle of a storm, but you could have left it at that. Why did you have my car towed and are now offering to do all the work for free? What's in it for you?"

"You know, short stuff, sometimes people do things just to be nice. No ulterior motive."

"Bullshit," I scoff. "Everyone wants something, so what do you want?"

His eyes flare and I mentally prepare myself for whatever dirty or degrading thing he is about to ask for. Instead, he surprises the hell out of me when he answers.

"Just say thank you."

I furrow my brows for a moment. It can't be that easy, can it? The sincerity that is plainly written across his face would disagree with my skepticism though. I nod slowly as I swallow back a sudden rush of emotions.

"Thank you."

Before I can think twice about it, I take a step forward and wrap my arms around him in a quick hug. As soon as my body touches his, my brain goes haywire. What the fuck am I doing? Why the hell am I touching him? Why the hell did I initiate it? I blame Cole and Kayla. They are making me a hugger and it's gross.

I go to pull away but before I can Dax pulls me tightly into him and buries his face into my neck. He takes a deep breath before he blows it out. I swear it feels like he just smelled my hair. I try to think about the last time that I washed it and feel relief when I realize I did last night, so it must not smell that bad.

He makes the hug last a lot longer than I was planning on. When I try to pull away again, his arms tighten just slightly. The gesture is surprisingly tender for someone who seems so detached with the women I have seen him with. They are always going out of their way for his attention, but he rarely returns it. Only by placing a hand on a hip or allowing them to sit on him or touch him. He is never the initiator, at least that I have seen.

"No problem," his gruff voice breathes out just above a whisper.

Then he reaches out and brushes a loose strand that has fallen from my ponytail and tucks it behind my ear. I can't quite name what emotion is dancing in his eyes right now, but it's like he has truly dropped his mask and I am seeing the real him for the first time. The only word that I can give it is intense. I bite the inside of my cheek and look down, trying to break whatever the hell is going on right now. Seemingly on the same page, Dax takes a step back as he clears his throat.

"So, I can start working on Bobby a little at a time. I am hoping it shouldn't take longer than two to three weeks."

I narrow my eyes at his intentional misuse of her name. "Okay. I work most days but anytime I don't, I will be here."

"You don't have to help, short stuff, really. There isn't much you can do, it's kind of a one-person job."

I can't help but feel a little disappointed at the fact that he doesn't want me here. I am sure that I will probably get in the way more than anything, but I see this as an opportunity to learn something that I need to know so that I can avoid more situations like yesterday.

"I know you probably don't want me in your personal space, but I really would like to learn. I have never had the chance to learn about cars and I think it's something I probably should know more about."

He nods at that, seemingly agreeing.

"Yeah, everyone should know at least the basics. Well, if you really want to help then you can. Just let me know."

"Okay. Well, I don't work on Tuesday."

"Then I'll see you on Tuesday, short stuff."

Dax tried to offer me a ride home, but I told him no and reminded him that I am very capable of taking care of myself. If I am being honest things were a little too weird with him today. I didn't think that I could handle a 15-minute car ride with him right then.

On Tuesday I went over to Dax's place, and we got to work. I quickly realized that there really wasn't anything for me to help with, so I made myself comfortable on the couch he had off in the corner and watched him work on Betty. Occasionally, I would ask a question but for the most part we sat in comfortable silence.

"I don't know anything about you," I blurt after a while.

He stops what he is doing and looks up at me, lifting one eyebrow in question.

"What?"

"I don't know anything about you, only what I hear. If I am going to be spending a lot of time over here, I want to know that you aren't some crazy psychopath that is going to kill me and wear my skin or something."

He lets out a sound that is a mix between a laugh and a choke.

"That isn't high on my to-do list, but I will keep the idea in mind. But that goes both ways. I don't know anything about you either. For all I know you sabotaged your car as an excuse to get close to me and try to seduce me," he smirks.

I gasp out a laugh before I huck a pillow at him. He dodges it chuckling before he re-focuses his attention on Betty.

"You wish," I mutter.

I sit there for a few moments before speaking up again.

"Okay, let's play question for a question then. I'll go first." I purse my lips and tap my finger on my chin considering my first question. "What is your favorite type of food?"

Dax barks out a surprised laugh. "Seriously? You want to get to know me to make sure that I am not a potential serial killer, and your first question is food oriented?"

I give him a very blank stare, my tone completely serious.

"Food is a very important subject."

He shakes his head at me like I am crazy but indulges me by answering.

"Mexican, specifically the taco truck on main street. What about you?"

"Same. I could live on only street tacos and margaritas," I joke.

"What's your favorite color?" I ask next.

"Turquoise," he says looking directly into my eyes.

I shift slightly trying to hide the blush that is creeping up my neck. Most people say my eyes are blue but if you really look you will notice that they are more like Turquoise. Though I have never met anyone that has ever commented on it. Then again, maybe I am reading too much into this and it is just a coincidence. Fuck. Maybe this was a bad idea.

"What do you want to be once you graduate?" He asks, obviously picking up on my uncomfortableness. I think about that for a moment before looking up to him with my completely honest answer in mind.

"Happy," I say with a sharp nod.

He pauses for a second before nodding his head in agreement. I think it's what everyone strives for, but only those who have felt like it wasn't in the cards for you can really appreciate what it would mean to be truly happy in life.

"Why do you only do underground fights?" I ask. "From what I have seen you are pretty good, so why aren't you competing? You could potentially have a real future in the UFC."

His casual expression falls, and he turns away, apparently ignoring my question. I accept it, he doesn't owe me anything. I just know that I am missing something here.

"I had a lot of anger issues as a kid, still do," he says with a shrug. "My dad bailed when he found out my mom was pregnant, so he wasn't in the picture and my poor mom was at her wits end with me. So, my uncle put me into some classes when I was 8 to keep me out of trouble." He laughs softly as if remembering something.

"Anyways, I got really into it, got pretty good too. Then in high school Chase and I crashed a fight at the gym on a Friday night. I was a young punk that thought I could whoop anyone's ass so when there was a last-minute drop out, I stepped in." He shakes his head. "I got the shit kicked out of me. But that only made me more determined. It made me work harder, longer and come back more often until I was the best." He pauses for a moment before continuing.

"I got so good that Cameron decided to train me my freshman year of college and set up a low-end league fight. I went in there and knocked my opponent to the ground in the first round. But when I am in there, and I am fighting, it's hard to switch it off. To be giving everything you have and then just stop. It's hard for me at least. I kept pounding the guy after the ref called knockout. When I was finally able to stop, he had to be rushed to the hospital and it took three security guys to get me off him," he says with a wince.

"They took my win, and I got a warning. A month or so later, same issue. A couple months after that, I did it again. I try so damn hard when I am in there. I guess you could say it's my therapy and I just kind of check out and go to a different head space. I became a liability, so I was put on suspension for three years. I guess to give you a short answer, I have self-control issues."

He looks down at his hands for a moment as if recognizing what they are capable of for the first time. He flexes them and looks back up to me.

"I have already blown my shot at the big leagues. Even with my suspension ending soon, I doubt Cameron would work with me again. I brought a lot of negative attention not only to my own name but to the gym.

"Uncle Marcus has been killing himself at the bar for years now. I have tried to drop out of school to help him more, but he refuses to let me. So, I will probably take over a good amount of the work there when I graduate to give him the break that he deserves."

"That is pretty noble of you," I comment. "Giving up your dream for your uncle."

Dax shrugs. "He was the closest thing to a father that I ever had. Besides, I am not totally giving up. I still get to fight on Fridays and train when I have free time. I have to keep fighting no matter what capacity that is in. I need to. I need it to breathe, to feel alive."

My breath catches at his words. I can relate so much to how he feels. You don't get it unless you are a fighter. The freedom and power you feel, not just over another person but over yourself. You feel like if you work your ass off and put your mind to something, you can do it, and no one can ever take that away from you.

"So, is all of that the real reason why your fight name is The Angel of Death?" I ask.

He gives me a rough nod before letting out a hollow laugh.

"Yeah, I mean, I am sure my tattoo didn't help but at the time everyone was saying how fighting me was like taking on death itself. Like I was the fucking grim reaper."

I nod my understanding and I pause before asking my next question "Do you think you have yourself under control now?"

He just shrugs. "It's been three years. I am older now."

"That doesn't really change anything though," I say dubiously.

"No, I guess not. I'm getting better, I think. I didn't lose control with you," he points out.

I scoff and shake my head. "Don't act like you took it too easy on me. I know you held back but we both know that I out maneuvered you in the end."

He shrugs. "You are a good fighter. Where did you train?"

I tense at his question before I will my body to relax as I pick at my nails casually.

"Back home."

The room goes quiet for a moment and for a second, I think that he is going to drop it but of course he doesn't.

"So, what are you running from then?"

"What makes you think I am running from anything?" I try for an unaffected tone, but even to my own ears it sounds anything but.

He cocks his head to the side and slightly narrows his eyes.

"Call it intuition."

I hold my face in an expressionless stare as I contemplate how much I am going to give up.

"My past."

He nods in acceptance and the game unofficially ends.

CHAPTER TEN

Aubrey

I am working out at the gym late night Friday when Cameron comes strolling out of his office.

"Hey killer. We are getting started downstairs in a few. People will be rolling in soon. Why don't you stick around?"

I shrug and nod, throwing one more hit to the heavy bag I was working over before I grab my stuff and head to the locker room. Since I am the only female member that they have ever had the gym only has one locker room, but fuck if I care.

I peel off my sweat drenched clothes before stepping into the shower. The water is lukewarm at best, so I decide to just worry about washing my body and getting out. As the water pours over me, I feel the faint sound of the door opening. Shit. Guess I am not alone anymore.

"Aubrey! What the fuck!" Dax snarls as he storms over to me. Shoving past me, he slams the shower off before throwing a towel at my face and spinning on his heel to look at the wall.

"Dude, what the fuck is your problem? I'm not done!" I snap as I wrap the towel around my body.

"Yes, you fucking are! The other guys will be down here any second and here you are taking a soapy shower in the middle of the room like the star of a fucking porno!" He snarls.

His fists are clenched at his sides while his body towers over me completely still and rigid. I snort a laugh at his bullshit and shake my head.

"Oh my god, just fuck off. All of you shower in front of each other all the time and in case you didn't notice, these are the only showers in the damn building," I say as I quickly dry off before slipping on my bra and panties and then a pair of grey sweats and a black t-shirt.

"Yeah, well you could have at least told someone that you were going to be in here so no one would walk in and see all of that."

"Sorry, princess. I didn't know that my body was so offensive to look at," I scoff as I brush past him.

I only make it two steps before his hand grips my bicep tightly, yanking me back until my body slams against his. I try to pull away, but his grip only tightens. Sure, I could probably maneuver myself out of his hold somehow if I felt like I was actually in danger but like I have said before, Dax Hart doesn't scare me.

His head dips down as his nose brushes against mine, his voice a rough grumble.

"Your body is a lot of things, but offensive is not one of the words I would use to describe it."

I feel dizzy having his mouth so close to mine. A fog settles over my head suddenly making me unsure of where I even am right now. Why was I mad? I can't even remember what we were fighting about.

"What words would you use?" I ask huskily.

His lips twitch just a bit at my question but the serious expression on his face remains as his head lowers another half an inch before his other hand just barely brushes the dip of my waist.

"Sinful, tempting…fucking perfect."

My breath catches as his green eyes flare with intensity. He leans in just another inch, his lips only a hairs width away from mine when my brain begins to finally start working. What the fuck, Aubrey? Are you seriously about to let this womanizing douche come in here, end your shower, man handle you and then kiss you? Fuck that.

Quickly, I rip myself out of his grip and take several healthy steps back. Dax doesn't move an inch, his body still hunched over like he is still bending over me. His head slowly turns to look at me, his face completely blank before he starts walking towards me until we are chest to chest.

Fuck. What the hell is he doing to me? I am screaming at my legs to run or my arms to push him or hit him, fucking anything. But I used up all of my energy in fleeing from him the first time. Now all I can focus on is the feel of his heavy heartbeat through his chest, beating in time with mine.

"Sounds like you are a bit of hypocrite then, huh? You had no problem watching me shower, you just didn't want other people to see me like that, right?" I rasp.

Something dark passes across his face. I am not sure if it was my words or maybe a thought that was triggered from my words but either way the heavily tense moment evaporates into thin air. Dax takes two steps away from me before he turns around and storms out of the locker room.

Breathing out a deep sigh of relief, I count my stars that what I said pushed him away. I don't know how much longer either of us would have lasted. *What the hell was that?* Shaking my head, I grab all of my stuff before I jog out of the locker room, doing my best to push that weird ass interaction as far away from my head as possible.

I dump my stuff inside Cameron's office so that no one tries to steal my shit before I head down to the basement where a decent sized crowd is already gathered. I catch Blake's eye as he plays bouncer at the side door that opens to the parking lot where everyone is paying their cover charge. He gives me a friendly smile and a head nod as he ushers in the next group of people. I give him a small wave before I slowly make my way through the room.

In the front row of metal folding chairs, I see a few guys I spar with taking up a majority of the row. When Cane sees me coming over he nudges the guy next to him to move over a seat before gesturing for me to sit. I give them a nod in appreciation before I take the seat.

Josh comes up behind me, his breath already reeking of stale beer as he slumps over my shoulder and giggles. I shit you not, the man giggles.

"Aubrey! You never hangout with us on Fridays! To what do we owe this great pleasure?"

"No work tonight and my workout ran late," I smirk as I watch him drunikly try to stand up straight.

"You on the card tonight?" He slurs.

I shake my head with a small laugh causing him to pout.

"Damn. I was hoping to make some cash. I'd bet my whole fucking paycheck on you. All these dumb kids that come here have no clue what a badass you are. They'd all bet against you and then I'd make so much fucking dough."

I laugh as I watch him stumble into a seat. "Maybe another time."

He continues to pout but nods before he turns to one of the other guys and starts rambling on about God knows what. Cane and I talk for a little while until the lights start to flicker before heavy metal music starts booming through the room. Soon, Dax emerges from the locker room and jumps up into the makeshift octagon that is in the middle of the room.

I have been to some nasty underground fights before, but this place is one of the better ones. It doesn't smell too awful down here and seems relatively clean. The octagon has a newish mat on the ground and a 7ft cage surrounding it. Dax bounces on his toes a little bit while Chase and Blake stand behind him, rubbing his shoulders and pumping him up.

A few more seconds go by before the song changes to Stronger by Kanye West and a young guy with a red mohawk comes out. I scoff at the song choice because a walk out song should tell you everything you need to know about a fighter, and I don't know if he could have made a lamer choice. I would be shocked if the guy is even 18, he looks younger. He is also looking awfully smug for someone without a lot of muscle or definition.

Shit. This is going to be a blood bath.

Both of the guys pop in their mouth guards and strap their gloves on before Cameron steps to the center of the floor and starts the fight. I look to the side and see Blake and another regular in the gym handling a shit ton of money as bets are practically being tossed at them from every angle. I am sure everyone is putting their money on Dax, at least if they were smart they would, because mohawk guy doesn't have a chance in hell.

I swing my eyes back over to the fight just in time to see Dax throw a nasty right hook to mohawks jaw. He spins around in a circle but manages to stay upright, though he already looks pretty disoriented. The kid throws a few wild haymakers and surprisingly enough one actually lands across Dax's eyebrow, splitting it open. I watch as Dax lifts his hand up to his face and sees the fresh blood on his white glove before a dangerous look flashes across his face.

Oh fuck.

Almost effortlessly, Dax throws out a left kick, complimenting it with a right jab to the ribs and then a left hook to the jaw. The kid drops to the ground, obviously knocked out but that doesn't stop Dax. Not wasting a moment, Dax jumps on top of the kid and attacks, throwing devastating blows at him in a steady rhythm. Left, right, left, right, left, right. Blood splatters across the mat with each swing and I am pretty sure that I just saw a tooth or two roll across the floor.

I recognize the look in Dax's eyes, or really lack of. His gaze is blank, almost robotic as he viciously tears the kid apart. If someone doesn't stop him soon he is going to kill the guy. Without thinking twice, I jump out of my seat and launch myself against the fence.

"Dax! Dax! Stop!" I shout.

He can't hear me though. The crowd's roars are so loud that my efforts are like trying to shout into a hurricane. My eyes quickly flick around looking for someone else to step in. I don't see Cameron anywhere, knowing that he would have stopped things already if he was in here. He must have stepped out. My eyes connect with Blake in the back of the room, catching the worried look he is sharing with me. Why isn't anyone doing anything?

Fuck it.

Gripping the fence tightly, I make quick work of scaling it before hopping down on the other side. I hear a few panicked voices call out my name, but I block them out as I run over to where Dax and the unconscious kid are sprawled out across the floor.

Squatting down next to Dax, I quickly grab his face in my hands and pull hard so that he is forced to face me. His fist freezes midair as he looks into my eyes. His normally emerald green eyes are currently an obsidian black while his face is hauntingly blank. It is like he isn't even here right now but somewhere dark and deep inside his mind.

"Come back, Dax. Come back. You aren't there anymore. You

are safe. Deep breaths," I say softly.

I don't actually know what he is going through at this moment, but I know when I am spiraling, those words usually do the trick to bring me back to reality. I can see the moment that my words sink in for him. The darkness in his eyes slowly starts to recede as he stares into my eyes. I keep demonstrating deep breaths while making sure to never break our eye contact or my hold on his face.

It seems to be enough to ground him because after several deep breaths he blinks a few times before he looks down at the unconscious kid underneath him. He practically scrambles off of him before throwing himself up against the cage on the other side of the octagon. Quickly, Dax shouts out for their on-hand medic to help the kid. The medic and a few other younger guys help get the guy out of the octagon and on to a stretcher before they take him back into the locker room.

Dax is standing a few feet away from me now and the crowd is going crazy with excitement and blood lust. Instead of reveling in the celebration, Dax and I are stock still in a silent stare off. No words need to be shared between us. Despite the fact that I fucking hate it, Dax Hart seems to be able to read me like a book. He saw everything the moment that he locked eyes with me. He sees that I get it. That I have been there. I have had my demons practically suffocating me, forcing me to claw my way out of the pits of hell and back to reality. I understood what he needed in that moment and nothing more needs to be said about it.

Suddenly, the gate opens and Chase bounds in excitedly with several girls as they rush Dax, giggling and pulling on him like they didn't just watch him spiral to a dark place. Like he didn't almost kill a man. I watch for a second, expecting him to lap up all the attention he rightfully deserves but instead he brusquely pushes his little fan club aside and strides over to me. He lowers his lips to my ear as he tries to talk over the crowd.

"Thanks."

I give him a tight smile and pat his shoulder before I make my way out of the cage. I get scathing glares from that redhead chick and her little group of followers that are always hanging all over Dax and Chase, but I couldn't honestly give a fuck. I don't even bother giving them a second look as I weave my way through the crowd. I quickly stop by Cameron's office to grab my stuff before I head home.

CHAPTER ELEVEN

Aubrey

The next morning, I wake up to an incessant knocking at my door. Seriously? I was lucky enough to not only get last night off but all day today as well. I had big plans like sleeping until one in the afternoon and ordering takeout.

Angrily, I yank off my blanket and stomp over to my door, ripping it open to see Kayla bright eyed and bushy tailed in a sports bra and a pair of fancy yoga pants with a high ponytail. I also see Cole standing behind her in a cut off shirt and a pair of basketball shorts with a sweet smile. What the fuck?

"Good morning, honey. You are coming hiking with us!" Mckayla announces.

I cock an eyebrow at her and swing my gaze to Cole. He throws his hands up in defense and points at Kayla.

"Don't look at me. I got the same wakeup call about a half an

I contemplate if a judge will sympathize to my case in Kayla's murder and deem it justifiable. I mean, who the hell wakes someone up on their Saturday off before 9am to go hiking? I don't think there is a person alive that wouldn't side with me.

I scoff before slamming the door shut. Unfortunately, Kayla being the sneaky little bitch that she is, sticks her foot in the way so that at the last minute it bounces back open.

"Nice try but you are coming with us. Non-negotiable," she smiles.

I wonder if she would look so chipper with a few less teeth?

I narrow my eyes at her I wish I didn't like her so much, then I wouldn't feel so bad at the idea of smacking her around a bit. Unfortunately for me, the girl has grown on me, so I won't be getting physical with her, today at least. In the short time that I have known Kayla I have learned that she has been spoiled all her life and doesn't understand the word no, so I am aware that this fight is a moot point.

Letting out a heavy sigh, I scrub my hand through my disheveled hair as I cross my arms over my chest.

"I will only go if you buy me breakfast," I finally concede.

"Done!" She agrees happily.

"Alright. Give me 15 minutes. I want to hop in the shower first."

"Pfft, that is stupid. We are going to get sweaty anyways. Shower after. Come on, throw on some clothes and let's go."

Holy fuck she is annoying. Why the hell do I put up with her again? I huff out an aggravated breath as I grab a sports bra, a black pair of running shorts and my off-brand tennis shoes.

Kayla slips some cash to Cole and pats his cheek.

"Be a love and grab some breakfast at the cart downstairs. They have these breakfast sandwiches that Aubrey loves."

Cole rolls his eyes like he is irritated to have to go but gives away his excitement at my coming with his trademark smirk before he heads downstairs. Kayla perches herself on the edge of my bed and scrolls through her phone while I get dressed.

"So, have you filed the report yet?" I ask.

Kayla looks up from her phone and grimaces before nodding.

"Yeah. I went home the other day and told my parents what happened. They took me down to the police station and last I heard Kyle was in jail."

"Good. Are you okay? I know it must have been hard to talk about it with your parents let alone the cops."

She shrugs. "I'm fine. It was a close call. My dad has insisted that I take some self-defense classes and carry a taser on me at all times from now on."

I chuckle at that until she pulls out a police issued taser gun out of her designer bag and waves it around.

"Oh fuck!" I laugh. "No one is gonna fuck with you now."

She smirks and puts it away before we head out the door to meet up with Cole. We run into him just outside the building.

"Miladies," he says with an exaggerated bow as he extends a couple of sandwiches to us.

"No, thanks. I am not doing carbs right now," Kayla says with a wrinkled nose.

I roll my eyes and shake my head.

"What does that even mean? Carbs are in everything."

"I am trying to stick to lean meats and leafy greens."

"Whatever, more carbs for me," I say as I stretch my hand out for the second sandwich.

Cole laughs and hands it over to me before he takes a bite out of his own.

"I don't get it, Aubrey. How can you always be hungry?" Kayla asks as we start walking towards the parking lot.

I shrug. *Because I spent years hungry*, I think to myself. Cole speaks up and throws an annoyed look at Kayla.

“Don’t be jealous just because she can out eat you and still have an incredible body.”

My eyebrows raise and an amused smirk crosses my lips. Cole winks like he is some playboy but the blush that begins to bloom across his cheeks proves it is nothing more than false vibrato.

“Damn right I am jealous! All I want to do is eat ribs and drink beer every day of my life, but if I did then I would need a forklift to get this ass out of bed every morning,” she says smacking her size two ass.

I shove her playfully and laugh. She is so ridiculously gorgeous, but she tries to pretend like she doesn’t know it. I don’t know if she says that stuff because she is fishing for compliments or maybe she is genuinely insecure. Either way there is no realm of possibility that Kayla could ever be considered fat.

After a quick drive, we end up at the Glenfield National Forest Park. Cole insisted on driving, saying it was the gentlemanly thing to do. Kayla nodded like it made perfect sense and I laughed because I don’t think I have ever met anyone quite like either of them.

Kayla is bouncing excitedly up the trail, going on and on about how the peak is a to die for view. Soon she starts going on about her latest hook up and how hung he is. The metaphors that she came up with had me nearly in tears laughing while Cole looked like he was going to die of embarrassment.

We have been hiking for four or five miles at least by now and despite my extreme physical fitness, I am fucking exhausted. For some reason though, us being so far into our hike seems to make Kayla catch a second wind. She turns around and grabs my hand excitedly as she tries to pull me up the trail faster. Unfortunately, my feet get tripped over themselves and by the time that I can get them righted, a rock decides to step right in my path, true story. I go down hard, twisting my ankle in the process.

“Oh my gosh! I am so sorry! Are you okay?” She asks as she

crouches down next to me.

Cole drops down on my other side and holds my injured ankle, gently moving it around to test my mobility. I wince when he twists it a half of a rotation. His sympathetic puppy eyes are on full display when he looks up at me.

"I think it is sprained. We should probably head back down to the truck," he says.

"Really?" Kayla whines. I swear she is a 4-year-old some days.

"Yes, really. She is hurt," Cole says shortly.

I push them away from me and slowly stand up.

"I'm fine, I've had much worse. Let's go," I say as I start hobbling up the trail.

After a few seconds, I hear their footsteps follow behind me. It doesn't take them long to catch up since I am going extremely slow. Cole comes up beside me and slips his arms underneath my legs before he swings me up into a princess hold.

"Cole, put me down. I have two feet, you know?" I snap, though there isn't much heat to my words.

"You are hurt, Aubrey. Let me help you."

I know Cole is serious when he uses my actual name. I grumble at his words. I hate needing help from people. First Dax with my car and now this? The thought of it all is enough to make me itchy. Despite my deep desire to tell him to fuck off and walk on my own, I relent. My ankle is hurting like a bitch. We are quite for a few moments before Cole speaks lowly into my ear.

"What did you mean when you said that you have had much worse?"

I tense at his question for the briefest of seconds before forcing my body to relax and giving him a casual chuckle and a shoulder shrug.

"Well, a sprained ankle is nothing compared to a broken arm from falling off your bike or your head being busted open after slipping in the shower."

Cole pulls back and gives me a dubious look like he sees straight through the horse shit that I am most definitely spewing.

"And have those things happened to you?"

Well, the injuries did. But that isn't how I got them.

I don't say that though. Instead, I shrug and look to the side. Cole lets out a heavy sigh, like he is frustrated I won't open up to him. It's nothing personal. I don't open up to anyone.

We finally make it to the peak after another half a mile or so and I finally see what all the fuss was about. It is breathtaking. You can see the whole forest and even some parts of Glenfield from up here. I haven't seen anything so green in, well ever. East LA isn't exactly known for its views.

"Damn," I whisper.

Cole sets me down on a rock before he sits next to me while Kayla plops down in front of us.

"I know right?" She grins.

We sit in silence for a while before Kayla turns around to face us.

"So, Cole. What is your deal?"

Cole's eyebrows furrow as he gives her a confused smile.

"What do you mean?"

"I mean, what's your deal, do you have a girl back home or something? I've thrown out the vibes to you and you have passed them all up which is no big deal but a girl in my psych class said that she asked you out last week and you said you weren't interested. So, what's your deal? Is there a girl, or are you just not into the whole dating scene?"

He hesitates for a moment as his eyes flick around briefly before he gives her a carefree grin and cocks his head.

"Why does there have to be a deal? Maybe I am just not interested in that girl. And you and I are friends. I don't want to mess that up by crossing a line."

"Hmm possible, I guess. So, you don't hook up with friends?" She asks again as her eyes bounce over to me, a mischievous smile playing at her lips.

Now I see where she is going with this, and I really wish that she would drop it. Cole hasn't made his attraction for me exactly hidden but I try to push it to the side whenever it does come up. I value his friendship, but I just don't think I could ever see him as anything more. It is kind of a shame because he would be the perfect boyfriend for probably 98% of women.

Shooting Kayla a poisonous glare, I turn to see Cole laugh stiffly before he shakes his head.

"Nah, I am not really the hook up type to begin with, especially with friends. I'm not into the idea of dating just to date. Guess I am just waiting for the right girl," he says with an easy smile as he looks at both of us.

"That's cool. I respect that," she says seemingly dropping the subject before she shoots me a loaded look. I don't know what is going on in that head of hers, but I think she needs to loosen her ponytail.

After a little while we decide to make our way back down. I didn't even try to argue this time with Cole. I jumped up onto his back and we were on our way. I got to say, I am pretty impressed that he was able to carry me the whole way with no complaints. He didn't even seem winded. He is lean and in good shape but nothing like the guys at the gym.

When we get back to campus, Cole wraps my ankle with some ace wrap that he had in his truck and hands me a few painkillers that he also happened to have. Kayla took off to take a shower and Cole insisted on carrying me up to my room since I am on the third floor and the elevator is currently busted. He has me hop up onto his back again before he starts walking.

“Gotta say, I could get used to you being wrapped around me,” Cole teases as he walks down the courtyard.

“Psh, I am sure you could, golden boy,” I laugh as I smack the back of his head.

He laughs and his blue eyes twinkle when he cranes his head back to look at me. I smile at him and look up to see that we are at my dorm building before I lock eyes with Dax. He is leaning against the wall, one foot resting against the building. He is wearing a black cotton t-shirt and dark wash jeans. He looks fucking good. It looks like he has been here for a little while and I notice that his dark gaze is intently trained on us. His eyes flick down to Coles hands that are holding onto my thighs and then over to my wrapped ankle.

“You good?” He asks, gesturing to my ankle.

“Ye-”

“Yeah, she is good, man. Took a little spill on our hike this morning. I think she will live though, right, darlin’?” Cole says, cutting me off before I could respond to Dax.

“I didn’t realize you guys were so close,” Dax says coolly as his eyes continue to flick back and forth between us.

“We-”

“Oh, we are really good friends. This is my girl right here,” Cole says, cutting me off again as he winks at me.

I furrow my brows and twist my mouth to the side. I know what he said is true, but he just made it sound like there is more to it, when there definitely isn’t. Obviously Cole and I need to have an uncomfortable conversation, but that conversation definitely doesn’t need an audience. My gaze swings over to Dax who is staring me down as if asking me to confirm or deny what Cole just said.

“He is one of my friends,” I say blandly.

Dax nods sharply once and pushes off the building, not wasting another breath on us apparently as he walks towards the parking lot. *Well, that wasn’t uncomfortable or anything.* Cole drops me off at my room and I thank him for the lift before practically shoving him out the door. I so don't have the energy to deal with all of that right now. Once he is gone, I take a long hot shower and spend the rest of the day just how I originally planned. In bed.

CHAPTER TWELVE

Dax

Left, right, left, right. Jab, uppercut, cross.

I repeat my sequence over and over again just like I have been doing for hours. The heavy bag swings from side to side at the impact of my hits and my muscles are screaming for a break. I should stop, but I can't. I can't because currently the bag has Cole Simmon's stupid fucking face, and I can't help but pulverize the damn thing.

Fuck that douche.

I used to think he was a nice enough guy but my opinions of him have severely changed. Fucker better hope he never runs into me on a bad day, or I will rearrange his fucking body. He has acted like a prick ever since the beginning of the semester, or should I be more specific and say since he has been following Aubrey around with stupid ass heart eyes for her.

Obviously, Aubrey can hang out with whoever she wants, God knows that I do. But I know her well enough by now to know that if she is looking for a casual fuck or even something more, she won't be able to get what she needs from Cole fucking Simmons. He is too soft, too weak. He has friend zone written all over him. He couldn't handle a woman like Aubrey.

Fuck, Aubrey. Just thinking about her sends my pulse racing. She is the most infuriating yet intriguing person that I have ever met. I have never gotten off to such a bad start with someone so quickly in my life. It took weeks just for her to not look at me like she wanted to detach my head from my body. The girl has quite a bit of issues, and I should know because I am the fucking king of issues.

I came by her place today to say thanks for last night. I wanted to talk to her more after the fight, but everyone stormed the cage, and she took off like a bat out of hell. I tried to follow after her, but Chase and a bunch of girls wouldn't leave me the fuck alone. They kept yammering on about how epic the fight was and all of that shit.

Epic is not the word I would use to describe me losing absolute control and almost killing a fucking child. Because that is what he was, a child. Cameron found out while he was getting bandaged up that the kid lied about his age. He was 16 years old and had no fucking business being in that cage, let alone with me.

Fuck. I really thought I was getting my shit handled. One step forward, three steps back, I swear.

If it wasn't for Aubrey last night, I have no doubt that I would have killed the kid. I was so far gone I wasn't even in the room. I wasn't looking at the kid in front of me. Instead, he was a faceless monster. He was the shadow of a man that destroyed my life all those years ago and I wanted to end him once and for all. I needed it. The darkness inside of me thrived off the bloodshed. With every fleck, it pounded its chest and begged for more.

Somehow Aubrey was able to bring me back. One moment, I was lost in my own personal hell and the next a siren voice was calling me out of the dark and into the dimly lit basement of Cameron's gym.

Come back, Dax. Come back. You aren't there anymore. You are safe. Deep breaths.

I can still practically here her sweet voice coaxing me out of the darkness, running off my demons with a few simple words.

I wanted to say thank you, genuinely. Maybe even explain where my head was at before she intervened. Fuck knows why I would want to explain myself. It isn't like I need to or anything. She is easy to talk to though. The way she looks at me sometimes, the way she talks, makes me feel like I don't have to explain myself. Like she already knows me better than I know myself. I think it is because we are one in the same.

I have her number and could have just sent her a quick text or even called her, but I wanted to do it face to face. It was the right way to do it.

Sure, keep telling yourself that.

It felt like I was waiting forever for someone to come in or out of her building before she finally showed up. I planned to slip into the building and ask around until I found her room. I didn't know what she was up to today but her coming back from an early morning hike with Cole, getting a motherfucking piggyback ride from him, was not what I had expected.

Instantly, I was fucking livid. I wanted to rip his arms out of their sockets for even daring to touch her. That initial thought sent my head spinning and made me a little slow to realize why he was carrying her. When I asked if she was okay, the little prick wouldn't even let her speak before he cut in, saying how she was all good, calling her fucking darlin', and then saying that she was 'his girl'.

Rearing my arm back, I begin attacking the heavy bag with a fucking vengeance at the memory. Scrawny motherfucker. I will snap him in fucking half if he refers to Aubrey as his anything ever again. I don't know why I feel this overwhelming sense of possession over Aubrey. She isn't anything to me, not really at least. But the thought of someone like Cole trying to get with her has me ready to fall into a murderous rage.

"Damn. What crawled up your ass?" My Uncle Marcus calls out as he props himself in the doorway of the garage.

I don't answer him as I continue raging against the bag with everything I have. I have been at it for over an hour, and I am still not fucking calm, but my body is ready to give out and I know that I need to stop. Taking a step back I let out a rough breath as I put my hands on my hips.

"I'm fine," I say shortly as I try to slow my breathing.

"Yeah, right. Look at you, you can barely stand up. I haven't seen you like this in years."

As soon as he says it, I notice that I am having a hard time standing up. My legs shake as I slowly make my way over to Aubrey's self-proclaimed couch before sinking down into it. I lean my head back against the cushion and inhale deeply. *Vanilla*. It even fucking smells like her.

I am so fucked.

"Does this have anything to do with Aubrey?" My uncle asks, nailing it right on the head. But how does he fucking know?

My head snaps up at the mention of her name before I look over to him. He gives me a knowing look, but I brush it off and shrug as I tip my head back up to look at the ceiling.

"I don't know what you are talking about."

Marcus snorts. "Boy, I may be getting older but I ain't stupid. I see the way you look at her."

I shrug, not choosing to answer as he continues.

"Does this thing with Aubrey also include Cole?"

My head practically breaks off my spinal cord with how fast I whip my gaze to his. How the fuck does he know so much? Maybe I don't give him enough credit.

Heaving an aggravated sigh, I lean forward and rest my elbows on my knees as I look down at the ground and run my fingers through my hair.

"I went to see her. To talk to her about something and she was coming back from a hike with Cole. He had his fucking hands all over her and," I pause and shake out my hands, just now realizing that I have been tightening them into fists with each word that I spoke.

"Ah. I get it. So, you have been too much of a pussy to go after what you want and now you are pissed that someone else is trying to take her?"

"You don't know shit," I spit aggressively as I look up to him.

I watch as his mirth filled gaze fades at my disrespect as a dark thunder cloud rolls over his face. Ah, fuck.

"Boy, don't think that just because you are grown that I won't knock your ass into line. You may be a man now, but I bet I can still get a few good licks in."

He isn't lying. Marcus is still in damn good shape, and he has a nasty temper like me, one that I was on the receiving end of more times than I can count growing up. Each time I deserved probably more than the last.

"Sorry," I mutter as I let my head sag forward.

Fuck. Why am I getting all twisted up over a chick like this? I have never dealt with shit like this before. I don't date. I hookup and I never go back for seconds. It keeps things less complicated that way. I like no strings and no feelings attached situations. Girls I get with always know the score and it just works. But Aubrey doesn't fit into any of that.

She is fucking gorgeous, no doubt about it. From the first moment I saw her I couldn't take my eyes off her. I catch the guys at the gym practically drooling over her daily. She is so fucking hot no other girls seem to compare.

I have imagined hooking up with her more times than I can count but the really fucking scary thing is that after the fantasy is over, she is still on my mind. She isn't just any girl that I will forget her name by morning. She isn't someone that I could ever imagine hooking up with and never speaking to again. As much as I hate to admit it, I have come to look forward to the days that we talk, crave it even.

I am so fucked.

The next Friday I stroll through the gym doors, fist bumping and nodding to people that call out to me. I am not on the card tonight. I was, but I just wasn't feeling it. I have been pushing myself harder than normal this week and I am fucking feeling it. Besides, the guy they had me up against is hardly challenging. He is a big fucker, but he is slow as fuck, and I have already handed him his ass too many times to count. So, I decided to just kick back and watch the others tonight instead.

Chase is talking with a few guys near the octagon downstairs when he sees me come in.

"Where you been, man? It's been a minute," he greets me with a half bro hug.

"Just been training, class, helping at The White Oak," I shrug.

Chase nods as he glances around the room. My eyes do the same and I furrow my brows.

"Where is Blake at?"

A look of irritation passes across Chases face before it fades into nonchalance as he shrugs.

"He is helping your fill-in get ready."

"Who did you get?" I ask as I notice the normal guys that would be willing to go up against Collins are all standing around or already look like they have fought.

Chase is quiet for a second before a smirk crosses his face. "You'll see."

Shaking my head at his weird cryptic answer, I turn to face the room where the lights begin to flicker, indicating the start of the of the fight. I take a seat in the front with Chase and some other guys as everyone gets settled. A lame song comes on that I know to be Collins walk out song. Sure enough, he steps out of the locker room, strutting like a peacock.

The guy is comparably my size. Except where I am solid muscle he is solid bulk. Don't get me wrong, his hits pack a pretty decent punch, but he doesn't have the speed to back it up. As long as whoever they have fighting against him stays light on their feet and can throw a decent punch, they will probably have a good chance at taking him down.

Once Collins is in the octagon, the music changes to Lose Yourself by Eminem. Sick beat. The bass is bumping through the room and the anticipation for the fight ratchets up as the next fighter comes out from the locker room. When my eyes lock on them, my stomach drops. What the fuck? Aubrey?

She is stalking towards the cage, a hard look across her face with determination flaring in her eyes. She is wearing a baggy t-shirt and a pair of spandex shorts with her hair up in a tight bun. I try to get her attention to see what the hell she thinks she is doing going up against a guy that is well over twice her weight and size, but her eyes are firmly focused on Collins.

"What the fuck, Chase? Why would you let Aubrey take my place? Collins is a tank. He is going to fucking destroy her!" I bark.

Chase rolls his eyes. "Relax. She volunteered. Besides, the cocky little bitch needs to be taken down a peg or two. Why does it matter anyways? What's it to you?" He asks with a questioning eyebrow.

I shrug nonchalantly. Doing my best to brush off his bitch remark as I turn to face Aubrey. Blake is standing in the corner behind her, talking in her ear as she nods resolutely. She reaches down and strips off her shirt, tossing it to the side. Instantly, the room fills with chatter and even a few wolf whistles. The sounds have me clenching my jaw in irritation as my eyes greedily take their fill. Fuck. Her body is fucking perfection. I have to shift slightly to hide the hard on that I now have.

Aubrey doesn't pay any of the vultures any mind, though. Her jaw is tightened in irritation, eyes narrowed into spite filled slits and body rigid with barely controlled anger. If Aubrey can stay out of the way and get a few decent hits in on Collins she may come out of this fairly unscathed. Either way though, if Collins hurts her too bad then I will have to return the fucking favor tenfold.

CHAPTER THIRTEEN

Aubrey

I narrow my eyes at Collins as we get into our stances. I am ready to beat this piece of shit into the floor. My workout ran later than expected again and I decided to stick around for the fights. I wasn't sure if Dax was fighting tonight or not and for some odd reason, if he was, I wanted to be here for him. For moral support or whatever. Don't know why the fuck I would even care, honestly. It isn't like we are friends or anything. We are barely acquaintances. But still, here I was.

When I walked through the basement door everyone was talking about how Dax bailed at the last minute on his fight and they were looking for a volunteer to fight his scheduled opponent, Eric Collins. I had seen the guy in passing but that was the extent of my knowledge of him. I was shooting the shit with Blake when Collins approached me, talking about how I was the new gym whore and how unfair it was that he hadn't gotten a taste.

I was ready to lay the motherfucker out when [illegible]se stepped in between us. He told me that if I wanted to fight, I would have to do it in the octagon. So that is exactly what I am fucking doing. Blake took me to the back and told me every useful piece of information he could give me on Collins. He was just as pissed as me about his bullshit comments, even more pissed at Chase for pushing me into fighting Collins. But no one ever forces me to do anything that I don't want to, not anymore. I'm gonna wipe the floor with this fucker.

From what Blake told me, Collins is slow as fuck, but his hits are brutal. I can't let him get too many swings on me or it will be lights out. Good thing I don't plan it. I am pretty quick too. Being small and light has some advantages, I guess. I just need to get in some good hits and then get out. I will tire him out and make him chase me, wear him down and then I will go in for the kill. It's the best shot I have.

My eyes flick out to the crowd to see a thunderous looking Dax in the front row next to Chase. Dax's arms are folded across his chest and his body looks to be riddled with tension. As soon as he sees that my eyes are on him he mouths to me 'what the fuck are you doing?'. I roll my eyes at him before turning back to face Collins.

Cameron steps into the cage, throwing me an uneasy look before he looks at Collins. I know what everyone is thinking. The guy is well outside of my weight class, obviously. Normally no one would be stupid enough to fight someone so far out of your own class but like I have said before, I never claimed to be smart.

At the word fight, a sense of calm sweeps over me as my adrenaline skyrockets. This is my sanctuary. My peace. Collins fucked up by mouthing off to me and now I am about to show him what happens when people fuck with me.

He reels his arm back and swings on me. I can tell there is quite a bit of force behind it, but it is so slow that I easily dodge it and he hits air. I jump back a few steps before I bounce around on my toes. Collins doesn't pause, advancing on me with several more combinations, all that I manage to outmaneuver.

It only takes a couple minutes of this for his movements to begin slowing down even more so. He sure doesn't have my stamina. Seeing a window, I slide into the left and throw a hit to his gut. I hear a rough breath leave his chest before I jump back. Unfortunately, it isn't quick enough, and he lands a hit across my cheek. The sharp sting that accompanies the hit tells me that the skin split open at that. Fuck.

Moving my hands in front of my face, I dance from side to side, waiting for another opening. When I get one, I throw my leg out and get a nice kick in to his ribs. While he bends down to cradle his now tender side, I wind my left arm back and pop him in the nose, causing the thing to explode in a gush all over the mat and himself.

He grunts in pain before his beady eyes turn near black. He throws a wild haymaker at me that I am just able to duck in time before I give him a nice uppercut. He stumbles back at the impact, working his jaw from side to side as he does.

A fire seems to light under his ass because in the next moment he charges like a raging bull. I go to duck his advance, but he anticipates it with a kick to my side. Fuck, that hurt. I step back quickly to maintain a healthy distance between us until I can catch my breath, but he follows me with a hit to my nose.

Eye for an eye, I guess.

Blood splatters across the mat as it runs down my face. For a moment, the pain doesn't even register though, my face is just fucking numb. I throw a blind hit just out of protection, but I only hit air as Collins leans back and kicks me square in the stomach. I stumble and despite my best efforts I fall to the ground.

Oh, fuck.

Quicker than I thought he would be able to, he straddles me. I am still a little dazed from that face shot to register it all, but I do have the good sense to get my hands up to protect my head. This motherfucker could probably give me a concussion with one hit to the temple.

He seems to realize that I won't be letting my guard down on my head, so he starts going for my ribs. *Hit. Hit. Hit. Hit.* Fuck, my ribs are screaming in pain. I swear I just heard one crack despite the roaring noise coming from the crowd. I keep one hand up while I dart the other out and pop him in the face, hoping that I can get another window and get out of this fucked up predicament that I have currently found myself in, but to no such luck.

Exhaustion starts to pull me under with each hit, my adrenaline is starting to wain as pain overtakes me. Fuck. Everything *hurts*. Suddenly, breaking through the heavy clouds of exhaustion a rough voice cuts in.

"Short stuff, you gotta get him off you. You won't be able to take much more. Buck him. Buck him off now. You got this. Fucking *fight*!" Dax roars into my ear.

I tilt my head back slightly and see that Dax is plastered against the cage right by my head. His face is dark with fury, but his eyes are heavy with concern. They urge me to fight, practically beg me to. Blowing out a determined breath I channel everything that I have into bucking him off me. Despite the insane pain it causes having my tender ribs slam against his as I move up and down on the floor, I keep at it.

It takes several tries before I am able to get any sort of gap between Collins and me. As soon as he raises up just high enough, I slip my legs out from underneath him and wrap them around his lower back. His head whips up before he tries to break free from my hold, but I only hold tighter as wrap my arms around the base of the neck and pull on him as hard as I can, effectively locking him into a guillotine.

"Atta girl," Dax booms. "Snap his motherfucking neck if you

have to. Don't you fucking let up for anything but a tap, baby!"

I let Dax's words of encouragement be a tether for my strength, forcing me to hold on with everything I can. I harness every moment of my life where I felt small, weak, outmatched and I put it into this hold. His neck strains under my hold and I can feel the moment where Collins begins to truly panic. He throws brutal hits to my sides in a desperate attempt to get me to loosen my hold, but nothing will stop me now. My body has become cold, I feel nothing except for determination and adrenaline.

Arching my back, I yank his head down even more, straining him to the max. My body shakes as I use every muscle that I have to keep this huge man in my hold. It pays off, though. Only a few seconds later I feel the soft pitter of a tap out against my ribcage. Tap, Tap. I keep my hold for a few more seconds to make sure it was a genuine tap out and not a slip of the hand. Sure enough, another harder tap, tap comes, and I quickly detangle myself and scoot out from underneath him as I go to stand up.

Looking around the room, I smile wide and proud at my hard-earned win. I turn back to give Collins a hand up but notice that he is already standing. He winds his arm back and nails me right in the temple. The shock of the hit sends me careening to the floor. I hear an animalistic roar sound out not too far away as I go down. At this moment I can't be sure if it was the crowd, an actual animal or maybe just my imagination.

I feel Collins heavy body back on top of me once again. I am so dazed from that hit that I can't even fight back. My stomach rolls with instant nausea as my head splinters into a debilitating pain. *Yep, concussion for sure.* I wait for the impending hits to come from Collins, but they never do.

Suddenly, his body lifts off mine before the floors shakes with a heavy thud. I slowly roll my head to the side and see that Collins is now the one pinned to the ground, and it is Dax that is on top of him. Dax is in his street clothes but that doesn't seem to be stopping him. His fists are pulverizing Collins's face and I honestly can't be bothered to help the cheat. Who the fuck hits someone after they tap out? A fucking sore losing pussy that's who.

Shit. I'm kinda impressed Dax got in here pretty quick. The gate is on the other side of the cage so he must have climbed it. *My hero*. I scoff to myself. I don't think he could drop the hero bullshit if he tried. In this one instance though, I am moderately grateful for it. Just this once.

It doesn't take long for others to storm the cage. Several guys swarm Dax, trying to pull him off an unmoving Collins but they don't get very far before Dax is back on top of him yet again. It takes three huge guys to peel Dax off Collins for good but that doesn't deter Dax. He fights wildly against his restrainers, his eyes that same obsidian black as he desperately claws to get back to his prey. He is practically feral at this point. I have never seen anything like it. And what does it say about me that I don't think I have ever been this turned on in my life?

While I was busy watching Dax's wild beat down, I didn't realize that someone had come up behind me. Blake's words are muffled at first before my brain can focus in on them enough to comprehend what he is saying.

"Aubrey! Are you okay? What hurts?"

"Everything," I snark with a dry laugh that I immediately regret as my ribs scream in pain.

Ouch. Fuck.

"Fuck, girl. You are one crazy bitch, aren't you?" He asks with a laugh of his own.

"You know it," I slur slightly.

Slowly, Blake helps me to my feet. Ugh, standing is worse. At first I was thinking maybe Collins just cracked a rib or two but now I know for sure that a few are definitely broken. I can't even breathe without the pain. That sucks too because ribs take fucking forever to heal and hurt like hell doing so.

"Dax! What the fuck is the matter with you! We never interfere in fights just because someone is losing, no matter who they are!" Cameron shouts as he steps into the cage.

His wild eyes land on Cameron as he lunges to break free from his restrainers, but thankfully for everyone's sake, it doesn't work.

"She wasn't fucking losing! She won! Collins fucking tapped and then hit her when she let him go. He is a fucking cheat, and he is going to die!" Dax roars.

"Yeah fucking right. She is just being a shit loser. Always playing the victim when shit doesn't go her way. Typical fucking woman," Chase scoffs with his arms crossed over his chest.

I practically get a shot of adrenaline from Chase's words and my anger is back in full force. I will fucking tear him apart! Dax looks to be having similar thoughts but before he or I can do anything, Cameron surprises the hell out of us all and whirls on him, decking Chase right across the face. He goes down hard and I fucking revel in it.

Cameron turns to face me like he didn't just knock someone out as he cocks his head to the side.

"That true?"

I nod. "He tapped out, twice. I waited for the second tap out just to make sure that it wasn't a mistake. He fucking tapped and then came at me."

Cameron's jaw tightens as his eyes sweep over the crowd. They land on a group of guys that were right up against the cage when Collins and I were on the ground.

"Did anyone see Collins tap out?" Cameron asks.

All the guys share tentative looks with each other before they turn to Cameron and nod solemnly. Cameron's nostrils flare at that as he turns to bark at the on-hand medics.

"Go patch him up. If he needs the hospital, dump him at emergency with the typical mugging story. As of now, Collins is never allowed back on my property. You cheat, you are eighty sixed! Got it?" He barks out to the room.

A round of nods and agreements sound out before Cameron pushes through the crowd and stalks off. Dax seems to have calmed down a bit, but he still forces his way out of the guy's arms. Instead of going after Collins again like everyone assumes, he rushes to me. His large hands cup my face tenderly, examining my injuries with a tenderness that I didn't think he would be capable of.

I am sure I look worse for wear. Obviously my nose is all fucked up, my cheek is split, and I am pretty sure he nailed part of my eye when his meaty fists clobbered the side of my head with that last hit. You wouldn't know that I looked like I just got out of an underground fight, literally, with the way that Dax is cradling my face, like I am the most precious thing in the world. An unsettling feeling settles in my stomach, and I don't know if it is from the concussion or from him. Either way, I do my best to push it down.

"You okay, short stuff?" His low voice rumbles.

I try to crack a smile but wince when it pulls at all of my injuries at once. *Fuck.*

"I'm good," I rasp. "Probably would be a hell of a lot worse off if you hadn't jumped in. Thanks for not minding your business. Don't make it a habit, though," I fake scold in an attempt to get his serious concerned eyes to settle but it doesn't work.

His frown deepens as he looks down at me.

"You need to be checked out."

"I'll be fine. A couple of ibuprofens and some water and I will be good as new."

"Fuck that. You are hurt. Plus, you probably have a concussion. You need to be watched tonight."

"I've had worse, Dax. Really, I'll be fine. Appreciate it, though."

“I seriously doubt that,” he scoffs.

Leveling him with a hard look I stare into his eyes.

“Trust me, I have.”

A dark look flashes across his face before he very carefully picks me up and holds me in his arms as he starts walking across the cage. He pauses briefly at the groaning Collins that is now being examined by one of the medics. Dax sneers down at him and I half expect him to give him a kick or go back to beating the shit out of him. To my and everyone else’s surprise, he doesn’t. He does, however, pause over Collins before he spits on his face and continues towards the cage door. Why was that a turn on too? I think I took one too many hits to the head. I am losing my fucking mind.

CHAPTER FOURTEEN

Aubrey

Dax barks at someone to follow us as we leave the cage before stepping into the locker room and gently depositing me onto one of the benches before he sits next to me. He takes my hand and holds it with both of his fiercely. The feeling that races through me has my completely thrown and I do my best to bury it and glare at Dax and the guy that followed us as he steps forward and takes a look at my face. I just want to fucking go home.

The guy steps up with a wet towel and carefully wipes away the blood covering my face. I wince a few times when he brushes over the cut on my cheek, but it doesn't take long for him to finish. He quickly applies some antibacterial cream to the split before feeling my nose, confirming that it is just bloody, not broken. Yay.

His hands lightly trail down my arms before moving over to my ribs. I hiss a sharp breath when he touches one of them and then [illegible]other and another as he makes his way down. He pulls away and shakes his head as he looks at Dax and me.

"He got you good. Without scans I can't say for sure but based on your reaction and the feel of things I would say that you have at least three broken ribs and several more cracked. You should really go to the hospital.

"No hospital," I groan as another wave of pain washes over me.

The guy grimaces and Dax's grip on my hand becomes almost punishing. I wiggle my fingers a little because I swear there is no blood flow left in my hand which causes Dax to instantly relax his hold.

It's your call but you are gonna be pretty damn sore for the next six weeks at least."

"Well, that sucksss," I say, my words slightly slurring at the end. The room feels like it is spinning, and my head is *so* fucking heavy.

Dax's brows furrow as he looks down at my pupils.

"I think she has a concussion too."

I shove his beautiful face away from me as I roll my eyes. I open my mouth to tell him that I am fine but suddenly find that I am unable to speak as my stomach's contents empty themselves all over Dax's shoes. The heaving part definitely doesn't help the hurt ribs thing either.

"Definitely a concussion," the other guy brilliantly surmises.

Dax finally lets my hand go before he kicks his shoes off and goes to his locker to put on a spare pair of shoes as the guy starts cleaning up my mess. I'd probably be more embarrassed if everything didn't hurt so fucking much. The guy and Dax share a few more words before he grabs a few more things from his locker and turns to me. Without warning, he scoops me up again and carries me out of the gym and places me into his car. I don't bother asking where we are going because I literally don't care. I just want to close my eyes.

"Hey, you gotta stay awake," Dax scolds as he starts the car up and slowly pulls out onto the street.

"Too tired," I groan.

"I know. Just stay awake for the next hour and I will let you rest a little. I am assuming you have had a concussion before?" He asks.

His tone isn't condescending or judgmental, just factual. Because getting a concussion as an MMA fighter are about as common as getting an STD from a hooker. Colorful comparison, I know.

"Yeah. Nothing more than an annoying headache," I shrug.

"If you are lucky. If you aren't, they are really fucking dangerous."

I don't respond, choosing to cradle my head in my hands. Fuck, this shit hurts. Dax wrestles around in the bag that he grabbed from his locker before he holds out a water and a bottle of pills out to me.

"Here. This should help. I got these last time I landed myself in the hospital."

I look at the label and my stomach turns. Hydrocodone. *Fuck that.* I toss them back into his bag like they are a poisonous snake, ready to turn on me any minute. Because that is basically what they are. People say that weed is a gateway drug, which doesn't have anything on this shit.

"Just take a half of a one at least. I promise it will help," Dax says softly as he turns into the parking lot outside of the dorms and parks.

"I'm not taking that fucking shit!" I spit.

His eyebrows raise at my aggressive tone, but he doesn't say anything more. Quickly, he gets out of the car and walks around my side to get my door, but I am already pushing it open. I go to get out of the car and almost eat shit on the pavement as my pain flares. Dax's strong hands catch me effortlessly before he picks me up *again*.

I don't even bother to protest because I literally don't have the energy to care about my ego right now. Dax carries me in silence, and I am ridiculously grateful for it. My head is killing me and all I want is sleep at this point. We make it up to my dorm room quickly and I turn my furrowed brows to him when he stops right outside of my door.

"How did you know where my room was?" I ask as I reach into my bag for my keys.

Dax looks down at me for a second before he takes my keys for me and shrugs.

"I've asked about you before."

He has?

"Oh yeah? What did you find out?"

When the door unlocks, Dax pushes it open before kicking it shut and carefully laying me down on my bed before he stands back to look at me.

"You are from California, though you won't tell anyone where exactly which is more than a little sketchy. You are here on a full-ride scholarship, so you are probably a geek, and you don't hang out with anyone besides Mckayla Blackburn and…" He pauses as his hands flex into fists by his side as his jaw clenches before he lets it loosen. "Cole Simmons."

Looks like someone isn't a fan of Cole. Which is honestly kinda weird. He is that nice guy that everyone can't help but like.

"Wow. You knew all of that before we started hanging out?" I ask as I settle back on my bed.

"I could have found out more if I really wanted to."

I snort. Of course, he could have. He is Dax motherfucking Hart. Anyone in this school, hell this town, would do anything to get on his good side.

"Not sure if I should be grateful that you didn't give enough fucks to find out more or offended."

He cocks his head slightly as his typical stony expression stays in place.

"Who said that I don't give enough fucks? I just didn't want to learn more about you from other people. I want you to be the one to tell me your secrets, not some gossipy bitches.

My stomach flips at his words as I see a flare of intensity flash in his eyes. I don't know what to say to that so instead, I change the subject.

"Can you get into my dresser, second drawer, and hand me a sleep shirt? Sports bras and spandex weren't exactly designed for comfort."

Dax nods as he turns to my dresser and quickly retrieves a baggy shirt before handing it to me and turning to face the wall. He is pretty respectful for a rumored manwhore. I start maneuvering my way out of my sports bra, but frankly it is a bitch to get out of on a good day and with my ribs hurting the way they do it is pretty fucking impossible.

"Ah, fuck. Shit," I curse as I get my arm stuck.

"Do you need help?" Dax asks hesitantly, still facing the wall.

I should tell him no. Tell him to leave and go home or something. But if I do I will be stuck in this thing all night and I really just want to get comfortable. Blowing out a frustrated breath I sigh.

"Yeah."

Slowly, Dax turns around and makes his way to me, keeping his eyes firmly on mine the entire time. Without breaking eye contact he reaches down and grabs the bottom band of my bra as he gently starts pulling it up. When I need to lift up my arms I hiss out another pained breath. He pauses as his eyes bore into mine.

"Sorry. Are you okay?"

The compassion and concern that I see in his eyes takes me by surprise for a moment. I never would have guessed that he could have a soft side like this, but I am seeing it with my own eyes tonight.

"I'm fine," I rasp, suddenly realizing that my breasts are totally bared to him and he has yet to even try to sneak a peak. I feel oddly impressed as well as slightly disappointed. Which is so fucking stupid.

Dax pulls the rest of material off my head and drops it to the floor. His eyes flare but they still never stray from mine. I don't even realize that he is moving towards me until his mouth is only a half an inch away from mine. As if he is waiting for me to make the final move. Maybe it is all the knocks to the head that I took tonight or the flat-out exhaustion, but I don't overanalyze my next move.

Leaning forward I brush my lips against Dax's, if anything but to satisfy the curiosity that I have caught myself having over what Dax may taste like. He always smells of leather and mint, but he doesn't taste like it. He tastes like sin and darkness. It is fucking addicting. I want nothing more than to surround myself in it, to revel in it for all of my days.

That single thought is enough to snap me out of this lust filled haze we have found ourselves in. Dax brushes his tongue along the seam of my lips but instead of opening up for him like my body desperately wants to, I push on his chest. He pulls back and looks at me questioningly as I shake my head.

"That shouldn't have happened," I say brusquely as I begin re-building the wall I accidently dropped.

His curiosity fades and what looks almost like irritation takes its place. He gives a sharp nod before holding out the sleep shirt for me to take. I keep my eyes on him as he stares down at me with a clenched jaw as I carefully slip into the shirt. No way in fuck am I going to ask him for help, not even if it killed me.

Dax turns on his heel and grabs my desk chair, spinning it to face me before he sits down. I furrow my brows at him as I lift my blankets and slide underneath them.

"What are you doing?"

"Watching over you. You can't be asleep for too long with a concussion. You need to be monitored."

I shake my head. I need him out of my space before I do

something stupid like invite him into my bed.

"I will set alarms. I'm fine. You should go."

"I'm not going anywhere, Aubrey. Just shut the hell up for once and try to get some sleep while you can."

Opening my mouth, I begin to argue until I see the fierce look slashed across his face. It isn't just one that brokers no arguments, it looks harsh, angry, maybe even hurt? I give him a soft nod before I settle into a comfortable position. Well, as comfortable as I can get.

I close my eyes just as I hear Dax rustling around in my room. I am about to open my eyes and ask him what the hell he is doing when I feel the cold chill of an ice pack press against my tender ribs through my sheet. I am about to thank him when I feel warm lips press against my temple, the same exact spot that Collins' meaty fist drilled into. The kiss lasts several seconds, and I don't miss the deep inhale Dax takes before he retreats.

As soon as his touch is gone, I miss it. Which only proves how important it was for me to end our kiss earlier or how it shouldn't have happened at all. Dax is dangerous for me. He makes me feel too much. I am not in control of myself or my emotions around him and those are two things that I can't afford. We need distance, I need distance. I can't let my guard down, no matter how much, for the first time, I want to.

CHAPTER FIFTEEN

Aubrey

When I woke up the next morning, my desk chair was empty, and Dax was gone. Of course, that was after he woke me up every fucking two hours like a damn drill sergeant. I swear if I could have physically gotten out of bed, I would have kicked his ass.

All of the times that he woke me up, we stayed silent. He would ask me what I would rate my pain, give me a fresh ice pack and some water and then try to convince me to take his pills. Each time I vehemently turned him down and told him to fuck off. The pain got so bad around three in the morning that I caved and took a couple of ibuprofens. It didn't do much, but it did take the edge off. Fuck. I haven't been messed up like this in a while. I think I went into that fight thinking that I would come out a little better off than I did. But what was I really expecting? Collins is pushing 300lbs, he is a fucking ogre.

Unfortunately, I have work today so I will have to get my ass out of this bed at some point, but I don't go in until four and I am only working until ten so it could be worse. I don't think I will be able to fall back asleep now, so I opt to spend my day watching trash tv and ordering takeout.

When it is time to get ready for my shift I very slowly peel myself out from my warm bed and make my way to the shower. Every step jostles my ribs as well as every breath. Thank God I have a high pain tolerance otherwise I think I would be curled up in a ball right now. I spend way more time than I probably should have in the shower, but the warm water felt so good I didn't want it to end.

Once I am out of the shower and dressed, I go to my mirror and pause. Fuck. I didn't realize I was looking that bad. The cut to my cheek is already starting to close but it is swollen and red as well as some lovely bruising surrounding it. I also have that same wonderful swelling and bruising around my nose, left eye and even at my temple. I look like I got in a fight and lost, bad. I mean, I did get in a fight but I sure as fuck didn't lose.

I rummage through my room and am able to find a bottle of concealer that Kayla must have left here the last time that she was over. I begin rubbing it on all of my problem areas which is pretty much my whole damn face. Kayla is a little paler than me, so it is a little too white, but it looks a hell of a lot better than it did. Still, I have a feeling Marcus isn't going to be happy with me being the face of his bar to his customers.

Walking into The White Oak, I do my best to keep my head down. I hatched this elaborate plan that if I keep my head down as much as possible and have Cole take all of the orders then I can probably hand out the food without anyone noticing my face too much. No one cares about the face of the person bringing your food, your eyes automatically go to the food, right?

Unfortunately, the one flaw in my plan was that I wasn't expecting Marcus to be tending bar front and center of the door. He sees me the instant that I step in through the door. He glances up casually before his eyes widen slightly.

"Damn, girl. What the hell happened to you?"

"You should see the other guy," I halfheartedly joke.

From what I remember of Collins face after Dax was done with it, I look like a pageant queen in comparison. Unfortunately, Marcus doesn't think my joke is very funny. His brows furrow and he looks like he is ready to ream me. Before he can say anything, Cole walks around the corner all smiles until his eyes land on my face. His eyes widen in horror as his mouth literally drops.

"Darlin'? What happened!" He nearly shouts as he rushes over to me.

I try to tell him to be careful or to stay back but he is too damn fast as he pulls me into a bone crushing hug. *Ow*. My body instinctually curls in on itself to protect my injured ribs, but it does little to help. Before I can tell Cole to get the hell off me, a rough voice shouts out over my shoulder.

"Simmons! Let her go! You are hurting her you, dipshit," Dax growls.

Cole quickly lets me go, still keeping his hands on my upper arms as he takes me in. His eyes are worried as they scan over my face and land on where my hands are cradling my ribs.

"Did I hurt you?" Cole asks.

The puppy dog eyes he is throwing me are too much and I can't bear to answer truthfully. So, I force out a smile and shake my head.

"No. You are fine."

"Don't fucking lie to him, short stuff. Only an idiot bum rushes someone that walks in looking as rough as you do."

I narrow my eyes as I look over my shoulder and sneer at Dax.

"Gee, thanks."

He rolls his eyes at me like I am being ridiculous before he settles a glare on Cole. Fortunately, Cole doesn't notice because his worried eyes have yet to leave me.

"Darlin', who did this to you? What happened?"

I shrug. "Fight night. Fucker was pretty big."

"And a fucking cheat," Dax snaps.

Marcus's brows furrow as he turns to Dax and calls him over. They share a hushed conversation that seems fairly heated based on Dax's face and the raising level of their whispers.

"You fought? Against a man?" Cole asks in disbelief.

I am a little offended that he seems so surprised.

"You knew that I trained," I point out.

"Well, yeah. But I thought you just like worked out and maybe sparred occasionally. I had no idea that you had intentions of actually fighting anyone, let alone grown men. I would have talked you out of it."

I let out an amused chuckle even though I am quickly becoming anything but.

"Oh yeah? You would have, huh?"

Cole gives me an exasperated look and shakes his head as his hands slip off of my shoulders.

"Come on, Aubrey. It is dangerous, clearly. Just look at your face. I don't even know what is wrong with your stomach but from the way you are favoring it I am going to guess that it isn't good."

He isn't wrong. The bruises covering my ribs are nasty and large. But fuck him for thinking he can tell me what to do with my spare time or my body.

"Fuck off, Cole. You are out of line," I warn.

He shakes his head vehemently, clearly not dropping this.

"No, I won't. I care about you too much to sit back and watch you get hurt like this. Promise me you will never fight again."

My eyes bug out. He can't be serious, can he? I am fucking speechless at the nerve of someone who is supposedly my best friend. Does he even realize what he is asking of me? That I need to fight to breathe, to live. No, he probably doesn't but that is irrelevant.

Dax butts in again before I can say anything.

"Chill out, Simmons. Aubrey held her own in a totally unfair fight. She never should have been up against someone like Collins, and she still won. She is a grown woman and can make her own decisions. She doesn't need you trying to tell her what to do. It's the 21st century, dickhead."

Well said, Dax.

Cole swings his narrowed eyes over to Dax as he crosses his arms across his chest.

"How do you know so much about this, Hart? I'm assuming you stood by and let this happen?"

Dax scoffs. "Of course, I was there. I dropped out of my fight last minute and she volunteered to take my place before I even got there. When I showed up the fight was already on, but I was there the entire time. Especially when Collins hit her after he tapped. He was the last man to disrespect Aubrey and last I checked he is in the ICU. So, you may want to change the attitude there, Simmons, before you share a room with him," Dax says in a low tone that holds nothing but promise.

"Enough!" Marcus snaps as he rests a hand on Dax's chest. "You," he says pointing to Cole, "back to the floor." "You," he says pointing to Dax, "back to the kitchen." Then his eyes swing on me and my stomach dips at the anger on his face.

Ah, fuck.

"You, go home and don't come back until you are all healed up. I don't need you scaring the shit out of our customers before they even get their drinks."

Fuck. It will take at least a week and a fuck ton of make up before my bruises will fade enough. I can't afford to not work for that long. I go to argue with him, but he holds up a hand, silencing me. I hang my head and turn on my heel to head back to my dorm.

I only make it a few steps out the door before a hand catches my elbow. I expect it to be Cole, probably apologizing for being a dick, but surprisingly it is Dax.

"Hey. We left in kind of a hurry last night and Cameron wasn't able to give you your winnings from the fight."

Dax holds up a rolled-up wad of money that looks like a ton. Slowly, I take it out of his hand as I examine it.

"It's three grand," Dax says.

My eyes bug out at his words.

"Holy fuck. Is the pot always so high?"

He shakes his head.

"Nah. That is a lot more than what the winnings normally are. The odds of you losing were 32 to 1. Paid off pretty nice," Dax smirks softly.

"Fucking a, I'll say. This is going to help with the whole not working thing."

"Sorry. I should have warned you about that. I could see if Marcus will let you cook. I could wait tables if you want?"

I cringe. "I wish but I am a shit cook."

He nods, not saying anything more but not leaving either.

"Thanks," I finally say after a little while. "For looking out for me yesterday and all night. You didn't have to."

His mouth twitches slightly before it straightens out and he nods.

"You got it, short stuff. Figured now we are square."

I nod at that. I like being even. Owing anyone anything is a dangerous game. My eyes involuntarily flick down to his lips as I think about a few things that I wouldn't totally hate doing to show my thanks but quickly brush it aside. I pushed him away for a reason last night.

"I opened this morning for Marcus, that's why I wasn't there when you woke up. I was going to go home and get a couple hours of sleep. You could come over a little later if you want?"

I furrow my brows at that.

"You are going to work on Betty today?"

"Nah. Not today. I was just gonna lounge out, watch some movies, make some dinner, ya know?"

Nodding, I pause. Is it bad that I kind of want to come over? Yes. It is definitely bad. I need space from Dax. Hanging out with him at his house, watching movies and eating dinner sounds way too intimate for me and the exact opposite of space. So, begrudgingly I shake my head.

"I think I am just going to go do the same."

Dax nods and ducks his head for a second but I don't miss the flash of disappointment that passes across his face. When he lifts it back up, the look is gone but I know what I saw. He stares at me with a hardened mask like he is forcing himself to detach. Trust me dude, I am trying to do the same.

"Alright. Well, I will text you when I work on Bonnie next."

I smirk at his intentional wrong name before I nod.

"Sounds good. Thanks again."

Dax nods his head before turning on his heel and heading inside while I slowly hobble back to campus.

CHAPTER SIXTEEN

Aubrey

My bruising slowly faded from the violent black and blue to a nasty looking green and yellow. It took 8 days before I could go back to work without Marcus shooing me away. The first few days were actually pretty nice. Besides class, I spent most of my time in bed resting. My ribs are still tender as fuck, but they are getting a little better every day which is good.

Over the last week when I wasn't resting I was hanging out with Kayla and Cole. Cole apologized the day after I left The White Oak for how he talked to me. He explained that he was freaking out because he didn't like that I was hurt, which I get and all, but he has to learn that fighting isn't something that I could ever just give up. Not for anyone. It saved my fucking life in more ways than one and I will be damned if I let anyone take that from me.

A few times I even went and helped Dax with Betty. Well, I call it helping. I am pretty sure that he classifies it as me bugging the shit out of him but whatever. He has taught me some basic things that I didn't know before which is cool and I feel like I have a good understanding of how Betty works now. I even gave Dax some ideas on alternate ways to fix things but much to my dismay, he ignored every suggestion. I mean, it is my car, shouldn't I have a say in things?

When I wasn't giving Dax helpful advice or learning about how to 'properly' change my oil, I mainly napped. It started off one day with me laying down on my couch (Because it is totally mine now) in Dax's garage. I closed my eyes for half of a second and I fell into a deep dreamless sleep. It was practically blissful.

Once I woke up, a soft blanket was laid over me as Dax quietly worked away on Betty. I didn't comment on the fact that he went out of his way to make me comfortable, and he certainly wasn't looking for a thank you either. He was just being nice which is something that I am starting to realize that Dax does a lot for others if you really pay close attention.

Now it has become practically a routine. I come over, shoot the shit with him for an hour or so, take a cat nap before either ordering take out or heading home. We have fell into a comfortable little routine that has alarm bells screaming inside my head, but I do my best to ignore them. I keep telling myself that as long as I don't cross any more lines with Dax, like kissing him while I am half naked in bed, then being comfortable hanging out with him is safe enough, for now at least.

I come walking in through his door on Friday afternoon, carrying a big bag of street tacos from that food truck he told me about a while ago. I see Dax standing over Betty as he works on something under the hood. I breeze past him and dump our food onto the bar top in the corner before I turn to him.

"Hey. So, I got street tacos, but before you start being all ungrateful and saying, 'you can't eat that shit,' just know that I have zero problem eating them all by myself, so your loss if you're gonna be a bitch."

I give him a mock scowl, waiting for him to crack a smile or give me shit for how much I eat but instead all I get is a grunt in response.

My joking attitude fades as I look at him more intently now. His eyes are blood shot and a little puffy. Has he been crying? Oh fuck. Something is definitely wrong. I cross the space between us and put my hand on his bicep. He tenses under my touch but doesn't push me away.

"Dax," I say gently. "What's wrong?"

"Just a shit day," he says quietly while continuing to wrench on something.

I nod in understanding. God knows I have had my fair share of days like that.

"You know you can talk to me, right? I mean if you want," I offer with a weak smile.

He looks me in the eye for the first time today and I suddenly notice that his emerald eyes aren't their usual vivid color. Today they look dull and sullen. He stares at me blankly for a few moments and I almost think that he isn't going to respond until he finally speaks.

"My mom died four years ago today."

His tone lacks any emotion. If I didn't know better, I would say that we were just discussing where to eat later. My heart aches at the pure pain that etches across his face with every passing second. I don't even think he is really here with me right now. He is stuck in his own head. He is fucking suffocating. I can practically see it, practically feel it.

Without thinking twice, I grab Dax and pull him in for the tightest hug that I can manage with my mangled ribs. He resists only for a second before he wraps his arms around my waist and buries his face into my neck. I feel hot tears hit my skin, but I don't acknowledge them, knowing that this silent comfort is what he needs right now.

I stand there stroking the back of his head gently like a child who needs to be consoled, because right now that's exactly what he is. I didn't even know his mom had died, and four years ago? He was only 18. It would have happened a little before he entered the UFC. Pieces of the puzzle start to fall in to place, giving me glimpses as to why Dax is the way he is.

After another minute or so, I take his hand in mine and guide him over to the couch before I push him to sit down. I sit next to him and pull his head over to rest on my shoulder where I continue to run my fingers through his dirty blonde hair. His eyes are closed as he leans into my touch, drinking in the affection that I am offering.

"What was her name?" I ask carefully, not quite sure if I should keep silent or not. It takes a few seconds before he finally responds.

"Maria."

His voice is rough like it has been raked over hot stones and the vulnerability layering it twists something inside of me.

"That's really pretty," I smile softly. "I bet she was gorgeous."

"She really was," he agrees.

He lifts a hand and pulls at the thin chain around his neck that I have noticed a few times. When he holds it out for me to look at it, I notice that it is a woman's necklace. It is a beautifully constructed silver angel with diamonds in the wings.

"This was my mom's. I gave it to her for her last birthday that we spent together. I thought it was perfect since I used to call her an angel for being able to put up with me. She always agreed. I like to wear it, makes me feel close to her."

I reach my hand out and hold it gently as I examine it.

"It's beautiful."

He nods. "I usually go and visit her grave at least once a week. But time has just gotten away from me lately, I guess. I woke up this morning and for a minute I forgot what day it even was. It's like I am forgetting her, and I fucking hate myself for it."

I pause for a second before I reach over and grab his hand, interlocking our fingers together. I wait to see if he is going to pull away but instead he squeezes my hand so hard my knuckles nearly crack.

"Dax, you aren't forgetting her. You are healing. She knows what is in your heart and so do you. The fact that you even feel guilty proves that you will always love her deeply.

He shrugs as he squeezes my hand tighter but doesn't say anything more. We sit in silence for a few minutes before I break it.

"Can I meet her?" I ask quietly.

His head lifts so he can meet my eyes, a confused look across his face. Trust me, I am a little surprised that those words came out of my mouth too. But I still want to.

"She is dead, Aubrey," he snaps like he thinks I am not listening.

I do my best to repress my eyeroll but know that I don't succeed.

"Yeah, I heard that part. I meant; can I go to her grave? Talk to her?"

Now he looks really confused as he looks at me carefully.

"Why?"

Now it's my turn to shrug.

"I'd really like to meet the woman that put up with you for so many years. Maybe she can give me some tips," I tease.

He is quiet for a few moments, and I am almost certain that he is gearing up to tell me to fuck off. Instead, Dax surprises the hell out of me by giving me a small smile and nodding his head. 20 minutes later we are standing in front of a headstone with a beautiful angel engraved into the stone.

Maria Hart
Loving Mother, Sister & Angel
April 23, 1980 – November 12, 2018

Dax moves over to stand in front of it, brushing his hand against the angel while holding his necklace with the other.

"Hey Ma," he says softly, his voice clogged with thick emotion. "I brought someone who wants to meet you. This is my friend Aubrey."

I smile at the introduction while I plop down, crossing my legs as I sit in the grass. I look up and smile at Dax and he returns it before squatting to sit next to me. I then turn to the head stone.

"Hello, Maria. It's really nice to meet you. You can call me Bree."

I look over to see Dax watching me with an intrigued expression, but still smiling. I reach out to grab his hand and squeeze it before continuing.

"I just wanted to let you know that Dax is still the pain in the ass that I am sure he was for you. But don't worry, I am working on him." I hear Dax chuckle at that, but I am too focused on my conversation to indulge him. "I am sure that he tells you enough, and you see it every day, but he loves you very much. I can tell that you were the best mom to him, and he could never thank you enough for that. Any kid would have been lucky to have you as their mother. Thank you for loving him so well."

Dax slowly pulls me into his side and tucks me against him, his arm draping around me while we sit there in comfortable silence. To my surprise, I don't try to pull away nor do I want to. Every time that I am with Dax a little bit of my resolve weakens despite how hard I try to keep it strong. We understand each other in a way that others just never would get. His darkness is the same inky black as mine. His broken jagged pieces are a mirror image of mine.

It's Saturday night when I get a call from Kayla.

"Hey, what are you up to? Psh, what am I saying, you are

probably in bed with cookie dough ice cream in your pj's, binging Netflix."

I look at the paused Netflix show before looking down at my pajama clad lap with a bowl of ice cream in it.

"No," I bite out. "It's chocolate peanut butter. Cole ate the last of my cookie dough."

She cackles on the other end.

"You are so predictable. Well, jump in the shower and put some effort in. We are going out. Tonight."

"Pass," I groan.

"Sorry, honey. That wasn't a request. I will be there in 15 minutes."

"So, I have 30."

"Same thing."

She hangs up at that and I roll my eyes and toss my phone to the side before I drag my butt out of bed and get in the shower. I swear, I need to kick that girl to the curb.

45 minutes later Kayla and I are making last minute touch ups in my mirror.

"We look so hot!" She squeals.

I slipped into a slinky black dress of hers with a deep v neckline that showcases my tits nicely. The dress hugs my waist and is paired with some sparkly heels, another contribution of Kayla's. She did my hair in bombshell curls that fall loose against my back. Thankfully with the help of concealer, my bruising is practically gone so I won't get the open-mouthed stares that I was getting before. Though tonight I may be getting stares for another reason because even I can admit, I look fucking good. Maybe I should try putting effort in once in a while if this is the result.

When Kayla showed up earlier, she was rambling excitedly about some frat party that is going on tonight that she scored an invite to. Apparently, she was told she could bring 'hot friends.'

What an honor to be included. I roll my eyes.

Jack asses.

Kayla loops her arm through mine as we make our way across campus. I am pretty sure she is just using me for stability while she attempts to walk in her sky-high heels. When we get to the party it is everything that I imagined a frat party on a Saturday night would be like. People are pouring out of the house and onto the lawn with red solo cups in hand. The girls have so little on that they could be mistaken for auditioning for an open spot at the playboy mansion.

When we step inside the house, the smell of stale beer, musk and sweat assaults my nose. Not the greatest but what do you expect when you cram this many people in to one small frat house that looks to be well over seventy years old.

Kayla pulls me in close, shouting over the thumping music. "I'm gonna grab us some drinks!"

I give her a thumbs up as she teeters off in her heels like a baby giraffe. I look around the room, checking out my surroundings. Nothing too exciting to report. Just a bunch of co-ed's humping and grinding on each other while they are in various states of intoxication. My bed and ice cream were way better than this.

CHAPTER SEVENTEEN

Aubrey

As my eyes sweep through the party they suddenly land on two green eyes that are steadily trained on me. He is wearing a black leather jacket, white t-shirt and dark wash jeans that make him look absolutely edible. Fuck.

Dax must be able to read my mind because when I look back up, he smirks at me before sauntering over to me. I mentally prepare myself for whatever he is about to say while I remind myself to keep my guard up. No matter how smooth and sinfully sexy he is I can't let him get to me.

Be strong, Aubrey.

"Hey Bree," he says, his voice smooth like honey.

Ah, fuck. I struggle not to physically shiver at the way my nickname sounds on his lips. He is totally fucking getting to me and this little acquaintanceship thing that we have going on is getting increasingly dangerous. Trying to brush aside the bubbling feelings inside of me I go for an air of indifference.

"I only let people I really like call me, Bree," I say coolly.

He smirks at me as he raises an eyebrow.

"Oh yeah? Do I not make the cut?"

"Nah. How does that feel on that inflatable sized ego?"

He barks out a laugh before shaking his head.

"Not good. I'll wear you down," he says with a wink.

My heart skips at that wink and my stomach drops at the determination in his words. As much as I don't want his words to be true, I fear they may be.

"Can I get you a drink?" He asks.

I am about to bite out some clever response when I see Kayla stepping up next to me.

"Hey!" I greet her, grabbing the drink she offers me and looping my arm through hers.

This move not only helps stabilize Kayla once again but also is the perfect excuse to get a few feet of distance between me and Dax. I turn back to face him as I raise my drink.

"I'm good, thanks."

Unfortunately, none of that discourages him. He takes a huge step towards me until I am practically plastered against him. He leans in close to whisper into my ear as he does.

"Do you want to dance?"

For a moment my mind short circuits. I am overwhelmed by the smell of mint and leather and *him.* Oh fuck. No. Not good. I'm not exactly sure where this sudden flirtatious side of Dax came from. Maybe it is because we kissed the other night and neither of us has recognized or talked about it since. Maybe it is because we have been spending so much time together.

Or maybe he really likes me.

No. Fuck that. There is no way in hell the playboy in him would ever let him settle down with one girl and I am not interested in being a one and done. I will not be just another woman that falls at the feet of Dax Hart. I will not be another statistic.

Steeling my resolve and thanking the big man upstairs that I was able to talk myself off of that bridge that I definitely almost jumped off of, I wipe my face clean of any and all emotion as I look at him head on.

"Nope," I pop, before turning and grabbing Kayla's hand as I drag her towards the dancefloor.

I start swaying to the beat, doing my best to shake off the creeping feelings that are trying to take up permanent residence in my chest. I'm also trying to ignore the hypnotic eyes that I can practically feel drilling holes into my back.

When I turn to look at Kayla, I see that her eyes are wide, and her mouth is hanging open.

"Uh, did you just blow off Dax Hart? That man is fine as hell! I would climb him like a tree in a heartbeat," she shouts over the beat of the song.

I snort. "Yeah, you and every other girl in here it seems." I pause for a second, trying to come up with an excuse as to why I just blew off the Adonis of campus. "He is just not my type."

I forgot for a moment that very few know Dax and I even interact at all. Cole knows that Dax is helping me with my car, but I knew bringing the subject up with Kayla would be opening the door to endless questions that I didn't want to answer, so I didn't bother. The only people that know we use the same gym are the guys at the gym, so I guess our acquaintanceship has been kind of on the down low.

She laughs while swaying her hips.

"Honey, he is *everyone's* type. I was at The White Oak last night and he had Charlene Johnson practically dry humping him at their table. Then they both *mysteriously* disappeared to the bathroom at the same time. She came out with the most satisfied smile I have ever seen. I'd kill to look like that after bathroom sex with a guy."

My ice runs cold at her words and my smile disappears. Right after he dropped me off at my dorm from the graveyard where I held his hand as he cried over his dead mother and spoke to her for hours, he went and fucked some random bitch in the bathroom of my fucking work? I shrug at Kayla so that she doesn't see the jealousy that is stewing inside of me.

I know that I have no right to be jealous. He is just fixing my car for me, he helped me out when I got hurt at fight night and we have talked a bit and hung out but it's not like we are together or anything. I don't even want that anyways. So why does hearing about him hanging out with me during the day and fucking random bitches at night feel like a knife to the gut?

Whatever, it doesn't matter. The important thing is that whatever I thought might be going on between us has been effectively blown to smithereens. All developing feelings I was starting to have for him are gone in an instant. Great, right? I am sure as hell not going to let Dax motherfucking Hart ruin my night.

A pair of strong arms snake around my waist before hands settle on my hips. My hackles rise and I am about to tell Mr. Dude Bro where he can shove his hands, when a familiar voice whispers into my ear.

"Darlin', I couldn't stay away any longer. You are driving every man in here crazy."

I turn around and smile up through my eyelashes. Cole is cute. His brown hair is perfectly quaffed, falling slightly in his eyes that only amps up his boyish charm. His dark Henley is clinging to his body, displaying his solid chest while his jeans are tight on his muscular thighs. His trademark twinkle plays in his sapphire eyes I can't help but want to keep it there.

"Just friends, golden boy," I remind him before I wrap my arms around his shoulders and begin swaying my body against him with the beat.

His smile grows as he tightens his grip on my hips, brining me in closer.

"For now."

"Forever," I say with a laugh as I shake my head and spin my hips.

We dance like that for a couple of songs laughing and smiling. His hands wander lower and lower until they finally land low, cupping my ass and tugging me in so our bodies are completely flush.

I raise a questioning eyebrow at him with an amused smirk across my face, but I don't push him away. I know it is probably fucked up that I am letting him do this right now. I know that he has a little crush on me. He has made it pretty damn obvious. I shouldn't be leading him on like I am, and I definitely shouldn't be using him to forget about how Dax screwing some bitch in a bathroom fucking hurts. But despite all of that Cole seems to be enjoying himself and all I want to do is have a good night. I will set things straight with him tomorrow, tonight I need the distraction.

One of Cole's hands squeeze my ass for a second and before I can even react, I hear a loud crash from behind us. I look over to see a broken bottle of beer on the floor as Dax stands above it, his fists clenched, jaw tight and eyes on fire directed right at Cole. Oh fuck.

I can tell just from there little interaction at The White Oak that these two don't get along and that previous tension only seems to ratchet higher when Cole notices Dax's glare before he pulls me into his side tighter and sends Dax a scathing look of his own.

Fuck. Really, Cole?

Within seconds Dax storms over to us, reaching down and yanking my arm to pull me from Cole's grip. I stumble in my heels for a few steps until I steady myself in front of him, shooting him my most poisonous look as I do.

"What the hell is your problem?"

"You are," he seethes before he closes his eyes and takes a deep breath. When he opens them again the fire is a little more contained but still there, nonetheless.

"Can we have a minute? In private." He spits out that last part while looking over my head at Cole. I don't have to turn around to see his reaction, I can practically feel the anger vibrating off Cole.

Internally I groan. I seriously don't have time for his bullshit. Fuck him.

"Nah, I'm good. Now I will ask again, what the hell is up your ass tonight, Dax?"

"Nothing," he shrugs suddenly acting like he didn't just storm over here and make a huge ass scene as he crosses his arms. "I just didn't take you for the easy type. Guess I didn't have you figured out like I thought I did. Apparently, you will turn into a whore for anyone if they give you attention for long enough."

I wind back and throw every ounce of power I can into a right hook to his jaw. He stumbles back a few steps and the whole room becomes deathly silent with only the music in the background making any noise. I stare daggers at him, daring him to talk shit again.

Are you fucking kidding me?

I can't believe that I ever thought there was something decent about him. That he was a good guy once you got underneath all of the bullshit. I thought…I don't know what I fucking thought but clearly I was wrong. There is a small number of things that can actually penetrate through my armor and calling me that word is just about the worst one.

I bury the hurt that I'm sure is splashed across my face at his nasty words. I straighten my stance and lift my chin up as I stare at Dax. He is standing at his full height, his face a perfect mask of composure. But the flaring nostrils and the near black eyes give him away. In that moment, I think of the one thing guaranteed to make his façade crack.

"C'mon, Cole. Let's head back to my place," I say coolly, reaching out and grabbing Cole's hand.

Cole's eyebrows shoot up his forehead before he nods and follows me out the door. When we get to the door, I turn around and lock gazes with the green-eyed jackass while he continues to shoot me the deadliest glare that I've ever seen. If I wasn't so royally pissed off, I probably would be intimated. Instead, I blow that fucker a kiss and stroll out into the night with Cole's hand in mine. I think I hear some shouting come from inside the party, but I decide to block it out as we head towards my dorm.

The farther we get from the party the more Dax's words begin to sink in. *Whore*. In my opinion, the nastiest word in the English language. It is one that I have been on the receiving end of more times than I can count. When your mom is the *whore* of Sunny Crest Trailer Park you get labeled by association. Just imagining being compared to her in any level has my stomach rolling.

Biting back the angry tears that are begging to escape, I let out a ragged breath. Cole slips his arm over my shoulders and tucks me into his side. I look up to see a soft smile and sympathetic eyes. I give him a weak smile before turning my eyes back down to the sidewalk.

When we get to my building Cole looks almost uncomfortable as he scratches the back of his neck.

"I'm really sorry he said those things to you, darlin'. That was really fucked up and I can tell it really got to you."

I wave off his sympathies. God knows that I don't need anyone's pity.

"It's fine." I pause for a second before deciding that I am not going to let that asshole ruin my night. He proved to be exactly the kind of person that I had first thought he was, so why am I all upset and surprised. Fuck him. I screw on an assuring smile as I look up to Cole.

"Do you want to binge some Harry Potter?"

The sympathetic look fades away from his eyes and mischief takes its place.

"Why, Miss Davis. Are you trying to get me alone in your room?" He teases.

I snort, releasing a genuine laugh before swatting his arm.

"Behave. Hands to yourself."

He chuckles and places his hands in the air in surrender.

"Yes, Ma'am."

Once we get upstairs, he pops in the Sorcerer's Stone while I grab the ice cream.

"If we keep making this a thing, I am going to have to walk sideways through my door," I call out before plopping down next to him on my bed.

I offer him a spoon and the tub of ice cream. He looks upset for a moment before he looks into my eyes.

"Don't say that. You are so beautiful. You don't even have a clue."

I clear my throat before turning back to the TV. We really need to have that boundaries talk. I think allowing him to get all handsy with me tonight may have blurred the lines and I need to fix that quick. But tonight, I just don't have it in me to get into it.

I know deep down that I was holding a teeny tiny flame for Dax ever since I met him, despite his asshole tendencies. Well, tonight Dax effectively snuffed that flame right out. I don't have time to deal with anything close to a relationship anyways and I have done the whole friends with benefits thing and casual hookups. I can barely handle my own emotional drama, why the hell would I want to take on anyone else's on top of that? Dax is an asshole but in the end this is all for the best.

Looking to the side I see that Cole is still staring at me with a serious look across his face. His eyes drop to my lips just for a second. My eyebrows raise slightly before I lean away just a bit. Cole must be able to read the look on my face because he pulls me in for a hug while he rubs soft circles on my back but doesn't try anything more. We stay that way for so long that my eyelids start to get heavy. Before I even realize it, I'm falling asleep to the smell of laundry detergent and pine.

The creak of the floorboards has my eyes springing open. They strain to see who is coming down the narrow hallway. I roll over on my side and tuck myself against the back of the musty couch, hoping that whoever it is will just leave. I'm never that lucky, though.

A strong hand buries into the back of my hair and rips me off the couch and onto the floor. I land on my hip and as much as it hurts, I quickly forget about the pain as the first slap comes. The sharp sting has my blood thrumming in my cheeks. I open my mouth to cry out for someone, anyone, but he is quick to cover my screams.

His dirty hand covers my mouth before shoving several fingers down my throat. I gag against the intrusion, but he only pushes farther. Tears begin to gather in my eyes as he continues shoving his fingers deeper until my stomach is rolling. I feel the bile traveling up my throat but before I can retch it up, a heavy fist slams across my face and all I feel is darkness.

Gasping for breath, I shoot up to a sitting position. I hold my throat gently as I greedily suck in the clean air. Even though I am safe, and it was nothing more than a nightmare I can still taste his fingers. I can feel the pain that each hit delivered. I can hear the impending footsteps sounding down through the quiet trailer, holding promises of pain and terror with each step.

A body moves next to me and for a moment, I panic. I fly out of bed and leap over to my desk where I pick up my lamp like a weapon, ready to beat the fuck out of whoever broke into my dorm room. Then the figure rolls over and I see clearly who it is. Cole.

Cole came home with me last night. We ate an entire gallon of ice cream and I crashed early on. Blowing out a ragged breath, I shake my head as I slowly place the lamp down.

Apparently Cole wasn't awake enough to witness my little freak out because when he opens his eyes he gives me a sleepy smile.

"Good morning, darlin'."

"Hey," I rasp with my best attempt of a smile.

He seems to notice how forced it is because his head cocks to the side gently.

"Did you sleep okay?"

I nod my head slowly as I walk over and sit on the edge of my bed.

"You?"

His smile widens as he sits up.

"The best sleep of my life."

I cringe at his words. Fuck. Letting him stay the night was most definitely a mistake. Doing my best to divert the conversation I laugh lightly.

"Well then I feel really sorry for you, because these twin beds are like sleeping on cardboard."

He chuckles as he leans forward and rests his elbows on his propped knees.

"What are you doing for Thanksgiving?" He asks.

I stare at him for a moment confused. Is Thanksgiving coming up? Is that something normal people keep track of? I have never had a traditional Thanksgiving before, so I don't really understand all the hype. The food that people normally have is pretty good, at least from the stuff that I have had before. But is the holiday something that I actively look forward to? Most definitely not.

"Probably working," I shrug.

"The White Oak closes."

"Oh, well then probably just hanging out here and getting some homework done, binge a little Netflix. What about you?"

"Come with me," he says.

"What?"

"Come with me, for Thanksgiving, to my house." His smile is shy but filled with hope as he looks at me. I go to tell him no in the nicest way possible, but he presses on. "I am driving home on Thanksgiving morning and staying the night then coming back the next morning. My family takes holidays very seriously and I promise my mom will stuff you full of home cooked food until you can't move. Come with me.

"We will have fun. My family will love you, and my little sisters will drive you crazy, but they are so cute that it is almost worth it. I want you to come with me, I can't leave you here all alone. Come."

The last word is softer than the rest of his persuasive argument. He says it almost like he is pleading. I still don't get what the big deal is.

I can't go, I don't know these people. And yeah, he is my best friend, and it would be cool to do something other than barricade myself in my dorm room, but I can't intrude on their family time. Besides, it isn't like me going home for a holiday to meet the parents exactly instills the boundary lines that I want to draw with Cole.

But what else am I really going to do? It's just dinner, right?

"As friends, right?" I clarify.

His smile twitches for a second before he nods and smiles.

Fuck it.

"Sure. Why not?"

Cole's face lights up brighter than any expression I have ever seen.

"Great! We are going to have a ton of fun. Trust me." He leans over and kisses the side of my head, holding it for a second too long to be considered just friendly. Fuck. We really gotta talk. Just not after I had a super shitty night.

Fuck this is a mistake. Me going home with him is not going to convince him that we are better off as friends. Neither was dry humping him in the middle of the dance floor last night, though. I am going to blame this all on Dax. If he wasn't such an asshole, none of this would have happened. Yep. Dax Hart fucking sucks.

CHAPTER EIGHTEEN

Dax

Red. All I saw was red as I watched her dancing with Cole. I knew she was unlike any other woman that I had ever met from the moment that I met her. Hell, that's what I liked about her. So, when she gave me the cold shoulder after I asked her to dance, I wasn't surprised or upset. I thought maybe things would be different between us after yesterday, though.

She pushed me away after we kissed the other night, but I thought that she was just scared since there is clearly more than a mutual attraction between us. Fuck knows it scares the shit out of me. No matter how hard I try and what I do though, I can't get her off of my mind. Maybe it isn't the same for her, though. Instead of being scared maybe she simply just isn't into me. That thought stung more than I would like to admit, but I didn't want to focus on that. I just kicked back with a beer and watched her move her outrageously sexy body to the music.

"Bro you are drooling," Blake jokes.

Him and Aubrey get along pretty well, and he seems to always be the first one to call me out when I watch her at the gym, The White Oak or fucking anywhere. If Aubrey enters a room, my eyes are like heat seeking missiles that land on her every time and Blake gets a fucking kick out of it.

"Fuck you," I grumble.

I tip my beer back and drain it before cracking open a new one. He is probably right, though. She is so beautiful it's not even fucking fair, but there is something else about her, something that almost draws me to her. I don't quite know what it is, but she gets me, probably better than I even get myself.

I have tried to get her out of my head, I mean she is so prickly and not anything like the women I normally get with, but that is the great part about her. She isn't just a quick lay. Which is also the scary as fuck part.

After I took her home last night, I was feeling down and horny as fuck just from being around her all day. I didn't even think about trying anything with her since the last and only time that we kissed she quickly ended it and told me to forget about. Like that was fucking possible.

So, I went to The White Oak and found someone that would take my mind off of the fucked up day I had and get Aubrey out of my head. Win, win, right? The shitty part is that the instant the girl's lips touched mine, it was Aubrey that popped into my head. I practically leaped away from the girl in front of me and told her that I wasn't into it anymore.

She got all huffy and stormed out of the bathroom but made sure to put on a good show for her friends and mine that were waiting for us to come out, no doubt to protect her ego. When I stepped out of the door, I felt like such a piece of shit for trying to replace Aubrey with another girl. It's not the girl's fault that I'm into someone else.

Maybe I need to take Marcus's advice and just go for her before it's too late.

I snap out of my thoughts and return my gaze to Aubrey. I can't help but smirk, she looks so fucking hot tonight. Her platinum locks are cascading down her back as her body sways, the tight dress she is wearing sliding up every once in a while when she gyrates her hips. She is temptation in the fucking flesh.

Fuck it. I am tired of being the creeper in the corner just watching her dance. I think it is time I show her how much better it is to dance with a partner. I go to take a step so that I can do just that, but someone beats me to it. I watch as Cole slithers his arms around her. Fucking snake.

My body goes fucking rigid as I watch with murderous contempt, waiting for Aubrey to push him away or send me some type of signal that she wants me to throttle his ass because I have been itching to do that ever since the other day at The White Oak, but she doesn't. She leans into him and puts her arms around his neck. I am fucking seething now, silently brewing with anger.

I stand there clenching and unclenching my fists, trying and failing to get a hold of the rapidly building anger inside of me. It's irrational. She isn't my girl. We are friends at best and based on her attitude tonight she doesn't seem too interested in becoming more. Maybe I should just stop driving myself crazy and let her go.

Fuck that.

She is gonna be mine, she just doesn't know it yet.

I continue to watch them very closely while I contemplate exactly how I can get Cole the fuck away from her. Then I watch as he slides his hands down to her ass and brings her into him. Still, she doesn't push him away and when I see his hands squeeze, it sends me right over the edge.

I am fucking done.

Before I even know what I'm doing, I shatter my fresh beer against the floor and am rushing towards them. Aubrey glances up at me, her look of confusion morphing to anger when I grab her arm and haul her away from Cole like I've been imagining for the last 10 minutes. But instead of crushing my lips against hers like I also fantasized, I yell at her.

After I tore into her about coming across easy, she dished it right back to me by leaving the party with Cole. Shit. That didn't go like I was hoping. Smooth move asshole. I didn't mean any of it either. As soon as the words left my mouth I wanted to take them back, especially when I saw the look on her face. But what the hell did she want me to do? She was driving me crazy. Making me jealous and shit. Fuck, I've never been jealous a day in my life. Guess I've never met anyone worthy of being jealous of.

Fuck this. I am not letting her just walk away from me. We need to talk this shit out. If she's going home with anyone, it's going to be me. I only manage to take one step towards the door before a flurry of red hair steps in front of me, blocking my path.

"Hey Daxie," the stage 5 clinger purrs.

I fucked her once and she has been practically humping my leg at every turn since. Even if I did go back for seconds and Aubrey wasn't on my mind twenty-four-fucking-seven, I still wouldn't touch her because not only was she a lousy lay, but the bitch is crazy as fuck. She is smiling up at me with what I am sure are well rehearsed fuck me eyes, but I don't think she realizes the crazy overpowers any sex appeal she would have had.

"Move," I say as I try to step around her.

She steps in front of me again, putting a hand on my chest.

"Don't be that way, baby. Come dance with me. Let's have some fun. You know we always do."

Her face breaks out into a low seductive grin that makes me groan. I can't deal with this shit right now, fuck, ever. I brush past her and head out the door without so much as a backwards glance.

When I step outside I look all around but don't see Aubrey or Cole anymore. Fuck, what am I even doing?

I clearly crossed a line with her based on her reaction. I have never seen her look so wounded. The look only lasted a few moments, but it was long enough to make me want to crawl into a fucking hole like the piece of shit that I am. She needs space. I'll go see her tomorrow and we will talk shit out.

Jumping into my car I fire it up before heading home. I need to get my shit together. This all has got to fucking stop. I can't fucking take it. Ever since I found out what Aubrey Davis tasted like I have been a fiend aching for more. We have to clear shit up and fast.

I wake up the next morning to a head splitting headache. Great, just how I wanted to start my morning. I pop a couple of ibuprofen before I jump in the shower. Once I'm dry, I pull on my leather jacket and slip into a pair of jeans before I stroll out the door.

As I'm heading towards campus, I replay the events of last night in my head. I can't believe I said that shit to her. Maybe I can get her to come over if I tell her I have something that needs to be done on her car. She is always interested in anything that has to do with that piece of shit. Yeah, that could work.

When I get to campus I throw my car into park and head towards Aubrey's dorm. As I come up to her building I look up to see that the light in the window of her room is on, so she has to be awake. While I am still looking up at the window I slam into someone before I can dodge them.

"Shit. Sorry, man," I say before I look down to see who I just bumped into.

Cole gives me a short nod and walks away without a word. Did he just come from Aubrey's dorm? And wasn't he wearing that too tight shirt last night? Shit. I spent last night beating myself up about what I said, trying to get the possibility out of my head that Aubrey really did take him home. Seeing him this morning is like a punch to the gut.

I don't know if I want to run to Aubrey and beg for her to forget about all of the shit that I said last night or knock Cole out for even daring to get near her. I decide the latter will probably just land me in even hotter water with Aubrey, which should be impossible at this point because it seems to be boiling right now.

I pull out my phone and shoot her a text.

Me: Hey I got a new part for Betty. Going to put it in if you want to stop by.

The typing bubbles pop up only a few minutes later. I watch my phone closely both excited and nervous to see what she has to say to me after the way I treated her.

Aubrey: Nope.

Nope? That's all I get? One word? Fuck. I decide it is best to try to shrug it off. I will let her be pissy and brush me off for now. I am sure in a couple of days she will calm down and things will go back to normal.

Looks like I was wrong since it has now been a week since the party and Aubrey has dodged me at every attempt that I have made. Even when we bump into each other at school she doesn't make eye contact with me. It's like I don't even exist in the same world as her anymore. I would never admit it to anyone but it actually kinda fucking hurts.

I know that all of this is my fucking fault but shit, did she have to rub Cole in my face like that? She has to know that I feel something for her. I have a reputation and it definitely isn't being at a chick's beck and call, fixing her car, taking care of her all night and talking practically all day every day. Especially not for a chick that I am not even hooking up with.

I decide to send yet another text. It's embarrassing how many texts and calls I've sent her over the last week that have all gone completely unanswered. Too bad for her, I'm persistent as fuck.

Me: Bree, talk to me. Please. I miss you.

Normally me opening up to anyone or talking about feelings is a hard pass, but me demanding her to speak to me or pretending that nothing happened at all hasn't worked for me so far, so I need to switch tactics. Though I am not really holding my breath for a response.

CHAPTER NINETEEN

Aubrey

Dax: Bree, talk to me. Please. I miss you.

I have probably re-read this text 10 times since getting it this morning. My fingers twitch, ready to remind him that I only let people I like call me Bree, but I resist. All other times he has reached out he has been a demanding asshole, talking about how I better hear him out and a bunch of other shit and even a few where he had the audacity to pretend like nothing ever happened. All of those texts were from the same douche who tried, and succeeded, at humiliating me in front of an entire party.

This text is different, though. This is from the Dax that only I see. The guy that I like spending time with. The one who spends all his free time fixing poor Betty and covers me with a blanket when I fall asleep on the couch and looks after me all night when I have a concussion. This is from the guy that I thought I was starting to feel something for.

I don't typically hold grudges, especially over careless words

I have had plenty thrown at me in my life to not let them rattle me too much. But despite my irritation, I have come to care about Dax's opinion, so his words cut deeper than most others would have. It doesn't even matter anymore. He is nothing but a playboy asshole and I am so done with him. Though, I am also sick of him badgering me, so as much as I would love to keep making him suffer, I respond.

Me: I'll be at your place at 5.

I try not to focus too hard on what I'm going to say, or what I am going to hear him say when I get there. I just want to get through one full day without Dax plaguing my thoughts.

Fat chance of that.

Cole wanted to hangout this afternoon, but I told him that I was going to Dax's to get him off my back. He told me that he didn't like the idea of me being alone with him when he blew up on me last time I saw him, but I honestly don't give a shit. Cole insisted on driving me and picking me up and I relented at that. If I don't have to pay for a ride then I will take what I can get.

We pull up to Dax's driveway a little before 5PM and Cole turns in his seat to face me.

"Call me if you need me. I'll be here in 5 minutes. Or I can just wait here. Whatever you want."

I roll my eyes. I appreciate what a great friend he is, but he can be so smothering somedays I can't fucking breathe around him.

"Will do, thank you." I pat his hand before I slide out of the car.

Cole drives away as I walk up to the door to Dax's garage. When I step inside, I see Dax beating up the heavy bag he has hanging off to the side. His back is to me, so he hasn't seen me yet. I am not really sure how to start this conversation off. I am not too good with touchy feely stuff and unfortunately I foresee that shit being brought up today. Feelings fucking suck.

I see an extra pair of gloves sitting off to the side and decide that it might be easier to listen to his bullshit if I can hit him when I want.

I start to pull them on as I shout out to him.

"Want to spar?"

His movements stop instantly, and his spine goes ram rod straight. He turns and looks over to me, his eyes slowly looking me up and down as if recommitting what I look like to memory. It makes me uncomfortable because a warm feeling spreads through my chest and I don't know how to deal with that.

"Hey, Bree. I-"

I hold up my hand, cutting him off. I lift my hands into a defensive pose and wave for him to advance me. He cocks his head to the side for a moment and throws me a 'you serious' look before he lifts his own hands and comes towards me.

Dax gets close enough to be within arm's reach and I take a swing, missing as he easily ducks it. I stay light on my feet, bouncing around as I wait for him to counter. Only he doesn't. He just stands there guarding himself. Guess I am the aggressor today. *What's new?*

"Look, Bree. I'm really-"

"Save it. I don't give a fuck about your bullshit apology. Just fight me asshole," I snap.

Okay maybe I do hold grudges. It looks like I have some pent-up anger about this whole thing. I go to strike Dax and am able to graze his lower jaw. Not enough to do much damage but enough to connect. He spins on me and wraps his huge arms around me, holding me tight against his chest in a bear hug. The smell of leather and mint infiltrates my senses, making me a little woozy for a second as he lowers his head down to my ear slowly.

"I just want to apologize about the other night. I was drunk and mad. I wasn't thinking. I am really sorry."

Doing my best to ignore the sincerity pouring through his words, I throw my head back for a head butt. Because of our height difference it only catches his chin but the resounding crack that it makes tells me that it hurt, nonetheless.

"Shit" he barks, quickly releasing me from his hold.

I whirl on him and land a kick just above his right knee that makes his leg buckle. Instead of falling to the ground like I was hoping, he only staggers to the side for a moment before regaining his balance.

"Tell me, Dax, what the hell do you think gives you the right to treat me the way you did?" He goes to answer but I cut him off. "You are the biggest womanizer on campus, maybe in the whole damn town. There is a different girl on your arm every time that I see you and you have a reputation of not even remembering their fucking names. You spend the day with me at your dead mother's grave and your night fucking some dumb bitch in my work's bathroom. Yet somehow, I am the whore when I dance with a friend? And I am just supposed to be okay with that!" I shout.

While he is absorbing my words, I throw a few jabs along with a couple of kicks. He blocks almost everything I throw at him, but I do land several good shots.

Obviously, there would be no competition if he was actually exchanging blows with me and not acting like a heavy bag, but I need this. Beating on him is finally releasing some of the anger that I haven't been able to release since last Saturday. I have avoided going to the gym because I didn't want to run in to him, so this release is much needed.

I have done a good job of avoiding him in general. Anytime him and his friends came into The White Oak I switched sections with whoever else was working with me and the few times he tried to corner me on campus I just kept walking like I never saw him. But I did see him, I always see him.

Dax is actually sweating right now and appears to be lightly catching his breath. Which makes me prouder than I can express. I continue my attack on Dax, though I don't have the stamina that he does and I'm running out of steam fast. I open my body up briefly to deliver a kick but as soon as I do I see that it was the wrong move.

He sees the opening and has me on the ground pinned underneath him before I can even blink. I do my best to buck him off my body and wriggle free like I did with Collins, but Dax is 260lbs of solid muscle and I'm fucking spent. On top of my exhaustion my ribs are also fucking killing me, and I wouldn't be surprised if I just took a step back in my healing process.

Heaving out an aggravated sigh, I tap out and he eases off of me quickly before laying on his back next to me as he faces the ceiling.

"How did you know about the girl at the bar?" He whispers so quiet that I barely hear it.

I turn my head to face him and lock eyes with those nuclear orbs.

"People talk, Dax. Especially about you. I have heard more stories about your exploits than I can even count. So, if you are so busy with every other girl in the world then why do you care what I do? And why would you tear me down like that in front of everyone? I thought you had a little more respect for me than that."

I let the disappointment and hurt bleed through my words. I want him to see how bad he fucked up and that I won't let anyone treat me that way, no matter who they are.

"I didn't sleep with her. I kissed her and I just…couldn't."

I blink at him slowly as I let his words sink in. Why does a small part of me feel relieved to hear that? It is strange as fuck. The stranger thing though is the insurmountable rage that I feel at the thought of him kissing someone else. Not that I thought I was the last girl that he has kissed over these last few weeks but now I know for sure that I am not. And that pisses me off. Before I can say anything he speaks again.

"I'm really sorry about the party, Bree. I didn't mean it. Not one word," he says looking genuinely ashamed.

I shake my head at his attempt to sidestep my question.

“Answer me,” I practically beg. “Why would you do that to me when you are out there living it up. Even if I was making out with every guy in the room, how is that any different from what you do? Why did you treat me the way you did?”

He blows out a deep breath as his eyes roam over my face before locking on mine.

“I think you know why.”

I turn my head to face the ceiling and let out a shallow exhale. Fuck. I can’t let his words get to me. I can’t let them mean anything. I shove and cram every single feeling that stirs at those words and the look on his face into the smallest box in the darkest corner of my chest.

“Well, I’m not your girl and you’re not my man. We shouldn’t have opinions on how we spend time with others, so mind your business and I will mind mine. And in case it wasn’t clear, I will drop your ass if you *ever* call me a whore again. Ever.”

He nods solemnly and opens his mouth to say something before I shove his shoulder lightly, trying to break the tension and hoping to end this conversation. He gives me a small smile and stands up offering me his hand. I take it and stand with him.

“Want to see how your baby is coming?” He asks.

I perk up at that and instantly the tension in the air melts away.

“Yeah.”

Dax nods his head for me to follow him. When I come over to stand next to Betty, I notice a brand-new set of tires on her.

“Dax, we didn’t talk about tires. I didn’t know you needed the money for them so soon.”

He shrugs. “Forget about it. I had these lying around anyways. Besides your old set were so worn you were ready to blow a tire, or four. I want you safe.”

He ducks his head at that last part as if embarrassed to admit that he cares about me. My heart warms and I pull him into a hug and kiss his cheek, selfishly lingering for a few seconds before I pull back.

"Thank you," I say softly.

Dax looks down at me intently before he lets a genuine smile spread across his face. After a few seconds he turns to look back at Betty.

"She should be all good to go by next week. I can probably get her back to you after Thanksgiving."

"Really?!" I ask excitedly.

"Yeah, just a couple more small things and she will be good as new...well she will be a hell of a lot better than how she used to be," he teases as I swat at his arm.

Dax shoves his hands into his pockets as he shifts his weight from side to side for a second. He looks almost nervous which doesn't seem right because this is Dax motherfucking Hart we are talking about.

"So, uhm. I don't know if you are doing anything, but Marcus usually puts on a hell of a spread for Thanksgiving and it's only the two of us. So, if you aren't busy, well...you know you're welcome anytime."

My smile turns down a bit at the fact that I won't be around. A low-key Thanksgiving with Dax and Marcus sounds really nice actually. I can't help but feel kind of touched that he would want me to come over.

"Actually, I won't be in town. I already have plans."

Disappointment flashes across his face before he schools it and nods.

"Oh yeah. For sure. Visiting family?"

"Yeah, well, not my family. I was just going to hang at my dorm, but Cole invited me to his family's place."

His eyes harden at the mention of Cole before he gives me a curt nod and sharp, "Cool."

Silence stretches between us for a moment until my phone rings. I look down to see that it's Cole.

"Hey, what's up?"

"Sorry to bug you. Marcus just called me in for the dinner shift. I have to be there in 30. I didn't want to leave you without a ride, so I can pick you up now before I head in?"

I almost tell him that I'll find another ride, but I look up to see Dax watching me with a stony expression and decide that our visit should probably be done for the day.

"Sure, that's fine."

"Alright, I'll be there in a minute."

"Okay," I say before hanging up. Dax is still staring at me almost expectantly. "My ride will be here soon." I explain.

He works his jaw for a moment before he speaks.

"Cole?" He asks, his tone terse.

"Yeah," I say softly. He raps his knuckles on the hood of Betty and moves back to his heavy bag without sparing me another glance.

"Cool. Catch you later then."

Then he starts wailing on the bag way harder than he was when I first arrived. The tension in the room has returned and it is so thick that you could practically choke on it. I slip out of the door wordlessly and wait outside for Cole.

I shouldn't feel guilty that I made plans with Cole. How was I supposed to know that Dax would invite me over? Before an hour ago we weren't even speaking. I don't feel guilty, he's just bummed he won't have a friend at dinner, and he isn't a fan of Cole, that's all. But the way my gut is churning tells me that's not all.

CHAPTER TWENTY

Aubrey

It's the morning of Thanksgiving and Cole has just finished loading up our bags into the back of his truck before we hit the road. He lives in a small town about three hours north of Glenfield. I insisted that if Cole was going to force me to spend a holiday with his family the least he could do was buy me road trip snacks. He happily agreed and proceeded to practically buy one of everything at the gas station on our way out of town.

The drive has been pretty nice. We have talked a little bit, listened to music a lot and just enjoyed the scenic drive. But as we get closer nerves start to pool in my stomach.

"I am kinda nervous," I mutter more to myself than anything.

Cole's eyebrows raise in surprise as he turns to face me before looking back towards the road.

"I don't think that I have ever known you to be nervous about anything, like ever."

"Yeah, well, I don't have a whole lot of experience meeting

the parents of my friends. I haven't really had that great of friends before you and Kayla."

I look out the window as I try to think about the last time that I met anyone's parents really. It was probably my last boyfriend's parents when I was 16. I went over to his house to hang out. They were nice enough at first but when they found out where I lived they called me trash to my fucking face and told me that I was never allowed to see to their son again. He bowed down and took it like a little bitch and that left a bad taste in my mouth about meeting anyone's parents, friend or not. It also left me with a distaste about boyfriends in general which is why I stuck to casual hookups for the last couple of years.

Before I know it, Cole and I are pulling up a long driveway that has a white moderately sized rambler with red shutters and a blue front door smack dab in the middle. The yard is beautifully manicured and there is even a front porch swing. See? Norman fucking Rockwell painting.

Cole kills the truck and undoes his buckle, scooting over to me. He tilts my chin up with his fingers forcing me to meet his gaze. Those ice blue eyes are intently focused on me as he speaks.

"They are going to love you." He pauses for a moment glancing down at my lips and then back to my eyes before he says softly, "Who couldn't?"

My eyes widen and my stomach drops. Ah fuck. I knew I should have faked the flu or something. Nothing good will come from this weekend, mark my words.

Something changes in Cole's face before he gives me that typical easy smile. He plants a quick kiss on my cheek as he slides out of his door.

"C'mon. If I know my mom she is probably watching us, trying to get a glimpse of the first girl that I've ever brought home."

He throws me a wink before he gets to my side to open the door.

When he does, I hop out after him as he heads to the bed to grab our bags.

"What? You have never brought a girl home? Not even a friend?"

He just shakes his head with our bags in his hands as he ambles towards the house. Sure enough, we don't even get to knock before the door swings open revealing a woman in her mid-40's with Cole's same light brown hair and smile. She is so tiny and petite that it makes me wonder how the hell she ever gave birth to Cole. Poor woman.

"Cole! I didn't realize that y'all were already here."

Her accent is much thicker than Cole's, but her voice comes out as sweet and smooth as syrup. He rolls his eyes at her as he leans in to place a kiss on her cheek.

"Nice try, Mama. Next time let me at least knock before you open the door. That way it doesn't look like you are spying."

She shrugs like she doesn't care either way if she was caught or not.

"Oh well, can't blame a mother for being curious."

She swings her gaze towards me, and I immediately freeze. This is the moment I have been dreading ever since I agreed to come. My mother was the farthest thing from the word, so to meet someone who has been described to me as the embodiment of the word is intimidating as fuck. I force out a polite smile as his mom keeps staring at me expectantly.

"Hello, Mrs. Simmons. I am Aubrey. Thank you for letting me crash your holiday."

Her smile brightens as the corner of her eyes crinkle slightly. Phew. That's a good sign, right?

"Oh, sweet pea, it is so nice to meet you! The pleasure is all ours!" She practically squeals before she hauls me into a huge hug, squeezing me so hard that my ribs ache. Fuck. I swear those things will never get better.

I awkwardly pat her back through the hug and look over her shoulder to see Cole smothering a laugh. I shoot him a dirty glare just before his mom pulls back slightly, while still holding my biceps in an iron grip.

"And none of this Mrs. Simmons nonsense. You can call me Renée, or Mama or anything else but!"

I smile and nod my head.

"Yes, Renée. Thank you again."

She flicks her hand at me.

"Please, we are all so excited to have you. Coley here hasn't stopped talking about you since the first day of school. On our weekly call you are all he talks about!"

I look over at him with a shit eating grin. His face is crimson as he ducks it in attempt to try to hide the flush. I nudge him in the side as I smirk.

"Weekly call huh, Coley? You call your family every week?" He looks appreciative that I don't harp on the whole I am all he talks about part.

"Of course. I am a proper southern son. Right, Mama?"

"Hmm I don't know. A proper southern son would come home to visit more often and wouldn't be only staying for one night."

He shrugs. "Well, no one is perfect, I guess."

I let out a laugh while Renée smacks the back of his head like he is a pesky child. Cole chuckles as he walks deeper into the house. Renée loops her arm with mine and drags me along to where I assume the kitchen is, if the smells we are following are any indicator.

Sitting at the kitchen island are twin girls with the apparent Simmons family brown hair but with green eyes like their mother. They can't be older than 7. They are hand mashing potatoes when they both look up and see Cole ahead of us. Their eyes light up and the squeals that emerge from their tiny bodies are so sharp, I am fairly certain dogs in California heard and are howling. They both jump into his arms, one on each side while screeching with delight.

"Coley, Coley! You're home!" They chant.

I sit back smiling at the scene before me. Cole looks so happy here. There is no doubt about it that he is a family man. He just fits here. I look out of the corner of my eye to see Renée studying me with a smile on her face as I watch Cole. I see that hopeful glint in her eye that makes me internally cringe. I wish that there was a polite way to tell her that things aren't like that between us, but I have a feeling that it would probably fall on deaf ears.

"Do you guys want to meet my friend?" Cole asks the twins and they both scream, "YES!"

He chuckles and sets them down before dragging them towards me. Suddenly being close to a stranger they revert back to being typical shy 7-year old's who are nervous in front of company.

"Aubrey this is Caroline & Carli. Girls, this is my bestest friend in the whole world, Aubrey."

His eyes sparkle with delight, and I can tell that everyone in this room means the absolute world to him. I crouch down to their level and give them my brightest smile.

"Hi there. It is really nice to meet you both. Cole has told me so much about his beautiful sisters."

They both snicker behind their hands blushing furiously. Guess the blushing thing is a family trait.

"Thank you miss Aubrey," Caroline says. Carli picks up her sentence. "It's nice to meet you too."

Damn. These have to be the most polite children that I have ever met. I hear a loud shout come from what looks like the family room on the other side of the house. Renée huffs and rolls her eyes.

"Harry! Get your butt in here. The kids are here!"

A few seconds later a man walks into the kitchen. I could have told you that he was Cole's dad immediately. He has brown hair, though it isn't as light as the rest of the Simmons, those piercing blue eyes though are all Cole. He wraps Cole into a big hug and says a few words to him before they break apart and look towards me.

"Dad this is Aubrey. Aubrey this is my dad, Harry."

I stick out my hand to shake his.

"Nice to meet you, sir. Thank you for having me."

He grabs my hand and kisses the back of it. I can't help but snort at the gesture. Looks like both of the Simmons boys are charmers. Renée tuts beside me as she rolls her eyes at her husband's antics.

"We are glad y'all could make it out!" Harry turns back to Cole with a smile on his face as he claps his shoulder. "I didn't think you would make it in time. The first quarter just ended."

Cole chuckles and shakes his head.

"I would never dare miss football on Thanksgiving. That is just sacrilegious. Aubrey, do you want to come watch the game with us? If not, I am sure Mama wouldn't mind the company."

I look towards Renée with a small shrug.

"If I wouldn't be in the way?"

"Heavens no, sweet pea. Take a seat. You can take over mashing the potatoes. The twins have been begging to watch the game anyway."

Cole gives me a soft smile before he and his dad walk out of the kitchen together, their heads bent together seemingly done in attempt to have a private conversation. I turn back towards Renée.

"Thank you. I am not too into football."

A look flashes across her face as she furrows her brows.

"Well that simply won't do. If you are going to be with my Cole, you will have to get use to the sports channel always being on. He has always been that way ever since he was a little boy."

"Oh, we aren't together. We are just friends," I correct quickly.

She gives me a mischievous grin before saying, "We will see."

Fuck. I think not taking no for an answer also seems to be a Simmons family trait.

CHAPTER TWENTY-ONE

Aubrey

The next 30 minutes are spent with Renée bouncing around from task to task so quickly it makes my head spin. I haven't seen one box or packet of pre-packaged anything. Everything looks like it was made from scratch. Damn, what can't this woman do?

When we all sit at the table, Harry prays over our food before we all dig in. The girls try to get away with filling their plates up with potatoes and rolls and when Renée notices she piles on the green bean casserole and turkey. They groan simultaneously and I can't help but be amused at having a front row seat to the show. It is like an out of body experience to watch this seemingly ordinary happy family enjoying a meal together. I don't think I have seen anything like it.

"So, Aubrey. Cole says you are from California," Harry says as he dishes more yams onto his plate.

I nod my head as I finish chewing. Why does everyone always

decide to ask you questions or address you when you have just taken a bite of something?

"Yes, I am," I finally say.

"Do you know any movie stars?" Carli asks.

My lips tilt up in a smirk. "No, I don't. But one time Robert Downey Jr. bought my coffee."

"Who is that?" Caroline asks with furrowed brows.

"Iron Man," Cole interjects with a smile as he winks at the girls.

"REALLY?!" The twins shriek.

"Mhmm. I think he was just irritated that I was taking too long to have the barista count out the dimes and quarters I was trying to pay with, but it was still nice of him."

Everyone chuckles at that and the sound releases some of the tension inside of me that hadn't quite released since I agreed to come here. As dinner goes on, I have to admit I think I might even love his family more than him. His sisters make horrible jokes that are so bad they are good while his dad sits back and watches quietly with a fond smile on his face. Renée tries to question Cole about his dating life while giving me a not-so-subtle side eye. It is almost funny because she is about as subtle as a dump truck.

"Mom, stop. Please," Cole begs while sending me an apologetic look.

"I am just curious, Cole. You are such a handsome man and so smart and caring. Any girl would be lucky to have you. Your father and I met in college."

"Oh, he has plenty of girls interested in him," I tack on with an easy smile.

"Really?" Renée asks with an excited gleam in her eyes.

"Yeah, our friend Kayla has shown interest, but he turned her down and I have seen several girls slip him their numbers at The White Oak."

Cole rolls his eyes as he takes a sip of his beer.

"Kayla and I would never work. We are way better off as friends and those other girls are not my type."

"Oh, yeah? Why, are they just too beautiful?" I ask with a challenging look and a small smirk.

I can't deny that I am having way too much fun teasing him with his family. Everyone has an amused smile on their face except for Cole who just looks irritated.

"Beautiful is nice. I prefer someone who is a bit prickly and sarcastic, though. Once you break through that shell, a really incredible person sits underneath."

His eyes burrow into mine seriously and I quickly break the eye contact to take a sip of my drink. Well, that certainly backfired. A few minutes later Cole and I start picking up the kitchen while the twins do the dishes and Harry rubs Renée's feet, saying she was on them too long today and that she deserved a break.

Once everything is all cleaned up, we all get settled onto the couches and watch some kid's movie that the girls picked out. After it is over, everyone starts heading for bed.

"Thank you again for having me. This was…well I have never experienced anything like this before. This has been the best Thanksgiving I have ever had. Thank you," I say.

The girls bounce happily, Harry gives me a sweet smile and Renée's eyes water before she pulls me into another bone crushing hug. Ow. Cole rubs his mom's back, as if reminding her that she needs to let me breathe. She pulls back and brushes away a stray tear and pats my cheek lovingly before going to tuck the girls in.

Cole says his goodnights before he turns to face me.

"So, we have the guest bed made up for you. My mom would probably have a heart attack if she knew that we have slept in the same bed before so I thought that it would be best if I took the couch."

"Oh no. Cole, this is your house. I am more than happy with the couch."

"Darlin'," he says as he fixes me with a serious look. "You clearly don't know Mama very well. She would beat me six ways to Sunday if I let you sleep on the couch. No arguments, let's go."

He ushers me to the spare bedroom, which obviously used to be Cole's bedroom. It is still decorated like a 17-year-old boy would have it who is obsessed with football, trucks and Lynyrd Skynyrd. It screams Cole and that makes me smile as I flop down onto his bed.

"Want to watch a movie?" He asks, gesturing to the TV in the corner.

I nod and he quickly flicks on a comedy before he bounces down next to me. I chuckle as I fly up a couple of inches while Cole begins to tickle me.

"Oh my god! Stop! I will fucking throat punch you!" I say in between labored breaths and laughs.

He laughs and finally stops before placing a quick kiss on my forehead. He raises his arm for me to lean into him and I look at him for a second, wondering if it is a good idea. But we have done this same thing at least a dozen times and it has never complicated anything before. I settle underneath his arm as we watch the movie play out.

About halfway through I feel a soft kiss against the top of my head.

"Thank you for coming home with me. My family adores you," Cole says softly.

I tilt my head up so that I can look at him better and smile.

"Thank you for inviting me, they are all so amazing. You are really lucky to have them in your life Cole."

He exhales a soft breath. "Yeah, I am lucky for a lot of people in my life."

I smile at him even though it is a little strained. Fuck things are getting way too intimate. I choose not to respond, instead focusing on the movie. The room is quiet for a few moments before Cole speaks again.

"My dad and I were talking about you earlier. While you were helping mama in the kitchen."

"All good things I hope," I tease lightly as I glance at him out of the corner of my eye.

He gives a small nod.

"He told me that he used to look at mama the way that I look at you when they first met. He also said that if I knew what was good for me, I wouldn't waste my time waiting for something when it's right in front of me."

My stomach sinks at his words as dread starts to creep in. This is what I have been trying to avoid for a while now. I feel like I have been pretty direct in telling him that I don't feel that way about him, but he seems to be pretty damn persistent. Or maybe I haven't been direct enough.

Looking back, I guess I have thrown him some mixed signals. Saying one thing but doing another. Dancing with him at the party, cuddling like this, hanging out practically every day. Fuck. I've been totally leading him on.

"Darlin'?" he whispers

"Yeah?" I ask warily.

"You know how I said that we could be just friends for now?" His voice is soft and shakes slightly with each word. I nod my head slowly.

"Now is over."

Before I can say anything, he slips his hand across my jaw and brings my lips up to meet his. I tense for a moment before my brain fully processes what is going on. I put my hands on his shoulders, ready to push him away when his lips move more urgently against mine, practically begging me to reciprocate. In that instant I seem to forget about all of the reasons I have in my head to not give Cole a chance.

His soft lips move across mine gently at first before the kiss turns more heated. His tongue gently sweeps against my lower lip, asking for access and I grant it, opening my mouth slightly for him. We aren't rushed or frantic. Everything about this kiss is tender and sweet.

When he pulls away, he peppers my cheek and neck with kisses, and I close my eyes and let out a soft moan doing my best to push away the brewing guilt of what this will mean for Cole in the morning and more importantly what it won't mean for me. His hands grasp my hips and gently lift the hem of my shirt up, his knuckles grazing against my skin. I shiver from the contact and grab the material ripping it off me in one fluid motion. I then reach behind me and unhook my bra tossing it to the side.

His eyes darken with lust as he takes me in. I know I should stop this. But right now, this feels like exactly what I need. Yet again, I am using Cole to distract me from my suffocating feelings, but he seems more than willing at the moment.

Cole's hands roam all over, as if memorizing my body. He lowers his mouth against my skin, kissing a hot trail from my mouth down my neck and stopping at my breasts. He looks at me once more before he takes me into his mouth. His warm tongue slides across my nipple gently sucking and flicking his tongue.

When he gently nips at me, I let out a too loud moan and grind my hips against him. I start to lift the bottom of his shirt as he helps, pulling it the rest of the way off revealing a chiseled six pack and a rock-hard chest. I forgot how good he looks without a shirt on.

I drag him back down to my lips as I greedily kiss him. I lift my hips and shimmy out of my jeans, and he thankfully takes the hint and goes for his belt buckle. Soon only two pieces of fabric are separating us. He lowers himself down to me, grinding against the spot I need him which earns him another throaty moan to slip past my lips. His hands go to the edge of my panties when a loud rap sounds at the door.

"Cole, you should probably hit the couch. You are lucky that I was the one that was getting a drink of water," his dad's voice says through the door.

We hear footsteps turn down the hallway a few seconds later and I bury my head into his chest and groan. I am fucking mortified. Cole chuckles and smooths my hair.

"It's okay, darlin'. My dad was our age once. He won't say anything."

"Ugh just go," I say, pulling the sheets over my face.

He tries and fails to pull the blankets down. Then the cheat goes to tickle my sides and I squeal forgetting about my embarrassment as he rips the blankets down and looks into my eyes with a sincere smile on his lips.

"This has officially been the best day of my life. Sleep well, darlin'."

He grasps my chin between his forefinger and thumb and tilts up so that I meet him in a chaste kiss. When he pulls away, he slips out of the room and down the hall. I close my eyes thinking about everything that happened today. I smack my hand across my face because I am so fucking stupid.

Now that the hormone crazed fog has lifted and I realize the gravity of what I just did, I can't help but feel thankful that his dad interrupted us when he did. I saw the look in Cole's eyes. This definitely meant more to him that just a little fooling around. He wants more from me, and I know for a fact that I can't give it to him. The reason I can't? Well, a huge one would have to be a pair of sharp emerald eyes.

Why the fuck did I let get things get so far? Like that is even a question. Deep down I know that I was reaching for something, anything to distract me from the thought that Dax had his tongue down some skanks throat just the other week. I was no longer the last kiss that he had and now he wasn't mine either.

As I toss and turn in bed, I can't help but wonder what Dax is doing, or more specifically, who he is doing. I am under no illusion that he will spend this entire break holed up at his place. He is Glenfield's most eligible bachelor. Everyone either wants to be him or be with him. Besides, it isn't like we left off on a great note anyways and I did just spend my night with my tongue in someone else's mouth, so I guess I have no room to talk. But still.

The idea of Dax hooking up with someone else turns my stomach sour. I know that I told Dax that we aren't anything to each other and that we shouldn't have opinions on each other's dating lives but what can I say, guess I am a fucking liar because I definitely have opinions.

CHAPTER TWENTY-TWO

Aubrey

The next morning, we have a freaking banquet of a breakfast. Renée made pancakes, French toast, eggs, bacon and hash browns. There are only six of us, but she cooked for an army of twenty. After we stuff ourselves and throw our bags into the truck, we say our goodbyes.

Renée tears up as she hugs and kisses us both and makes Cole promise to come home soon for a weekend to which he dutifully agrees. It's not like it is a hardship. His family is fucking awesome. I would have killed to have a family like this growing up.

Cole goes to start the truck and looks over to me with a soft smile, I try to return it, but I know that it doesn't look genuine. He tried to kiss me this morning, but I casually stepped out of his path. If it bothered him, he didn't let it show but every time that he looked at me with those damn stars in his eyes, it made my stomach twist. I hate that I am going to hurt him. I hate that I let things get out of hand and now he has these expectations that won't be met.

He tries to talk to me the whole ride back, but I hardly respond, being too lost in my own head. We pull up to campus after a few hours. Cole parks before getting out and jogging around to get my door. I give him a tight smile and nod my head as he grabs my bag. We head up to my room in silence.

When we get inside and the door thunks shut Cole blurts out, "Okay, talk."

Knowing I need to rip off the band aid, I sigh and walk over to sit on my bed as I pull my knees into my chest. Cole comes to sit next to me and is patiently waiting for me to speak.

"Cole, we shouldn't have crossed that line. You know I care about you, but you said it yourself. Hooking up with friends complicates things. I don't want to damage our friendship; you are too important to me. We are better off as friends."

Cole's patient look is immediately erased with one of panic and worry. He drops to his knees in front of me and quickly takes my hands in his.

"Darlin'." His voice is so thick with emotion that it looks like he has to physically swallow over it before continuing. "I've never said it out loud before. I think I have made it pretty clear with my actions, but some things just need to be said." He takes a deep breath as his Sapphire eyes meet mine.

"I am in love with you, Aubrey. I have been since the first day that I met you. You drew me in instantly and I just had to be near you. You're stunning obviously, that's what first got my attention but two sentences out of your mouth and I knew you were like no one I had ever met, and I had to see more of you. And then you mercilessly friend zoned me," he says, giving a teasing smile as I give him a sad one in return. "But I was ok with it, because it meant I got to spend all of my free time getting to know you even better and I just fell harder.

"All those study dates and lazy days with ice cream and movies, every moment spent with you was my new favorite. I was starting to think that we would be just friends forever. And then yesterday happened and it was like everything was falling into place.

"Aubrey, this is more to me than just a fling or casual dating. I am all in. But I know that all of this time you have been seeing me as just a friend while I have been falling deeper and deeper in love with you. So, I'll give you a chance to catch up. Let's just keep this casual, no labels or expectations but maybe now I can kiss you once in a while and you won't reject me?"

The last part comes out as teasing, but I can tell he is being serious. I open my mouth to tell him that I can't do that. He must sense what I am about to say because he apparently decides to switch methods and grabs my face with both of his hands as he pulls me in for a kiss. This time I have enough sense to not kiss him back before I put my hands on his chest and gently push him away.

Cole's eyes flutter open and they stare at me, big, sad and vulnerable.

"It's not just about things moving fast for you is it? It's Dax?"

His tone is accusing, and I wince at the sound, hating myself more with every second. I go to tell him that Dax has nothing to do with us, but he holds up a hand to stop me.

"Please don't try to deny it. I see the way you look at him, and the way he looks at you. It's okay. Everything I said is true, it would be impossible for me to be the only one to notice how incredible you are. I understand that you have feelings for him, I've known for a while, I guess. I just…don't you see that I am the better option? I would never hurt you. You would always be my number one priority."

"I know, Cole," I say quietly not able to make eye contact with him.

"But you still want him, don't you?" His tone hardens and a disapproving look crosses his face.

I just shrug and stare at my nails, trying to look anywhere but him. He lifts my chin to meet his eyes and I see the pain swimming there. It guts me to know that it's all because of me.

"It's okay, you know. You don't have to make a decision right now. I would just like to be considered."

I stare at him for a moment before I shake my head and sigh.

"Cole, you deserve so much better. So much more than I can give you. Putting this weird thing between Dax and I to the side, I still don't think that you and I are a good idea. I don't want to lose you in my life, though."

He nods his understanding as he cups the side of my face.

"You won't lose me. I will always be here, no matter what. I am not giving up on you Aubrey. Just think about it, I can give you so much. We could be so great together."

With that, he stands and kisses the top of my head before striding out of my room. There is that trademark doesn't take no for an answer bullshit again. I hope he will at least back off now. I don't want our friendship to be ruined just because he can't get past this little crush.

Sometimes I wish that I could just like Cole. He is good, kind, safe. A life with him would be simple, easy and dare I say a bit boring, which wouldn't be bad considering the life I have led so far. But Dax is fire. He is fierce, powerful, and all consuming. I know that if we did give things a shot, he would care for me with that same intensity. He would protect me with everything that he possibly could. But the problem with fire is, if you get too close you always get burned.

I have successfully managed to avoid both Cole and Dax for a whole week. I don't want to deal with seeing Cole give me those puppy dog eyes, begging me to feel a way that I just can't for him.

I also don't want to deal with Dax because I just don't even know how to. We left off on a weird note and I don't even know where his head is at let alone mine.

Maybe I am getting ahead of myself. I mean, Dax has never specifically said that he wants more with me, that isn't his style, so why would I be any different? I know that he is attracted to me and that he is a bit possessive of me, okay more than a bit. But for all I know, this really could all be just one big game for him, a challenge that he wants to conquer. As much as that would suck, I wouldn't be surprised.

That doesn't seem right, though. The way he looked at me in his garage tells me that he feels *something*. That's it. I'm done hiding like a coward. I will call him on Monday, get Betty back and see how things go. I am sure once I am around him, I will be reminded of the broody asshole that he is and then I can get over these ridiculous feelings. That still leaves me with the whole Cole issue, but that is a problem for another day.

On Saturday, I am woken up by my phone ringing nonstop. I think I miss about 8 calls before I finally accept defeat and answer.

"What?" I groan into the phone.

"Hey, sleepyhead! Get up! I'm on my way over to pick you up!" Kayla says cheerily. Who is she, Snow-Fucking-White? Who gets up *willingly* on a Saturday at 7:30am and is happy about it?

"Kaylaaa," I whine. "Can't you come and bug me in like three hours, at least?"

She snickers like I'm a silly child. "No. Get up. You have 15 minutes."

Then she hangs up on me. Fucking bitch. I seriously need to drop her ass. I get up begrudgingly, knowing that if I don't she will just come banging on my door until I answer.

35 minutes later, Kayla bounds through my door before perching herself on the top of my desk, making herself right at home.

"Ever punctual I see," I say with an unimpressed look on my face.

"Always, honey," she responds, tossing me a saucy wink. I roll my eyes before grabbing my purse and heading for the door with her in tow.

"So where are we going at this ungodly hour?"

"We are having a girl's day!" She squeals.

"A girl's day? For what?"

"Like we need a reason! But I have a date tonight with Jeremy. You remember him from the clay banks?"

"No, I don't. You never introduced us. You were too busy keeping him to yourself," I tease.

She snickers and shrugs.

"What can I say. Anyways I always did girl's days with my friends on the day of a date. And since we are now best friends, I figured it was mandatory that you accompany me to get ready!"

"Okay. I am going to pretend like that makes sense. So, what do we need to do? Why are we doing this so early? Don't you just need to get dressed and stuff?" I question as I slide into the Barbie Mobile.

She throws her head back laughing so hard that I swear I see a few tears.

"Oh my gosh, you are adorable. Honey, we have an appointment at the Spa in 20 minutes. We are getting Mani-Pedi's, Massages, Waxing. The works."

I look at her dubiously as she starts the car and takes off.

"You do all that just for a date? What if he is a dud? That's a lot of work to gamble on some dude."

"That's just part of being a girl!"

I shrug and look out the window.

"Not where I'm from."

She laughs again, shaking her head.

"Well, you are with me now."

After one deep tissue massage, two hands and two feet perfectly manicured and being waxed within an inch of my life, we eat at some hoity toity bistro in the salon where the chef salad costs more than I used to spend on groceries for a week back home. Good thing Kayla's dad is footing the bill. Thank you, Papa Blackburn.

Once we are done with lunch, Kayla insists we need to find her a new outfit. We head to a mall that I am pretty sure you need a black credit card just to enter. I glance down at my band t-shirt and ripped jeans before catching a judgy look from some stepford wife in a designer dress and an oversized frilly hat that belongs in the 19th century. I roll my eyes and trail after Kayla as she practically gallops into a store.

After a few minutes of browsing through racks Kayla pipes up.

"So, do you have any plans for tonight? All dolled up and nowhere to go," she hums.

"Nah. Probably just going to go home and admire their handiwork," I say inspecting my nails that are freshly slathered in shiny red polish.

"Honey. You know I say this because I care, but you need to get out there. This is college. We are in the prime of our lives. You have been down ever since you got back from break. Did something happen?" She asks with her eyebrows raised like I am a petulant child refusing to fess up.

If that is what she thinks of me for not gossiping then that is exactly what I am, because I am not taking the bait. I haven't told a soul about Cole and me, nor do I plan to. I also haven't told anyone about the moment Dax and I had shortly before break. For all she knows, I am still royally pissed at him about the party which makes me feel sort of bad that I am keeping things from her. But I don't share personal shit like that with people, friends or not.

I roll my eyes at her as I turn to look at a rack filled with clothes

I would never wear in a million years.

"Kayla, I'm fine."

"Well, you need to go out and have some fun. Would it really kill you?"

"Probably," I deadpan, getting more than a little irked that she won't just fucking drop it.

She rolls her eyes at me exasperated and huffs.

"Nope, it wouldn't. Promise me you will go out tonight, even if it is just for a bit."

I sigh heavily, weighing her words in my mind. I guess it wouldn't kill me to be a little social, but just a little. I would honestly try anything to get me out of my own head right now. If I eat another gallon of ice cream, I am pretty sure I am going to need to go up a pant size.

"Fine, I will go do something outside of my room tonight."

"Yay!" She claps before turning around and sifting through a rack of dresses. "Oh my gosh get over here! You have to try this on," she says, thrusting a red dress at me.

I hold it out to look at it. It is really pretty actually. I don't wear dresses, like ever, but that doesn't mean I can't appreciate one. It comes just above the knee and has a side slit up to almost mid-thigh with a plunging neckline. It's totally gorgeous but maybe a little bit much for the local bar across town that I was thinking about hitting up.

"Uh, I think this may be a little much for a night out by myself."

She shoos at me like I am a pesky fly.

"Be quiet and try it on."

I relent and go into the dressing room. Once I slip on the dress, I am impressed. It fits like a second skin. The deep red compliments my blonde hair and the plunging neckline leaves little to the imagination. This isn't normally my style, but maybe for one night it could be. I step out and Kayla's eyes widen before she breaks out into a huge smile.

"Yes! It's perfect I love it! You have to get it."

I nod my agreement then check the price tag and nearly choke on my tongue. $400 for a dress! Rich people are crazy. I begin to take it off right then and there, other customers be damned.

"I can't believe you let me try that on! I probably depreciated it just by touching it!"

Kayla rolls her eyes at me like I am being dramatic before she saunters over to me. She glances down at the tag before she scoffs and swats at the air.

"Don't worry about it. My treat."

"Kayla, this is not a treat. This is $400! That is like a month's rent where I come from."

She snorts. "Where the hell did you live? A cardboard box?"

I wince at that. She is closer than she probably realizes. She seems to miss my reaction to her words because she carries on.

"Well, where I come from, this is a treat. Seriously Aubrey, you have no idea how deep my pockets run. You are probably my only friend that doesn't, nor do you care. That's why you are my best friend. You care about me, not my money. That right there earns you the right to be pampered once in a while. Most people just think that I'm an obnoxious spoiled rich girl but not you."

"Well, that's not true. You are pretty fucking obnoxious," I tease lightly as she shoves me, chuckling softly.

"Please let me do this, I want to."

I don't know why but I concede and give her a small nod.

"Thank you, Kayla."

She kisses me on the cheek and smiles happily.

"Of course, Honey. Now come on, next stop is shoes!"

Oh fuck, here we go.

CHAPTER TWENTY-THREE

Aubrey

Later that evening, I am standing in my room inspecting myself in the mirror. I am wearing my $400 dress, still can't even believe I own something so ridiculously expensive, and the matching heels. I told Kayla that I was happy to wear my chucks and she looked like I just proposed we go on a murder spree.

I even curled my hair and did my makeup tonight. Not gonna lie, I look pretty fucking hot. I get out my phone and order a ride before grabbing my purse and fake ID as I head out the door. I decide to hit up a local club that Kayla said was really popular.

When I arrive at Club 22 the energy is palpable. The room is dimly lit with lights flashing in sync to the music. Drinks are being expertly poured at the bar and hordes of people are mixed on the dance floor, writhing and grinding together. Fuck yeah. This is what I am talking about.

I make my way to the bar and order three tequila shots because

I plan on having a good ass time tonight. As I am waiting for my drinks, I feel a meaty hand grab my ass. I whirl on the offender ready to drop his. I pause for a moment when I see a large hand clasp the creep's shoulder. When my eyes move up they catch a familiar pair of emerald eyes. He is staring daggers at the back of this guy's head but speaks to me through clenched teeth.

"I am trying not to save you. But you better do something before I do."

This time I don't hesitate. I wind back and throw all of my weight into one solid punch to the jaw, effectively knocking out the handsy asshole. He falls to the floor in a pathetic heap that I don't even care to give a second look at.

When I look up, I see Dax's surprised expression with a twinkle of pride in his eyes as he easily steps over the douchebag before standing next to me.

"Nice hit."

I nod at him wordlessly before I turn back to the bar and toss back one of my shots.

"So, where are your friends?" He asks

"Not here," I say casually.

I throw back the next shot, reveling in the burn that runs down my throat before settling warm in my stomach. Dax's brows furrow at that.

"I don't like that. There are creeps around here. Case and point," he says as he points towards the still unconscious guy on the floor.

I can't help but giggle as I shake my head. I think it is safe to say that the tequila is already hitting me. Might as well do another just for good measure!

"Well thanks for the concern, Dad, but I'm a big girl. I think I will be alright."

I toss back my final shot before slamming the glass down on the bar top. I pat Dax's cheek condescendingly before I sashay off to the dance floor. I try to lose myself in the song, ignoring the sharp green eyes that I can feel staring holes into my back.

Of course, he is here. The one night that I try to get away from everything, he is here. If that isn't a giant ass sign from the universe then I don't know what is. I turn around to see that Dax is still staring right at me. His face is intense and protective like he doesn't want to let me out of his sight.

Fuck it. When our eyes lock, I crook my finger towards him. Within seconds, he is striding purposefully over to me. That same intense expression is still fixed on his face but when he is only inches from me, I watch as his eyes darken. I lift up my arms and curl them around his neck as I continue dancing.

He looks hesitant for a moment before he reaches out and grabs a hold of my hips, digging his fingers into them so hard that I will probably bruise but I could care less. Someone bumps into me from behind and Dax yanks me into him even closer in response. I am now pressed tightly against his chest and my breath hitches at the contact. I look up to see his eyes bathed in desire and something else I can't quite name. Sadness?

We stay that way for a couple of songs. Our bodies never break contact while he has me practically panting as I grind against his leg. Fuck it has been fucking forever since I have gotten laid. All this time spent with Dax has made that painfully obvious because right now I am like a bitch in heat.

Once the current song ends, Dax brings his lips down to my neck, just hovering. I shiver as his breath skates across my skin.

"It's late. Let me drive you home," he murmurs roughly.

I nod my head probably faster than I should have before he laces our fingers together and guides us through the club. Much to my delight he doesn't try to drop my hand once we are free from the crowd, he actually squeezes just a little tighter like he is worried I am the one that will pull away. Not tonight.

He opens the car door for me before he climbs into the other side of his mustang. My head is still floating from the alcohol as I remember how good his hands felt on my body. After the second song they wandered down to my ass and stayed there for the rest of the night. Fuck. I wonder what I would have to do to get him to touch me right now.

Since we ran into each other, we haven't brought up the awkward fact that I have been avoiding him like the plague this last week, which I am completely relieved by because how the fuck do I explain that?

I am sorry I have been avoiding you. I just came to the realization that I am super into you and want more, though I know that isn't your style and I will probably just end up being a one-night stand for you. But I am weirdly ok with that if I can at least have you once.

Yeah, fuck no.

We drive in comfortable silence as he drives back to campus. Everything is different with him. There is no need to talk just to talk and silence with him never feels intolerable. When we spend time together like this it feels special, like we get each other and know what the other needs. As we get close to campus, he clears his throat.

"You look really nice tonight, Bree."

His voice sounds strained and is unusually soft for the man that normally commands attention and dominance the moment he steps into a room. I give him a small smirk as I look up at him through my eyelashes.

"Thank you."

When we pull up just outside of my building, he puts the car in park. Dax turns to look me in the eyes, and I notice that the same conflicted look is still there. He visibly swallows as if there is a lump he is trying to work past. When he speaks next his voice is barely above a whisper.

"You look more than nice, Bree. You are...fucking breathtaking."

My breathing stalls for a moment and my heart does a backflip. It's not his words really, he is always feeding me and probably every other girl in town lines and other bullshit. But it's the earnest look on his face that has me feeling like I am free falling. The emotion brimming his eyes is something that hits me hard, and damn if I don't almost believe him. I give him a small smile as I continue staring into his striking eyes. I wonder what those eyes would look like if I dropped to my knees and-

"So, where was Cole tonight?" He asks, watching my face closely.

"Cole?" I ask, suddenly confused. I was thinking about what his eyes would look like if I wrapped my mouth around his-Fuck. What was the question?

"Yeah. That place can have some shady characters, as you already found out. I know that you can take care of yourself, but a man shouldn't let his girl be put in those situations to begin with."

His tone is even and stiff, like the words are painful for him to even utter.

"His girl?" I question, as my eyebrows furrow

He shrugs. "I just assumed that after spending the holiday with him and his family you guys decided to give it a go."

Does he sound almost…sad? Is he seriously jealous of Cole? I know he freaked when I danced with Cole at the party, but I assumed it was just because I refused to dance with him. He wouldn't get upset like this over someone he just wanted a hook up with, right?

"We are not together things are…complicated. But we are not together."

His face remains impassive as he says, "So, you are single?"

"Yeah."

The air is charged for a moment and neither of us hardly breathe. I don't know who moves first but before I know it, Dax's lips are pressed against mine, his body leaning over me, pinning me to the seat. I groan as his tongue strokes my own. *Fuck.* Yes. This. This is the way every person deserves to be kissed.

Dax's hands are cupping my jaw, but they soon start traveling over my body, brushing against my breasts before continuing down. His fingers skate against the exposed skin of my upper thigh and I moan in anticipation.

"Dax," I whisper breathily. "Touch me, please."

"You got it, baby," he says hoarsely before his fingers deftly pull my soaked panties to the side as he slips a finger inside.

We both let out simultaneous groans as he pushes deeper inside of me.

"Fuck, baby. Are you this wet just for me?"

Normally I would give him shit. Tell him something so that it doesn't go to his head, but I am buzzed, emotional and fucking horny right now. I will say or do whatever it takes to get off right now.

"Yes. Fuck yes, Dax."

His fingers pick up their pace as his thumb comes down and starts swiftly rubbing circles against my clit.

"Say my name again, Bree. Tell me how bad you want me," his hoarse voice rasps into my ear as he sucks on the sensitive flesh just behind it.

"Dax," I moan. "I want you so fucking bad. Make me come, Dax."

A growl rumbles in his chest as he hits that magical spot before stroking it quickly. I shatter apart, shouting his name as I fall apart in the front seat of his car. My pussy spasms around his thick finger for several seconds like my body doesn't want to be done with him.

When I have come down from my earth-shattering orgasm, he slowly withdraws his hand before sucking his finger into his mouth as he rests his forehead against mine, never breaking eye contact with me. Fuck. I'm ready to go again.

We sit there for a moment in the fogged out car, the only noise being our labored breathing.

"Can I take you somewhere?" He whispers gently as he lifts a hand up to gently brush against my cheek.

I nod. Because right now I would do whatever he said. I suddenly see what the big deal is. I only made out with Dax and got finger fucked by him and I am fucking addicted. I want more of him more than I want my next fucking breath.

Dax presses a chaste kiss against my lips before blowing out a breath, pulling away and starting the car.

CHAPTER TWENTY-FOUR

Dax

They aren't together. As soon as she told me that she wasn't with Cole I knew that I had to take her here. I can't wait any longer now. I am not missing my window with her again. I wasn't sure how Aubrey would react when I told her that I have feelings for her but with the way she just kissed me and then used my fingers to get off, I would say she will take it better than I thought.

Fuck. I can still taste her. It was just a tease. I want the real thing, I need it. Shit. The sexy moans that she made, the way she said my name had me ready to nut in my pants. Pushing my straining cock to the side, I will it to calm the fuck down. If this goes well we will have plenty of time to get naked. I want to do this right with her.

It only takes a few minutes to get to our destination. I pull off to the side of the road before putting the car in park and turn towards

She looks around, obviously seeing nothing but tall thick trees and highway.

"Uh, for what?"

I jump out of the car and stroll around to her side so that I can open her door. I offer her my hand and she takes it as she climbs out. She looks around skeptically before turning back to me.

"Come on," I say tugging her hand.

I lead us down the side of the road for a few hundred feet until I find the tree that I marked years ago. I am about to start tugging her down the wooded path when I realize that she is wearing ridiculously high heels. I bend down slightly and offer her my back before I look over my shoulder at her.

"Need a lift?"

She shrugs and without any warning, jumps onto my back, almost taking us both down in the process. I stabilize us after a second and look back at her with a surprised expression. She is choking back a giggle as she loops her arms around my neck.

"As graceful as a swan," I joke.

That earns me a full bellied laugh that makes my heart jump out of my chest for a moment. I almost forgot how much I love to hear her laugh. I walk us through the brush, being careful to move branches out of the way so that they don't scratch her. After a little, we finally make it to firmer ground when I slip her off my back, committing to memory how great her toned body felt wrapped around me.

When I look down at her, she is staring up at me like I have lost my mind.

"Close your eyes. I want to show you something." She raises her eyebrows in a 'yeah right' motion. So, I decide to tack on, "Please."

She huffs out a quick breath before she closes her eyes. Then I take hold of her hand, lacing our fingers together as I lead her past the brush and to the clearing. I position her just right and stand back where I will be able to see her reaction.

"Okay, open."

At first, she looks confused but then when she takes in our surroundings, she gives me the most breathtaking smile I have ever seen. Her eyes widen in awe and the look of appreciation she gives my special place makes my heart constrict. Fuck she is so beautiful, it's not even fair.

"What is this place?" She asks, amazement shining in her captivating turquoise eyes.

I get it. I felt the same way the first time I saw it too. The 30ft waterfall is cascading over the rock edge that surrounds the swimming hole. The water shimmers in the moonlight and the forest around us makes it feel like we are the only people in the world.

"It's where I come to think. My mom discovered this place one day by accident. Ever since I was a little kid she would bring me out here. This is where we had all of the important talks in my life. Like when she lectured me about girls, or when I asked where my dad was and…this was just our special place, I guess."

I let out a slow breath before continuing.

"This is the one place in the world where I feel truly at peace. Where I can remember clearly the words that my mother and I spoke about when she told me about the man that she wanted me to grow up to be. Anyways, I wanted to bring you here because I think we are well past due an important talk."

Aubrey looks out over the water, letting my words hang for a moment before she quietly speaks.

"About what?"

I give her a 'you know what' look before I take her hand in mine and lead her over to the rock that my mom and I used to sit at. I have never felt so vulnerable in all my life, but if there was ever a time to open up to another person, it is now. Bree turns to me, seemingly waiting for me to start talking. I clear my throat once, twice, three times, trying to buy myself some time and come up with the perfect words to say. Finally, I decide that I don't need to give her pretty words, she just needs the truth, no bullshit.

"Bree, I like you. I really fucking like you. I think that I have since the night you basically told me to fuck off for beating the shit out of that creep outside of The White Oak. I knew from that first second that you were different. Then I got to know you more and even though you infuriated the fuck out of me, I liked you that much more. You didn't take any of my shit, or anyone else's for that matter."

She lets out a short snort at that and I grin at her before pressing on.

"There has always been something about you that I've felt drawn to, and it scared the shit out of me for a while, still does, honestly. So, I tried to tell myself that you were just another girl, that what I was feeling was lust not…something more. I tried not to think about you. Even tried to hook up with other girls just to get you out of my head."

She winces at that omission, and I kick myself for being so stupid. No one could ever compare to her.

"I haven't opened myself up to anyone since my mom died. I loved her more than anything in the world and she left me, not by choice but she is gone all the same and it damn near killed me. I know that I could never live through a second heartbreak like that, so I took my heart out of everything. I pushed everything down and built-up walls so tall that no one could ever climb them." I pull my lip through my teeth and look down at the ground. This baring your soul shit is harder than it seems.

"The point is, I've never had a problem living my life like that, until I met you. I spent so much time trying to fight what I feel for you that when I was finally ready to tell you how I feel, you were going away with Cole. I gotta tell you, that fucking sucked." I let out a sharp humorless laugh and shake my head.

"The idea of you with anyone but me, it drives me fucking crazy. It makes me fucking murderous. I-" I pause for a second, noticing how my hands have turned to fists as my teeth are practically bared while I speak. Blowing out a deep breath I shake my head before I look back up to her.

"So, I guess what I am trying to say is…give me a shot, give us a shot. Let me show you that I can be more than the detached asshole that I am with everyone else, that I can be the man my mom would be proud of, a man that *you* would be proud of."

I watch her carefully, but she doesn't react. She doesn't speak, she doesn't move. She is just…frozen. My stomach is twisting with nerves and my knee is bouncing wildly.

How can she have nothing to say after all of that?

"A shot?" She asks curiously.

I nod and swallow.

"To show you how good we can be. How well I can treat you. I want a shot at calling you mine."

A soft smile spreads across her face.

"I would like that," she says as a slight blush blooms over her cheeks.

I feel like a hundred pounds have been lifted from my shoulders and it's like I can finally breathe for the first time in what seems like weeks. I let out a huge breath and wrap her up into a hug, smiling into her hair before inhaling. *Fuck.* I have missed the smell of her. I pull back realizing she has some explaining to do, though.

"So, you said you and Cole are complicated."

She nods slowly as she turns to look back out over the water. I pull her face gently back towards me.

"Un-complicate it."

My tone brokers no argument, and she must be able to tell because she blows out a breath and runs a hand through her silky hair as she nods.

"Cole told me that he loved me-"

"Yeah, no shit," I huff, my tone bitter. "Anyone can see that, baby. Except maybe you."

She rolls her eyes at my attitude and continues.

"He wants us to be together. He is my best friend and really wonderful and-" I cut her off

"So why aren't you together?" I snap. I can't listen to her mooning over him for another second without flipping the fuck out.

"If you would let me finish a fucking sentence maybe you would know, asshole," she huffs throwing me an irritated glare. I sweep my hand out for her to continue.

"He isn't you."

My heart stalls for a second. Damn, I didn't see that coming. The troubled look in her eyes tells me that I shouldn't start celebrating just yet though.

"Did you tell him that?" I ask.

"He already knew apparently. I told him that we were better off as friends but I don't think he really accepted it. He said that he wasn't giving up on me. I have been avoiding him since then."

I twist my face in displeasure at that. At least I wasn't the only one that she was avoiding. Did something more than the whole feelings talk happen during that weekend away? More questions flood my mind, and I can't stop them from spilling out.

"Did you guys sleep together?"

"No," she says urgently.

Thank God.

"But," she starts. Oh fuck. "I don't want there to be any secrets between us. We did kiss and fool around a little bit. It stopped quickly and it will never happen again, obviously. He is great but he is just not the guy for me."

My anger flares at her words. Just imagining Cole kissing her, touching her, has me ready to drive to his place and beat the living shit out of him. Motherfucker putting hands on my woman. Fuck no.

Doing my best to calm my temper I blow out a rough breath. I fucked up too. Aubrey didn't do anything that I haven't in attempt to avoid my feelings for her. I have no right to be pissed. I still am, though.

Steering the conversation to safer topic, I look into her eyes as I speak.

"So, are we doing this?"

"I'm in," she says with a nod and a smile.

I don't wait one more second. I dive in, grabbing her face in my hands and pulling her lips to meet mine. The instant they touch, a small jolt of electricity hits my lips and I pause only for a moment at the reaction. I slowly move my mouth across hers, tasting every inch of her. I nip her lip and she parts slightly for me. I delve my tongue in and slowly tangle mine with hers.

Fucking *finally.*

My hands bury into her soft hair, and I tilt her head up slightly to grant me more access. As I am exploring every inch of her mouth, she wraps her arms around my shoulders and brings me into her until we are chest to chest, her hands dig into me like she is holding on for dear life.

Suddenly, she pulls her mouth away from mine before she moves away all together. I open my eyes to see her kneeling in front of me, her hooded eyes practically sparkling under the moonlight. Before I can say anything, her hands go to my belt as she quickly undoes it. Oh fuck.

Her smooth hand wraps around my rock-hard cock before she pulls me out of my boxers. She makes a noise in the back of her throat when she looks down at it and I can't help but smirk. Not to sound like a douche but that is usually the reaction I get. Aubrey looks up at me once more, slowly licking her lips before she lowers her head down and covers my tip with her mouth.

I groan into the night sky as I rest my hand on the back of her head. She bobs up and down, running her tongue over the sides before she sucks on the tip. Shit, yes. I can't help but push her head down a little farther to take me deeper. Most girls can't take me all the way which is fine because getting your dick sucked in any capacity feels fucking great.

I should have known that Aubrey would be the exception, though. She blows out a deep breath through her nose before she shoves my cock so far down her throat that I see stars. Holy fuck. I'm pretty sure the tip of my cock just touched her stomach. My hips involuntarily buck against her. I wait for her to gag and push me back, but she only takes me deeper. Fuck, this woman is perfect.

Aubrey starts doing this swirling motion with her tongue that has my eyes rolling in the back of my head. Weaving my fingers through her silky hair, I tighten my grip on her before I begin to fuck the shit out of her mouth. She takes everything I have to give, relaxing her throat as she reaches up and starts massaging my balls. Fuckkk. My pace quickens as she begins swallowing around my cock. The restriction of her tightening throat has me shooting my cum down the back of her throat.

She takes every drop, sucking me dry until I am fucking drained. Slowly moving off me, she releases my head with a pop before she gives me a look like the cat who got the cream.

Fitting.

I reach down and grab her head, crushing my lips against hers, loving the fact that I can taste myself against her tongue. Fuck. This woman will be the death of me, I swear to God. She is amazing and infuriating and beautiful and stubborn as fuck and finally *mine*.

CHAPTER TWENTY-FIVE

Aubrey

Monday morning, I am sitting in the cafeteria at a table off to the side still thinking about that night with Dax because damn. In the car and by the lake were both two of the hottest experiences of my life. I love getting off, who doesn't? But I also love giving pleasure. There is something so powerful about having a man weak and vulnerable. It is almost a rush to control when they will find their own pleasure, to put it off until you want it to happen. Maybe I am just a megalomaniac, though. Either way, it was hot as fucking hell.

We eventually went back to the car and Dax drove me back to campus, dropping me off at my door and leaving after a couple more scorching kisses. Things with Dax are so much more than I ever thought they could be. Where kisses with Cole were nice and sweet, with Dax it is like coming up for air for the first time.

I texted Cole this morning and asked him to meet me for lunch

This isn't something that could have been discussed over the phone, but I know we have to talk since last time we did he really did most of the talking. I am super fucking nervous to have this uncomfortable conversation again, but I don't think that he heard me last time and now that Dax and I are officially giving this thing a shot, I need to be transparent.

My feelings for Cole are real. I really care about him and next to Kayla, he is the best friend that I have ever had. But what I have with Dax is so much more than I know it could ever be with Cole. At the end of the day, I know without a doubt that Cole is not the man for me, and it isn't fair for him to sit around waiting for me with false hope.

"Hey, darlin'," Cole says smiling as he comes around to sit next to me.

He boldly tries to drop a kiss to my lips as he does, and I turn my head at the last second so that it lands on my cheek. Yep. He definitely didn't get the message last time. His smile slips but only for a second before he fixes it. Though unease now fills his eyes.

"I think that I didn't express my feelings with you properly last time we talked," I say.

I work my throat for more to come out but find that the words keep getting stuck. I don't want to lose my best friend.

"Okay?" He quickly prompts as if his nerves want whatever words I am about to say out there as soon as possible.

"We are friends, Cole, and that is all we will ever be. We aren't a good match, it's for the best."

He immediately shakes his head.

"No. You didn't even take any time to think about it. It's only been like a week! You haven't even given me a chance to prove to you how great we would be together."

"Cole…I-"

"No, Aubrey, look at me." He demands.

I keep my eyes fixed on the food in front of me that is suddenly completely unappealing.

"Aubrey," he snaps.

I glance up quickly at the sudden harshness of his tone. His eyes are darting back and forth, racing all over my face. The panicked look tells me that he is trying to figure out how to hold on to me. I don't know how to tell him that he never really had me, not like that.

"I really care about you, Cole. I do." I start. "You are my best friend but that is all that will ever be between us. I think in time you will see that. In time you will find someone who you feel so much for that your feelings for me will pale in comparison."

His eyes close at that for a moment as if letting the words wash over him. He doesn't accept it though, shaking his head more furiously this time.

"He isn't the best choice for you, you agreed. He is going to hurt you!"

I don't have to ask who Cole is talking about. Apparently he is still stuck on the idea that it is only Dax keeping me from being with him.

"You can't know that-" I begin but he cuts me off, grabbing my hands pleadingly.

"I can," he quickly says. "I also know that he will never be able to love you like I do, never be able to give you the life you deserve. Aubrey, when I took you home you stepped into my family like you always belonged there, right by my side. I was in love with you before we went home. But after that, I knew you were it for me."

His words break me, and I hope he knows how much it hurts me to do this. It's my own fucking fault. I let this go on for way too long and I have no one to blame but the bitch in the mirror. I squeeze his hand sympathetically.

"I'm sorry," I whisper, down casting my eyes once more.

After a few tense seconds, I peek up to see that his face has crumbled. He looks crest fallen and his eyes shimmer with unshed tears. All I want to do is wrap him up and take away his pain, but I know I can't. Resignation strikes across his face as he looks down at our intertwined hands.

"Choose me," he whispers so softly that I can barely hear him. After the words are out, he looks more confident as he meets my eyes and raises his voice slightly. "Choose *me,* Aubrey."

I swallow deeply and give him a subtle headshake. "You deserve to be more than someone's second choice. You deserve to be someone's everything, to be the air that they breathe and the heart that keeps them going," I say, trying to keep my voice soft to ease the blow of my words.

"I'd be your hundredth choice if it meant in the end that you were mine," he says as his voice starts to quake "You are all that for me, Aubrey. You are everything."

I slip my hands out of his grip and move one onto his shoulder, trying to provide more comfort but also trying to show that he can't change my mind on this.

"I'm sorry, Cole."

Like a flick of a switch, his eyes harden, and he shrugs my hand away. He digs his fingers into his disheveled brown hair and tugs for a moment before dropping his hands into his lap.

"You are making a huge mistake."

His voice comes out rough and condemning. All I can offer him is a small shrug and a deepening frown. He slams his hand on the table so hard that it makes me jump.

"Un-fucking-believable!" He shouts. "He is going to break your heart, remember that. *When* he does, remember that I never would have done that."

Cole pushes away from his seat as he rushes out of the cafeteria, slamming into the doors as he goes. Now that I am sitting here alone, I can feel the unshed tears burning and begging to be released. I close my eyes and fight them back. The knot in my stomach twists tighter as I realize the best friend that I ever had just walked out of my life, and I don't think I will ever get him back.

I make my way out of my last class of the day when I see Dax standing right outside, one leg crossed over the other and a cocky smirk on his face. His eyes light up when he spots me, and I smile back as I make my way over to him.

"Hey beautiful," he says before leaning down and giving me a soft peck.

He pulls back and smiles at me sweetly while tucking a piece of hair behind my ear.

"Hi," I breathe out.

It's then that I look around and notice the whole hallway has practically come to a standstill around us. I shoot a few of the onlookers scathing glares before I turn back to Dax.

"Looks like we will be the talk of the town by the end of the day."

Dax's eyes sparkle with mirth as he continues to stare at me, not giving the people around us the time of day.

"Well, let's give them a show then."

He grabs me by the waist and dips me back, enveloping me in a deep passionate kiss that is just as mind blowing as our first. When he brings me back upright, he tosses his arm around my shoulder and starts ushering me towards my dorm.

I smile up at him before looking in front of us to see that the same redhead that I've seen hanging all over Dax at The White Oak and the clay banks, I think I heard her name was Julie. Her eyes are aimed straight at me and if looks could kill I would already be burned at the stake. I am not going to waste my time on some petty chick though, so I break our eye contact before leaning up on my toes and kissing Dax on the cheek. I hear a huffed grumble come from behind us as we pass her, but I am too focused on the feeling of being wrapped up by Dax.

Once we get outside my building, he stops and grabs my hands.

"So, I was wondering if you had any plans Saturday night?"

"No, I don't think so. Why?"

"Well, I want to take my gorgeous girlfriend out on a date," he replies, warmth flooding my stomach as he gently caresses the back of my hands.

"Girlfriend?" I ask, raising my eyebrow in a challenging look. "You are pretty full of yourself to think that me giving you a shot translates to being your girlfriend," I tease.

He lets out a soft growl and grips my hips, hauling me into him. His head bends down until our noses brush against each other as his breath fans over my face.

"Make no mistake, Aubrey Davis. When you agreed to giving us a shot you agreed to the whole nine yards. We are doing this thing for real. I have never had a girlfriend before and I will probably fuck some shit up, but I am not going half ass on anything with you. So, be prepared for the full boyfriend package. I am talking dates, romantic gestures, cuddling; the whole shebang."

"Sleepovers?" I ask, only partly teasing. I could definitely get down with nothing but me Dax and a bed all night.

Dax groans as he pulls me against him even tighter.

"Fuck yes."

I stand on my tip toes to brush my lips across his.

"We will see how good this date is first," I wink.

He chuckles bringing one of his hands up to caress my cheek.

"I guess I better bring my A-game then."

I nod biting my lower lip. His eyes lock in on the movement and he descends pulling my lip from my teeth and sucking it into his own mouth, gently nipping and kissing it as he does. I press my body flush to him and can feel his growing cock, hard against my stomach. At least I know I am not the only one affected. I grind my hips into him, reveling in the friction.

Unfortunately, I hear someone come up next to us and clear their throat. Irritated, I break away to see Kayla standing there with her arms folded and an amused look on her face.

"Well, hey there kids. Please, don't stop on my account. This is better than porn."

I snort and shake my head.

"Dax, this is Mckayla."

She shoves an extended hand in between our bodies for Dax and he moves one of his hands to shake hers, still holding onto me tightly with the other one.

"Nice to meet you. I have seen you around a couple of times. Blake has talked about you too," Dax says.

Her cheeks pink at the mention of Blake as she tries to swallow a shy smile. That surprises the hell out of me. She is the last girl to get shy about a guy's attention. She is the girl that would usually bask in the attention, so this reaction has piqued my interest. I'll definitely be asking about that later. Look at me, wanting to gossip about boys and shit. I'm almost like a normal 19-year-old girl. Almost.

Dax turns back to me.

"I gotta head out. I have to get to the gym. I will call you later," he says wrapping me up in one more dizzying kiss.

"Alright," I say as we break apart.

He shoots me a wink and gives a head nod to Kayla before he saunters off towards the parking lot. I turn back to Kayla and see that the teasing look has left her face and I am met with a sad smile. I cock my head in question.

"Can we talk?" She asks.

"Sure," I say, the confusion evident in my tone.

We make our way up to my room and I settle onto my bed while she stands at the end, staring at me for a minute like she is choosing her words carefully.

"Why didn't you tell me that something was going on with you and Cole? Or you and Dax? We are supposed to be best friends. I have tried over and over to get you to open up, but you always shut down. So, I tried giving you your space hoping that you would offer up the information willingly and you never do." Her face is curious like she is confused, but the hurt is clear in her eyes and a stab of guilt runs through me.

"There wasn't anything going on with Cole and me, not really at least."

"That's not what he says," she snaps back. "I ran in to him during lunch. He was storming out of the cafeteria and looked really upset. I took him aside and asked him if everything was okay. Obviously, it wasn't. He said you two were practically together and then you showed up this morning telling him that you chose Dax over him. Mind you, the same Dax that publicly shamed you in front of everyone, the same one with an out-of-control temper and a player reputation."

The guilt that I briefly felt slips away at Kayla's brash and demanding tone. I jump up from my bed to stand in front of her.

"Hey, that's bullshit. Cole and I were never together. He wanted to be, and I told him that I couldn't. Then he told me to take time and sort out my feelings. I did, and because they don't align with his that makes me the bad guy? And who the fuck are you to judge Dax. You don't even know him!"

She scoffs and rolls her eyes.

"Please, I know enough."

"Aren't you the one who thought I was crazy for not wanting to hook up with him?" I throw back.

"Yeah, Aubrey, to hook up not date. I thought you were smarter than falling for the same crap that he has used on hundreds of girls before you."

"That isn't who he is, not with me. He is different. I am not just some girl to him, we care about each other," I say, the anger fading from my voice and vulnerability taking over.

"Well how the hell am I supposed to know any of that when you won't fucking talk to me!" She shouts.

It's the first time that I have ever heard Kayla swear and it stuns me into silence. She shakes her head like I am a lost cause and grabs her purse from my desk.

"Whatever it doesn't matter what I say, you have clearly made up your mind. Don't come crying to me *when* he breaks your heart. Yeah, not if, *when*."

With that, she walks out of my room and slams the door shut. I flop backwards onto my bed and stare at the crack in my ceiling intently. I don't understand why Kayla is so insistent that I shouldn't date Dax. She is always all over my case to hook up with guys, but suddenly it's a bad thing that I actually like a guy? My anger at her resurfaces, rearing its ugly head.

Just because I don't want to sleep around like her doesn't mean I am doing anything wrong.

Even as I try to hold on to my anger, I can't fight off the uneasiness creeping in. The two closest people to me found out about my relationship with Dax and reacted horribly. Granted they both had their personal reasons for their reactions. But they both voiced similar concerns. That Dax *will* break my heart. And as much as I try to tell myself that they are wrong, a tiny voice in my head agrees, and keeps whispering, "*Run.*"

CHAPTER TWENTY-SIX

Dax

I have been training every chance that I can get this week, gearing up for another fight next Friday night. The money is great at fight night and all but it's more than that for me. Every fight I get tougher, quicker, smarter. Up until a few months ago, my dreams of rejoining the UFC were nothing but a distant memory.

After spending so much time with Aubrey lately, things have started to change. The last few fights that I have had I had good control over myself. I didn't let the darkness drag me under and I didn't send anyone to the hospital. Progress.

I don't know if Aubrey is a direct result of my change or if it is just a coincidence, but one thing is for sure, everything has changed since she came into my life. I have opened up to her about my former dreams and she asked me if it was something that I would still want to go after. Am I pussy if I am too afraid to admit it? That I want it more than anything in the fucking world? Well, almost anything.

It's probably a lost cause to hope for anyways. I would need a gym to sponsor me at least and after the shit that went down years ago I am not sure that Cameron would want to stick his neck on the line for me again. My suspension technically ended two weeks ago, and I guess I won't know for sure unless I talk to him.

Fuck it. I'll sit down with Cameron next time I am in the gym and talk it out. If he understandably doesn't want to back me then maybe I can start looking for other sponsors. Someone has to be willing to give me another shot, right?

I have been in the gym so much this week that I have barely gotten to see Aubrey. I may sound like a pussy, but I have fucking missed her ass. It's Saturday night and I am on my way to pick her up for our first date. My leg is bouncing as I pull up outside of her building. I planned a romantic as fuck surprise for her tonight. I hope she likes it.

It doesn't take me long to get into her building and knock on her door. When she opens it, I struggle not to swallow my tongue. *Holy fuck. I think she is trying to kill me.* She is wearing a body-hugging blue lace dress that dips low on her chest and hits about mid-thigh. I look down to see that she is also wearing a pair of heels that make her legs look like they go on for miles.

As I ascend my journey, I settle on her cleavage and start to feel myself getting hard. The thin straps of her dress show off her creamy complexion and suddenly all I can imagine is tearing it off her. Her hair is done in some up do thing that displays her neck, begging for me to bury my face into it.

"Like what you see Mr. Hart?" Her voice husky as she speaks.

I swallow and nod furiously. I told her to get all dolled up, but I wasn't expecting her to be this…stunning. I know I look pretty good in my black slacks and white button up, it's one of my only outfits that doesn't consist of jeans or workout shorts, but she is fucking showstopping.

The only other time that I have seen her dress up was that night in the club and it took me a bit to realize that it really was her. The Aubrey I know is more comfortable in sweats or jeans than a tight dress and heels and I really dig that about her, but tonight I am really liking this other side of her. My woman is fucking drop dead gorgeous. *My woman.* Fuck, I love the sound of that.

"You are…Fuck. I'm speechless," I say shaking my head in awe.

"Thank you. You clean up pretty well for a rough and tough fighter," she jokes.

I toss her a wink before wrapping my arm around her waist as I haul her into me. My mouth claims hers before she even has a second to resist. I am probably going to have lipstick all over my face by the time I am done with her, but I don't give a fuck. I would cut off my own fucking arm if that meant that I never had to stop kissing her.

After a short yet familiar drive, I park the car as Aubrey looks over to me.

"We are having a date at the gym?" She asks with a cocked eyebrow.

I can't help but smirk at her. You can appreciate at least one thing about Aubrey, she doesn't sugar coat shit. If she doesn't like something or isn't impressed, you bet your ass you will know it immediately. I walk around the side of my car and open her door for her before offering my hand. She takes it and watches me closely as we make our way inside.

When I unlock the door, she gasps softly, and I smile as I walk around to face her. I asked Cameron if it was cool to bring Aubrey here for our date after hours. He gave me a ton of shit for taking so long to lock her down, but he finally relented.

Aubrey seems to be most comfortable in this place. Not sure if it is the gym itself or just the comfortability of it that reminds her of another time and another place. Either way I thought that this would be a good place to have our date at.

Blake however, thought that Bree wouldn't be super into hanging out in a smelly gym after hours and sparring all night, so he suggested something a little more romantic. I am glad that I listened to him because her initial reaction tells me that he was right. He helped me string up those fairy light things around the place since I thought Cameron would chop my balls off if I lit candles anywhere and burned the mats. Then I ordered an expensive ass dinner, because expensive translates to romantic in girl talk, right? I have it all set up at a little table to the side with a bottle of champagne and a single red rose in a vase.

John Hughes doesn't have shit on me.

"Dax," she breathes softly. "This is kinda perfect."

"Just kinda?" I tease.

"Well, I can still smell Goldstein's god-awful aftershave so," she shrugs, and I bark out a rough laugh.

"I know. Fuck, I aired this place out for almost an hour but once that guy uses that stuff it basically gasses out the whole building."

She chuckles as I walk her over to the table. I went for Italian food because I figured who doesn't like pasta, and with the way my girl eats I figured she would appreciate it. I think I guessed right because by the time I glance up from my plate to look at her she has already inhaled half of her plate. I can't help but smirk. Most girls would probably be uncomfortable eating on a first date, but of course that isn't Aubrey. I swear she could out eat two other women and still be hotter than both of them.

We talk for a while and bullshit about everything and anything. She is so easy to talk to it is kinda crazy. I have never felt such an intense connection with someone before. Never felt like I could show them the dark jagged parts of myself and have them care for me all the same. I thought that chance died with my mother, but the way Aubrey makes me feel…fuck she makes me feel too much.

I walk up behind her and wrap my arms around her waist, tugging her in close to me. She turns around and smiles up at me before she leans on the tips of her toes and brings her lips up to meet mine. I grab the back of her head to take control of the kiss, gently dragging my lips across hers before slipping my tongue into her sweet mouth and slowly stroking and savoring every bit of her.

After a few moments she breaks away and I groan with displeasure.

"I think it's time to head to your place," she whispers into my ear.

I perk up at that and look back at her, searching for any doubt but all I see is desire. I slowly ease her down me, enveloping her delicate hand in my large calloused one before we turn and walk to the car. The car ride back to my place is silent and the air is charged with anticipation.

We keep exchanging side long glances but nothing more than that. It's like we both know that if either of us makes a move we won't be making it home and she deserves better than a quickie in the back of my car. Then again…No, Fuck. Keep driving, dickhead.

When we get to my place, I open the garage door and pull her up the stairs that leads to my loft before I stand to the side and let her step in first. I follow behind her and as soon as I shut the door, I slam her against the wall and pin her in with my arms before descending on her mouth. I move my hands to her hips and grip tightly, hardly able to control myself. Her arms go around my neck, pulling me deeper into her. My hands drift to just below the curve of her ass before I lift her up. She immediately wraps her legs around me as I begin walking us down the hallway, never breaking the kiss.

As soon as we step through the door to the bedroom, I kick it shut. Then I drop her onto my king size bed and take a few steps back to admire the sight of her *finally* being where I have fantasized for so many nights. Slowly, I stalk towards her like a hunter to its prey. Her dress has lifted high on her thighs and my gaze flicks down to the newly exposed skin. I need more.

I climb on top of her, my fingers grazing where the hem of her dress lies. I caress her silky skin, momentarily getting lost in the feeling of her before I pull her dress up and over her head, tossing it to the side before reaching down and unclasping her bra as I throw that to the side as well.

Sitting back on my heels, I pause for another second to admire the view, my cock twitching in anticipation as I take my fill. Her smooth breasts are sitting on full display, showing off her soft pink nipples that are making my mouth water. I lean over and pull one into my mouth, swirling my tongue against it as she lets out a breathy moan. I graze my teeth gently causing her to yelp.

"Oh, fuck. Dax," she moans.

I bite back a groan of my own because that sexy little moan has me ready to cum in my fucking pants like a little bitch. She is so fucking hot. Moving my mouth across her breasts I begin my descent, leaving a trail of kisses down her body until I am met with a pair of black lace panties. I run a finger over the noticeably wet fabric.

"Mmm," I growl. "You are drenched for me, baby."

She lets out a little whimper and nods her head almost frantically. Smirking to myself, I grab the delicate fabric and shred it off her body, discarding the scraps to the side with ease. She gasps in surprise and makes eye contact with me, her eyes blazing with need. I hold her gaze as I run a finger through her soaked pussy.

Her breathing is now ragged as she mewls, "Please."

I quickly sink a finger into her and the moan that comes from her fills the entire room. Her walls clamp down around my finger hard before I begin to pump in and out of her while her hips start grinding against the palm of my hand, practically begging me for more. I push another finger inside her before lowering my face down to meet her perfectly bare pussy.

Slowly, I run the flat of my tongue through her lips, making sure to put extra pressure against her clit. She gasps as her fingers dig into my hair, practically drowning me in her arousal. You won't hear me fucking complaining, though. Aubrey tastes like raw undiluted sin. I curl my fingers inside of her, rubbing that sweet spot as I lick every inch of her, making sure not to waste a single drop of her taste.

Her legs start to tremble as I continue my assault on her pussy as she cries out.

"Dax, Oh…Oh my god…I'm gonna…"

Her walls begin throbbing around my fingers as I lick and suck every ounce of her release. When her body goes still and she blows out a deep breath, I flick my eyes up to meet her gaze as I pull my fingers out and flatten my tongue one more time before licking her from top to bottom. Her eyes darken as she watches me slowly ease up before grabbing my belt and dropping my pants and boxers in one move.

Aubrey's eyes are steadily on my rock-hard cock as I move to my bedside table and roll on a condom before climbing on top of her again. I press my lips against hers as my cock nudges against her wet pussy.

"You ready for me, baby?" I whisper against her lips.

"Fuck, yes," she breathes out.

I know that I should ease into her. She is so fucking tight, and I am far from average, but I can't wait another fucking moment. I push myself into her faster than I probably should have and bite out a sharp curse at the feeling of her pussy practically strangling my cock.

"Fuck, baby. Your pussy is so tight. Shit," I hiss as I begin to slowly thrust in and out of her, savoring the feel of her silky walls gripping me perfectly. Fuck. I could die right like this, and I'd be fucking happy. I never want to be anywhere but buried inside her again.

"Dax," she moans before looking me dead in the eyes. "Fuck me."

I lose all control from the look in her eyes. I begin to frantically thrust into her like I will die if I ever stop. Right now, it feels like it. Bree moans her approval and meets me for each thrust. I slip my hand down to her swollen clit before I start rubbing quick circles while continuing to snap my hips against hers.

"Yes, baby. Fuck. Tell me who this pussy belongs to," I growl out as her pussy clamps down on me again.

"Me," she snarks, despite her eyes rolling into the back of her head.

I raise my hand and spank the side of her ass hard. She yelps at that and clenches on me at the impact. Oh fuck. My dirty girl likes to get spanked.

Moving my hand away from her clit I hold on to the headboard while keeping my other hand on her ass as I continue driving into her tight pussy. She whimpers at the loss of contact but maybe she won't be such a fucking smart mouth next time.

"I'm not going to ask again, Bree. Tell me who this pussy belongs to, or I will punish you."

"Promise?" She groans as she looks up at me through her thick eyelashes.

My hand cracks against her ass harder than the last time. She shouts out in pain but then her pussy practically soaks my cock, proving how much she is enjoying herself.

"Ah, fuck. Dax."

I rear my hand back again and slap her already heated skin. Her back arches into me as her mouth opens on a gasp.

"You," she breathes out. "I'm yours. Fuck, I'm yours. Just don't stop!" She practically begs.

All it takes is one more slap and her pussy convulses on my

cock, drenching me as she shouts her orgasm. Shit. She feels too tight, too good. Too fucking perfect. I reach down and pinch her clit which makes her scream out even louder and makes me lost it instantly as I empty myself inside of her.

When I begin to slow my movements, I look down to see that Bree has a dazed and satisfied looking smile on her face. I slowly pull out of her and roll on to my back, hauling her into my side as I do. She wraps her arms around my torso and smiles against my chest. My heart is still beating so fucking hard that I think it's ready to burst out of my damn chest. Can you die from mind blowing sex? Because if so I think I am on my way out of this world.

As I catch my breath my mind races with the fresh memory of finally having her fully after imagining it so many fucking times. I have had a lot of sex in my life, a lot of good sex. But fuck, one time with Bree and I know that nothing and no one will ever compare. I know in this moment that I will never want anyone else.

Her breathing softly evens out as she drifts off, still firmly wrapped up in my arms. When I know that she is fully asleep, I bend down and kiss the top of her head before whispering against it.

"I'm fucking ruined."

CHAPTER TWENTY-SEVEN

Dax

Not even a few hours pass by before muffled whimpers wake me up. My eyes blink open, flicking around the room wildly looking for the owner. When my eyes catch on a sleeping Aubrey my brows furrow as I watch her clench her shut eyes tight like she is in pain.

"No, stop. Please," she mumbles against my chest.

"Baby," I whisper as I rub her back. "Wake up. It's just a dream."

The instant that my hand rubs against her back, her body tenses before she begins to thrash.

"No! Get off me! Help! Someone help!" She wails, her eyes still firmly closed.

My stomach bottoms out at her words and the pure terror in her words. I shake her more aggressively to try to get her out of whatever hell she is currently trapped in, but it doesn't work. The more I try to coax her awake the harder she fights, the more she cries. It tears my fucking heart out.

When I watched over her while she had her concussion she made a little noise here and there in her sleep. Not much, just some murmured words and light whimpers. I thought she was just having a bad dream. It sure as fuck wasn't like this. One of my hands is cupping the back of her head gently, making sure she doesn't hit it on the headboard.

What demons are you fighting, baby?

Knowing that shaking and shouting won't get her out of this, I choose to wrap her up in a safe but tight embrace. She fights against me, but it isn't too hard for me to hold her against me. I drop my mouth to her ear as I whisper softly the same words that she once told me.

"You are safe, Bree. You aren't there anymore. You are safe. Come back to me, baby. Come back to me."

I repeat this over and over again and finally, her struggles begin to lessen, and her cries stop altogether. Her face is still twisted up in what looks like pain and fear. I press a featherlight kiss against her temple as I continue to hold her tight. I don't know what she is battling or what kind of horrors she has faced. All I know is that the monsters from her past don't stand a chance. She has a new monster in her corner now. One that will beat, gut and kill any motherfucker who dares look at her.

I wake up to a screeching noise piercing my ears. I must have forgotten to turn off my alarm. Groaning, I roll over to try to grab my phone and turn it off, but suddenly I smell smoke. I spring out of bed and rush out to the living room where I find Aubrey standing in the kitchen, wearing one of my t-shirts and cursing like a fucking sailor over a pan that looks to be on fire.

Biting back a smile I jump into action. I rush up to her, grabbing a towel and wrapping it around the handle of the pan and moving it to a different burner as I push Aubrey back a few feet. She huffs throwing her hands in the air and stepping back as I grab the fire extinguisher that I keep in the kitchen before I put the fire out quickly.

Once the smoke has cleared, I wrinkle my nose and look down at the charred black culprit of the kitchen fire.

"Sweetheart, what the fuck *is* this?"

"It *was* pancakes. I poured them and then I had to pee. I was gone for literally 30 seconds and then they fucking caught fire like I was cooking with gasoline!" Her tone is near a shout and most people would probably assume that she is angry, but I see the disappointment in her eyes.

I step away from the stove and scoop her into my arms, stroking her back slowly as I place a kiss on the top of her head. She lets out a loud sigh while I hold her before her arms wrap around me. After a few moments, I pull back to look at her and watch as she quickly swipes away a lone tear.

"I should have known. I've never been a good cook. I'm self-taught with not much practice. I'm not proud to admit that this isn't my first breakfast related fire. I just...I wanted to surprise you, I guess."

She looks to the ground, shrugging it off like it's no big deal and it doesn't bother her, but I can tell that it does. I can't help but smile at her, though. She looks up at me, an irritated look resting on her face.

"What?" She snaps.

"You really like me," I state grinning ear to ear.

She rolls her eyes heavily and shakes her head as she shoves me away from her.

"Of course, I do, dipshit."

My smile stays in place as I grab her face in my hands and crush my lips against hers. I pull back, still cupping her face in my hands. Memories of last night come to the front of my mind. At first, they are sexy and pleasure filled, but they soon turn to what came after. The way Aubrey looked as she desperately fought whatever nightmare she was in. The pain she seemed to be in.

Her broken cries that made her voice sound more defeated than I had ever heard before. I am dying to know what she dreamed about last night, to know what evil plagues her thoughts. But I know her almost as well as I know myself by now, so I know that she won't answer. In fact, if I give away that I witnessed an extremely vulnerable moment like that, she might pull away from me. There is no way in fuck I will let that happen, so I decide to push it to the side for now and enjoy the day with my girl.

"Get dressed. I'm taking you out for breakfast before you attempt scrambled eggs and burn the whole fucking place down."

I turn on my heel and run down the hallway, snickering as a wet dish rag comes soaring at me.

"Asshole!" She shouts, though I hear a hint of amusement in her tone.

Aubrey

After breakfast, Dax and I spent the rest of the day in bed. Holy fuck. Sex with him is out of this fucking world. I am not a virgin by any means, and I have had really great sex before. Well, at least I thought it was great sex. Now looking back none of those times hardly hold a candle to Dax.

The weird part is that after the sex, the warm glowy feeling that you usually get during sex didn't go away. I have never felt anything like it before. Despite my efforts to keep myself at least a little guarded and ease into things with Dax, I find myself falling for him more and more every time that we are together. I have started to wonder when I will just admit that the falling has already ended, and I am already there.

Not today, apparently.

Dax handed me the keys to Betty and said she was good to go so I was able to drive her back to campus Sunday afternoon so that

I could get caught up on homework. On Monday, my day goes by very uneventfully and very lonely. I head back to my dorm to get dressed for work as I get lost in my thoughts. Once I got back to my room and my Dax bubble burst, the memories of the last week came flooding back. Two of my best friends, hell my only friends, are no longer talking to me. It fucking sucks.

I know that there is probably no repairing things with Cole, at least anytime soon if ever. He needs space and I have to respect that. But I miss Kayla, I get that she was hurt that I didn't open up to her. That just isn't who I am, though. I wish she would understand that I never tried to hurt her. It's just that the idea of cracking myself open for others to see the scarred and bloody mess physically makes me ill.

Maybe I should drop by her dorm before I have to head into work? A knock comes from my door, shaking me out of my thoughts. Crossing the room, I turn the handle and open the door to reveal the very girl I was just thinking about in the flesh.

"Hey," Kayla says meekly with a halfhearted wave.

I stare at her for a few heavy seconds before I decide to just say fuck it. I throw my arms around her and hug her tight. I used to despise physical contact outside of the gym or the bedroom but with people like Kayla, Cole and Dax, I don't mind it as much. It's only been a week of not talking but I have missed this bitch. She wraps her arms around me as she lets out long sigh. Kayla pulls back and holds on to my arms tightly.

"I am so sorry for everything I said. I was such a bitch."

I shake my head.

"No, I am sorry. I didn't mean to hurt your feelings. I am just not used to sharing that kind of personal stuff. It was nothing against you," I say as I pull her into my room and shut the door.

"You shouldn't feel obligated to tell me things you aren't comfortable with just because we are friends. If you want to tell me things then you can on your own time. No pressure," she promises.

I blow out a sigh of relief because as much as I would love to promise to be more open, I don't know if I can actually commit to that right now.

"Thank you. I am sorry that I hurt you."

Kayla looks down for a moment, wringing her hands almost nervously.

"Well, if we are being honest, that isn't the sole reason that I lashed out that day."

"Oh?" I question.

"I was jealous," she says softly.

"Jealous? Of what?"

She huffs as she tosses her hands out wildly.

"Of you, duh. You don't even try, and you have two of the hottest guys on campus at your feet. Anyone with two eyes can see how in love Cole is with you, always has been. And Dax…he is the love 'em and leave 'em kind. Girls are just a way to pass the time for him. But when I saw how jealous he got over you at the party, I knew something was up.

"I go out with guys all the time. I put myself out there and all I ever am is a one-night stand or a steady booty call. I want someone to look at me the way just one of them looks at you and here you are with your pick! And then you never even told me about it. I was a raging jealous bitch, and I am so sorry."

I can't help but want to laugh. Jealous of me? No one in their right mind would be jealous of me. I am a bruised and broken shell of a person that can hardly feel normal feelings without being ready to break out in hives. Yeah, the thought of a rich beautiful girl like Mckayla Blackburn being jealous of trailer park trash Aubrey Davis is straight up laughable.

"Kayla," I start. "You have so much going for you. I think you need to take another look in the mirror. You are stunning and confident with a heart of fucking gold. Not to mention your bank account is pretty huge," I tease with a wink. She rolls her eyes with a small smile but doesn't speak.

"Any guy would be lucky to even talk to you. So, if these fuck boys aren't willing to put in the effort for a girl like you then fucking forget them. They aren't worth it. Hold out for the guys that are worth it."

She gives me a sad smile and a shrug.

"Yeah well, I guess I haven't met any of those yet."

"What's up with Dax's friend, Blake?"

I remember how odd she acted when Dax brought him up. I know Blake really well too. He is a great guy. I don't really see him with girls. They hang around him, but he doesn't pay them too much attention.

Her eyes brighten just a bit, and a pink tinge stains her face before she looks away and shrugs again.

"He is in my biology class. We are always partners for group projects. He is really nice and hot obviously, but that's it."

"That's not it. Didn't you hear Dax? Blake has talked about *you*, to his guy friends. You and I both know that guys don't talk about how cool girls are with their friends unless they are into them."

She doesn't look very convinced and that is too bad because now that I think about they would probably be great together if the vibes are there. Blake would probably worship the ground that Kayla walks on and she would love every moment of it.

Clearly Kayla wants to be done with this conversation though because she looks uncomfortable as hell. So, I decide to switch topics and try to be a little more open with her.

"Dax and I had sex," I blurt.

Okay. I guess a lot more open. Hey, as long as I am not talking about my past or the feelings that I can't quite name for Dax then I am good.

Her eyes widen with shock, then they turn to excitement. "What?!" She screeches. "When? Where? How was it? He's huge isn't he? Oh, he has to be he is Dax Hart-Breaker for a reason. Girls wouldn't willingly sign up for that shit if he wasn't!"

I smirk about to answer some of her questions when I pause.

"Wait. Is that like a nick name or something?"

Her excitement fades and she seems to realize that I have never heard this before. She schools her features to a casual look.

"Oh yeah. Uh, I think it's just something some of the girls he has been with call him. Since he never does serious…until now, of course," she adds on.

I nod my head as I turn away. I knew that he had been with a lot of women, hell I have had my fair share of fun before I came to Whitman. But to hear that your boyfriend's proclivities were so well known that he has a group of women out there calling him a heart breaker is something else. It plays into my fear that my heart might not be very safe in his hands that much more. It is a stark reminder to make sure to keep my growing feelings self-contained.

The next day that I don't have work, I decide to swing by Dax's house after class. I find him beating up the heavy bag in the garage, like usual. He is only wearing work out shorts and fuck if it isn't a drool worthy sight. His muscles ripple as he reigns down blow after blow against the defenseless bag. His breathing is labored as sheen of sweat covers his rock-hard chest. I watch as one bead of sweat slowly rolls down his shredded abs before it disappears down the front of his shorts. Never thought that I would be jealous of sweat.

Dax chooses that moment to realize that I am here, while my eyes are still firmly trained on where that bead disappeared to as I bite my lip.

"Hey baby," he says, sauntering up to me with a knowing smile.

I look up to him with a mirth filled smirk as he approaches me.

"Hey."

When he gets to me, he picks me up from the back of my knees as I wrap my legs around his waist, kissing his full lips. His lips move against mine before he presses his forehead against mine.

"I missed you," he whispers.

I throw my head back and let out a laugh.

"Babe, it's been like two days."

He groans. "Don't remind me, that is two days too long. Stay tonight?" He practically demands.

I nod and he smirks before kissing me senseless once more. He carries me over to *my* couch before laying me down as he hovers over me. He starts kissing my neck, gently sucking and nipping. I close my eyes and hum my approval as his hand snakes down to my legs, slipping underneath the fabric of my leggings when his phone rings.

He ignores it as his hand keeps moving over my soaked panties. Just as he goes to peel the fabric away from my legs, his phone starts up again. I glance at it and back to him, raising an eyebrow in question.

"Ignore it," he grumbles

I reach out to slide his shorts down when the phone rings a third time. He drops his shoulders in exasperation and sighs. He rolls off of me and walks over grabbing his phone.

"What!" He barks into the phone. "I'm fucking busy," he snaps at whatever poor sucker decided to call him. Then his expression morphs from pissed to shocked. "Are you serious?" A slight pause then he roars. "Fuck yeah! When?" Another pause. "Hell yeah I'm in, let's do it! Thank you!"

He hangs up the phone and beams one of his rare dimple exposing smiles.

"What?" I ask.

"That was Cameron," he grins. "I went and talked to him last week. Now that my suspension is over I asked if he would be willing to sponsor me. I had given up on my dream to rejoin the UFC but lately I have felt this push to get back at it. I figured that if he said no, I could try training at other gyms and see if I could find someone who would work with me. But Cameron agreed to sponsor and train me. He has a fight lined up for me this Saturday."

I am speechless for a moment. I jump to my feet and tackle him in a hug. Holy shit! He has a regulation fight coming up! Holy fucking shit!

"That is fucking amazing! Congrats!"

"Thank you. Will you come?"

I roll my eyes and punch his arm.

"Are you fucking kidding me? Like I would miss it! Can I bring Kayla? We were supposed to hangout this weekend."

"Sure. I will have Blake and Chase keep an eye on you guys. Gotta keep my girl safe."

I shoot him an irritated look as I hold a warning finger up to his face.

"We both know that your *girl* can handle her own."

He chuckles and nods his head as I smile. His smile starts to slip and a sense of vulnerability seeps in.

"Do you think that I can do it? That I can keep it together?" He asks.

I don't hesitate, I nod my head as I hold his face in between my hands so that he has to look at me.

"I do. You can do it, you just can't let your demons hold you down, Dax. You can't let the darkness drag you under. You have to fight to stay above it. If you believe you can do that then of course you have what it takes. The only thing that can get in the way of your dreams is you."

He looks at me for a moment as if he doesn't totally believe me before he nods and drops his forehead against mine.

"I can do it if you are there for me. With you in my corner, I don't know what I couldn't do."

I smile softly before I lean up on my toes and close the distance between us. He cups my face lovingly as his lips move gently against mine. The kiss is sweet and full of passion and unspoken promises. But as soon as his tongue strokes against mine it turns darker and way more delicious.

Letting out a soft moan as I deepen the kiss, I grind my pussy against his thigh as I tilt my head up. Dax makes a deep thundering noise from his chest before he snakes his hands down my back and over my ass as he lifts me into the air. I wrap my legs around him instantly as he begins walking while our tongues battle for dominance.

I assume that he is about to either carry me upstairs to his bed or maybe drop me down on the couch. I don't expect him to lower me to my feet just to the side of the couch before he takes a step back. Disappointment fills me for a moment, but it is short lived when Dax spins me around and shoves me over the arm of the couch.

Before I can say anything, Dax peels the top of my leggings down until they are bunched up around my sneakers. I have never been so thankful for no buttons in my life. Dax runs one of his large hands up and down my spine before it palms my ass.

Leaning down over me, his breath tickles my ear as his low voice growls against my skin.

"Do you have any idea how many times I have pictured bending your ass over this couch?"

I hum under my breath and am about to give him a smartass reply when his hand comes down and spanks me. Ah, fuck. Why does that feel so fucking good? Maybe all the years of getting beat up in the cage has conditioned me into liking getting roughed up in bed. This is honestly the first time that anyone has ever tried anything like it before, but I am fucking here for it.

"You like that don't you, baby girl? It is supposed to be a punishment, but your greedy little cunt practically weeps for me when I spank your ass. Do you think your pussy would like to be spanked too?"

I groan at his words which causes him to let out a deep chuckle.

"Yeah. I think my pussy would love that, because don't forget, it is *my* pussy. You said so yourself," he says as he pushes two fingers inside my already soaked pussy.

"Asshole," I grouse as I bite back a moan. I don't want the cocky fucker to know just how much I am enjoying his thick fingers as he works me over fucking perfectly.

"Asshole, huh? You giving me hints, baby?" He asks as he withdraws his wet fingers and slides them through my ass cheeks.

One of his fingers circles my asshole gently, never applying enough pressure to go in but making sure that I am a fucking panting mess. I wouldn't be surprised if I have stained his couch by now.

"Dax," I groan. "I need-"

"I know what you need. Tell me, baby, has anyone ever taken you here?" He asks as he applies a little more pressure.

"Yes," I moan as I bite my bottom lip.

His finger withdraws quickly, and I whimper at the loss of contact before his hand cracks across my ass cheek. I buck against the hit, feeling both pain and pleasure rush through me simultaneously. Turning my head, I look over my shoulder to see Dax's face thunderous.

"Never again, you hear me? The only person to ever touch you again will be me. The only man that will ever be inside this pussy is me, the only man that will ever be in this ass is me. You are mine, Aubrey Davis, and I am about to prove that."

Without any other warning, Dax thrusts a finger inside my ass. I gasp at the sudden intrusion before my gasp quickly turns to a moan. Dax slowly thrusts in and out of me a few times before he adds another finger and then another. Fuck.

"Shit, baby, I can barely feel my fingers. You think this ass is ready for my cock?"

I bite my lip and nod frantically. Frankly, if he doesn't get his cock in one of my holes I am going to fucking combust. Dax chuckles lowly as he continues thrusting his fingers in me.

"Such an eager thing. Alright, baby. I will give you what you need. But I'm not wearing a condom. I want to empty myself in you and make sure that you can feel me for the rest of the day. You good with that?"

"Fuck! Yes," I shout. "Just fuck me!"

"Good girl," he says before withdrawing his fingers.

Dax steps away completely for a few seconds before he comes back. Cold liquid hits my ass, causing me to tense up. He runs a warm hand on my back in a soothing gesture as his other hand spreads the liquid.

"Easy, baby girl. Just want to make sure you are ready for me."

"I don't know if I am relieved or irritated that you had a bottle of lube at the ready in the garage. How many bitches have you fucked in here?"

His hand snakes around to the front of my throat, pulling me up so that I am forced to look at him. The move should terrify me, any manhandling should really, but with Dax I have never felt safer. Instead of filling me with fear all it does is set flame to the burning embers inside me.

"None. Only you baby. Just you."

His words give me a stupid amount of pleasure but I don't get too much time to relish in it before I feel Dax's thick cock press against my ass. I've had more than my fair share of ass play in the past but never with a man Dax's size and not in a while. Even with the lube it is going to be fucking tight.

Dax inches in agonizingly slow. The pain flares for a few

moments before it fades and need outweighs it. I wiggle my hips to encourage him to go deeper and when he is finally seated in me we both groan in pleasure. His cock pulses inside of me several times as he suddenly stills.

"Shit, baby. I don't know how long you expect me to last with your ass squeezing the life out of me like this."

"Just make me come," I demand as I wiggle my hips again, the previous discomfort completely forgotten and all that remains is pleasure and the feeling of being so fucking full.

Dax begins slowly moving his hips as I push back against him. Normally I like to fuck for a while, but I can already feel my orgasm building. It's been building ever since he bent me over. The hand that isn't resting on my throat creeps around my stomach and down to my clit. I could fucking sob with relief when his fingers start perfectly rubbing me. I moan my approval which only spurs him on more, his thrusts becoming deeper and more frantic.

My pussy begins convulsing, my orgasm so close I can practically taste it.

"More," I beg. "Just a little bit more."

At my plea, Dax's fingers stop moving and pull away from my pussy before coming back down over my clit with a sharp slap. Instantly, I see black. The scream that is ripped from my throat sounds foreign as my body shakes and shutters around his cock. Dax lets out a feral growl behind me as I feel his hot cum coat the inside of me. Both of our orgasms seem to last forever, and I feel ready to die of complete and utter bliss. What a fucking way to go.

CHAPTER TWENTY-NINE

Aubrey

The week goes by in a blur. Dax has been training his ass off for his fight coming up tomorrow, so my time has been split between working, hanging out with Kayla and school. Cole is still massively avoiding me. He even traded off all of the shifts that we had together at work, so I think it's safe to say that our friendship has been officially burnt to a crisp.

Pushing aside the disappointment that fills me about my and Cole's friendship, I shoot off a text to Dax.

Me: What are you up to?

Dax: Training. What's up?

Me: Do you have time for dinner?

Dax: Always have time for you baby. I'll pick you up in 20.

I get ready in record time. I honestly was expecting him to blow me off so once I am ready I rush out the door to wait for him in the parking lot. Can you tell that I am excited to see him? Ugh, I've become one of those needy bitches.

When Dax pulls up, he gets out of the car and starts walking towards me. The second I see him my stomach flips and I can't fight the smile that spreads across my face. I run towards him and jump into his arms. He catches me easily as I bend my head down to kiss him. He lifts one of his hands to cup my face as he moves his full lips across mine eagerly.

"Wow, we better get out of here. My girlfriend will be here any minute," he teases.

I smack his arm and jump down.

"Easy there, playboy. Let's go, I need to be fed," I say bounding up to his car.

"Yes, dear," he replies with a smile before shutting my door.

15 minutes later we are sitting down at Rocco's on the other side of town with supposedly the best Pizza around.

"You guys seriously call this Pizza? Pathetic. You should try some from this little hole in the wall place I used to go to back in California. It would change your life," I say inspecting the slice in front of me before deciding what the hell and taking a bite.

"I've never been outside of the state line, so I'll take your word for it," he shrugs.

"Never?" I thought I was the only one that never left their hometown.

"Nope. No need, I guess."

I open my mouth to tell him that we need to fix that soon when a shrill voice pierces the room.

"Daxie! Oh my gosh, I didn't know that you were going to be here. We have an extra seat if you want to join us!" Julie says before pointing at the group in the corner.

I look over to see a table with Chase, Blake and some other girl in it. Dax glances over and gives the guys a nod before turning back to Julie.

"We are good."

His voice is short and the not-so-subtle hint to fuck off is clear, at least to everyone but her. She sticks out her bottom lip like a 4-year-old while twirling a lock of her fire engine hair around a manicured nail.

"You are no fun. Well maybe I can come by tonight and remind you how much fun we have together," she says giving him her best seductive smile as she leans forward ever so slightly to give him a full access view of her cleavage.

I ball my fists in my lap, trying to talk myself out of knocking this bitch out. Why is it a bad idea again? I can't seem to remember. Ah, yes. Jail time and losing my scholarship. Yeah this bitch isn't worth that shit. Dax's eyes narrow at her immediately, irritation written plainly across his face.

"No."

The smirk falls from her lips, and she looks genuinely confused.

"No?"

"No, you can't come by. You can, however, fuck off. I would like to get back to my date with my *girlfriend*," he says nodding at me.

I don't even try to hide the smug grin that comes to my face when he introduces me as his girlfriend. Her gaze flicks over to me, her nose scrunching up in displeasure before she turns back towards him with a cool shrug.

"Okay, Daxie. You know how to reach me, day or night." She draws the last part out and runs her hand across his arm as she walks away.

I scoff and roll my eyes, damn this bitch is desperate. Dax grimaces as he looks at me like he is embarrassed that I even had to experience all of that. I guess I can expect more run ins like that now that I am dating Dax Hart-Breaker.

"I'm sorry about that. She's a fucking handful," he says.

"Sounds like you would know," I snap back, not even trying to hide the accusation in my voice.

"Baby-" he starts but I cut him off with my hand raised.

"Forget it."

He reaches across the table to hold my hands, and as much as I want to be a petty bitch and pull away, I don't.

"No, listen. She was nothing. Just someone that I hooked up with literally once. She was just a way to pass the time, baby. I swear."

My eyes flick up to him and narrow. I was going to drop this but if he really wants to do this, then let's fucking have it out.

"Is that how you will talk about me when we break up?"

I try to keep my tone hard and angry, but I think my fear peeks through a little too much. A look of pain flashes across his face as he slowly withdraws his hands before slumping back into the booth.

"When?" He questions, his voice soft as he looks at me.

I just shrug, trying to keep up my I don't give a fuck attitude, even if it couldn't be further from the truth. My gut is twisting painfully at the thought of my life without Dax in it. He has quickly become a huge chunk of it, practically everything, which is scary as fuck.

"They call you Dax Hart-Breaker for a reason."

The hurt look slides off his face and a pissed one takes its place, his jaw ticking.

"Really?" he grits. "You are going to listen to petty bitches that are pissed I didn't fall in fucking love with them? You look like you have something on your mind, so please, don't hold back."

My eyes narrow a fraction at his attitude. Motherfucker.

"Fine. You scare the living shit out of me. Most of the time I think that I know you, but the Dax that I know wouldn't touch that bitch with a ten-foot pole. You have a nasty reputation, and I am not one to cast stones with my glass house of a past, but you have to see it from my point of view. You have never been in a serious relationship and honestly, neither have I. Neither of us know what the fuck we are doing here, and it is fucking terrifying. I feel too much for you and I fucking hate it! I want to believe that I am special and all but sometimes I just don't know."

The condemnation left my voice somewhere along the way and I am left feeling vulnerable and exposed. It makes me itchy as fuck. I squirm in my seat a little like I can get rid of the feeling if I do.

"You have the power to crush me. No one has had that in a long time. Just don't…don't make me regret trusting you," I finish with a whisper.

All of the irritation seems to melt off him as he reaches for my hands again and rubs small circles on the back of it.

"Baby, you can trust me." He swallows for a moment before continuing. "You have that power too, you know. I'm really fucking scared too but being with you is worth it."

My eyes soften at that. I give him a half of a smile and he returns it. We sit in silence for a few more minutes just looking at each other before he speaks again.

"Ready to get out of here?"

"Definitely."

We jump up from our seats and intertwine our hands as we head for the door. I look over my shoulder as we go to see Julie glaring daggers at us, her fists balled into fists on top of the table. She looks pissed that she didn't rattle us like she intended. Fucking bitch.

When we get back to campus, Dax walks me back to my room and buries his hands into my hair, bringing his face close to me. Every time he kisses me it feels like the first time all over again and I can't help but feel that everything in my life has led me to be right here at this moment. Holy fuck. I am turning into some sappy schoolgirl.

Dax breaks the kiss and hovers just over my lips smiling.

"So, I will see you tomorrow?"

I smile. "Of course. I will be in the front row screaming my fucking head off for you."

He grins and kisses me one more time before leaving. I stand at my door watching him leave, knowing that I can't keep denying it. I am totally in love with Dax motherfucking Hart.

CHAPTER THIRTY

Aubrey

I am currently staring at my full-length mirror, trying to decipher how I feel about Kayla's latest round of dress up. I'm wearing a pair of black skinny jeans and a sparkly black and silver tank top, since I vetoed the leather skirt and a shirt that made me look like every other ring bunny. She says that this is how everyone dresses to fights and I argued with her since I have been to my fair share of entry level UFC fights back home, but she wouldn't hear of it. Pick your battles, I guess.

When we pull up to the gym that the fights are being held at a town over, I look around, surprised to see just how packed it is. Cars are overflowing from the parking lot and out onto the street. I know there are quite a bit of fights lined up for today, but it is still a pretty impressive turn out.

It takes us a little, but we are finally able to find a spot. After parking quickly, we make our way to the front door where Blake is waiting for us. Before I even get a word out, he is stepping up to us and ushering us past the bouncer at the door. I go to say thank you but realize that he isn't even looking at me. No, his eyes are firmly set on my gorgeous best friend and by the fuck me eyes she is sending back to him, I'd say the attraction is more than mutual.

Before they go at it right here in the middle of the room, I grab her by the arm and pull us farther inside so that we are out of people's way.

"I got to make sure a few other people get in. I'll find you," Blake says to Kayla before walking back outside.

"Oh my gosh! Did you see the way he looked at me!" She shouts as she smacks my arm excitedly.

I nod my head and give her a knowing smile before I look around the place. We are crammed like sardines in here, but the energy is so wild that you can physically feel it in the air.

"I am going to go to the bathroom before he gets back!" Kayla says in my ear.

I give her a thumbs up as she weaves her way through the crowd. Slowly, I work myself through the masses before coming to the edge of the octagon where a fight looks to be wrapping up. At least I sure hope it's almost done because the scrawny kid on the ground pouring blood like a fire hydrant doesn't look like he will last much longer. Forget losing the fight, this kid looks like he will be spending the night in the ER.

Suddenly, I feel a large hand grab my ass. Seriously? What the fuck is it that makes men think they are entitled to touch anyone's ass just because they want to? I turn around quickly to see some drunk college kid with a grin plastered on his face while he lightly staggers in place.

Without hesitation, I throw a punch right over his left eye and then grab the offending hand by the wrist and twist, effectively dropping drunky to his knees. He lets out a sharp yelp and struggles to break his hand free, but I just apply more pressure when he does.

From this angle I could snap his wrist like a twig, and for a moment I consider it until I feel a hand on my shoulder. *Why the fuck does everyone think they can touch me tonight?*

"Easy there, champ," Chase drawls.

I sneer at him and roll his hand off my shoulder. I still haven't forgotten how he set me up for that fight with Collins or the bullshit sexist remarks he made when it was questioned if I truly won or not. Dax doesn't talk about him often and he has yet to bring me around him, thank fuck. I know that they have been friends ever since they were kids so it isn't like I expect Dax to drop his lifelong friend just because I can't stand his fucking guts.

Narrowing my eyes at Chase, I apply just a bit more pressure to drunkys wrist just to be a bitch before I drop it. When he attempts to stumble upright, I kick him in the side, toppling him back over. I feel several sets of eyes on me as I do but that's nothing new when I publicly drop some guy in front of all his friends. It is the 21st century and yet people are still surprised when they see a woman stand up for herself and not stand by to get sexually assaulted. Motherfuckers.

Turning on my heel, I face the octagon once more to see that the scrawny kid is finally knocked out. Someone drags him out of the cage and a swarm of people come in, cleaning all of the blood off the floor as quickly as possible before the next fight begins. Turning my head, I see Kayla making her way towards me with Blake's arm draped around her.

Shit. That was fast.

When they reach me, Blake gives me a smirk before whispering into Kayla's ear, causing her to giggle like a pre-teen. They are so cute together already, I could puke.

A guy jumps up into the octagon and starts doing what seems to be a very well-rehearsed introduction for Dax's fight. Apparently, the guy Dax is fighting is named Chad Bronson and it's his first official fight. In the back corner I see some guy around Dax's age with a buzzed head make his way through the crowds. They don't give him much love, but he doesn't seem to mind. He looks arrogant, like this won't even be a sweat. I don't know this guy, but I've been the one trying to land a blow on Dax Hart before. I don't think he knows what a challenge it is going to be.

I know the instant that Dax enters the room, not because of the introduction or his signature music but because I can *feel* it. He doesn't look out into the crowd or pay any attention to the people shouting and cheering around him. His eyes are firmly locked on his opponent, stalking towards him like a predator.

The fight starts almost as soon as Dax enters the cage. Chad comes in charging quickly. Dax easily side steps him while he bounces on his feet, waiting for him to make the next move. Chad's eyes blatantly flick to Dax's torso before he pulls back to swing. Dax anticipates his move and dodges the throw before countering with a left hook to Chad's jaw. He stumbles back a few steps, clearly dazed before trying to shake the stars away.

Chad begins to advance once more but you can tell that he's pretty disoriented and definitely isn't as coordinated as he once was. Dax lets Chad make his way almost right up to him before giving out a punishing kick to the ribs that drops Chad to his knees. Dax accompanies it with a right hook to the face that hits so hard, I swear I just saw some teeth fly out into the crowd.

That seems to be all she wrote for Chad. His body drops to the mat with a resounding boom despite the noise in the room. The second he hit the floor the whole room erupted. Dax immediately stepped away from Chad like he was on fucking fire.

Good job, babe.

Dax throws up his arms in celebration when he is officially announced as the winner, and I scream my fucking head off for him. He must be able to hear me because his eyes flick to the side and lock on mine before he winks at me. Dax jumps out of the cage and accepts his congratulations as he walks towards me.

"Nicely done, Mr. Hart," I say in my most flirtatious tone.

He gives me a panty melting smile, before he sweeps me up into a sweaty bear hug. He starts carrying me around the room like I am a trophy that he just won. I shout at him, demanding that he put me down, but I don't really mean it. In this moment there is no where I would rather be than in this man's arms. I am so fucking proud of him.

I am wiping down some tables at work one night when Dax comes in through the front door, head whipping around the room until his eyes land on me. A huge smile breaks across his face and he runs up to me before picking me up spinning me around as he kisses me. I chuckle against his lips as he deepens the kiss. Thankfully the place is pretty dead so there aren't many people around to see Dax's form of greeting, except of course Marcus who is bartending.

"Dax! She is working. Can you at least save that stuff for when she clocks out?" Marcus's voice is more resigned like he knows that he is asking too much from Dax. The acceptance of it all makes me chuckle.

I have passed by Marcus a couple of times at the house, but we haven't spent much time together outside of work. I don't know for sure, but I don't think that Marcus has a problem with us together which is a huge relief since he is really the only family that Dax has left and one of the most important people in his life.

Dax slowly puts me down before turning to him.

"Sorry Unc, but I just got an amazing phone call." He smiles at him before swinging his gaze back to me. "Cameron called. He has a fight scheduled for me after New Year's. If I win, there will be another one after that and so on and so on. Bree, he says that if I keep up this steam then I could get a shot at the title one day!

"Oh my god! Dax! YES!"

Now it's me who jumps him. He catches me as my legs wrap around his waist and I pepper his face with kisses. Dax has had two more fights since that first one that I went to. Both times I was front and center for, screaming my head off in support of my man. Both times he annihilated the competition.

Marcus comes around and clasps Dax's shoulder and I begrudgingly climb out of his arms. Dax turns to Marcus as they share a short man hug.

"That is awesome, kid. I'm so proud of you. Where will the fight be?"

"This one is in Birmingham but if I move onto more, who knows." He looks over to me and smiles. "Looks like I may have the chance to cross the state line soon." He winks and I laugh as he wraps me up into a hug.

"I am so proud of you, babe," I murmur into his chest before he pulls me back to look at me.

His smile is big, and his eyes shine with excitement that his dreams are coming to life. He looks ready to say something and opens his mouth slightly before he closes it and gives me one more kiss. He talks with Marcus and me for a bit while we work and eventually he heads home.

I am so excited for what this means for Dax. He has worked so fucking hard for this and even though he had to conquer some obstacles he is doing it. He just had to get out of his own way. Seeing him go after his dream makes me feel like maybe I could do the same. I just have to figure out what that dream is, I guess.

It's the last day of classes before winter break and I am so fucking ready. Finals have been kicking my ass but thank fucking god, I just finished my last one and am now headed back to my room to grab my bag. Dax convinced me to stay at his place over break instead of hanging out in the dorms. Marcus is going out of town to visit his new secret girlfriend's family so we will be completely alone for break. I am really excited to have that much uninterrupted Dax time. I could pass on the holiday part.

I am walking down my hallway when I stop dead in my tracks and see something completely unexpected outside of my door. Cole. He is standing there with his shoulders hunched and hands buried into his jeans. He has a nervous expression on his face and when he looks up at me, I have the sudden urge to run up and hug him. I have missed him more than I realized. I tried not to think about him, but it's been hard without my best friend. I slowly walk up to him and stop a couple feet away from him.

"Hi, Aubrey," he says softly.

Aubrey not darlin'. It's just a subtle reminder that we will never be able to get back to being the old Aubrey and Cole. It's probably for the best but it fucking sucks all the same.

"Hi," I reply in an equally gentle tone.

The tension in the air settles around us as the silence stretches. Cole just stands there staring at me like he is not quite sure how he got here to begin with.

"Do you want to come in?" I ask finally.

He nods but doesn't say anything. I unlock my door and open it for him, but this is Cole, and he could lose his southern gentleman card if he let me hold the door for him, so he takes it from my hand and gestures for me to go in first.

When he comes in and shuts the door he just stands right in front of it facing me with his hands reburied in his pockets. I stand in front of him not sure what to do or say. He finally speaks after a little while.

"I am heading home for the break."

I smile at the thought of how happy his family will be to see him.

"That's awesome. I am sure Renée is excited to have you back so soon."

"Not soon enough in her opinion," he offers with a halfhearted chuckle.

"Can't blame a mama," I mimic in my best Renée impression. We both laugh a little more genuinely at that and I give him a small smile. "Well, tell them all I say hi and Merry Christmas."

He nods. "They asked if you were coming. They wanted you to come. My sisters adored you at Thanksgiving and loved that braid you showed them how to do with their hair. The whole family wanted to know why you wouldn't be coming."

"What did you tell them?" I ask, suddenly nervous at how his family's opinions have probably changed about me now.

He shrugs. "The truth. That I am in love with you, and you are in love with someone else."

I blow out a heavy breath as I look up to him regretfully.

"Cole I-"

"It's okay," he says interrupting me. "Really, it is. I was upset and needed space, but I miss you. I miss our study sessions that consisted more of movies and ice cream than actual studying. I miss talking to you about literally everything. I miss working with you. I just…miss my best friend."

I take a small step forward, crossing my arms across my stomach in attempt to stop the rolling feeling that has begun ever since I saw him in the hallway.

"I miss you too. This has been really fucking hard for me. I have tried to give you your space, but you have no idea how many times I picked up the phone just wanting to hear your voice or tell you a story about something stupid Kayla did or something that happened at The White Oak. Then I would remember that we aren't friends anymore…" I trail off as I wrap my arms around myself even tighter.

"I don't want that, Aubrey," he says shaking his head. "I want us to be friends. I will get over my feelings. I don't want to lose you from my life."

I smile and nod my head.

"I don't want that either."

He reaches into his pocket and pulls out a black box with a bow on top. His hand nervously spins it around in his palm before looking up to me.

"I got you something," he says offering it forward. "Merry Christmas."

Fuck. Well now I feel like an ass. I cringe as I look from the box to him.

"Cole, I-I didn't get you anything. I'm sorry. I didn't-"

"Aubrey, I don't need anything. It wasn't really planned. I just saw it and thought of you. Don't over think it."

Slowly, I reach out to take the box from him. His eyes watch me carefully and my heart thunders in my chest as I carefully open the box. My breath catches when I look inside. Laying against the cream leather interior of the box is a stunning silver necklace that has what looks like a bird pendant with the feathers made up of dozens of tiny red rubies. I look up to Cole in surprise. This thing is way too nice. There is no way I can accept this.

"It's a phoenix," he says quietly. "They are supposed to be the symbol of new beginnings. I figured since that is what brought you here it was fitting. I was also hoping that we could have a new beginning."

Despite my best efforts, my eyes start to water as I throw my arms around his neck, hugging him close to me. His arms almost immediately wrap around me and hold me tight. I feel him let out a long exhale and I have a feeling that this is as much of a relief for him as it is for me. I lean back and he smiles at me before taking the box out of my hands.

"May I?" He asks gesturing to put the necklace on me.

I nod as he pulls it out while I spin around, lifting my hair out of the way for him. He clasps it together and lets it drop. It hangs around my neck at the perfect height settling in the center of my chest. I look down to admire it and look up to see that Cole is staring at me with an intense look. Fuck. Can we really do this? Just pretend that his feelings aren't there? I want to say yes but the way that he is looking at me, with so much love and care, makes me think otherwise.

"Just friends?" I ask hesitantly.

He gives a small sad smile and nods.

"For now."

I sigh heavily.

"Cole."

He chuckles softly but it isn't exactly a happy sound. It sounds more remorseful than anything. Slowly, he steps forward and places a chaste kiss on my cheek.

"Merry Christmas, Aubrey."

Cole holds his lips against my cheek as he murmurs to me before he carefully pulls away, looking down at me with those sad expression filled eyes before he turns and walks out the door.

CHAPTER THIRTY-ONE

Aubrey

I pull up to Dax's house an hour later just as he makes his way outside. Betty gives her own greeting in the form of a backfire noise as Dax comes up to my door. He shakes his head and chuckles as I get out of the car.

"Damn, I should have just gotten you a new car for Christmas. Then we could have junked this scrap metal."

I slap my hand over his mouth quickly as I hush him.

"Shh, she will hear you and if you hurt her feelings, she won't start for me."

We both laugh as I drop my hand before Dax bends down to press his lips against mine. I smile into him and wrap my arms around his neck as he slightly dips me backwards. Fuck. I have been with some good kissers, but Dax motherfucking Hart blows them all out of the water. We break apart eventually and he smiles down at me happily. His eyes flick down to my neck as he cocks his head slightly. I guess he noticed my new present.

"I haven't seen this before. It's nice," he comments as he holds the pendant between his fingers.

I nod and decide to be honest about where it came from. God knows I already keep enough to myself. I can open up about this stuff.

"Cole gave it to me for Christmas."

Dax drops it in a flash and rips his hand away like the necklace physically burned him. His brows furrow and an irritated look crosses his face.

"Excuse me? When the fuck did this happen?"

I roll my eyes and shrug at his sudden attitude.

"About an hour ago. He came by and said that he wants to be friends again."

I turn around to grab my bag and the bag that has Dax's Christmas present in it. Dax yanks my bag out of my hand and slams the car door with a hollow laugh.

"Yeah, sure. *Friends*. Who the fuck does that little shit think he is? He knows that you are my girl, and he gets you fucking jewelry? I should fucking kick his teeth in!"

My brows dip as I feel my own anger starting to rise inside of me.

"No, you shouldn't. He is my friend, and he gave me a Christmas present. Babe, we need to get something straight right the fuck now. I *am* your girlfriend, but I am *not* your property. I will be friends with anyone I want. You have to accept that and trust that I would never do anything to hurt you or our relationship."

"I trust you just fine. I however don't trust Mr. Just Friends to keep his fucking hands to himself."

I roll my eyes and shake my head before opening my car door, tossing the bag in my hand back inside haphazardly before I snatch the one Dax is holding and toss it in as well.

"Okay, well I am fucking done with your jealous bullshit. I am just gonna hang on campus for break. Let me know when you are done being a prick."

I lower myself into my seat and go to shut the door when his hand stops it. Despite how much I would love to swing the door shut and crush his stupid fucking fingers, he is too strong. Dax stares at the ground for a few moments, silently stewing before he brings his eyes up to mine.

"I'm sorry," he says quietly. "You are right. I can't control who you are friends with. It's just…fuck. You are fucking everything to me, Bree, and he wants you. You hanging out with him again makes me nervous as fuck. It makes me scared fucking shitless that maybe he could take you away from me."

Honesty drips from his words and it's the worried expression in his eyes that make me get out of the car and step into his arms.

"Dax, we were good friends for a while before he ever admitted he had feelings for me. He never tried anything then and he won't now. I am not going anywhere, and no one is stealing me. The only person that could get rid of me is you."

He hugs me tight and nods his head, burying his face into the crook of my neck as he blows out a deep breath.

"If he pulls anything, and I mean fucking anything, I will stomp his ass into the motherfucking ground," he grumbles into my hair.

I let out a sharp laugh as I shake my head.

"Deal."

The next couple of days are a mix of Dax and me working out at the gym or in the garage and fucking like rabbits, but you won't hear me complaining. Dax surprised me the first day I stayed over with an early Christmas present of a new pair of UFC regulated gloves. They are dark purple and black, and I fucking love them. Dax and I are sparring lightly one day in the garage when he speaks up.

"Hey, baby?" He asks as he picks up his water bottle before throwing me mine.

"Hmmm?"

"Have you ever considered teaching self-defense classes? I mean, you are really good, obviously. I think more women should be able to defend themselves in dangerous situations and I think that you could be that person to teach them."

I look at him thoughtfully and nod.

"I agree. I have never really thought about it honestly but it's not a bad idea. I would love to have the opportunity to do what others did for me."

"Which is?" He pushes.

I know he has been dying for me to open up to him, but it is so fucking hard to let down the walls that I built up so high. What if he looks at me differently? Worse, what if he pities me? I couldn't handle that. But he deserves more. So, I decide to let him in, even if it is just a little bit.

"Take young girls in that don't know how to defend themselves and give them the skills they need to survive."

"Survive?" He questions softly.

My eyes beg him to not push anymore and thankfully he doesn't. He just pulls me into his arms and kisses the top of my head tenderly.

While my head is tucked under his chin he whispers into my hair, "Someone attacked my mom, and she couldn't defend herself against him. That is how she died."

Stilling my breath, I don't dare move a muscle. Dax never talks about his mother, he never brought up the cause of her death and based on how close they were I imagine that it is still too painful for him to think about let alone talk about with others. I am not sure if that is all he has to say about it, so I just stand there, silently holding him, allowing him time to continue if he wants to.

"She was working late at The White Oak. Her and Marcus used

to run it together. I begged her for the car one night because I wanted to go to some party. She finally relented and said she would walk home. It was only a quarter mile walk to work from our house. One that she had done a million times before. If I would have known what was going to happen, I never would have taken the car. I-I never thought in my wildest dreams that anything would happen to her."

His breath catches as I feel his lips press against the crown of my head.

"He tried to mug her. She wouldn't give him her purse and so he stabbed her. Left her bleeding out in the middle of the street. By the time someone found her and called the paramedics it was too late. The worst part is that I didn't even find out until the next morning. I was too fucked up at the party. Marcus called me about fifty fucking times and every single one went unanswered. I was partying while my mother was dying because I insisted on having the car. Then Marcus was dealing with the death of his sister all on his own because I was passed out drunk."

He spits the last part out with disgust. I can tell just in his voice that he is disappointed in himself, that he feels in a way responsible. I hug him tighter before he pulls back to look at me. I see watery tears building up in his eyes as he brushes a loose piece of hair behind my ear.

"I wish that someone would have trained her, shown her how to defend herself. She never listened to me and would never have let me show her anything. Maybe, if she would have taken a class or something she could have gotten away. Maybe she would be here to this day.

"She died not far away from where I first met you, where that piece of shit grabbed you. I didn't even know you, but I had this overwhelmingly urge to protect you, like I wish someone could have for my mother."

"Babe, I am so sorry that you went through that."

He gives me a sad smile and a small shrug.

"I wish I could say it's okay, but it isn't. So that is my own selfish reason of why I think you should do something like that. You have a talent, a gift that you can share with others. You can change lives and save them, plus you will get paid to wail on people," he jokes lightly which causes me to laugh.

"I will think about it," I say.

He smiles and captures my lips in one more kiss before turning to the heavy bag and letting out a ton of what looks like pent up rage and heart ache.

Christmas morning is here and even though it's just Dax and I, we make our way out to the living room and exchange Christmas presents by the tabletop dollar store Christmas tree he picked up the other day. I hand him the small box with the present that I agonized over. I don't have a ton of money saved up since Betty hit the bank account pretty hard, even though I am fairly certain Dax was only charging me half of what everything really cost. I wanted his gift to be something special, something that actually meant something. I also am a little nervous that I may have crossed a line to get this present made. So, I really fucking hope that he likes it.

He opens the box and looks down at the contents. The smile that was on his face slides off as a serious expression takes its place. He pulls the keychain out and holds it up so that he can look at it better. It has a set of angel wings on it and the words around the keychain say, 'God has you in his arms, I have you in my heart' and then in the middle is a picture of his mom. I found it at his house a few weeks ago. I swiped it, got it copied and slipped the original back into his side drawer before he even realized it was gone. He glances up to me for a second and then back down to the keychain for another moment before he returns his eyes to me.

The look on his face is not the happy expression I was hoping for. Fuck. I rush to explain.

"I found the picture. I thought that it would be nice for you to have something easy to keep with you at all times so that you can always have her close. So that even on the days where you aren't able to make it to her grave or you don't feel like you are remembering her in the right way, you have her with you." I pause for a second as I fiddle with my fingers as I look down to my lap before glancing back up to him.

"I'm sorry, it's weird isn't it? I shouldn't have gone through your things. I'm sorry."

I go to take it from him, but he rips it out of my reach and cradles it protectively to his chest.

"No," he snaps. "No, this is incredible. I love it." He looks deeply into my eyes as his words soften. "So much, thank you, baby."

He leans over and hugs me which makes me breathe a sigh of relief. Then he hands me a small velvet box with a red ribbon on it. My heart thumps wildly in my chest in anticipation. I never really got gifts growing up besides the guys from the gym here and there. Most of the time that stuff was just essentials like clothes and food and stuff like that. It was embarrassing for so many people to know that my mom spent all of our money on drugs instead of food and other essentials, but the guys were always good about not saying anything, they would just hand me a box and walk away which I appreciated more than they knew. I miss those fuckers.

I go to open the box, but Dax places his hand over mine before I do.

"Wait," he says quietly. He looks nervous as he pauses for a moment and swallows before continuing.

"Bree, I have been hooked on you from the first moment that I saw you. I knew you were different immediately. You are so beautiful and amazing and smart and fucking *strong*. I admire the hell out of you. You make me want to be a better person and I really think that every day I spend with you, I become one. I've never felt like this about anyone before, ever. Everything with you is special and scary and fucking perfect. I've been trying to find the right time to say this, but I chicken out every time."

He blows out a heavy breath as looks directly into my eyes causing my heart to thunder in my chest.

"I love you, Bree."

I am shook to my core. I know that I have been fighting my feelings for him for a while now. Usually, I can bury my feelings and put up an impassive front but with Dax it's fucking hard. As crazy as it sounds, I trust Dax. I know that he cares about me deeply, I know that he is extremely protective of me and only wants the best for me, but for him to admit that he loves me? It is the final blow to my defenses, and I know that I can't hold back any longer. All my walls drop at once and it's like he can almost see it because his face visibly softens while his eyes remain intently trained on me in anticipation.

"I love you, Dax."

Relief washes over him and he gives me the most brilliant smile that I have ever seen as he pulls me in for a kiss. My stomach flips as our lips brush and I can't help but groan into the kiss. I start slowly crawling into his lap to straddle him as he pulls away and chuckles, urging me to open the box. I shoot him a dirty look since he is being a serious pussy block right now. He smirks, not at all bothered by my evil look as he nods towards the gift again.

Sighing dramatically, I lift the box top to reveal a white gold bracelet with a rectangle plate on top, engraved in it is 'Forever'. I freeze for a moment as I take it in before I look up to Dax to see that he looks almost bashful, which can't be true because I don't think that Dax Hart has the capability to be bashful. But his head is ducked like he is nervous to see my face with a small smile on his lips. I tilt his chin up so that his eyes meet mine straight on.

"Dax…" my voice cracks as I speak. I swallow hard, trying to clear it. "This is the most amazing thing that I have ever received in my entire life, ever. Thank you, babe."

With so much emotion being passed between us there is only one thing that I can do in this moment. I set my box to the side and this time I successfully jump into his lap. He accepts me quickly and splays his hands across my ass as I straddle him. I work my way up and down his neck, trailing quick urgent kisses.

"Bree," he murmurs softly before running a hand through my hair and pulling to move my neck to the side to give him better access.

I tilt my chin to the side for him as I sigh happily and run my hands over his tree branch like arms. Dax being ever the alpha male doesn't let me stay on top for long before he is lowering me onto the floor before leaning over me. His hard cock rubs against my soaked sleep shorts and I let out a tortured moan at the contact. He gives me a cocky smirk before he peels my shorts off as well as my panties before he dives his head down and feasts on me like I am his favorite meal.

His mouth is punishing and unrelenting as he expertly works me over, his tongue moving in quick motions, applying just the right amount of suction until I am screaming my release all over his face. When my legs stop shaking Dax rips his shirt up from behind him, revealing his perfectly sculpted body. I can't help but run a hand over his tattooed arms before going down his rippled abs. I don't even know how he is real the guy looks fucking photoshopped.

Dax frees his cock from his shorts as his large hand grasps it, stroking a couple of times before he pushes his way into me. I let out a gasp as my body adjusts around his thick cock. We had the talk about coverage after the time in the garage. I'm covered on birth control, and he went and got an STD test to prove to me that he was clean, so ever since we haven't bothered with condoms.

"Fuck. I can never get enough of your pussy, baby. You are fucking perfect," Dax groans as he thrusts into me deeper. I moan as the tip of his cock rubs against my g-spot.

"Right there!" I gasp.

Dax reaches down and hooks both of my legs over his shoulders before he grips my thighs in his hands and leans back as he fucks me in the air. Holy fuck, I don't think I have ever felt anything so deep in my life.

"Shit. Fuck. Dax. God yes!" I cry out.

"Yeah, take that dick, baby. You are such a good girl."

His words of praise are like a match to a stick of dynamite. He pulls me in just a little closer, causing my clit to grind against his pelvis, causing me to shoot off like a rocket. I shout out my orgasm as Dax spills himself inside of me.

We take a few moments to catch our breath before we look at each other and smile. Dax presses his lips against mine before I nip at his lip. His eyes instantly darken with a threatening promise of punishment to come. Merry fucking Christmas to me.

CHAPTER THIRTY-TWO

Aubrey

The rest of the break was spent with Dax training every day for his big fight coming up. When he would get home for the day, we would have dinner, have sex, a lot of sex, and then hang out. We fell into something really domestic and really easy. We were practically living together, and I wasn't completely petrified with fear at the idea. Dax makes me feel safe and loved. Two things that I had never felt truly before. My nightmares had even stopped for the first time in, fuck, years.

I went home Sunday night so that I could get myself ready for the new semester. It was oddly sad to say goodbye to Dax and I could tell that he was feeling the same way. He kept insisting that it was fine if I stayed over again, but I insisted on coming back. As much as I didn't want to I knew it was for the best, at least right now. Dax's fight is coming up the following Saturday and I know he has to throw himself into every minute of training that he can get for it. I don't mind. I am so proud and so fucking excited for him.

On Monday I had a new class schedule and didn't know anyone in my classes, which was honestly fine by me. I finally got to my last class of the day, American history, when I made my way to the back of the class and took a seat. Class was just about to start when a familiar brown head of hair rushed in the door. Cole searched the room for an empty seat until his eyes fell on me, a small smile spreading across his face as he hurried over to claim the empty seat next to me.

"Hey, Aubrey," Cole says as he plops down next to me, pulling out his things.

"Hey, Cole. How is the family?"

He beams a huge smile as he turns to me.

"Awesome! We had a ton of fun. The girls entered a gingerbread house making contest and actually won! And Dad and I sat around and got fat while Mama stuffed us with so many Christmas treats. I swear I think I gained twenty pounds," he says as he rubs his ripped stomach.

I roll my eyes and shove his shoulder lightly as he chuckles. That familiar twinkle returning to his blue eyes, I haven't seen that in what seems like forever. Class goes by pretty quick before Cole and I walk out together. A silence that had never really happened to us before descends on us and I find myself trying to think of what to say.

Finally, I just decide to blurt the first thing that comes to mind.

"Did you hear about Dax's fight this Saturday?"

Cole slightly winces and I realize that Dax is probably the last thing that he wants to talk about. But he is my boyfriend and a big part of my life and if Cole is going to be my friend again, he will have to get used to Dax being brought up in conversation.

"Yeah, I did. Pretty awesome," he says quietly.

"Are you going to come? I know a lot of people from campus are coming."

He shakes his head softly and gives a small smile.

"Nah, I've got to work. I am covering so Marcus can go with too."

"Oh, yeah. Right. Of course."

The longer we walk the more awkward things get. I am desperately trying to figure out what topics are safe to talk about and which to avoid when Cole looks at me and chuckles.

"Shit, Aubrey. You don't have to be so awkward. Stop thinking too much and just talk, we have always been able to talk about anything. I am not going to fall apart if you talk about your relationship or what has been going on in your life that doesn't include me. This will only not be weird if you don't make it weird. So, knock it off," he says lightly as he bumps his shoulder against mine. I blow out a breath of relief and nod smiling at him as I tell him about the latest guy I sparred with at the gym.

The first week of the semester flies by. Kayla and I hang out most days since Dax is training and Cole even joins us a couple times. Especially with Kayla being there, things weren't even a little bit awkward between Cole and I. One night we went out and got pizza at Rocco's, well, Cole and I got pizza while Kayla got a salad. Who the fuck gets a salad at a pizza place?

A few other times we had some study sessions/movie marathons that were really relaxing and much needed. Everything seemed to be back to somewhat normal. Except for the fact that being Dax Hart's girlfriend has caused quite a bit of buzz around campus. Random people that I swear I have never even seen before know my name and are inviting me to parties and events left and right. Is this what Dax deals with every day? It's kinda fucking annoying.

When the day of the big fight is finally here, Dax and I hop into his car and head out. It's only a little over an hour drive so we were able to grab an early dinner before we left. Well, I ate while Dax watched me since it was obviously too close to the fight for him to eat anything. He won't admit it, but he is super nervous for tonight. I know that for a fact because his knee has been bouncing for the last 45 miles non-stop while his hands white knuckle the steering wheel. I place my hand on his knee to stop the motion.

"Babe, relax. You got this. You are a badass and if you stay sharp and trust your instincts, you will do great. Stop psyching yourself out."

He looks at me and releases a long breath before nodding.

"I know, this is just big. I don't want to fuck up."

"I understand, but trust that you are a better fighter today than you ever have been before. You pummel that guy into the ground and as soon as you hear the ref call the match, get as far away from him as you can and look for me. I will be the crazy bitch yelling her ass off for you."

I say it with a wink and place a quick kiss on his cheek. He gives me a cheeky smirk and winks before taking my hand and kissing it tenderly. He doesn't let go of my hand the rest of the ride and that's fine by me. I will be whatever kind of support he needs.

We arrive at the gym that is hosting the matches today and park. Dax quickly meets up with some other guys from the gym that are also fighting today as they all head back to the locker room, but not before he hauls me against him one more time and crushes his lips against mine. He pulls away just as quickly and gives me a sexy smile and a wink before he jogs to catch up with the guys. I recognize a couple of people from campus and then my eyes find Blake and Kayla sitting in the front row.

"Kayla! I didn't know that you were going to be here!" I say as I come up to them to hug her. She gets up excitedly to hug me back.

"I didn't know either. Blake showed up at my dorm this afternoon and asked if I wanted to tag along."

Her cheeks are beet red, and I can't help but give her a teasing smirk as she swats my arm. I chuckle at her before saying hi to

Blake. Kayla thankfully saved a seat for me, so I have a perfect view of the octagon.

We watch a couple fights, some more exciting than others. So far every guy from our gym has won their match. I know that Cameron is an incredible coach, but I am blown away at the dominance all of the guys present just by stepping through the door. They are fucking machines.

After a bloodied guy is helped out of the octagon and he hobbles away, I hear Dax's intro music play and my adrenaline spikes in anticipation. Dax stalks from the locker room as he makes his way to the cage. His head is up, shoulders back and eyes looking straight ahead. He wears a stony-faced expression that gives absolutely nothing away. He looks serious, lethal and ready to get shit done.

That's my man.

His opponent comes out shortly after. He is just as huge as Dax with cannons for arms. The guy has a buzz cut and looks to be older, maybe in his early 30's. He is built like a fucking tank and for the first time at one of Dax's fights, I am a little nervous. Out of all of Dax's fights that I have been to, one thing is always the same, he never loses. Until now though, Dax has never been up against an opponent who looks so formidable.

I glance over at Dax to see what he thinks about this guy, but his face remains impassive. He doesn't even size him up like the guy is clearly doing to Dax, obviously trying to intimidate him. Dax doesn't even blink he just stares deep into the man's eyes, ready to go to war. The ref goes over the rules quickly before he signals for the fight to begin.

In seconds, the man is coming in hot, swinging wildly with what looks to be a ton of force behind each punch, but they all hit air. Say what you want about Dax Hart, but the man is lightning quick. With every jab, hook or kick that his opponent sends him Dax anticipates it, dodging and side stepping them all. The first-round ends before

I know it and Dax has yet to throw one hit. That isn't usually his game, so I am a little confused why he didn't take any of the several of the openings that he had.

Blake gives me an easy smile as he settles his arm around Kayla's shoulders.

"Just wait."

I narrow my eyes questioningly before I turn back to face the cage. The second round starts up and it is immediately apparent that Dax's opponent has slowed down quite a bit. Even though his movements are a little more sluggish, the intensity in his eyes has not let up. He throws a wild right hook that lacks any true follow through and Dax dodges it easily before he finally makes a move. He takes advantage of the opening that the man just left and is quick to deliver a punishing jab to his ribs combined with a follow up left hook to the jaw that hits so hard the man literally turns 180 degrees before dropping to the ground.

The whole gym erupts into a frenzied roar, but Dax doesn't stop. He straddles the guy and pounds his face into the floor, just like we talked about. After only a few hits the ref declares the fight a knockout and Dax jumps away from him quickly before he practically runs to the other side of the cage, breathing rapidly as he looks down at his unconscious opponent. Dax's eyes frantically search the crowd until they land on me, a wide smile breaking out across his face exposing his mouth guard. I jump up and down screaming and cheering like a mad woman just like I promised, and I can see the pride shining in his eyes even from all the way over here.

Dax is officially announced as the winner before he makes his way out of the cage. I run over to meet him at the exit, not giving him a seconds notice before I climb him like a tree, peppering his sweaty face with kisses. He grins into my neck and continues walking with me wrapped around him.

We make it away from the crowd and stop just in front of the locker room when Cameron comes jogging over to us with a huge smile on his face. Dax lowers me to my feet as he approaches before lacing our fingers together

"Dax!" he shouts. "That was perfect! Exactly what we talked about. Arturo's blows would have been lethal if he would have landed one, but he has no stamina. He has been a force to be reckoned with for some time in the Heavy Weight class. I'll be working on your next fight soon. Great job, kid!" He says clapping his hand on Dax's shoulder before heading back to the octagon to be with his next fighter. Dax turns to me, and I swear that my face is going to crack from how hard I am smiling.

"Babe, I am so fucking proud of you. You have no idea!"

He gives me a huge smile and dives in, capturing my lips with his. The kiss starts out sweet and tender but quickly turns passionate and a little wild. He digs his fingers into my hair and pulls my head back, kissing the spot behind my ear and working his way down my neck until he reaches my collarbone as I let out a small whimper. His eyes lock with mine for a second before something in him seemingly snaps. Dax throws me over his shoulder and opens a supply closet to the left of the locker room, shutting the door behind us as he steps inside.

"Dax! What the fuck are you doing? There are people literally everywhere!"

He doesn't respond, though. His eyes are hooded, looking at me hungrily. His face serious as he recaptures my lips with his. This time his hands snake up the front of my shirt peeling it away from my skin and tossing it onto the floor. He kisses hot trails all over my body making my breathing become ragged.

"Dax," I say, my voice breathy and hoarse.

I am not really sure what I am trying to say to him at this point, because I can't deny that seeing him up there shirtless and dominant didn't make me crave him like he is clearly craving me. I decide to say fuck it as I reach for his shorts, pulling them down while he works at the buttons of my jeans.

Once he has slid my jeans down my legs, I hook my right leg around his torso as he drives into me without skipping a beat. His pace is near frantic as I arch my back into him as he moves. Holy shit, this man can fuck. Dax reaches a hand in between us as he rubs fast circles over my clit before nipping at my ear.

"Fuck, you feel like heaven, baby," he groans in my ear.

"Shit. Dax," I gasp.

He lets out a feral growl as he nips he even harder this time.

"Say my name again. Shout my name as you come on my cock, Bree."

My body starts to quake as Dax continues circling my clit before he sinks his teeth into the tender skin of my shoulder. I go off like a fucking rocket, screaming out his name as I shake uncontrollably.

"Dax!"

His pace becomes hurried as he slams into me faster and faster until he is growling out his own release. He places a gentle kiss against my tender skin that he just buried his teeth into before he breathes me in slowly. After a few moments, he pulls his head back to look at me as he smooths my hair to the side, kissing my temple with a loving smile.

I unwind my leg from around him as he slowly eases back. Our combined orgasms begin running down my leg but lucky for us this storage closet has spare rolls of toilet paper and paper towels. Dax quickly gathers some toilet paper before he hands it to me.

"I'll let you clean up for now since we have a bit of a drive ahead of us. But I am going to fill you up again later."

I smirk, not fully understanding why that turns me on so much. Guess I am just freaky like that. Dax stares down at me for a moment before he grips the back of my neck tightly and brings our heads together until our foreheads are resting on each other.

"I love you, Dax Hart," I whisper.

"I love you Aubrey Davis," he replies touching the bracelet he got me that is now a permanent fixture on my wrist before he adds, "forever."

CHAPTER THIRTY-THREE

Dax

I just finished up another fight and fucking won. I feel on top of the motherfucking world. Every fight that I have had since I re-joined the MMA, I have won. I am tearing through my opponents so quickly and brutally that MMA commentators are actually starting to talk about me. There is word that everyone should 'be on the lookout for Dax Hart' and fuck if that doesn't feel amazing. Bree wasn't able to make it this time because she had to work but she is meeting me at my house so that we can celebrate, preferably naked.

Bree and I have practically been living together over the last few weeks now that we are well into the new semester. I have been trying to think about how to bring up making it official, though I don't know if it is a good idea. She can be skittish about that kind of thing, and I don't want to spook her until I know that we are in a really good place.

Although I feel like we are already there, I can't help but feel like there are things that she is holding back on, important things. I mean, fuck. She still hasn't even told me what town she grew up in, I don't know anything about her family or if she even has one and more importantly, I have no idea what plagues her nightmares. Thankfully it seems that they have stopped, but I will never forget the fear splashed across her sleeping face those first few times that she slept over.

I know that I need to just trust that when she is ready, she will tell me. But I have never claimed to be a patient man and I feel like there are still things between us, keeping us at arm's length and I fucking hate it. Chase and I are just coming back into Glenfield when he starts getting hyped up all over again about the fight. Since Bree couldn't come and Blake had a date with Kayla, I invited him. We have been kind of on the outs ever since he set up Bree to fight Collins. I'm still pissed at him about it, but he has been my best friend for as long as I can remember.

"Man, you fucking killed it tonight! We got to celebrate! Let me call some people and we will hit up Club 22 or something." He gets out his phone to start making calls when I shake my head.

"Nah, man. Just drop me at my place. Aubrey is waiting for me."

He gives me a side eye look before shrugging.

"Yeah and I am sure she will still be waiting for you in a couple hours after we have partied a little."

I shake my head again.

"No, thanks. I just want to get home to my girl."

Chase lets out a long exhale that tells me something is up. We have been best friends since we were ten years old, and he is about as subtle as a damn freight train.

"What?" I ask half exhausted and half irritated. He shakes his head a bit as his mouth quirks up into a twisted scowl.

"Man, I wasn't going to say anything because I thought you'd be done with her by now, but you need to cut that chick loose."

"Excuse me?" I ask, my tone instantly turning dark at how he refers to Aubrey like she is some flavor of the week. Chase clearly doesn't pick up on this though because he continues on.

"Look, I get it, man. She's pretty hot and has a banging body. I am sure that she has been a fun lay. Plus, she was the first girl since seventh grade who hasn't completely fallen at your feet, which was probably a rewarding challenge, but you are Dax motherfucking Hart. There are hordes of women out there chomping at the bit just to be near you and you are wasting all your time on that stuck up bitch."

"Pull over," I grit through clenched teeth.

He shoots me a confused look before shrugging his shoulders and continuing to spew his shit as he pulls over.

"All I am saying is that you have become pretty lame since you got with her. I miss the old Dax that would stay out all night chasing pussy with me. You never want to go out anymore and I need my wingman back. I guess you don't have to dump the chick if you really want to keep her around. But at least come out and let loose a little with me. I know Julie would be willing to have something on the low so you can still be public with Aubrey."

I don't even hesitate. I punch him so hard in the face that his nose cracks and instantly sprays the dash with blood. I hit him two more times before smashing his head into the steering wheel.

"You stupid fuck! If you ever speak about Aubrey that way again, I will fucking kill you!" I roar in his face.

He is barely conscious as he just sits there, groaning as he holds his face. I am sure he is just as shocked as I am that I just pulverized his face. But he crossed so many fucking lines in just a few sentences that even over twelve years of friendship can't justify it.

I grab my shit at my feet and get out of the car slamming the door shut. It's a little cold for February but I see a diner up ahead and march towards it. I give Bree a call to see if she will come pick me up and she says that she will be here in 15 minutes.

When she pulls up, I bound up to her and meet her at the front door. I pull her into me until our hips are flush as I begin devouring her mouth. She lets out a little yip of surprise before snaking her arms around my neck and returning my kiss with an equal amount of intensity. I pull back and look down into a pair of dazed turquoise eyes that I have become fucking obsessed with. I love this girl so fucking much, I swear if I didn't have her, my heart would fucking stop beating.

"Let's go," I say softly.

She nods and threads her hands with mine as we head out to Betty. I take the keys and drive us back to my place. When we get there, I go to get out of the car before Aubrey says something.

"So, are you going to tell me why I had to come get you at a diner in the middle of bumfuck nowhere when Chase was supposed to drive you home?"

Her tone is patient like she is asking a child to fess up to eating all of the Halloween candy. I just shrug and look out the window.

"He wanted to go out tonight. I wanted to come home to you. We decided to split off in separate directions."

"Uh huh," she says, clearly seeing through my bullshit. "And when you guys decided to 'split off' was that before or after you got into a fight that ended with blood sprayed all over your shirt?" She asks with a raised eyebrow and a 'don't fucking lie to me again' look. I glance down at my shirt and sure enough I got caught in the crossfire of Chase's exploded nose. I exhale heavily and look at her.

"We got into a fight about you," I say, debating on how much I want to tell her.

"He doesn't like me," she says, more like a fact than a question. "I know, if I am being honest, I kinda hate his fucking guts. But I put up with him for you."

"Well, you won't have to anymore. After the way I beat his face in, I am pretty damn sure that our friendship is over, and good fucking riddance."

Aubrey's eyebrows raise in shock at that before she blows out a breath.

"Geeze, was the shit he said really that bad?" I give curt nod and she returns it. "Okay then, well fuck him. Let's talk about you. I saw the live stream of your fight in between tables. You kicked ass, babe!"

I manage to crack a smile as I peck her lips.

"Thank you, baby. It sucked not having you there with me. It's like I can feel when you are in the audience watching me. It makes me go harder than usual."

"Aw, trying to impress your girl?" She teases as she gets out of the car.

I chuckle as I trail after my dream girl while she heads inside. Man, fuck Chase. He is supposed to be my best friend and if he doesn't realize that I have never been happier than I am with Aubrey, then he doesn't deserve to be my friend. Aubrey ambles into the kitchen grabbing a couple of beers for us and I can't help but think about how I am looking at my forever.

The next day I am sleeping with Aubrey tucked into my chest when my phone rings. I groan as she buries her head under the pillow and turns away. I peek one eye open and reach for the offending device.

"Hello?" I say groggily.

"Hey, kid! Nice job last night," Cameron says, dude sounds so chipper he must already be on his third cup of coffee this morning.

"Thanks, Coach. I appreciate it."

"Well, I wanted to let you know that some folks at the UFC

reached out to me. You have gained a lot of attention. They want you to fight David Sanchez in LA two weeks from Saturday. If things go your way there, who knows what is next."

"David Sanchez, really?" Sanchez is a legend and way out of my league, or so I thought. But hell, I am up for a challenge any day. "Let's do it. I will be ready."

"Alright we'll talk soon," he says before hanging up.

I lower the phone and sit there for a moment stunned. Is this really my life now? Did that just happen? Excitement overtakes me as I reach over for Bree and pull her until she is on top of me.

"Dax? What the hell!" She shouts grumpily.

I drag her face down and kiss the hell out of her for one to shut her up and for two because I am so fucking excited. When I finally pull away, I smile up at her as I cup her flushed cheek.

"We are going to LA, baby. And it's a big one!"

My excitement is practically emanating out of every pore of my body, but I see that she isn't sharing my enthusiasm. Her face is almost instantly blank and emotionless. I can practically see the wall that she just threw up.

"California? You got a fight there?" She asks in an unaffected tone.

"Yeah, in two weeks. You will come with, right?" I ask, my voice almost pleading.

I've never had to ask her to come to a fight before. She has always been all over coming to any of them that she can. Then again, this is cross country and back to her home state, maybe things are different this time. She rolls out of bed and starts to get dressed, avoiding eye contact with me.

"I don't know, Dax. I probably have to work, plus I can't exactly afford to jet off to LA right now. But I will catch it online. You know I will be rooting for you."

My brows dip at the blatant brush off. She really isn't going to at least try to come with? She could ask Marcus for the time off. I'll pay for her plane ticket, whatever it takes. I just want her by my side.

The few moments that I have taken to think over everything were a few moments I clearly didn't have because when I glance back up, Bree is already fully dressed and reaching for her purse to head out the door. Something is up. I sprint out of bed and put my hand on the bedroom door, slamming it shut just as she began to open it. She lets out an exasperated sigh still staring at the door.

"Baby," I say in a confused tone. "Talk to me."

I grab her hand and drag her over to sit on the bed. She begrudgingly lets me pull her over until she is sitting by my side. She is staring at the carpet in front of her while I stay silent, letting her think over whatever the hell is going on inside that beautiful mind. She finally looks up to me with watery eyes.

"I can't go there, Dax. There is so much that I haven't told you, some that I am not sure I will ever be ready to tell you. There is nothing left for me there. I just can't."

Nodding slowly, I lace our fingers together as I scoot even closer to her.

"So, I take it from your reaction that you grew up in LA?"

Her eyes flick away from me as she gives a terse nod before quickly wiping at her eyes. Bree never cries, like ever. I'm not exactly sure what happened in her past or what has her so rattled that she feels like she can't even go back to that city, but whatever it is, I will be there for her every step of the way. I will protect her with my dying breath from everything, including her demons.

"I will be there. Don't think of it like you are returning home, think of it as you are going there for me, with me. I need you there, baby. I never fight the same when you aren't there. You are all I need. You don't have to tell me anything if you don't want to, I am not interested in your past. I am interested in *our* future." I pause for a moment and then add, "Please." I pour every drop of emotion into my words, hoping she can see how much it will mean to me if she comes.

After a few painfully long seconds she reluctantly nods her head and whispers, “Okay.”

I kiss her temple and pull her in to my side.

“Thank you, baby. The past can’t hurt us, and I will be right by your side to protect you from now until forever. Now let’s get these clothes back off you,” I say with a waggle of my eyebrows as she chuckles when I lift her up and flip her on her back.

I am so relieved that I will have my girl in the crowd cheering me on. I couldn’t have done any of this without her. If it wasn’t for Bree I never would have even attempted to get back into the circuit. I owe her fucking everything.

My suspicions are now obviously correct that she is hiding what seems to be a lot from her past. We all have secrets and things that we don’t want to relive twice, I get that. I just wish she felt as safe with me as I do with her to share that kind of stuff.

CHAPTER THIRTY-FOUR

Aubrey

I am zipping up my suitcase when I start to have a mini panic attack. Dax is in the parking lot waiting for me so that we can catch our flight to California. Fuck, I don't think I can do this. I ran like a fire was lit under my ass from that place. I swore to never go back and yet here I am showing back up six months later.

I don't know why the idea of being back there is so debilitating. Like Dax said, the past can't hurt me. Not anymore. It isn't like being in the same zip code will suddenly turn me into that weak scared little girl that I used to be. That girl died a long time ago. I've grown, I've changed. I am strong as hell now and a fucking fighter to the bone.

The thing that terrifies me the most about this trip is that it just serves as a reminder of all of the things that I have yet to share with Dax. It's selfish and unfair to keep so much emotional baggage from him when he has already got on the ride, but what if he learns the truth and wants to get off? That scares the fucking shit out of me.

I don't want Dax to look at me like some broken girl. I don't want him to see me as the trailer park kid. I want him to see me as just Aubrey, *his* Bree. But if I want a future with him, I know that I have to start opening up to him. I guess it started with admitting that I am from LA. It is more than anyone else could get out of me. That is all just the tip of the iceberg, though. Okay, that's it. I have made up my mind. I am going to tell Dax everything. I will tell him all of the dirty details of my life and hope to hell that he still loves me by the end of it. Yep. I am going to tell him…soon.

A few hours later, Dax and I are sitting in our seats on the plane, getting ready to take off. Neither of us have ever flown before so I am very nervous, and Dax is doing that thing where he acts like Mr. Cool and Confident but bounces his knee like a toddler on a sugar high.

Once we take off, we both relax a little but the previous dread that I have been feeling ever since Dax got that phone call sets back in. What if I run into someone that I know?

Come on, Aubrey. The city has over 2.5 million people.

I already looked up where we will be staying and where the fight is. We are so far away from Sunny Crest trailer park that we might as well be in another state, thank God.

We land smoothly and make our way to the outside of the airport and hail a taxi, well, I do. Dax is standing in the middle of the damn road looking around seemingly overwhelmed by the amount of people around us. LAX at its finest.

"Dax! You coming or should I go do weigh in for you?" I call out.

He laughs and shakes his head as he jogs over to me. We place our bags into the cab and jump in before we head to our hotel. Dax insisted on paying for my flight and his hotel room was already covered so none of that came out of my pocket, thankfully. I still feel guilty as hell to just tag along like a leech, though. I eventually gave up arguing with him about it around last week. It's not like I really had the money to blow anyways.

We get up to the room and only have enough time to drop off our stuff before Dax has to change. Weigh in is being held just downstairs so thankfully we don't have to drive anywhere to make it on time.

Soon we are walking down to the conference room where everything is being held. We don't say a word until we step into the elevator.

"I am nervous," Dax says softly under his breath.

He rarely ever acknowledges his nerves, even if I can see them plain as day. I know that there has been a lot of pressure on him lately as more and more attention is focusing on him. But that is just part of the gig, everyone wants to know about the undefeated rook who is absolutely tearing through his opponents.

"This is fucking huge, Bree. I mean, people are recognizing me just by my face. MMA commentators are talking about me. I am fucking fighting a guy that just a few months ago, I used to watch on the TV at home. It's all a lot. I don't really know what I am doing."

Dax really does look nervous. I get that he feels all this pressure to live up to all those big dreams that he has had built up in his head for so long, but I don't think he understands how much raw talent he actually has. Yeah, he may not win tomorrow against Sanchez, but everyone fucking knows it will be close regardless. Dax will fight with everything he fucking has in that cage. I just can't let him beat himself before the fight has even started.

"Hey," I say quickly, stopping him from pulling himself down any further. I grab a hold of the back of his neck with both hands and make his eyes meet mine.

"You need to knock that shit off right the fuck now. I get that you are nervous and that is okay, but you need to remember who you are. You are Dax motherfucking Hart. You are the epitome of cool, calm, collected and cocky as fucking shit. No one and nothing rattles you. You were born to do this. You are a natural and you are going to prove it tomorrow night. But tonight, you focus on three goals. Don't let the shit talking rile you up, try not to be too much of an asshole to the reporters and make weight."

He still looks hesitant until I add, "And I will be just to the side, right there with you the whole time. Once we are done, we will go out and have a drink, well, I will. You have to stay all sober and shit, so you get to supervise," I smirk as he gives me a small smile in return.

I stand on my tip toes and place a soft kiss on his full lips. That seems to help ease some of the tension because when we break apart, he stands a little taller and puts up that impassive mask of his that I am far too familiar with. The elevator doors open, and he struts out with that commanding authority that people absolutely flock to.

Weigh in goes by smoothly. Dax was stoic and intimidating as hell. He gave thoughtful and respectful answers to the reporters while Sanchez talked shit and threw jabs about Dax's lack of experience every chance that he could. He tried to rattle Dax and it thankfully didn't work.

The fact that Sanchez even tried to fuck with Dax like he did just proves to me what I already knew, he is worried about Dax. A new fighter that comes through the ranks tearing up guys this fast almost always makes it to a title fight. I am sure that Sanchez had his heart set on taking the title for himself. Commentators have speculated that whoever wins this fight will go on to fight Joseph Bernstein, the current heavyweight champion, for the title. So, the pressure is on for both of them.

As soon as Dax and I are out of the conference room, he lets out a deep breath as I hold his hand tightly. He squeezes it in return while we walk down the street until we find a little dive bar. I practically drag him inside, promising to have him in bed in two hours or less.

We take a seat at a small table in the corner. The place is pretty busy, but it is Friday night in the good part of LA, so what did we expect? Dax orders a beer for me and a seltzer with lime for him, such a chick. We both unwind after the pressure of the day and are talking about the guy that wouldn't stop snoring next to Dax on the plane when something catches my attention out of the corner of my eye.

I am laughing as my eyes flick over to see what caught my attention. I freeze when I notice at an older yet familiar man not a hundred feet away from us. His head is now shaved, and time hasn't been kind to him, but the snake neck tattoo tells me that it is *him*.

All of the color drains from my face as my heart plummets to the sticky bar floor. The familiar man must feel my gaze because he glances over to me, our eyes locking for a few moments before his expression changes from curiosity to a deep sinister grin. It sends chills down my back, and I physically shiver from the effect.

Dax notices my quick change in attitude and turns to see the man I am currently locked in a staring contest with. Dax looks back to me and then back to the man just as the guy gives me a small smile and a wink before he strides out the door with a couple other guys all in matching leather jackets with that familiar patch that is permanently burned into my brain.

I sit there frozen, unable to move, unable to breathe. I briefly considered the possibility of running into someone I knew. I never would have imagined that I would run into *him*. I haven't seen him in seven years, but he is the monster that has haunted my dreams ever since.

"Bree? Did you know that guy?" Dax asks, breaking me out of my trance momentarily. I numbly nod my head up and down, but I don't speak. I don't think that I physically can.

"Who is he?" He asks.

I turn to face Dax as my vision begins to blur with the burning tears that are brimming in my eyes. I don't answer, I just stare at him. I don't even know how to explain how I know that man. This was a part of my past that was never going to be up for discussion. Everything but this. Not this.

Dax is immediately concerned by the look on my face as he reaches out a hand to cup my cheek.

"Are you okay?"

I shake my head no and he quickly pulls out a couple of 20's, throwing them onto the table before pulling me into his side and walking us out of the bar. His arm is wrapped protectively around me as his eyes scour the streets as if he is looking for him. Good luck. Dax will never find him. He is a shadow, a ghost. You'll never be able to find him, not unless he wants to be found and if he does, then you are already dead.

CHAPTER THIRTY-FIVE

Aubrey

We make it back to our hotel room in complete silence. As soon as we step through the door, I crawl into the bed jeans and all before I curl my legs up against my chest. I close my eyes tightly, desperately trying to convince myself that this is all just a bad dream, that I am not really in the same city as that monster, the same city block.

“Baby,” Dax says, crouching in front of me. “Talk to me, you are scaring the shit out of me.”

My eyes slowly open but I don’t say anything. I just stare at him and blink.

“How do you know that guy?” Dax asks.

I blink again.

“Baby, please,” he begs, his emerald eyes clouded with concern.

I let out a strangled breath and shake my head.

“Dax, you have one of the biggest fights of your life tom

You need to get your sleep and this story is too heavy and too long," my rough voice cracks as I speak, quickly folding under the mounting fear I feel deep in my bones.

"I don't give a shit about the fight. You are my number one priority, always."

His eyes shine with so much sincerity that I have to close my eyes again. Fuck. I take a deep breath and realize that the big man upstairs must have decided that today is the day that I come clean. Here goes everything, I guess.

"I grew up in a shitty run-down trailer park on the other side of the city. My mom is probably still there. My mom has always been a party girl, but she came from a decent home. One night she hooked up with a couple of guys at a party and found out she was pregnant a few weeks later. She wasn't even sure who the father was and of course none of them wanted a thing to do with her after that night. Her parents kicked her out when she told them she was pregnant, so she was left at 17 years old homeless with a baby on the way and no fucking clue how to live her own life let alone raise another.

"We lived in a beat up one-bedroom single wide trailer. She said that the move to Sunny Crest was meant to be temporary but working double sometimes triple shifts got tiring for a teenager with a baby. She got into drugs when I was about 4 and soon realized that she could make more money having sex than working all day at the diner. Our trailer quickly became a revolving door of *clients*. Some of them were fine enough…some weren't.

"Darryl Jones, the guy at the bar, was one of mom's regulars for a couple years." I pause for a second to try to keep my voice from shaking but the emotion clogging my throat is so thick it is hard to choke back.

"I would sleep on the couch most nights since mom usually 'took care of business' in the bedroom. When Darryl first started coming around he didn't pay me too much attention. But the older I got the longer he would linger in the living room after he was done with my mom. When I was 11, he started sitting next to me for a while, he would tell me how pretty I was and most of the time we would end up watching a movie together even though he scared the living shit out of me. It wasn't long before the movies no longer held his attention, and he would t-touch me."

I stop for a moment to catch my breath and look to see Dax's reaction so far. Instead of the expected disdain or revulsion all I see is compassion and heartache. He squeezes my hand gently, silently urging me to continue.

"I was young, scared, weak. I told my mom about it, but she didn't care. She told me not to do anything to upset her best paying client so I quickly learned that she wouldn't help me. I was just a kid. I didn't know where else to turn. I was taught from a very young age that all bringing the cops around does is cause trouble. Even at 11 I knew better than to include them especially with Darryl Jones involved. When I knew him he was the roadmaster for the Snakebacks MC. He was powerful, untouchable and dangerous as fuck.

"Every night I would close my eyes and just hope that it would be over soon, I hated being so powerless but what could I do, you know? A few times I tried to fight back or push him away. He didn't like that, and I paid for my disrespect in blood and bruises. I quickly learned that if I just shut down, it would end faster than trying to resist."

My breath becomes choppy as I continue.

"Until one night when I was 12. When Darry came out to me he didn't even try to put on a movie. He went straight for my pajama bottoms. He told me that my mother was old and used up. I tried to push him away, to stop him, but he was too strong. He...he..." I swallow roughly and shake my head as I lower my voice to a whisper. "That was the first time that he done *that* to me."

I know that I don't have to explain to him what I mean, the wince that he gives me is indication enough that he understands.

"When it was finally over and he left, I ran. I was bleeding so much, and I was fucking terrified. I was terrified of him. I was terrified that it would happen again. I was terrified that that was all my life would ever be. So, I just…ran. I kept going until I hunkered down against the side of a building a few miles away. I was only wearing a baggy sleep shirt that was slightly torn from my struggling and it began to rain. I knew that it was unusually cold that night, but I felt nothing. I was just numb.

"After a little while, a man came out of a door a few feet away from me. I was so fucking scared that I fell on my ass before I scrambled to my feet and attempted to hide like an injured animal. I didn't know who he was or what he was going to do to me. All I knew was that I couldn't let him do what Darryl just did. I knew even then that I wouldn't survive it a second time. The man seemed confused at first until he saw my torn shirt, the blood trickling down my bare thighs and the general look of terror that was in my eyes."

I shake my head and close my eyes as I feel several large tears stream down my cheeks. I have never shared this story with anyone, ever. It is just as painful as I thought it would be. Fuck.

"It was an MMA gym," I let out a dry laugh as I shake my head. "Of course, right? I stumbled upon an MMA gym during fight night and the owner, Gary, came out thinking that I was a druggie or something. When I told him how old I was he cursed under his breath and asked if I had anywhere safe to stay the night. I told him no and he brought me inside, after a fuck ton of coercing. I wasn't exactly in a trusting mood, but he was very kind and spoke very softly to me.

"He made sure that he kept a good amount of distance from me at all times, gave me a fresh t-shirt and some way too big sweatpants and even got one of the fighters' girlfriends to sit with me while fight night carried on. As odd as it sounded, I wanted to be around people. I didn't want to sit in a quiet room that I didn't know. I wanted the noise, I needed it.

"I sat there for what felt like hours as I numbly watched people beat the living shit out of each other. Some were fighting out of rage, some out of fear, but to all it was a release, an escape. I wanted that. I wanted to escape, to feel powerful, to feel free.

"Gary let me sleep on the pull-out couch in his office that night and even gave me some left-over pizza. The next morning when I woke up, him and some of the guys were already training. I hung around for a bit and they even stopped what they were doing to show me a few basic self-defense moves. When I knew I couldn't stay there any longer, Gary and the guys offered to train me for free. I just had to take it seriously and show up on time every day.

"For three weeks, I showed up every day right on time. I learned a lot in such a short amount of time and even started becoming friends with a lot of them. They took me in when I needed help, let me join their family. Some of the other fighters weren't too much older than me at the time which was nice to have some people that were relatable at least in age. No one actually knew what happened to me. Obviously they came to their own conclusions but at the end of the day they all knew that I just needed help."

I cringe and my stomach sours as I think about the next thing that happened. Fuck, it may have been seven years, but it feels like it has been seven minutes. I remember everything…vividly.

"One day I didn't make it, though. I was late for school and stupidly forgot my change of clothes at home. So, after school I tried to sneak into the trailer and grab my stuff quickly before slipping back out. Of course, who do I find sitting on the couch, almost like he was waiting for me?" I ask dryly as Dax clenches his jaw, a white-hot fire burning in his eyes as he waits for me to continue.

"He grabbed me by the throat instantly. My mind panicked for a moment. I froze under his touch, petrified with fear. Then a thought came to me, I did the first thing that the guys told me to always do if you are out matched. I grabbed the closest thing to me to use as a weapon which happened to be a glass ashtray and hit him over the head with it. I thought it would be enough to get away from him so that I could run. Unfortunately for me he recovered too quickly and had tackled me to the ground almost instantly. He was so mad, he just started raining punches down on me. I tried to fight, to use the skills that the guys had taught me, but I was only into the basics at that point. I basically only knew how to throw some simple jabs and block, obviously not well enough, though.

"When I felt him tear my jeans off, I felt like I was going to die. I wanted to if it meant that I didn't have to live through that again. I fought, bit and scratched with everything I had but it wasn't enough. He was…in…me and I eventually just shut down. I felt so defeated, so broken. I stared at the front door, wishing there was a way that I could get to it but knowing that I wasn't that lucky.

"As if my wishes conjured him, my friend Julian from the gym stepped up to our porch and peeked in through the side window. Gary sent him to look for me since I was running late, I guess he had a bad feeling and wanted to make sure that I was okay."

I shake my head as I look up to the ceiling briefly before looking back to Dax.

"I will never forget the look of horror that washed over his face when he realized what was happening. He was only 15, we were just kids. I am sure that it was the last thing that he expected to see. Julian kicked down the door almost immediately and ran at Darryl, tackling him off me before throwing a brutal punch to his temple. It instantly knocked Darryl out and Julian wasted no time helping me stand before getting me as far away from Darryl as we could. Despite my protests, Julian called the cops, and he rode with me in the ambulance to the hospital.

"One broken nose, two fractured ribs, a concussion and a face full of bruises later, I landed myself a spot in the hospital for a week. With Darryl's obvious ties to the Snakebacks and the extent of my injuries it landed him ten years in prison. Guess he got out early or something since that was only seven years ago," I trail off for a moment, looking at the ground before I glance up to Dax.

His fists are tensed into balls so tight on my thighs that his knuckles have turned white. His jaw is clenched so hard that I am sure it could cut steel in this moment. Anger is literally vibrating off his body. I know he is trying to keep it together for me, but it looks to be a losing battle.

"As soon as they let me out of the hospital, I practically lived at the gym. I would rarely go home and I lived and breathed MMA. They were my family, my chosen family. They were the only people that had ever gave a shit about me, they practically raised me. It was hard to come to Glenfield and leave them behind but if I stayed, I would always be haunted by my past. I wanted more for my life, and they wanted more for me too."

I blow out a breath and nod my head signaling the end. Fuck, I expected to feel relieved after finally getting all of it off my chest but instead I feel raw, weak and uncomfortable as fuck. I look to Dax expectantly, but he doesn't say anything. He just stares at me. I don't know if I actually want to know what he is thinking right now. Does he look down on me? Does he see me as a victim, a weakling? That would be the fucking worst.

Then after a few minutes, he pulls me into his arms, holding me so tight, like if he holds on just a little bit tighter he will be able to protect me from all of the past hurt all these years later. We stay like that for a while before he murmurs into my hair.

"I am so proud of you, Bree." I pull back and give him a confused look as he continues. "You went through something horrible at a young age and you didn't skip a beat. You learned how to protect yourself when someone else should have been doing that for you. You kept on moving, you didn't let the bad times define you, you let it drive you. That is just one of the many things that made me fall in love with you. You are so strong and brave. You are a true fighter."

Damn. That wasn't at all what I expected. But I can't deny the relief that washes through me at his words

"I'm scared. I have been scared for years that he would find me one day and-"

"Shh," Dax soothes softly as he runs his fingers through my hair. "He can't hurt you anymore. I will never let anyone hurt you again."

I give him a watery smile that makes his hardened face soften ever so slightly.

"I love you, baby," he says gently.

"I love you," I whisper.

Dax crawls into bed next to me and tucks me into his side, slowly stroking my arm. I am almost asleep when he whispers, "I'm here. I'll always be here to protect you."

I burrow my face deeper into his chest and fall into the heaviest sleep of my life.

CHAPTER THIRTY-SIX

Dax

I woke up the next morning feeling like absolute fucking shit. It wasn't just the lack of sleep, though that part didn't help. I knew Aubrey had a rough background, but I had no fucking clue that it was all of *that*. I am sure there is a fuck ton more too, she only told me about two nights really. Knowing that I was in the same room as the man that broke not only her body, but her spirit, has me ready to explode. My temper is a ticking time bomb, and I am not sure how long I will be able to keep it in check.

Everything that Bree told me last night just confirmed what I already knew. This girl is resilient as fuck, she is more badass than anyone I have ever met, and I think I fell in love with her even more if that were even possible. I could see the concern on her face like she actually thought that what she went through was going to push me away. Clearly, she doesn't understand how deep my feelings for her run. I meant it when I said that I am in this forever with her, and it feels so fucking good to know that she trusts me enough to tell me the good, the bad and the super fucking ugly.

We say our goodbyes an hour before the fight, and she leaves me with encouraging words and a heart stopping kiss. I have to get down to the locker room and mentally prep and warm up while she heads to the arena with Cameron as her escort. Knowing that we are in the same city as that piece of shit, I wasn't taking any risks. Cameron is getting one of the trainers from the gym to sit with her so that she isn't alone, just in case.

My time to unleash all of my anger is almost here. I'll admit that I was nervous just yesterday that I may not have enough in me to take down Sanchez, not anymore though. I feel almost sorry for the fucker because I have never felt so amped up in my whole life. I am going to fucking annihilate him.

I am standing at the entrance of the walkway to the cage when I hear Sanchez's music play before he struts down his side, working the crowd and preening at the attention. I just bounce in place and shake my head, cocky bastard. Once he is in the cage my music plays and I waste no time. I walk steadily down the path to the octagon, my eyes zeroed in on Sanchez. It's too slight for anyone else to probably notice but his cocky smirk slips just a bit when he sees the daggers that I am throwing him. We stand in front of each other ready to start and I take a moment to picture Sanchez as the prick from last night. He's fucking *dead.*

Taking every ounce of rage that I was trying to contain last night, I let it all fly at the commencement of the fight. Sanchez throws a light punch to test his reach and I immediately counter with a hit to his ribs. He grunts and jumps back to the side as he rears back for a jab that I easily dodge. I don't wait for his next move as I storm towards him, throwing out a fake left jab before bringing my right leg up for a kick against his knee. I hear a loud crack, but he surprisingly doesn't go down. Unsurprisingly, he does his best to keep weight off of it as he winces in pain and begins slowly hobbling backwards.

Come back here, you little bitch.

I don't let him get too far before I throw a quick leg and jab combo, ending with a right hook to his jaw that hits so hard his entire body spins in a full circle before he collapses to the ground. I go to continue this fight on the ground when the ref quickly rushes to Sanchez, somehow stopping me in my tracks. The fight is immediately declared a TKO and the crowd goes fucking nuts. The sound is damn near deafening, but I couldn't give a fuck. With my chest rapidly rising and falling, I look out to where I know Aubrey's seat is and see her going absolutely ape shit, jumping and yelling her head off.

One solid punch to the face and I took down one of the stars of the Heavy Weight class. The ref holds my hand up in victory and if it were possible, the crowd gets even louder. Some reporters jump into the octagon and rush to interview me. I keep it respectful and brief. I am not big on all the show boating like most guys. I come to fight and prove that I am the best, and damn if I didn't just do that. I just surprised even myself.

I told Aubrey to meet me at the locker room after the fight and when I get there, I see her standing outside of it in her black skinny jeans and sexy red tank top that I have no doubt she borrowed from Mckayla. Thank God that she did because she looks so fucking hot. Bree sees me striding towards her and runs at me, leaping into my arms and capturing my lips quickly and possessively. I grab under her thighs to keep her up and plaster her to me as I walk us into the locker room. After a moment we break the kiss and she jumps down, breathing heavily.

"I am so proud of you, babe! That was amazing! I have never seen anything like that in my entire fucking life!"

I smile and open my mouth to speak when the door bursts open and Cameron comes in frantically with a giant grin on his face.

"Kid! That was insane. They are going to be talking about that knockout for years to come. Unbelievable!"

"Thanks, Coach. Couldn't have done it without you."

He shakes his head and grips my shoulder.

"Well, I have some news and then I will leave you two to your celebration," he says with a wink making me chuckle and Aubrey groan in embarrassment as she tucks her head against my chest. "I was approached right after you left the cage. It is confirmed that two months from now you will be in Vegas fighting Joseph Bernstein for the title."

Everything around me goes quiet and the room stills. Wait, did that really just happen? Could they really be bringing in an amateur like me up for the *title*?

"Believe it, kid," Cameron says, seemingly reading my mind.

I let out a whoop and pick Aubrey up, spinning her around. As I spin her, she keeps chanting, "Oh my god!"

When I set her down she kisses me deeply and the pride shimmering in her eyes warms my entire fucking body. It makes all of this so much better to know that I have her in my corner through it all.

When we get back to the hotel we barely make it through the door before Bree is naked. I have no idea how she got her clothes off so fast, and I don't give a fuck, I am just thankful I didn't have to tear them off her body. Adrenaline is pumping through my veins harder than ever before. Maybe it is because of the big win I just pulled off, maybe it is because I am up for a title fight in just two months or maybe it is because I have the sexiest woman alive in front of me right now. Either way I am so fucking ready.

I reach for my pants and quickly drop them as I whip off the shirt that I threw on in the locker room. As soon as my cock is free from my boxers Bree's mouth is swallowing me whole.

"Holy fuck!" I shout out as her warm wet mouth sucks me deep.

Her tongue flicks against my tip before running along the length of my cock before she shoves me down her throat. I place my hands on either side of her head as I thrust against her. Fuck. I've had more blow jobs than I can count but my woman can suck a fucking dick.

When I feel that tingling at the base of my spine I quickly dislodge myself from her perfect fucking mouth.

"That's not where I want to come, baby girl," I say as I grab her hand and pull her up until she is standing as I walk over to the bed.

Bree follows me over to the bed as I lay down, grip her hips and lift her until she is on top of me.

"Now, be a good girl and ride my fucking face, baby."

Her eyes flare with lust as she practically scrambles up me until her thighs are resting on either side of my head. She wastes no time in practically suffocating me with her pussy and I can't help but groan as she does. When I flick my tongue out to brush against her clit before diving in she lets out a throaty moan that has my cock jerking. *Soon, buddy. Soon.*

As my tongue picks up its pace Bree begins grinding against me with shuddered movements. It is hot as fuck. Most women are self-conscious about sitting on a guy's face but not my woman though. She shamelessly uses my face to get herself off and I couldn't be more fucking willing.

Her breathing comes in short labored bursts and her legs tremble before her sweet tangy flavor coats my tongue. I focus on her clit, drawing out her orgasm for as long as possible before I lick her clean from top to bottom.

When she slowly lifts off of me, she looks down at me with hooded eyes and a satisfied smile. I smirk at her as I slowly lick some of her taste off of my lips.

"Hop on my cock, baby. Show me what you got."

Bree's eyebrow arches at the obvious challenge, but I know my girl, she never can say no to a challenge. She wastes no time sinking down onto my cock, causing us both to groan out in pleasure until I am fucking buried inside of her. Fuck. Yes.

Her hips begin gyrating in a motion that has my eyes rolling into the back of my head. I am all for being the alpha male and nine times out of ten I prefer to be on top, but Bree has me reconsidering that because I have never had a woman ride my cock like this before.

My hands grip her hips tightly as I begin to lift her up and down, helping push her down farther with each thrust. Reeling my hand back I clap it down on her left ass cheek and watch as her back arches and she lets out a blissful moan.

"Dax! Yes! More," she begs.

I smirk and take a fuck ton of pleasure it watching my woman go practically boneless for me. Spanking her ass again as I help speed up the pace she gasps as she reaches behind and begins massaging my balls.

"Fuck yeah, baby. Just like that. Pull the come right out of me."

She moans at my words as her walls constrict around my cock. I spank her one more time as my other hand makes quick tight circles over her clit which sends her catapulting over the edge as she screams my name so loud the front desk probably heard her.

One more brush against my balls and my body is shuddering as my cock jerks inside of her, coating her walls with my cum. I keep fucking her as I fill her with every last drop until I am fucking drained. As soon as I finish, Bree collapses on top of me in a heap. I wrap my arms around her and bury my face into her hair as our breathing eventually slows down.

Slowly, I lift her off me before laying her down on the bed. I quickly walk to the bathroom and grab a towel, wetting it down with warm water before coming back out to her. Bree is right where I left her, gorgeously naked on top of the blankets with a sated smile across her face. My inner caveman beats his chest in pride that I was the man that put that look on her face.

Crawling up the bed in between her legs I take the towel and gently clean her up. Once she is clean, I roll her over onto her stomach and slowly run my palm over her reddened skin on her ass. I softly massage it before peppering it with kisses. She mewls like a sleepy kitten at the contact before pulling me down to curl around her. I smile against her as I close my eyes and fall asleep with a cheesy ass smile on my face.

The next morning, Bree decided to show me around LA a bit, the real places to see, not the tourist trap stuff. I think she was nervous at first to run in to Darryl again, but she has one of the top Heavy Weight fighters in the UFC currently by her side, no one will be getting to her. I asked her if she wanted to go visit her old gym while we were in town. She looked surprised that I would want to go with her which just made me roll my eyes. This girl seriously doesn't get that I would follow her to the ends of the earth.

A little after lunch, we roll up to a building with bold black letters out front spelling 'Knock Out'. When we step inside, a man behind the desk looks at us and his eyes widen. His face tells me that he is in his mid-50's but he is so in shape that I am sure he could pass for late 30's.

"No fucking way. Is that my little princess?" The man asks, his eyes zoned in on Aubrey.

She lets out a wide smile and a mock eye roll.

"Easy there, old man. I can still whoop your ass," she shoots back.

He barks out a loud laugh as he walks around the counter towards her.

"I'd like to see you try, Bree. What the hell are you doing here? Aren't you in college in bumfuck Alabama?" He asks as he gives her a big hug.

"I am, but my boyfriend had a fight last night downtown, so I tagged along." She looks up to me and smiles. "Dax, this is Gary, my oldest friend, and I mean that in both ways," she says as he elbows her. "Gary, this is-"

"Dax Hart," he finishes for her before putting a handout for me to shake.

"Nice to meet you, sir," I say as I shake his hand.

"It's great to meet you. We all stayed late here and watched your fight last night, un-fucking-real. I haven't seen a knockout like that in I don't know how long."

I dip my head in thanks but Aubrey cuts in before I can speak.

"Have you heard, Gary? Dax is scheduled to fight Joseph Bernstein for the title in two months!"

I can practically hear the pride burning through her words. I love that she seems more excited than even I am, and that is hard because this feels like my every dream coming true. Gary's eyes widen and a big smile crosses his face.

"No shit? Congrats! I have always hated that punk. I hope you wipe the fucking floor with him."

I let out a rough laugh and shake my head.

"I don't know, he is the champ for a reason. I am gonna do my best, though."

Gary rolls his eyes and shoots Aubrey a look.

"Ah, a modest one. How overrated. Doesn't he know that it isn't being cocky if it's true?"

She laughs. "Oh, don't worry. He doesn't lack any in that department. I am surprised his ego fit on the plane here."

I send her a warning look and swat her ass before I smile. She just giggles before she looks over Gary's shoulder and her eyes widen.

"Julian!" She screeches before she takes off running and slams into a guy who looks to be about my age.

He is a few inches shorter than me with short brown hair and lean muscles. I am guessing he is probably a welter weight. I recognize the name immediately from what she told me the other night. This is the guy that saved my woman. If he hadn't done what he did, who knows what would have happened to her.

His eyes sparkle when he sees her and he catches her mid jump, spinning her around as they hug. I try to tamp down my jealousy, but it doesn't work very well. I don't ever want to see another man put his fucking hands on what's mine, ever. The respect and gratitude I had for him protecting her evaporates as my jealousy takes over. I am about to storm over there and tear his fucking arms out of their sockets when Gary places a hand on my shoulder.

"Don't worry about that one. Those two are like siblings. Nothing more."

I give him a sharp nod and look back at them. I don't buy it. I don't think it is possible for a man to not want Aubrey. Soon, she is dragging him back to meet me and I admit that I squeeze his hand a little harder than I probably should before I sling my arm around Aubrey possessively. To his credit, he doesn't bat an eye, just smiles affectionately at her and respectfully at me. I'm still watching him, though.

We spend a good amount of the day hanging out with the guys at the gym. Aubrey even sparred with Julian and won their first round. I shot the shit with the guys that were training, and the craziest part was that some of them were asking for my autograph. Gary was boasting about how I was the future champ and how the younger boys needed to take lessons. It was fucking surreal.

I asked Aubrey if she wanted to visit her mom down the road, but she shut that idea down real quick. Fine by me, honestly. I am not sure that I would have been able to hold my tongue if I came face to face with the woman now knowing what I know. What kind of mother could constantly put her daughter into dangerous situations like she did and not give a shit? I clench my fists at the thought of her. Fucking bitch.

We grabbed some street tacos from a little taco shack that makes the tacos back home taste like dirt before catching our flight home. Aubrey passes out on my shoulder on the plane, and I smile down at her as I watch her sleep. I can't help but think about how much has changed since we got on the plane Friday. Anything that was separating us before has been obliterated. It was scary as fuck for me to open up to her at first just like I am sure it was hard for her, but now it just feels amazing.

We make it back to my house a little while later and start unpacking. I cleared out a couple of drawers for her in my room so that she can have somewhere to put her stuff. It is also my not-so-subtle hint at wanting her to move in. Maybe I can just move her in without her even realizing and avoid the inevitable freak out that she will have over it.

"I am so grateful for you, baby," I say as I put away the last shirt in my bag.

She looks surprised for a moment, like she has never had those words spoken to her before. I guess I am going to have to say it more often. She gives me a melting smile as she zips up her suitcase.

"I am grateful for you, Dax. You know everything about me now and still, here you are. I never thought that I would find someone like you. Someone that would love the broken jagged pieces of me just as much as the rest. I didn't think that what we have even existed. So, thank you."

I stride over to her and cup her face in my hands, running my thumb over her smooth skin as I pull her in for a gentle kiss. This girl is fucking everything, and I can't wait to spend forever with her.

CHAPTER THIRTY-SEVEN

Aubrey

It is the following Sunday and Marcus is closing down The White Oak early tonight to have a party for Dax to celebrate his huge win in LA and his shot at the title. It is such a big deal, and I am so fucking proud of him. The next few months are going to be intense training as he gears up for the fight. I even had to talk him out of dropping out of school several times because he wants to spend every conscious minute at the gym. But to drop out three months before he graduates is so asinine, even he saw the light.

Because of our little impromptu trip to California, I pushed off my American History project and now it is due tomorrow, so I have to head back to my dorm to finish it up today. If I stay at Dax's, I know that I won't get anything done.

"What time do you want me to pick you up tonight, baby?" Dax asks while holding me as I try to escape to my car.

I shake my head.

"Don't worry about me. I am not sure what time I will get done. I know things are starting at 8. I promise I will get there as soon as possible."

He sighs and nuzzles against me, placing kisses up and down my neck making me giggle as I try to squirm away, but his arms lock down around me even tighter.

"Well hurry, if you take too long I am going to break down your door and drag you out with me whether you are finished or not." His face grows a little more serious for a second. "This night is for both of us. I wouldn't be here if it wasn't for you. You challenged me to want for more, to get my shit together and go after my dreams. I never would have been able to pull myself together if I didn't have you by my side." He strokes my jaw lovingly as he looks deeply into my eyes. "This is just the start for us, Bree. The possibilities are endless. And I swear I am going to spend my life taking care of you and spoiling you rotten."

I laugh at that.

"No, thank you. I can take care of myself, and I don't need to be spoiled. But I will take having you by my side."

"Forever," he whispers as his nose grazes mine and he gently kisses me one more time. I reluctantly pull away and get into the car to head back to campus.

I then spend the next ten hours barricaded in my room, pouring every ounce of energy I have into this project that I should have been working on for weeks now. Procrastination at its finest folks. I look up to my clock when I hit save and see that it is 8:15PM. Not too bad, I'll take a quick shower and be there before 9.

Once I am out of the shower, I give my hair a quick blow dry and throw on a pair of jeans and one of my band t-shirts. I check my phone as I am leaving and see that I don't have any messages or calls from Dax which is kind of odd since we usually can't stop talking. He must have been trying to leave me alone so that I would actually get some stuff done. I do see that I have a missed call from Kayla and Cole. Whatever, I will see them in like three minutes.

Ever since Dax told me about his mom, I stopped walking to The White Oak and started driving. He never asked me to do it, but I could practically see the relief in his eyes every time he saw my car in the parking lot. I would do anything to put his mind at ease. Besides he is protective as fuck enough as it is, which I secretly love but will definitely never admit to.

When I pull up to The White Oak I can hear the music bumping from outside and see that the parking lot is packed. Sometimes I forget just how popular Dax is, how many people are desperate for even a moment of his attention. To me he is just Dax, my Dax. He is kind of an asshole but a hot asshole, so I will keep him around.

I open the door and walk in to see throngs of college kids swarming the space. I look around for a few moments but don't see any sign of Dax or Kayla. I make my way to the front of the crowd and see that Cole is bartending. We make eye contact, and his eyes widen as I give him a wave. What the fuck? He stops what he is doing and rushes over to me quickly.

"Hey, have you seen Dax?" I ask.

"Let's go to the break room for a second. I need to talk to you," he replies, ignoring my question.

"Yeah, ok. Just let me say hi to Dax so that he knows I made it. He is probably fucking pissed that I am already an hour late."

I step around Cole and start weaving my way through the people when Kayla frantically rushes in front of me.

"Hey, Kayla. Have you seen Dax?"

I try to step around her to look towards the back of the bar, but she mirrors my movement. When I glance over my shoulder, I see that Cole is standing right behind me with his hand on my elbow, gently pulling me backwards. I furrow my brows. Something is definitely up.

"What's going on guys?" I ask warily.

They exchange grimaces as they look to each other for a moment. I take their momentary distraction to peek around Kayla. My eyes instantly land on what they were trying so hard to keep me from seeing.

Dax is sitting in a corner booth with Chase and some other girls, and there straddling Dax's lap with her tongue down his throat is Julie. She is grinding on top of him while his hand is resting on her ass. Ice fills my veins as I blink slowly, trying to wake up from this horrible dream. This can't be real, right? There has to be some logical explanation. That can't be my Dax cheating on me in plain sight at a party that he knew I would be at just hours after we were in bed together and he was telling me he would love me forever.

It fucking is him though and it is fucking happening. Bile fills my throat, but I quickly shove it down before I storm past Kayla. I hear her and Cole shouting for me to stop but I can't, I don't know if I could physically stop at this point. Chase is the first to see me and he gives me a smug grin and raises a questioning eyebrow, but I don't have time for his bitch ass tonight.

I spin to face Dax and grab a handful of Julie's red hair before I rip her off him and toss her onto the floor. She lets out a yelp before her body slams to the ground and I can't help but give her a solid punch to the face before I turn back to my piece of shit boyfriend.

A confused Dax looks up at me as if he doesn't understand where his make-out buddy went. *Un-fucking-believable.* Before he can say anything, I punch him with everything I can, making his nose explode from the impact.

"Woah!" he shouts as blood begins to pour down his face.

"How could you!" I roar in his face.

He just sits there blinking while attempting to hold his bleeding nose. Did this asshole really think that I wouldn't catch him? Or does he just not give a fuck? Based on the lack of excuses or explanations

I would guess the latter. Well, fuck him and fuck this. I knew all of this shit about love was complete and utter horseshit. A guy like Dax could never settle down with one girl and I clearly needed the harsh reminder considering the naïve bubble that I was living in.

I rip the forever bracelet off my wrist and throw it at his face. He makes no move to grab it while he looks at me blankly with a haziness cloaking his eyes. I look around at all of the beer bottles on the table and shake my head. Great, he is so shit faced that I can't even effectively yell at him. I close my eyes and blow out a long breath.

"You said that I could trust you," I say quietly, the anger still oozing from my words. "You said that you wouldn't crush me. But no one has ever hurt me like you just did, not even *him*. Don't ever come near me again."

I turn around to see Julie standing there with a Cheshire grin on her rapidly swelling face while her phone is pointed straight at me as well as some of her cronies' phones. I snatch her phone from her hand and smash it under my foot before I head butt the bitch.

The screech that she lets out could probably be heard from all around the world, so I decide to do everyone a favor and shut the bitch up by pulling my knee up and burying it into her stomach until she gasps for air.

I shoulder check some other bitch out of my way as I begin to storm towards the door. Kayla and Cole flank me on either side, each wrapping an arm around me. I brush them off and hold my head high as I march out of the bar even though I can fucking *feel* all of the eyes on me. Dax already made me look like a fool. I won't let all of these fuckers see me crumble.

Just before I go through door, I glance up and make eye contact with Marcus. Sympathy and disappointment fill his expression as he shakes his head sadly and wipes down the bar top. Yeah, I am disappointed in him too. But most of all, I am disappointed in me.

I pull out my keys and try to put the key in the lock three times before I step back and realize that I am shaking so bad that I can't even put the damn thing in. Cole cautiously wraps and arm around my shoulders and walks me over to the passenger seat of Betty before he goes around and gets into the driver's seat. Kayla gets into her car and follows us back to campus.

When we get there, Cole jogs out like normal to get my door. I stand to get out as everything suddenly hits me all at once. I can't push it away anymore. The hurt is absolutely debilitating, and I crumble into a heap on the parking lot ground. I let out harsh loud angry sob as Cole immediately scoops me up into his arms and starts carrying me like a child. I cling to his shirt and bury my head into his neck as I bawl my fucking eyes out.

We make it up to my room and Cole sits down on my bed, still cradling me when I notice that Kayla has followed us in. She immediately walks to my mini freezer and pulls out a gallon of ice cream. When she tries to offer it to me, I turn my head away and burrow deeper into Cole. I can't do anything but cry right now and I know for a fact that Cole holding me is the only thing that is keeping me somewhat together.

At some point I hear the door shut and I assume it was Kayla that decided to head home. Cole only moves once to lay down and once I get settled underneath his arm we don't move an inch all night. I stay pressed against him like he is my lifeline.

I inhale the smell of laundry detergent and fresh pine until my breathing evens out. My tears finally run out hours later and for the rest of the night I lay there numb. I can't believe I was so stupid to willingly give my heart up to someone like him. Everyone told me this would happen, and I didn't listen. I believed the lie. I fell for the bullshit. I can't even convince myself to be angry at Dax anymore, this is just who he is. If he walks like a duck and quacks like a duck...then I am clearly a fucking idiot if I expect him to be anything other than a fucking duck.

CHAPTER THIRTY-EIGHT

Dax

I wake up and instantly regret it. Holy shit. I have never been this hungover in my life. I look around to see that I am in the breakroom of The White Oak. Did I pass out in here last night? What the fuck?

I go to stand but fall back down instantly. I feel shaky as fuck and my stomach is rolling. My heartbeat thunders in my chest like a motherfucking drum as my mouth waters. Oh fuck. I quickly lean over the trashcan to the side and puke for what feels like fucking hours. When I finally stop, I rest my head against the wall. Damn. I didn't think I even drank that much last night. Although honestly, when I try to think really hard about last night it's pretty much all a blank. Guess it was a hell of a party then. Fuck I am going to need one hell of a hangover cure to shake this shit off.

Slowly, I try to stand again and am thankful that I finally can without collapsing, progress. I hold on to the wall as I open the door and carefully make my way through the bar. When I step out from the back, I see sunlight streaming in through the front windows while Uncle Marcus is getting ready to open the place.

"About time that you woke up, princess," he says gruffly, not looking my way.

"What happened last night?" I rasp, my voice hoarse and my throat dry as fuck. I walk over to the soda fountain and pour myself a water, downing it in two gulps before refilling the cup and repeating.

"You made the biggest mistake of your life, that's what." I furrow my brows in confusion and look at him before he continues. "You know, I thought that I raised you to be a better man. I damn well know that if your mother was alive, she would beat the hell out of you after the shit that you pulled."

He shakes his head in disgust and my temper flares at the mention of my mother.

"What happened?" I grit out.

I walk over to one of the stools at the bar top and lower my pounding head into my hands as I try to think about what happened last night. I remember getting to the party and the place was already fucking packed. Everyone was there. Even Chase.

"Hey, man," Chase says as he walks up to me with his shoulders hunched and his hands buried in his pockets.

I glance at him skeptically. I thought that I made it very clear that I never wanted anything to do with him again. I am pretty sure that pulverizing someone's face and then taking off on them is a universal sign for that. Chase must be able to read my mind because he lowers his head in resignation.

"I'm sorry for everything I said. I was being an ass. I guess I didn't really understand how strongly you felt for Aubrey. I get it now and you had every right to beat the hell out of me. I would have done the same. But we have been friends for over a decade, man. Don't let me being a dick ruin that. I am really sorry."

I watch him carefully for a few moments. Chase does not own up to his shit easily, if ever, so this is big for him. He must have realized he really fucked up. And he is right, I have missed the fucker. As long as he never opens his mouth about Aubrey again, we are good.

I give him a nod, accepting his apology as he claps my shoulder and hands me a beer with a relieved smile. I accept it and drain it in quickly. We shoot the shit for a while and have a couple more beers while I wait for Aubrey to get here. I am about 5 minutes away from hauling her over my shoulder and dragging her here whether her stupid project is finished or not. I might have to walk though because I am already feeling kinda fucked up.

*Julie has been annoying as shit tonight. She keeps scooting towards me, trying to get as close as possible. I keep shrugging her away, but the bitch is persistent as fuck. I grab another beer before I head to the bathroom. Then...*nothing.

I must have blacked out after that because no matter how hard I try, I can't remember one more tiny detail until I woke up this morning. Just before Marcus goes to speak, my phone dings with a notification. I pull it out and see that I was tagged in a video.

I click on the notification and the screen changes to what looks like the party from last night. The video starts off directed right at me while Julie is grinding on top of my lap. We are making out like the world is about to end while my hands cup her ass.

Oh my fucking god.

My eyes widen and my stomach drops to the ground at the sight. Suddenly, Julie's hair is ripped backwards as she falls to the floor. I don't have to keep watching to know who ripped her off my lap, but I can't look away.

Bree comes into view looking absolutely furious. She screams at me, asking how could I. Shit, I am thinking the same fucking thing right now, but Dax in the video has zero reaction, he just stares at her. Bree rips the bracelet that I gave her for Christmas off her wrist and throws it at my chest.

Then she takes a breath and says, "You said that I could trust you. You said that you wouldn't crush me. But no one has ever hurt me like you just did, not even him. Don't ever come near me again."

The venom and raw pain in her words literally knocks me on my ass. I almost fall off the barstool before I bury my fingers deep into my hair and pull fucking hard. What the fuck! This cannot be happening. This has to be a prank or something.

As I am trying to run through plausible scenarios in my head, Marcus comes up next to me and sets Bree's bracelet down on the bar top before clapping my shoulder. He shakes his head as he looks at me, disgust plainly written across his face.

"I will always love you, but I am so disappointed in you."

He walks away and heads back to his office, his door shutting with a solid thud.

Well, no hangover cure needed. I am fucking stone cold sober. I sit there in fucking shock for another moment before I jump into action. I have to see her. I need to explain that I don't remember any of that. That it wasn't me, that's not who I am anymore. I would never do anything to hurt her, especially not something so publicly humiliating. She is my fucking world. I can't lose her. I fucking can't.

I jump in my car and break every traffic law to get to her as fast as possible. When I get to campus, I race up to her dorm room and pound my fist against the door almost desperately until it finally opens. Only it isn't Bree that opens the door.

Cole steps through the door and shuts it behind him before crossing his arms over his fucking shirtless chest. What the ever-loving fuck is this little shit doing in my woman's bedroom half naked? I clench my fists into balls at my sides, channeling all of my self-restraint so that I don't knock him the fuck out right now.

Focus, Dax. Bree.

"What the *fuck* are you doing here?" I ask in my most threatening tone.

I've got to hand it to him. His face stays completely unfazed by the impending threat of my fists. Either he is really fucking brave or really fucking stupid.

"I could ask you the same thing," he scoffs.

"I am her boyfriend," I snap back.

I am fucking seething now. This piece of shit clearly spent the night with Aubrey. If they did anything more than sleep, I will fucking tear him to shreds.

He lets out a humorless chuckle as he shakes his head.

"Not after last night you aren't."

His words shake off some of my rage for a moment and I remember that I am the one who fucked up here. I came to beg for fucking forgiveness, not start a fight with Cole Simmons. I have way more important shit to do. Images of the video from last night flicker through my head, instantly filling me with remorse and disgust in myself.

"I don't remember anything from last night. I wasn't in my right mind," I mumble even though I sure as fuck don't owe him an explanation.

"Clearly," he replies sharply.

Alright, I am officially fucking done with him. I go to move around him so that I can talk to Bree, but he blocks my path. I cock my head to the side to figure out if Cole is really stupid enough to pick a fight with me. Is he for real?

"You aren't going in there. She is asleep, finally. After spending the first half of the night sobbing and second half of the night numbly staring at a blank wall because of how badly *you* destroyed her."

His words gut me. To think that Bree was hurting so bad, and I wasn't there. No, worse. To know that she was hurting so bad because of me slices me fucking deep. How could I have allowed something so awful to happen and ruin the best thing that I have ever had in my whole fucking life?

"You need to leave her alone, Dax. You and I both know that she is tough as nails. She can take practically anything that is thrown at her and keep on moving, but this?" He shakes his head solemnly. "It will take a while for her to recover from this, and you have to fucking let her. Do the right thing and let her go. You were never good enough for her anyways and you sure as hell proved that last night."

Instead of getting angry at his words, I lower my head in defeat. Fuck if he isn't right. I fucking blew it. I broke an already broken girl. I've never fucking deserved her. She is too good for anyone in this life. She is a dark jagged beautiful angel. Despite the fucking shit life that she has led she has a heart of fucking gold. And I fucked it all up.

I turn around slowly as I make my way back down the hallway. Before I round the corner I look over my shoulder at Cole.

"You don't deserve her either," I say hoarsely, emotion catching in my throat.

He nods and shrugs.

"Probably not. But I am a hell of a lot better for her than you."

He's right. I fucking hate his guts, but he is right. I was the first person that Aubrey ever trusted with her heart, and I stomped on it right in front of her. Fuck. I still don't get it. I don't even like Julie. I haven't found a single woman attractive since I met Aubrey, it's always been her. If I didn't see the video for myself, I would tell you that I would never have done that, no matter how drunk I was. But the evidence is out there for everyone to see how I carelessly threw away my entire fucking future.

I decide to blow off classes today before I get in my car and just drive. I start to head home but it only reminds me of all the times that Aubrey and I spent together there or about how I was trying to get her to move in just yesterday. I just can't go back there right now.

I could go to the gym and train for a while, but I really don't fucking want to be around anyone. Besides, what if she shows up? Despite my earlier plan to beg for her forgiveness and apologize, I'm not really sure that I could face her. Cole was right. I have to let her heal. I have to let her get over the hurt that I caused.

I drive until I find myself at the all too familiar cemetery up the road from my house. I blow out a ragged breath and walk up to my mom's grave. Slowly, I slump down to the ground as I take a seat before I put my head in my hands.

"Hey ma," I rasp softly. "I am sure you already know, but I fucked up. I lost her. I need her so fucking bad, but even I know that I don't deserve her."

CHAPTER THIRTY-NINE

Aubrey

I wake up late in the day, my eyes puffy and throat dry. Hours of constant crying will do that to you, I guess. I blink blearily when I hear a voice come from a few feet away.

"Hey, how are you feeling?"

Cole is standing in front of me with a coffee outstretched in one hand and a bag of something delicious smelling in the other. I sit up and accept the coffee as he sits next to me.

"So, I guess since you are here it means that all of that really happened last night?" I ask quietly, staring at the floor.

Cole grimaces and squeezes my knee in answer. I let out a choppy breath before I shake my head, physically shoving all of the pain and hurt down.

"It's okay, Cole. I'm fine. I get knocked down. I get back up. I guess I was just surprised. But I am good. I'm over it."

He gives me a dubious look and his voice is surprisingly curt

“Darlin’, stop. I don’t know who you are trying to convince, but you are definitely not good and it’s okay to not be. I know you have been strong your whole life but in this one moment you don’t have to be, lean on me. Let yourself fall apart. I will catch you every time.”

Slowly, I lean up and move until I am curled up in his lap, straddling him as I bury my face into his neck.

“You were right, he broke my heart,” I murmur.

Cole pulls me back and looks at me, his sapphire eyes swimming with so much emotion as what looks like pain flashes across his face.

“I wish I wasn’t. I would do anything in the world to take away this hurt,” he says almost desperately.

I nod sadly before shrugging.

“I guess the egg is on my face in the end though, huh? I am sure everyone is talking about what an idiot I am.”

“No. You are not the one in the wrong here, darlin’. He fucked up. He is the fucking loser here. Not you. You are-you are fucking perfection,” he whispers softly before he slowly leans forward brushing his lips against mine.

When I don’t pull away he deepens the kiss before he takes hold of my face gently, bringing me closer to him. I move my lips against his and can’t help but compare. There is no spark like with Dax, it doesn’t make me feel like my heart is going to beat out of my chest. I don’t feel like this is the end of life as I know it. But look where all of that got me. Maybe I was never in love with Dax. Maybe we just shared wild passionate crazy lust. Regardless of whatever we had, I want absolutely no part of it ever again.

The next several weeks go by pretty fucking painfully. There are times that are harder than others, but I try to bury it all. Despite my best efforts though, I still find myself laying in bed late at night thinking of him, of all the memories and promises that we shared. Then I remember what bullshit they all were, and I cry my fucking eyes out. Even though I would never admit that to anyone.

Cole has stayed glued to my side ever since that night and I am really grateful for the distraction that he provides. We haven't done anything other than hold hands and the occasional soft peck here or there. I think that he is letting me process things before he tries to be anything more than friends, and with our history, that is probably for the best. As much as I would love to make him happy and give myself fully to him, I just don't think I ever could. I thought I would be over Dax by now, but he occupies my mind almost constantly.

I haven't seen him since that night. Cole told me he tried to come see me the morning after, but he turned him away. I was in no shape to see Dax at the time, and I am thankful for Cole doing that. Honestly though, I am surprised he gave me up so easily. I figured he would have thrown himself at my feet and said all of the cliché bullshit about how it was just a mistake or a lapse of judgment. That it would never happen again, and how he only loves me. But instead, I got nothing. Maybe he was done with whatever little game he was playing with me, and this was the easiest way for him to duck out. I guess I never really knew the real him.

It has now been 52 days since we broke up and the big title fight is tomorrow. Obviously, me knowing exactly how many days it has been and what is going on in his life proves that I am definitely not over him. Maybe I am destined to be hung up on the asshole forever.

I am meeting Cole for lunch at Kramer's after classes today. It has become a regular thing for us over the last few weeks. Unfortunately, my appetite hasn't been up to much lately.

When I step inside the shop, I see that Cole is already seated with a big smile on his face as he sees me walk in.

"Hey!" He says enthusiastically, jumping up from his seat before kissing me on the cheek.

"Hey," I reply with a smile, trying so fucking hard to show people that I am okay on the outside.

We both get some ice cream and mindlessly chat for a little before the mood suddenly changes.

"So, darlin', I actually wanted to talk to you," Cole says while reaching out and grabbing one of my hands. His thumb lightly strokes the back of it as he does. I look up to him and see that there is a seriousness behind his eyes.

"How are you doing?" he asks tentatively.

I screw on my smile as I nod.

"I am doing a lot better." I continue nodding before I add on, "I am good," just to really sell it.

How am I supposed to tell him that I feel like I am walking around without a heart because Dax played hackey sack with it before tossing it in the trash?

Cole sighs heavily as he shakes his head.

"You're not. I know you, Aubrey. We are best friends. I have learned your tells by now and you are lying. So how are you really?"

My façade cracks slightly at him calling me on my bullshit and my smile drops until it vanishes completely.

"I wish I was better," I say honestly.

He nods, worrying his bottom lip between his teeth before he looks up.

"You are never going to get over him, are you? You are never going to love me like you love him."

He phrases the latter more like a statement than a question, like he already knows the answer.

"I wish I could," I say under my breath.

"You are going to take him back, aren't you?

I just shrug.

"He doesn't even want me back, so it's irrelevant either way."

I don't know if I would take Dax back if he asked. Could I really hold my own self-worth so low to allow someone who hurt me, slaughtered me, back in for seconds? But if life continues like this without him, do I even have a choice?

"If he asked, would you be with him again? Would anything stop you from being with him?"

I can tell that Cole is asking for his own sake and I can't blame him. He is scared that if we ever got together, and Dax came back asking for another chance that I would drop him and run to Dax. And I can't in good conscious ease his fear because I don't know what I would do. My silence must speak for itself because he nods to himself as if finally understanding that there will never be an us.

"I know I said it before, but you have to know that if you give him your heart again he is going to break it."

I sigh knowing the truth in his words now more than ever. Shrugging softly, I tilt my head slightly.

"Maybe, but it's his to break."

Cole winces slightly. I can tell that my words hurt him and I fucking hate myself for that. But I have been lying to myself and everyone else, pretending that I am not still in love with Dax, and I hate myself for that just as much.

"I love you, Aubrey. I think I always will," he says earnestly.

The finality of his tone makes this feel like goodbye. I wish it didn't have to be this way but for both of our sakes, it is probably best. I squeeze his hand and give him a sad smile.

"I wish I could love you the way you love me, more than anything."

He seems to take a small amount of comfort in that. He stands up, places a kiss on the top of my head and walks out of the shop. I know that us stopping whatever weird limbo thing we have been in is for the best, but as I glance around the empty ice cream shop, the cold sets in and I have never felt so fucking alone.

Kayla texted me a few hours later and said that she was coming over. We spent the night watching bad horror movies and eating junk food while we talked about Cole and Dax. She agreed that Cole and I parting ways was in the best interest of both of us but as far as Dax goes she didn't really have much opinion. She told me that I needed to listen to my heart. I told her that I couldn't do that because my heart has proven herself to be a traitorous bitch.

In the morning, we are woken up by a hard knock on the door.

"If it isn't Channing Tatum, don't answer it," Kayla murmurs with her head still buried into the pillow.

I let out a laugh and get out of bed as I walk over to answer the door. I am absolutely shocked to see Chase standing in the hallway with a sullen expression.

"Chase?" I ask confused. "What do you want?" My tone turns hard so fast that he actually grimaces from the intensity that it holds.

He can't seriously think that I have forgotten about all the times that he has treated me like shit, right?

"Hey, Aubrey," he says, scratching the back of his neck awkwardly. "Uh, can I come in?"

"No," I reply instantly before I slam the door in his face.

Un-fucking-believable. He knocks again and when I don't answer he starts talking through the door.

"Aubrey, please. I need to talk to you. It's about Dax. I-I, shit. I fucked up."

That gets my attention. I reluctantly open the door, narrowing my eyes on the piece of shit.

Talk," I grit out as I cross my arms defensively across my chest.

Chase brushes past me and steps into my room where a groggy Kayla sits up, looking at our intruder with the same amount of venom that I am. Girl power.

"I fucked up," he says again. I raise an eyebrow, prompting him to continue. "I don't like you. That hasn't been a secret." I scoff at that. "I thought that you were just a phase for Dax, a challenge and then he would move on. But he didn't, and then I thought maybe he just forgot what else was out there. I missed my best friend. He never hung out with anyone but you and when he did all he did was text you or talk about you."

Oh, I get it. So, not only was he embarrassed that a woman took him to the ground in front of all of his buddies, but he was also jealous that his best friend didn't want to stay attached at his hip all the time. How fucking pathetic.

"How did you fuck up?" I ask, hoping to skip to the fucking point.

Chase grimaces as he wipes a hand down his face.

"I slipped a ton of E into his beer and then had Julie come on to him. It was supposed to relax him so that he would just go with the flow. I must have given him too much because he was a fucking zombie. He couldn't speak, couldn't stand. His uncle and I had to put him in the breakroom to sleep it off at the end of the night because he didn't think that he could carry him up the stairs at home. Dax had no idea what he was doing and if you look close enough at the video you can see that he wasn't even engaging with Julie. It was more like he was just sitting there unable to move."

I stand there for a moment absorbing all of this information before I erupt.

"You drugged him!"

Before he can respond, I swing back and punch him across the face making him drop to the ground cradling his jaw as he continues.

"He is completely miserable without you," he says from the floor, watching me carefully like he expects me to attack him again. Not the worst idea. "He won't eat, won't sleep, won't even hardly leave his house. He doesn't even lay in his bed anymore. He insists on sleeping on the couch in the garage. Says it is the only thing that still smells like you. Cameron called me this morning and told me that Dax looks like shit and can barely stand up straight. He has run himself into the ground and now there is no way he will even be able to fight, let alone win. It will all be over in two seconds."

"If he has been so miserable without me then why hasn't he tried to talk to me since that morning? If he really isn't guilty then why hasn't he tried to explain to me-"

"Explain what?" Chase cuts off as he stands up. "Dax thinks that he got black out drunk and cheated on you. What is there to explain? In his eyes he fucked up and he has convinced himself that he doesn't deserve you or your forgiveness. But there is nothing to forgive! It wasn't his fault, it was mine."

So fucking true. I punch him on the other side of the face this time and he falls down again. I can't believe this piece of shit is the reason all of this happened. Dax didn't cheat on me. He was drugged and taken advantage of at the hands of his best friend and a desperate bitch.

"So, you haven't told him what you did? Does he even know that he wasn't in control that night?" I bite out.

Chase just shakes his head, looking ashamed.

"Well, what the fuck do you want me to do about it? I have no way of getting a hold of him. You know he turns off his phone this close to a big fight and if he is in as bad of shape as you say, I doubt a fucking phone call will fix anything anyways."

He shrugs. "Can you go to Vegas? You might make the fight if you leave right now. You could see him before."

I shake my head and toss my hands out at my sides.

"Even if I could jump on a plane and fly across the country, I have no way of paying for such flight or making sure that there is a flight that could get me there on time or that it would have any open seats."

"Maybe not commercial," Kayla pipes in. "But a private jet would do the trick."

I roll my eyes at her.

"Good plan, Kayla. Do you have a private jet we can borrow?" I ask sarcastically, but she just stares at me with a serious expression. "Wait, you do?" She shrugs like it isn't a big deal as she stretches. "How fucking loaded are you?" I ask incredulously.

"Very," she says before crawling out of bed. "I will call the pilot. We can probably land by 5PM."

"The fight starts at 8PM. I will call Cameron and make sure that they have floor tickets for you. You have to get there before the fight starts," Chase says.

I nod my head and let everything that just happened in the last 5 minutes soak in.

"Wait is this really happening?" I ask the room.

I have imagined every possible scenario for why Dax did what he did. None of them included him actually being innocent. None of them included him being fucking drugged by someone that was supposed to be closest to him. I will be so fucking pissed if I wake up and this was all a dream.

"This is happening, and we don't have time to pack bags. We need to get to Glenfield Airport, like now," Kayla says.

"I'll drive you guys, it's the least I can do," Chase says.

"I'll fucking say," I snark before grabbing my purse and heading out the door to board a private jet to the UFC heavy weight championship where my ex-boyfriend/hopefully soon to be boyfriend again will be fighting. How fucking weird is my life?

CHAPTER FORTY

Aubrey

We get to the airport in 35 minutes. Unfortunately, there is some delay with getting our flight approved and it takes almost two hours before we are cleared to fly and those were two hours that we didn't have. Our estimated land time is now 7:30PM and I am sweating it. We still have to try to make it to the arena and I have to convince them to let me back into the locker room before the fight starts. I am bouncing my knee nervously when Kayla puts her hand on it.

"Calm down, it is going to be okay."

"It's not. I can't believe that I automatically assumed the worst of him. I should have talked to him. We should have worked it out before I just jumped and cut him out of my life."

"Well, to be fair, honey, you walked in on him making out with another girl while she dry humped him in the middle of a bar. In normal circumstances, there is no other conclusion to draw."

"But nothing about us is normal. I should have known."

"What are you going to say to him?"

"I have no fucking idea. I just need to see him. I feel like I can't breathe another second without him."

She nods her head and pats my knee before sitting back into her plush seat and scrolling on her phone. Of course, the streets are gridlocked once we land. We finally hail a cab and arrive at the fight at 8PM on the dot. Shit. Let's hope that Dax can pull himself together for the biggest fight of his life.

Cameron said that he left the tickets at will call so we race up to the booth and get our tickets before we haul ass to our seats. When we get to them, I look up to see the first punch being thrown and it isn't Dax who is throwing it. Bernstein lands a hard hook to Dax's jaw, causing him to stumble backwards.

I can see what Chase was talking about, Dax looks like shit. I am at least two hundred feet away from him and I can still see the dark circles deep under his eyes and the gruff stubble of his unshaven face. Instead of looking energized and ready, he looks exhausted and weak. He has enough common sense to get his hands up to block any more incoming blows, but defense is not his game. He ends fights with his deathly blows, and he won't last too many rounds in this condition.

Bernstein lands blow after blow on Dax and I can see that it is starting to wear him down. I am screaming my head off, shouting Dax's name, desperately trying to get his attention but the arena is roaring loud so of course, he can't hear me. Bernstein wraps his arms around Dax before lifting him into the air and slamming him onto his back. The whole stadium ohhh's as the floor vibrates from the impact. Bernstein jumps on top of him to continue his attack when the first-round ends. The ref has to pull Bernstein off before Cameron rushes over to Dax. He helps Dax to his feet briefly before Dax collapses to the ground. Cameron scoops him up and practically drags him to their corner while I frantically try to think of how I can get their attention.

I put my fingers in my mouth and let out the loudest whistle I can manage, which I will admit is pretty fucking loud. Dax's head lulls slightly in our direction and Kayla and I start jumping up and down, waving our arms like lunatics. It seems to do the trick because those hypnotic green eyes lock onto mine and widen in recognition. I know screaming will do no good, I can hardly hear myself think right now. Obviously, it isn't like he can leave the cage to talk so I decide to just mouth to him, "I love you."

A look of surprise crosses his face as he mouths, "Forever." He turns back to Cameron and says something as he nods his head. He looks like he just got a shot of adrenaline as he slowly starts to jump in place, fire returning to his eyes.

When the second round starts, Dax comes in like a bat out of hell. Before Bernstein even realizes that Dax is coming for him, he has already landed a 1-2 combo followed by a nasty kick to the ribs. Dax is moving a little more sluggish than he normally would, but he is like a whole new fighter compared to the first round. The element of surprise is soon lost though as Bernstein begins to throw a few good hits that knock Dax back just as the second-round ends.

Dax goes back to his corner where Cameron quickly patches up a cut that he caught across his eyebrow. Cameron is talking to him animatedly, but Dax's eyes never leave mine. I mouth to him, "You got this," and he nods before he kisses his fist and points it towards me causing my heart to stall for a moment.

The third round begins similar to the second, with Dax coming in like a mad man. This time Bernstein is ready and blocks one of Dax's jabs before countering with a hook. Dax winces but that is the only indication that it actually hurt him.

As quick as lightning, Dax cracks Bernstein across the face, causing him to stumble back. Bernstein is able to throw out a hook that makes Dax pause in his assault. They begin trading close contact jabs, each giving as good as they are getting until Dax lifts his knee up and smashes it into Bernstein's side. Bernstein stumbles a few steps again as Dax advances on him, delivering a strong head kick that knocks him to the ground.

Dax jumps on top of him and quickly wraps him up in an arm bar. Bernstein fights like hell to get out of it but it is no use. I can see the veins in Dax's neck throbbing as he holds onto the guy with everything he has. Bernstein's arm is bent back at an unnatural angle and looks ready to snap in half. The ten second warning sounds as Bernstein struggles to keep it together until the next round. Dax's body strains even harder as he bends Bernstein's arm back even more and it is just enough to push him over the edge as Bernstein frantically taps out.

Dax releases him quickly and jumps to his feet. The ref comes over and holds Dax's hand up in the air and the crowd goes fucking insane. The overhead introduces him as the new Heavy Weight Champion of the world and tears of pride spring to my eyes.

After Dax gives a brief interview with the news casts that rushed into the cage, he makes eye contact with me again. He scales the cage and jumps it instead of going out the door like a normal person before he comes face to face with me. His smile is wide, but his eyes are hesitant. I take the lead and throw my arms around his neck and kiss him with everything I have. In this one moment, everything is perfect.

"Meet me by the locker rooms in a few minutes," he says into my ear before he slips me a V.I.P pass that Cameron probably gave him.

I nod as he grabs my face and crushes his lips against mine once more before walking back to the locker room. I beam at Kayla and give her a hug before I tell her that I am heading back to wait for him.

I am walking down the hallway, weaving around people crowding the walkway when someone bumps into me. I turn to glance at them but before I see them, I am shoved sideways through a door that leads to some sort of room. I whirl around to come face to face with the devil himself. Darryl Jones gives me a sinister grin and licks his lips.

"Well, well, well. Little Aubrey Davis. You sure have grown into a very delicious woman."

His eyes are hard as he smiles and I can't help but feel like that weak little girl again under his gaze, but only for a moment. Instinct kicks in and I go to punch him, but he catches my fist midair. I kick my leg out to strike him, but he anticipates that too and side steps it while pinning my body to the wall with his.

Darryl grabs me around my throat and slams my head into the wall. The force of it causes me to see stars. I struggle to get my bearings when he pulls my head towards him until our noses brush before he slams be against the concrete wall once again. This one knocks the wind out of me and sends a sharp pain ripping through my head. I feel a light trickle run down the nape of my neck and I don't have to check to know that it is blood.

"I was hoping you would be here. When I saw you were the up-and-coming heavy weight stars' personal whore in LA, I banked on it. I even got us a more private room to take care of some unfinished business."

His slimy voice makes my skin crawl. I look up into those eyes that have haunted my nightmares for near a decade. Apparently he doesn't like my lack of response because he draws me away from the wall again before slamming me back against it. I swear to fuck, I am about to puke or pass out. I am not sure which will happen first.

"You cost me a lot of good years by running your little mouth. I've been counting down the days until I'd see you again," he grins as his eyes slowly slide down my body.

"Go to hell," I spit with what little voice I have, while his hand tightens around my throat.

His grin slips slightly at my defiance, and he pulls me forward until I am nose to nose with him before he throws me back so hard the instant my head touches the concrete everything goes black.

CHAPTER FORTY-ONE

Dax

I cut all of my interviews short or completely blow them off before I get dressed quickly into a plain t-shirt and jeans. Aubrey is here, and she said that she loved me. She kissed me. I don't know what happened to make her come and I don't fucking care. I know that I don't deserve her, but I do know that I need her, and I will spend the rest of our lives making this up to her.

I stand outside the locker room and look around. I don't see her anywhere and she should definitely be here by now. Maybe she just came to support me and got swept up in the moment. Maybe she doesn't want anything else from me. The thought makes my heart sink, but I keep swiveling my head back and forth, trying not to let all of my hope die too quickly.

I see Cameron walking up to me with a confused look on his face.

"Hey, kid. Congrats again. Is Aubrey alright?"

I cock my head. “What do you mean?”

“I just saw her being carried out of here towards the hotel. She looked passed out. Did she get drunk or something?”

My spine straightens at his words, and I am instantly on alert.

“Who was carrying her? What did they look like?”

“Bigger dude, bald head. He had a snake tattoo on his neck.”

My blood runs cold, and I take off running towards the entrance of the hotel. He came for her, just like she feared. I wasn’t there to protect her like I swore I would. Shit, shit, shit.

My feet pound the marble floor as I make my way through the hotel lobby. I am spinning in circles looking frantically for any sign of either of them, but I see nothing. I rush up to the closest receptionist, a young guy about my age. He seems to recognize me as his eyes widen and a smile breaks out across his face.

Before he can say anything, I rush out, “Is a Darryl Jones staying here?”

“Oh, uh. Sorry, Mr. Hart but I can’t disclose that information,” he says slightly stuttering,

Maybe I look as pissed off and terrified as I feel.

“What room is he in!” I bark.

“I really am sorry. I-”

I cut him off and grab him around the throat, not hard but enough to show him that I could crush his windpipe in a second if I wanted to.

“He is dangerous and just took my unconscious girlfriend to one of these rooms. I need the room number and the key right the fuck now, and if you get in my way you will regret it.”

The guy’s eyes are wide and frantic as he nods his head up and down quickly. I release my hold on him and he gasps, struggling to breathe. Maybe I would feel bad if Aubrey’s safety wasn’t dangling by a thread, just out of reach. He scrambles around and seems to find the information he needs before he gives me a key.

"Room 621, sir."

I take it and nod before I take off running to the elevator. I look over my shoulder to him and shout as I step into the elevator.

"Call the police! If they don't get here soon there will be a dead body."

Probably not the smartest thing to shout because now it will be pre-mediated murder with plenty of witnesses, but I could give fuck all about any of that. I just have to get there.

The elevator takes what feels like a fucking lifetime until I finally reach the 6th floor. I sprint out, following the room numbers until I find 621. I put the key in, but the door only opens two inches before the chain stops it. Those two inches allow noise from the room to filter out into the hallway and I hear Aubrey screaming and struggling. *My girl.* Fuck no. No one will hurt her ever again.

I step back and kick the door as hard as I can, causing the chain to explode into a million little pieces across the floor. The first thing that I see is Aubrey laying on the bed, desperately trying to fight off Darryl. He has ripped her pants practically in half and has his own unzipped. There is a fuck ton of blood on the bed coming from what looks like Bree's head while Darryl's hand is wrapped around her throat, causing her face to turn blue as he applies more pressure. She doesn't stop fucking fighting, though.

"What the fuck?" Darryl growls as he looks towards me.

I charge him and cross the room in three steps before I tackle him to the ground. He goes down hard as I land on top of him. I pin him down by his throat just like he was doing to Aubrey and start landing hit after hit across his face. He struggles underneath me, trying to wiggle and buck me off of him but my iron grip doesn't give him much room.

My rage is white hot and blinding. All I see is this sick fucker that needs to fucking die. I briefly look up to check on Aubrey for a second, realizing that she may not be. But my little fighter has color already returning to her face and is watching us with a hard expression like she wishes she could get in on this. Of course, I spend too long staring at Bree and Darryl uses the moment to his advantage before he grabs the landline phone and hits me over the head with it. It catches me off guard as I fall backwards.

Darryl doesn't waste a second before he jumps on top of me and lands a few hard punches before reaching into the back of his waist band. His hand whips around with a gun pressed against my chest. I grab his wrist to try to turn it away from me or get it out of his hands, fucking anything. I hear a screech come from Aubrey and feel the impact of another body landing on top of us. We tumble onto our sides as she is now also reaching for the gun. In our awkward three person struggle I suddenly hear a loud bang before we all fall still.

I look down and see red quickly coloring my white shirt just over my stomach, but I don't feel anything. I feel numb. Everything seems to slow down, and my gaze collides with those beautiful turquoise eyes that I am most definitely fucking obsessed with. She must see the blood beginning to seep out of me because she instantly turns back to Darryl, does some twist maneuver with her wrist and turns the gun on him. In the same second I hear three consecutive pops and watch as Darryl's body slumps next to me, warm blood spreading between us. Aubrey drops the gun and scrambles over to me.

She whips her shirt off and places it over the hole in my stomach, trying to stop the bleeding. I have never seen her look so terrified. Even when we first saw Darryl back in LA. Maybe I am worse off than I feel. But I don't really care. All I can smell is her. I inhale deeply and smile. Lifting my hand up I caress her soft skin. My touch smears some blood across her cheek but if she notices she doesn't say anything. She just looks at me with equal parts love and fear.

Soon, I hear muffled shouts and several pairs of heavy footsteps.

I lift my heavy head to see police officers bustling around the room as well as paramedics behind them. Glad the guy at the front desk took my threat seriously. I never thought Aubrey would be the one to kill Darryl, though.

I look at her one more time as they load me onto a stretcher. I bring our intertwined hands to my pocket and urge her to grab something from it. She understands and does. She pulls out her bracelet and tears start free falling down her cheeks.

"Forever," I croak before everything slowly fades away. I feel no pain or fear. I was there for Aubrey when she needed me, and for that I have no regrets.

I try to pry my eyes open, but they are too damn heavy. I hear a faint beeping in the background and an angelic voice.

"Dax?"

The sound gives me more strength and I work to finally lift my eyes open. Everything is blurry and it takes a couple of blinks before things start to come in to focus. I see white walls with a window on the wall to the side of me. There is a sterile smell in the air and that beeping is coming from some machine next to me. When I look to my left, I see Aubrey sitting next to me, gripping my hand with puffy eyes and a tear-streaked face.

"Are you okay, baby?" I rasp.

She lets out a short dry laugh.

"Are you okay? You are the one who has been out for two days."

I look at her confused.

"Two days?"

"Yeah," she shakes her head solemnly. "You lost a lot of blood. The bullet ruptured your liver and they had to do surgery to repair it. With the combination of the beatings that you took in the first-round and the shock of everything else they were worried how long it was going to take for you to wake up. You scared the hell out of me, asshole!"

Fire returns to her solemn eyes which made me breathe a little easier. My little fighter.

"I am so sorry, baby. I got there as fast as I could, but it wasn't enough. He should have never even touched you." I grab her hand and squeeze. "I will never forgive myself."

She squeezes back with a barely there smile.

"You couldn't have stopped it. He told me that he had always been planning on coming for me. It was only a matter of time."

I swallow hard.

"Did he hurt you?"

"He threw my head against a wall a couple of times, and it knocked me out for a little bit. When I woke up, he was trying to get my clothes off in the hotel room and I started kicking and fighting. That's when he resulted to trying to tear them off. You came in pretty quick after that."

Anger washes over me at the thought of someone, especially him, touching her, hurting her. I hear the beeping in the background speed up and it must be my heart monitor because I can feel the adrenaline coursing through me. Aubrey places a calming hand on my chest.

"Easy there, tiger. It's okay. He can't hurt me anymore. He can't hurt anyone ever again."

I look up to her, asking a question with my eyes that she seems to understand.

"Yeah," she nods. "He is dead. I was in cuffs for a little while until I explained everything."

"Are you okay?" I ask tentatively.

"I am fine. As bad as it sounds, I am fucking relieved. The fear of him one day coming for me was always in the back of my head. Now he is nothing but a memory, and I refuse to give him one more ounce of power over my life."

I pull her arm towards me, and she leans over and kisses me deeply. My heart soars at having her in my arms again and then it stops at the reminder of how stupid I was to have lost her in the first place. I break the kiss and hold my nose to hers.

"Bree, I will never be able to forgive myself for what I did to you, to us. I understand if you never want to see me again. But please know that I love you more than anything, you have changed my life, changed me. I will love you forever no matter what."

Her smile is so soft and sweet that it makes my gut twist with hope.

"Babe, Chase came and talked to me. He is the reason I came to the fight."

"Chase?" I ask suddenly thoroughly confused. He has been thrilled over our breakup even though I have been slowly dying.

"He drugged you at the party. Slipped a shit ton of E in your drink. He wanted you to cheat on me, to 'let loose and have some fun' apparently. He didn't realize the amount he gave you was going to knock you on your ass like it did. Apparently, you couldn't speak, walk or do anything really. Julie put on a little show at my expense, but you couldn't even participate with her even *if* you wanted to. You were too out of it to know what was going on, let alone stop it from happening. It is not your fault."

I am shocked at her words. My own best friend fucking drugged me? I shake my head because it couldn't be true, but then again, it makes fucking sense. I didn't just feel hungover the next day, I felt like I was coming down from a bad trip. I don't remember anything after a couple of beers that Chase had been feeding me. The video made it seem like I was into it but thinking back on what I saw, Julie was the one making all of the movements. I was just sitting there like a statue. It makes perfect fucking sense.

"That son of a bitch!" I bark out before I blow out a deep breath and shake my head. “I wouldn’t, I couldn’t ever do that to us, Bree. Not willingly.”

“I know, babe,” she says as she kisses the back of my hand. “I should have known all along, but I was shattered, I couldn’t think straight. But you are not to blame, maybe just pick some better friends,” she says lightly attempting to break the dark mood. *Yeah, no shit*. Chase is fucking lucky that I am half-way across the country in a hospital bed right now.

“I love you so fucking much. I never realized just how much until I lost you.”

“Me too,” she says shyly.

“Come here,” I say pulling her to lay on the bed with me. She looks at me like I am crazy.

“No, I will hurt you.”

“I don’t give a shit,” I spit out. “Get your sexy ass over here now. I need to hold my girl.”

That gets her to move as she slowly curls up next to me while I put my arm around her. Her head nestles against my chest as I rub small circles on her back. I have never felt so peaceful in my entire life. Knowing that I have Aubrey back, suddenly nothing else matters. Then I remember that I am the new Heavy Weight Champion and that feels pretty fucking good too.

EPILOGUE

Aubrey

One year later

We are back in Vegas tonight. Arturo Cortez is challenging Dax for the Heavyweight title, and it's definitely gonna be a well matched fight. There have been many that have tried to steal the belt, but Dax has remained unshaken. Commentators are saying that Dax is the pound for pound king who is practically impossible to beat. Considering ever since the UFC signed him, he's been undefeated, I would say that is a fair assessment. Dax is not arrogant though. Shocking, I know. He knows that one day he will lose, and when he does it will only make him better. But he is still Dax motherfucking Hart so he's still a cocky ass more days than not.

The rumor mill came up with the craziest stories about what happened the night he took the title. It ranged from, he saw me from a deranged fan. They got part of that right, he did save me, though I will never admit it to him. I remind him constantly that I don't need saving and that I took care of Darryl by myself in the end. Though if we are being honest, I was fucking terrified and as tough as I tried to act, I silently prayed that Dax would somehow save me. And then he did. I knew for sure in that moment that he would be my forever.

When we returned to Glenfield, Dax rightfully beat the shit out of Chase, and he took it surprisingly well, for a little bitch, at least. Dax has not spoken to him since, thankfully. Life is too short for toxic fuckers like that.

Kayla and Blake are finally officially dating and are probably the most head over heels in love couple that I've ever seen. He worships the ground she walks on, and she loves every second of it. We have even gone out on a few double dates at Kayla's insistence. Though I didn't really see what the big deal was since we all four hang out all the time anyways, but whatever keeps her happy and off my back, I guess.

Cole and I were never really the same. We were able to work together but things were always a little strained and tense. As soon as he graduated he headed back home after he was offered a job in his hometown. I bet his family loves having him so close.

Dax graduated and is a fulltime UFC fighter while I just finished up my sophomore year at Whitman U. I am going for a business degree and my goal is to open my own gym for women. It is going to focus heavily on self-defense and how to use a woman's smaller body to her advantage. For now, Cameron is letting me hold self-defense training classes at the gym twice a week which is great experience for me.

The fight has just started, and Cortez comes in with wild haymakers. Every swing or kick he throws is packed full of power and I can see why they think he will be the one to finally take down Dax. The man is an absolute animal, but Dax is smarter. He throws a couple of halfhearted jabs to keep Cortez distracted while Cortez wears himself out fast.

This dance lasts for a couple of rounds and I almost have a feeling that Dax is just dragging it out based on the way Cortez is slowing down. His connections on Dax are good and it is overall an entertaining fight, but I can practically see the moment Dax decides to finish it. Cortez gets a good connection to Dax's side and Dax grunts before he spins on his heel and delivers a roundhouse kick right to the jaw. It's an instant knock out.

I jump to my feet screaming and shouting until my voice is hoarse which is pretty normal for me at these fights. Nothing gets my adrenaline up like seeing Dax win big. I look over to see Cameron jump down from the cage as he quickly strides over to me.

"Hey, come with me," he says, before taking my arm and escorting me up the stairs and into the cage.

I follow along and see a smiling Dax standing in front of me inside the cage. His abs are covered with a sheen of sweat, and I have to consciously remind myself not to swallow my own tongue. I will never get used to how good looking this man is. I look up to those sharp emerald eyes and see a cocky twinkle in them, like he knows exactly what I was thinking.

When I get close to him, he picks me up and spins me around in a circle, carrying me around like I am the prize he won. Dax sets me down onto my feet and smiles at me before he leans down to my ear and whispers, "Sorry."

I am about to ask him for what but then someone hands him a microphone and he drops to one knee. *No*. He wouldn't dare. Not in front of all these people. We have talked about marriage casually, but he has to know that I will die of fucking embarrassment if he is going to ask me in front of all of these people.

"Aubrey," he says into the microphone for the whole arena and anyone watching on TV to hear. Fuck my life.

"You are my best friend, my number one fan and the love of my life. It has always been you and it always will be. I swear to love you and cherish you and make sure you never run out of cookie dough ice cream."

I chuckle softly as tears begin welling up in my eyes. Then he pulls a little black box out from behind him and pops it open, revealing a stunning cushion cut halo diamond ring with more diamonds encrusted around the band. The thing is fucking huge. I jokingly told him that he could just get me a ring pop and I would be happy, but I really wasn't joking. I would marry this fucking man with a shoelace on my finger.

"Will you do me the extraordinary honor of marrying me?" He asks, hope shining in his eyes with a nervous smile on his face.

I bite my lip to hold back the megawatt grin that is ready to spread across my face. I begin nodding like a fool before I tackle him to the ground, kissing him all over as he laughs. I think the whole crowd laughs at the fact that I just pinned down the Heavyweight Champ, but I don't care about anyone or anything else other than this man in front of me.

When I finally get off of him, he slips the ring onto my finger, and it fits perfectly. He grabs my face and pulls me in for an earth-shattering kiss that is fucking everything. It is filled with promises and hope and love. I never thought that a life this good was in the cards for me. I always thought that some people just drew the short end of the stick and that was just the way it was. I wish I could go back and tell that girl how wrong she was.

He finally breaks the kiss and smiles at me, cupping my cheek lovingly. I return it and whisper into his ear, "I love you, Dax

Hart."

"I love you, Aubrey Davis, forever."

EXTENDED EPILOGUE

Dax

Two years later

"Alright, gentleman. We've been over the rules. Protect yourselves at all times, follow my instructions at all times. Touch gloves, if you wish," the ref says between me and Barrett.

We both stare at each other, neither of us extending our hands as we each assess the other. It's been five months since Jacob Barrett, and I have been in the Octagon together. Last time, the motherfucker stole my belt. I had been undefeated for almost two years. I knew it couldn't stay like that forever, I knew someone someday was going to take me down. I just didn't expect it to be the twenty year old from the Hamptons. The kid looks like he is better suited on his daddy's yacht or attending an Ivy League college than getting his face bashed for a living.

I thought I had the fight in the bag, how could I be undefeated for nearly two years and not get a little cocky, right? I was the

Heavyweight Champ of the world and in my head, some twenty year old kid that probably trained in between fencing lessons wasn't going to be changing that. Fuck was I wrong.

The thing is this kid has some power. He's built pretty wide, and his arms are like cannons. Barrett is constantly bouncing on the balls of his feet, making him lighter and his kicks lethal. And fuck, his hits. Never felt anything like it. Those fuckers took my breath away. We circled each other for the first few rounds, learning each other's moves and openings for possible takedowns. By round three, he ended me with two hits. One to the ribs, which broke two in the process and one to the button, which knocked me out for a solid five seconds, giving me my first knock out in my professional career.

I've spent the last five months training, healing and sharpening my game for this moment. Thank fuck my wife is just as passionate about the sport as I am, or I don't think we'd be married after the last several months. I can't help but smirk slightly as I think about the pep talk Bree gave me in the locker room.

"You walk into that Octagon like you own it, because you do. That is your fucking kingdom, Dax, and that kid stole it from you. Are you gonna take that lying down?"

"Fuck no," I snap, her words riling me up just like she knew they would.

"That's fucking right," she agrees. "You're gonna wear him out, play touch and go for a couple of rounds. Don't hesitate, if the opening is there you fucking take him. We know his takedown defense is shit. Drop the fucker and go to town. He's all stand up, but grappling is where you dominate. Weigh him down and finish him."

"Bree, are you cool if I do the coaching?" Cameron teases as he crosses his arms over his chest.

She shoots him a fake irritated look before turning to me. Wrapping her hands around the back of my neck she yanks me into her, crushing her lips against mine in a kiss that is full of heat, passion and dirty promises to come if the way she is sucking on my lip is anything to go off of.

When she pulls back, she smirks at me as she takes a step back.

"I'll let you girls chat. I love you, give him hell," she says, as she makes her way to the door. She pauses slightly, her full ass popping out in those leather pants as she looks at me.

"Oh and babe? If you don't win, you're sleeping on the couch. I only screw winners."

I bark out a laugh and shake my head as she chuckles to herself and heads out the locker room.

I snap back to the man in front of me, more than ready to bring him down. I don't dare break eye contact with him, even if I can feel Aubrey's eyes drilling into my back as the ref asks if we are ready.

This one's for you, baby.

Barrett comes at me hard and fast. I'm able to sidestep him as I bounce in place before ducking a right hook. I throw out a jab that lacks any real follow through. It's more to just test my reach and keep me out of his until he wears down a little more. Unlike the last time we fought, Barrett doesn't seem to be wasting any time getting a feel for my movements or assessing me. I don't know if it's eagerness or cockiness, but I can see it in the way he moves, his emotions and adrenaline are not controlled. He thinks I'll be an easy takedown, an easy win to keep his belt.

He swings wide and I take the opportunity to kick his left leg. His leg buckles for a moment before he rights himself, a fire flaming in his eyes as he seems to be getting frustrated that he hasn't been able to land a hit on me. Not seeming to care about keeping his distance anymore, he barrels towards me as I wrap my arm around his neck. I try to wrap him into a guillotine, and I almost get him when he starts going to town on my previously injured ribs.

I wince in pain as his fists drive into the same spot over and over again. I lift my knee to his stomach, connecting well but it's not enough to stop his assault. Another hit, harder this time from Barrett has a breath escaping me as I feel a pop. Fuck!

Having no choice but to let him go, I release the guillotine and bounce back, trying to put some distance between us as my ribs scream in pain. If the little shit re-broke my ribs, I'm gonna be pissed.

Barrett comes for me again and I don't hesitate to throw out a left kick to his torso. He grunts as he winds back and lands a solid shot to my jaw that has me stumbling back just as round one ends and the ref pushes Barrett back to his side. I do my best to stand tall as I walk over to my side of the cage.

Bree is looking up at me with concern as I spit a mouth full of blood onto the ground as Cameron and Derek rush inside the octagon. They set up my stool before I take a seat as Derek begins smearing some Vaseline against the cut on my eyebrow while Cameron's mouth is moving rapidly. I do my best to focus on his words, but it sounds like he's underwater as the roar from the blood thirsty crowd fills the stadium.

The conversation Bree and I had this morning plays over in my head as Derek finishes bandaging me up as best as he can before giving me a few small sips of water. I've got to get him down. I doubt I even won that round. The fucker came to fight tonight and if I don't get him to the ground soon my ass is smoked.

A hollow echo breaks through the deafening stadium as the familiar wooden blocks slap together twice, indicating the end of the break. Despite my body's protest, I stand up as smoothly as I can in an attempt to mask any and all weaknesses while Cameron and Derek quickly grab their things and shuffle out of the octagon.

My ribs are fucking killing me already and based on the smug smirk Barrett is giving me from the other corner of the cage, he knows it too. If I want a shot at taking him down to the ground, I need to do it with as many bones intact as possible. With a plan in mind, I advance towards Barrett, he comes in hard with another hit to the same ribs, but I don't allow myself to react, instead I hit him low on his left side, causing him to shift his weight and giving me the opening I need to sweep his feet out from under him.

He lands with a solid thunk, and I immediately pounce on him. He rolls me off of him quickly as he takes the top position, at least that's what he thinks. While he is throwing jabs at my ribs and stomach, I begin bouncing, bucking my hips up. It only takes a few times before Barrett loses his balance and falls to his side where I don't hesitate to strike.

I stretch my legs out before wrapping them around Barrett's torso. I'm able to get my right arm around the front of his neck when I feel him begin to panic. He knows what comes next, unfortunately for him, there is no getting around it now. Holding my right arm in place with my left, I move my legs down to his legs. I extend as long as I possibly can, effectively flattening him out into a rear naked choke.

Barrett throws a frantic elbow, but it just barely misses his mark. His fists are raining down on any part of my body that he can possibly reach but it's all for nothing. I know it. He knows it. The crowd knows it. I keep my hold on him tight, bearing down just a little more to encourage him to tap. If he doesn't soon he's just gonna pass out.

Finally, a reluctant tap to my bicep has me unwrapping myself from him and pushing him to the side as I take a few deep breaths before standing up. When I do, I feel the stadium physically vibrate as the crowd shouts in celebration.

I did it. I fucking did it.

I look over to see Barrett struggling to stand before I walk over to him and offer him a hand. He narrows his eyes at me, and for a moment, I think he's gonna snub me. But eventually, he reaches out for me, and I help him to his feet as I pat his back.

"Nice job, kid," I say into his ear.

"Enjoy it while it lasts, old man. I'll be coming back for my belt real soon."

I smirk at him as I nod. "We'll see."

From there, everything moves in a blur. Cameron and Derek rush over to me, all smiles and shouts as they quickly slip a black and gold UFC shirt over my head as Barrett and his team walk into the middle of the octagon where the ref is waiting. We all shake hands as the Heavyweight belt is placed around me.

Missed you, baby.

All around us is a rush of fans, reporters and officials before the announcer's voice booms through the stadium.

"Ladies and gentlemen, we have the time at three minutes and nineteen seconds in round number two. He is the winner by way of submission and the NEW Heavyweight champion of the world, Daxxx Hart!"

Somehow, I hear Aubrey through the deafening crowd as she makes her way past security, like the little shit she is, before rushing into the Octagon followed by Cameron, Derek, Blake and a horde of reporters. Bree jumps into my arms, and I catch her easily, despite the slight twinge I get in my ribs from the movement. I've got too much adrenaline pumping right now to feel much more than power. Tomorrow will be a different story.

"Congratulations," Cameron smiles as he gives me a hug and claps my back.

I nod and smile as Blake comes to do the same.

"Seriously, bro. You had me worried for a hot second. Thought I flew out all this way for nothing."

I scoff as I push him away. "Thanks for believing in me fucker."

"Always," he laughs, though I can tell it doesn't quite reach his eyes.

He isn't the same guy I knew in college. We're still good friends and get together when our schedules line up, which isn't much when Bree and I live in Glenfield as she finishes up her degree at Whitman and he is living out in New York running a private security firm. Just because we don't see each other a ton, doesn't mean I don't catch the way he doesn't smile as much, or ever really. People probably think it's because of the seriousness of his job, the responsibility of being one of the most elite security companies in the country. Bree and I know, though, he hasn't been the same since everything with him and Kayla went down.

Bree tried to stay in touch with Kayla after everything, but she pretty much ghosted her. I know it hurt her, even if my wife is still too damn stubborn to admit she has feelings like the rest of us. We talk for another few moments before Bree and I share a look. Lust is heavy in her eyes and my cock has been straining in my shorts ever since she jumped into my arms. There is usually only one way to get rid of all this adrenaline after a fight, or at least, only one way that I prefer to.

Taking her hand in mine, we make quick work of exiting the octagon and heading for the locker room. We only make it a few steps down the aisle before Bree lets go of my hand and shouts, "Holy shit!" She takes off and jumps into the arms of a huge guy standing to the side of the walkway. My eyes keep moving up until they finally get to his head. Fuck. This dude's gotta be at least 6'5, maybe 6'6.

6'6 or not, the man is holding my wife, so unfortunately, I'm gonna have to beat the shit out of him. I cross the distance between us in three long strides, my fists hardening into balls at my sides as I reach them. He glances up at me before an amused smile crosses his face.

"Ah, fuck. Look what you did now, Squirt. The Heavyweight Champ is about to beat my ass," he laughs as he slowly lets Bree go.

I quickly yank her into my side as I glare daggers at the guy.

Bree just laughs, though.

"Aw, don't be such a bitch. I thought you were one of the best tight ends in the league."

The guy snorts. "I'm a tight end, not a linebacker. My skill isn't going toe to toe with people, it's running and catching a ball."

Bree laughs as his words sink in for me. Now that I'm up close, the guy does look familiar.

"Caldwell, right? You play for the Seattle Crusaders?" I ask.

He looks at me and nods with a barely there smile.

"Sebastian and I grew up together," Bree supplies. "He's from the same shit hole trailer park that I am. We used to play football together in his yard until he got too cool to hang out with eight year old's."

"To be fair, I was thirteen and had just started playing competitively. Couldn't risk hurting the trailer park squirt in a pickup game."

Aubrey narrows her eyes at him as a pretty red headed woman chuckles softly next to Sebastian. He glances down at her, slipping his arm around her shoulders.

"This is my wife, Erica."

"Nice to meet you, Aubrey. Seb has told me a lot about you," she says sweetly before turning to me.

"And congratulations! I've never been to a fight before, but I see the hype, that was amazing!"

I nod my thanks as Bree speaks.

"So, where is the little one? I thought I heard that you had a kid," she asks.

"Twins," Sebastian breathes out with a heavy sigh that has his wife smacking his arm before smiling at us.

"They are at home with a friend. Seb heard about your fight and thought it would be fun to come and see if we could find you," she says.

Bree's eyes bug out as her eyes flick over Erica with what looks like pure panic.

"Twins?! Dear god, you poor fucking thing."

Sebastian rolls his eyes at her. "What? You telling me you don't have any little shit heads punching people in your future?"

"Fuck no!" Bree laughs as she shakes her head. "Are you kidding? Could you picture me as a mother? Hard pass. If any of our friends ever have kids, I'll be the cool aunt, but that's where I draw the line."

I chuckle as I kiss the side of her temple. I'm glad that Bree and I have been on the same page about that from day one. Some people want kids, but some don't and it's fine either way. We got asked a million times when we got married when we were going to start having kids and it used to piss Aubrey off. Maybe they assumed because we did the whole shot gun wedding thing one of the weekends we were in Vegas that she must have been pregnant. They didn't know we really did it because she refused to wear a wedding dress and do the whole big ceremony thing. Elvis officiant and all, it was fucking perfect.

Aubrey hasn't even graduated from college yet and we still get asked when she is going to start having kids. You never hear anyone ask me that, though. Sounds sexist as fuck if you ask me.

Sebastian laughs at her response as he nods. "Alright, fair enough. Maternal isn't the first word that pops into my head when I think of Aubrey Davis."

Erica smacks Sebastian's arm as Aubrey laughs but it's me that cuts in.

"Hart. Aubrey Hart," I say proudly as I grab her hand and kiss the ring that I put there two years ago.

She rolls her eyes as she looks at me and I can't help but smirk as I smack her ass. Heat fills her eyes at that, and I suddenly have the urge to get as far away from everyone as possible, pro-football player or not.

"Say no more," Sebastian says with a knowing smirk. "Congratulations, again. If you're ever in Seattle let me know."

"Will do," I say before I scoop Aubrey into my arms, tossing her over my shoulder as I jog off to the locker room.

I can hear Sebastian and several other people laugh as I do but I couldn't give a fuck right now. I kick the locker room door open, thankful that it's empty before laying Bree down onto the smooth wooden bench to my right. She makes quick work of peeling her pants off as I yank my shorts down. I'll make love to her in the hotel later, right now I need to fuck.

I reach down and run my finger through her pussy before pushing inside as far as I can with my wraps still on, finding her absolutely soaked already. Guess she's ready for a quick dirty fuck too.

"Dax," she moans as I add another finger.

"Yeah, baby. Tell me what my dirty girl needs."

"You, I need you to fill me up. Shove your thick cock into me and make me cum."

A low growl rumbles in my chest as I withdraw my fingers.

"With fucking pleasure."

I suck on my drenched fingers as I line up my cock to her pussy, not wasting any time before I burry myself inside her.

"Fuck yesss," she groans out as her hips lean up to meet mine.

"We gotta make this quick. Derek's gonna come looking for me to take my wraps off," I say as she nods quickly.

My hands go to her hips, gripping tightly before I start thrusting. Fuck. Almost four years together and I will never get over how good she feels. Her pussy strangles my cock like a vise every fucking time. I watch as she slips her hand down before quickly rubbing tight circles against her clit.

Releasing one of her hips, I quickly slap her hand away. Her eyes shoot up to me, her mouth parting probably to tell me off when

I bring my hand down to spank her clit directly this time. Her parted lips drop into a full o as she moans, her pussy spasming on my cock as she does.

"You love having your pretty little pussy spanked, don't you, baby? I can feel you practically convulsing already."

She whimpers as she closes her eyes and nods her head, wiggling her hips in encouragement. I smirk to myself before giving her a soft tap that I know won't be even close to what she's looking for. As predicted, her eyes shoot open in irritation.

"Don't fuck with me, Dax Hart. You may be Heavyweight Champ, but you could still be sleeping on the couch tonight. Now make me fucking cum."

I can't help but bite back my smug smirk as my fingers slowly rub against her swollen clit in big steady circles. I feel her pussy soak my cock even more but the irritation on her face says she isn't appreciating my teasing. I apply a little more pressure this time, forcing a needy moan to slip past her plump lips. Fuck. That sound goes right to my cock, and I can't help but be grateful she is so on top of her birth control because I couldn't pull out of her if my life depended on it.

"Dax, for fucks sake. If you don't make me cum right now, I'm gonna-"

Her words are cut off when I give her the sharp spank she's been looking for, immediately causing her to detonate. Her screams echo in the locker room as her body shudders and shakes, squeezing me so tight I have no choice but to empty myself inside her.

It takes us both a few seconds to catch our breath before we get dressed. When we are done, I look down at her, brushing the stray hair clinging to her sweat dotted forehead before placing a kiss against her lips.

"I love you, Aubrey Hart."

"Forever," she promises.

A heavy knock comes from the door causing us to share matching smirks before I shout, “Come in.”

THANK YOU

Thank you for reading Jagged Harts!

Reviews are huge for Indie Authors like me so if you have the time to leave one, I would so appreciate it!

Review Jagged Harts on Amazon

Review Jagged Harts on Goodreads

If you enjoyed this, check out some of my other books!

Inevitable – A second chance mafia romance

Undeniable – A single dad mafia romance

Untouchable – An enemies to lovers mafia romance

The Alphalete Series

The Walls We Break – A single mom sports romance

The Loyalties We Break – An ex-boyfriend's best friend sports romance

To keep up with the latest releases, giveaways and more make sure to sign up for my newsletter and follow me!

Newsletter

Instagram

Tiktok

Facebook Reader Group

Facebook

ACKNOWLEDGMENTS

First off, I want to give a huge shout out to all of my readers. You all are the literal backbone behind everything that I do. I can't express enough how much your support means to me. From reading a book of mine, to leaving a review or posting about my work on social media, I wouldn't be anything without you all. I love you endlessly.

To my amazing Beta and ARC readers, thank you so much for taking the time to read my work and make sure that I don't sound like a total idiot. Most of my books are still half word vomit when they make it to my Beta's and still in need of minor tweaking when my ARC readers get their hands on it. Thank you so much for everything you do for not only me but the entire book community. You are incredibly beautiful people.

To my friends and family, thank you so much for your unconditional love and support through every book. From the first word to the final period, you all show me nothing but compassion and encouragement. And sorry if you read this and are related to me because this book is definitely the steamiest one that I have written yet. I'd feel worse but I warned you not to read my books. I love you all.